Home
to
Pickleberry

B. C. Dombrosky

To Mom, my first reader.
To Dad, my first critic.
To my golden fox, may you never lose your fire.

A demon and a child sat at a table.

The demon didn't look like a demon. His face was familiar and comforting to the little girl with the dark ponytail. He appeared to her as someone who provided love and protection. The little girl, who had never known love, would have gladly accepted the demon in any form he chose to appear to her. But life was a little easier when he smiled at her wearing the face of a kind, elderly man.

Scattered upon the table before them was an array of colored papers and crayons. They'd already worked through a stack of papers, building stories and creating creatures and monsters. The demon worked strategically to help the child create a world where these creatures could live—a red-tinted world where they were free to play any sort of game they wanted, no matter how much it disappointed their mothers.

The child loved this. She loved telling stories and she loved having someone listen to them.

By the time she'd used the last of her colored paper and was left with only white sheets, her heart was swelling so full it seemed to spill from her face in the form of a contagious smile.

She took a sheet of paper and a red crayon. With care and consideration, she drew one curved line, then another, and then filled the space in with red. She presented to the demon a crudely colored heart as large as her head.

"Is this for me?" he asked. His voice was raspy, like air being pressed through an opening too small.

"Because I love you!"

"Oh," the demon said, holding the paper appreciatively and then crumbling it into a ball and tossing it over his shoulder. He leaned close to the child and pinched her cheek. "I think you can do better than that."

The child knelt in the grass looking at the ground. Her knees were red and itchy, but she paid them no mind. The grass was just tall enough to hide her from prying eyes and easy enough to be pressed down so she could have a clear view of the work she was doing. With her demon standing to the side so as to not block the light, she set to work.

She'd stolen her mother's sharpest knife and tucked it in the sleeve of her jacket. After a tiring chase, she held it ready in her hand.

Before her lay a dead rabbit. She was lucky that something so small had taken such little force to kill, but now she was unsure about taking the next step.

The knife trembled in her little hand.

"Go on, dear," said the demon. "It's only a small cut here." His long fingernail traced an imaginary line for her to follow.

The child nodded but didn't move.

"You do love me, don't you?" asked the demon.

She met his face with tearful eyes. "I do love you," she said.

He gestured to the dead animal.

With a shaking hand, she pushed the knife into the soft body and cut. It took several tries to cut deep enough as she had no experience dissecting animals. After a few cuts, she set the knife aside and plunged her fingers into the rabbit's inner cavity. Her hand emerged holding a tiny heart. She turned, eyes red, and presented the heart to her demon.

The demon placed his hand over his own empty chest and with the other he petted her coarse hair flat. "That's my girl." He smiled.

"Haven't I collected enough for you?" the child asked her demon during recess. She was older now and a few years into school. She'd been sitting under her usual tree with a notebook and a red pencil. None of the other students or the teachers seemed to notice when she wandered off.

Her demon settled next to her under the tree, enjoying the shade. "You know I value the collection you've started for me more than anything. I just think it's missing something," he said.

He pulled a rabbit from the inside of his trench coat like a magician would from a black top hat. Unlike the soft white rabbits known to accompany magicians, this rabbit looked like its body had been twisted and encased in bark. He gave it a scratch under its chin and placed it in the grass, where it thumped around stiffly. It didn't move like a rabbit. It moved like a dried branch that had fallen from an oak years ago and was better suited to be kindling rather than a pet kept in a demon's pocket.

"What kind of something?" she asked, scribbling mindlessly at her paper and not acknowledging the rabbit that hopped awkwardly around her legs.

"Something… bigger?"

"Bigger?"

Her demon nodded.

"Like… a dog? I've done that," she thought aloud.

"No. No, bigger than that."

She pondered, not looking up from her notebook. "A horse?"

"Mmm, not quite." His eyes seemed fixed across the playground to a group of kids playing Four Square.

When she couldn't guess anymore, she looked to the demon and followed his gaze. Her grip tightened on the pencil and she swallowed hard.

"You're scared," he said.

She lowered her eyes.

"You have no reason to be."

She didn't speak and made no motion to move.

"Dear," he said, pulling her gaze to him. "Don't you love me?"

She felt her eyes go misty. She allowed herself a mere nod.

"Excellent," he said with an excited smile. He waved his hand at the children and their game, and the ball flew from its original path and diverted completely off course to the tall grass at the back of the playground.

"I've got it!" yelled a blond boy.

Her demon lowered his reach to the rabbit, which jumped into his sleeve and disappeared. Once his sleeve stopped twitching, he looked to her expectantly and the child pushed herself to her feet.

She followed the boy deep into the grass far from the sight of the teachers and other students. The ball was nowhere to be found, but the boy continued to look.

She found a rock, small enough to fit in her hand but large enough to land a solid blow to the back of the boy's head.

As she stood over his still body, blood oozing from the wound on the back of his head, the demon appeared over her shoulder. He presented her with a knife.

She didn't move.

"No one loves you like I do, dear. Remember that. If you love me, you will make me happy." He pushed the knife toward her.

She watched the blood fall from the back of the boy's head and trickle over the ground.

"You do love me, don't you?"

She took the knife into her trembling hand. She rolled the boy onto his back. His chest rose and fell steadily. She lifted his shirt and the knife shook harder in her hand.

"His chest will be stronger than that of a dog or rabbit. You will have to strike hard," said the demon.

She nodded. She raised the knife over her head but held it there, trembling.

"Do it," he said. "For me."

She squeezed her eyes shut tight and swung her arm all the way back to gain momentum. As she began her thrust something grasped her wrist, stopping her mid-swing.

Her demon pulled the knife from her hand and pulled her into a tight embrace. "There, there," he comforted her. "I know. I know. Now go tell your teachers he fell and needs help."

The child ran off to get help, wiping tears from her eyes.

The demon loomed over the boy, smiling at what could have been. This wasn't the time. Still, in his heart he knew there was nothing this child wouldn't do for him. Utter devotion. Willingness to go to the end of the earth for his desires. A demon could only be so lucky to call that unconditional love.

Part One

The Unfortunate Life of Naomi Novak

September 3, 1969

This town is fucked.

I suppose it has always been fucked, but whatever rose-colored glasses I've worn since birth have been lifted. I can't afford to ignore the obvious now.

My entire life, I've had a sense of pride in the place I call home. Or at least I used to. I always thought the stories my Pa told me were bullshit, put there to keep kids from wandering into the woods or down streets where dopeheads camped out. Turns out there are things much worse than LSD and grass in this town.

There are monsters here. People who don't look like people anymore, beasts and witches; they hide from the obvious but I've seen them. Vampires have their fingers in everyone's pie, buying land, building buildings. It seems so harmless, but to what end? Even the leadership of this fucking town is corrupt. And I don't mean your old-fashioned political corruption. I mean monsters are running this place and people are none the wiser. I guess I used to be like that—ignoring the rustling, the shadows, the coincidences. It's impossible for me to ignore what I've witnessed.

His name was Barry and he was an ugly motherfucker who lived at the edge of Black Bile. He had no family, no friends, and no community. I don't know if he isolated himself or if the community did it for him, but I only knew about him by stumbling upon him. He must have lived alone in that shack for decades, but was more than happy to have a person to talk to. Aside from his little twitches and ways of acting, he was an all right guy. He collected whatever he could pull from the dirt. Trash, sandstones, regular old rocks, it didn't matter. If he could dig it up, he put it on a shelf.

The thing is, I could have let him be, but he was nothing but skin and bones. I couldn't live with myself knowing he was out there surviving on acorns and God knows what else. It became a thing for me to wander out his way a couple times a week, bringing him whatever I could talk my wife into making.

This went on for months, until it didn't. The last time I saw him he was a shell of the skeleton he used to be. Like any fluid, any life, that had existed in him was drained. I didn't stick around to figure out what happened. Black Bile opened up and dragged him and his shack to what I assume has to be hell. All I know is there is no body or house left for me to plead my case for sanity.

When I get so brave as to mention it, even my own wife shakes her head in embarrassment. I've learned to keep my mouth shut, since no one in this perfect little town wants to know what the true cost of perfection is.

The wolves and the witches and the vamps tend to keep to themselves. I guess it's whatever human parts are left in them. Or maybe they're up to something worse? I don't know.

Barry was a no one here, but who's to say they stop at no ones? There are other parts of this town that aren't managed. Monsters who can't govern themselves and have to be kept in line. Since no one else wants to wake up to what is happening, I guess it will have to be me.

I'm not stupid. I know one man can't save the whole town. But there is something just too special about Pickleberry to keep the freaks out. I have to protect my family. But these fucking monsters… I have to understand them. Maybe if I understand them, I can manage them.

If I don't at least try, this town is completely fucked.

Chuck

1

In times of discretion, the best place to hide is the most obvious.

If you're sending edibles to your out-of-state friend, you don't gut a teddy bear to hide the gummies. You buy a large bag of Starbursts and mingle the goodies in with the others. Not that this is to give you advice on how to illegally send drugs to your friends. This is just to say that if you're a hybrid human-something-not-human, the best place to be is out in the open. Somewhere boring, mingling with the other gummies.

Naomi Novak was an expert at mingling with humans.

She sat in a coffee shop in the middle of a sunny afternoon in a moderately busy town called Springfield, waiting for her appointment to arrive. On the table before her sat a cup of Earl Grey tea, long gone cold, a pocket-sized notebook, and the local newspaper. She'd been thumbing through the newspaper, pretending to be interested in the tea. The truth was she couldn't drink it, but spending endless hours in a coffee shop without something on the table drew odd glances. This was about blending in, after all.

Not that she was a stranger to odd glances, given her looks.

Naomi had low, flat eyebrows over round, dark brown eyes framed by full, dark lashes. Her skin was dull and colorless. Her lips were full—perhaps the only appealing thing about her face at a mere glance.

She always wore black. Black pants, chosen at random because they were clean and available. Long-sleeved shirts to cover the heinous, attention-grabbing tattoos—not chosen, but gifted to her whether she liked them or not. She spent no time on her makeup and little more on her nearly black hair, which is why she settled for something choppy and short, easily trimmed with a pair of kitchen scissors, and slicked back from her face with her hands multiple times during the day.

Today she kept it out of her face with a pair of dark sunglasses because she needed her hands to take notes. She'd flipped through all the local news stories and found nothing interesting. The city wasn't without crime or trouble, but Naomi didn't care about burglaries or drug busts. She kept her eyes out for the details people might glance over. With nothing better, she settled on the obituaries. Maybe she knew someone in there? Or maybe there was something about someone's death that didn't add up.

She looked out the window. The sun was passing the afternoon mark and she wondered if she'd been stood up.

When she looked back to her paper, a woman was sitting across from her.

Naomi didn't jump. She didn't even flinch. While she didn't recognize the woman, she was used to frightening figures appearing unannounced out of thin air—even when they weren't the clients she was expecting.

The woman's face was hidden behind a black veil that covered an oversized black hat. Below the hat she wore black sunglasses, a high-collared, long-sleeved blouse, and gloves. There wasn't an inch of skin visible. "I never pictured a coffee shop to be the place I'd find you."

Naomi thought her a bit over dramatic. "This is a brave outing for you."

The woman nodded. "With the advancements of SPF and UPF in clothing, we're becoming quite a brave race." She settled her hands on her lap. "I assume you know who I represent?"

"I can guess," Naomi said, with a pointed look at the clothing. "You must be new."

"I've represented The Den for many centuries, but I've recently taken up work under a different management. Lanora Del Rio. You may call me Nora if you like, but I doubt you ever will." She didn't offer a hand to shake.

"And why is that?" Naomi asked.

"That would imply we're going to be friends. I have no desire to spend any more time around you than necessary." She suppressed a shiver.

"But a phone call wouldn't have sufficed?"

"I've heard a lot of talk about you and curiosity got the better of me, I admit." Nora looked her up and down from under her sunglasses. Her nose scrunched. "I should have made the phone call, in retrospect."

Naomi leaned back in her seat, trying not to roll her eyes.

"We have another job for you." She reached for Naomi's notebook, noticing the scribbles.

Naomi snatched and pocketed it.

Nora smirked. "Do you think you have secrets from us?"

"I would like to humor the idea that I do," Naomi said.

Nora shook her head and reached into the black purse that hung from her shoulder. "Oh, I think I'm going to have fun overseeing you." She retrieved an envelope and held it in the air for Naomi to accept.

Naomi took the envelope. A chill of goosebumps crossed her skin as her hand brushed Nora's.

She took a moment to consider the image the two of them presented. "We look like a gothic lesbian couple after our intimate wedding in the local graveyard."

"I married my fourth husband in a graveyard." Nora pondered for a moment. "I ate his heart on our first anniversary."

Naomi grinned politely. Or she attempted to—she was sure it came out as a wince.

Nora giggled and was gone as suddenly as she'd appeared.

Naomi looked around the busy coffee shop but found nothing amiss except for the envelope in her hand.

Before she could open it, she was interrupted by a man who looked as though sleep and pressed clothes were foreign concepts.

"I'm so sorry we're late," he said.

"Mr. and Mrs. Wiggins," she said, tucking the envelope into her coat. "No need to apologize."

"Adele and I have been having a hard time keeping track of things lately," he said.

"Mr. Wiggins—"

"Please, Edgar."

"Edgar, no need to explain. Have a seat."

She indicated the booth across from her and they slid into their seats.

Edgar and Adele Wiggins were what Naomi imagined loving parents would look like. They wore wrinkled sweaters in coordinating colors. It was as though they were so conditioned to be alike, they didn't have to put any effort into it. They both were average in looks and carried a bit of love weight around the middle, but the simple rings on each hand told Naomi they were far past the point of caring. Aside from homely and comfortable, the couple shared a general look of exasperation about them.

"Has anything changed since we met last week?" Naomi asked.

Adele didn't speak and she hardly looked up from her lap. She shared the same red and puffy eyes as her husband, who made an obvious effort to keep his voice calm and collected as he responded, shaking his head.

"No one will listen to us still. The local law is making us out to be a laughingstock. They're saying we're overreacting, or that Ava is making it up. She's nine…" His voice broke a bit. He cleared his throat and composed himself. "We're out of options."

"I understand." Naomi nodded.

Adele spoke up. "Did you find anything?"

Naomi retrieved the pocket notebook Nora had been interested in. "I did some digging into the guy, Pete Hartman. As I'm sure you're aware, these allegations are very serious, and I can't just jump into a job without knowing for certain."

"We understand," Edgar said.

"It's both fortunate and unfortunate that I did find some evidence that will help your cause." Naomi flipped through her notebook until she found a dog-eared page with times, dates, and a brief sentence next to them. "I won't go into detail considering the evidence was more for my benefit than yours, but I can say I have witnessed Pete Hartman in various suggestive acts, but not limited to these alone. First and foremost, I witnessed him in the children's section of the local department store buying various packets of children's undergarments and toys. This could be harmless if he had a family of his own or even showed a willingness to donate such items, but that isn't the case. I later witnessed him in his home stowing away these garments and goods in locked cabinets."

"Why would he need children's undergarments?" Adele asked.

"He could be interested in forcing his victims to change them in order to hide evidence."

"Evidence?" Adele whimpered. She hunched forward, sobbing softly into her hands.

Edgar pulled his arm around his wife and nodded for Naomi to continue.

"The difficulty with this case is that Mr. Hartman isn't a trophy collector; ironic, considering he has walls filled with actual trophies. But he keeps no evidence linking him to his victims. If he's making the children change clothes, he's very good about disposing of the old clothes, as I couldn't find them. Also, he doesn't take photos or things such as hair, toys, or something else that would link him to his crimes."

"He was probably coached," Edgar spat and for the first time, Naomi watched hatred spread over his kind face. "He has friends in the local precinct. He coaches all their boys. The more they play, the more scholarships and… Why wouldn't they want to keep him around? He wins trophies for them."

"Ed, let her continue," Adele said.

"I'm sorry." He wiped away tears.

"It's okay. I won't go on much more than to say I have nothing to present that will help your case with law enforcement. Considering his connections, I would have to find something indisputable. I mean, I would have to literally catch him in the act, but he's far too careful for something like that."

"So, it's a lost cause? Our Ava…" Adele sobbed again.

"However," Naomi continued. "While I don't have enough evidence to convince law enforcement, I have found more than enough evidence to believe your claims myself. Which leaves us with a few options."

"We're listening," Edgar said.

"My question to you is what would you like to come out of this?"

Edgar swallowed a hard lump. "I don't know. We never got that far. We simply wanted someone to take us seriously and to do something. If he's hurting Ava, who else is he hurting? Or has he hurt?"

"I'm not in the business of *willingly* ruining lives just because I can." The statement hung in her mind for a moment. It was a half-truth, but there was no reason they needed to know that. "But given that I'm convinced, I can do more to resolve this problem with no connection to the two of you. I simply ask: do you want him to be caught or would you like me to resolve the problem?"

Adele and Edgar exchange uncertain glances. "He'll never be caught," he said.

Naomi nodded in agreement.

"What would you do?" Adele asked.

"The less you know, the better," she said.

Adele didn't press. Instead, she looked to Edgar and gave him an approving nod.

"It will be cash up front," Naomi said. "Once the fee is paid, I can set to work, and we'll never see each other again."

Edgar pulled an envelope from his sweater pocket as the mention of payment had been predetermined. The envelope was folded in half and worn. He slipped it across the table and then grasped tightly to Adele's hand.

Naomi pocketed the envelope without counting its contents. "I know nothing I do will undo what has been done to your daughter, but maybe you'll rest easier knowing he can't hurt anyone else."

They nodded uncertainty.

"It has been a pleasure doing business with you."

Taking the hint, the couple left the table in such a rush they nearly took out a waitress carrying a tray of drinks.

For the sake of appearances, Naomi lifted her abandoned cup of tea to her lips. She wondered if karma was real, if it was truly possible to do enough good that it would balance out the bad and make redemption a possibility.

When she considered the envelope she'd received from Nora, the optimism left her. She winced at the coldness of the tea against her mouth

September 21, 1969

I often wondered if morality was really a thing. We evolved from animals. Animals don't consider the home life of the animals they catch and eat. They don't give two shits about whether it had kids or if it was just a baby. Animals live meal to meal. I gotta eat to live so I live to eat. Or something like that. Where along the way did we start adding right and wrong into things? And who gets to decide?

I shoot a man because he's shooting at me. Does that make me as horrible as him or do I suddenly have the high ground because he fired first? I guess it depends on who you ask. There are too many factors in life for things to be black and white. We're bound by duty and obligation to determine the value of valueless things.

Maybe monsters exist peacefully in this town. Maybe it was their town to begin with and we humans moved in, taking it over, building houses and schools where there used to be big open nothingness. And the monsters just kinda evolved around us. Maybe I can live with that. Maybe I can turn a blind eye to blood banks in the hospital, but at what point do I start shooting? And does that make *me* the monster?

This town makes me question myself. It makes me question if I'm disrupting some sort of natural balance in the world. There are so many more of them than there are of us. And far fewer of us *know* about them. I'm learning this the hard way. No one seems to see the shadows moving or their true faces. Maybe they can't see what I can see. Maybe they're ignorantly, or willingly, blind.

All I know is I can't live knowing I'm the only one seeing things and just do nothing about it.

Chuck

2

His home was what you expected from an elementary school P.E. teacher and high school football coach. His walls were covered with an unnecessary amount of sports regalia. His furniture all matched and was several decades old. His kitchen appliances were limited to a microwave and a coffee maker. Naomi imagined he didn't spend much time at home to use any of it.

People like him tended to be clean and tidy—to purposefully give the impression that their lives were completely and utterly vanilla. Who would suspect the guy with one bookshelf full of autobiographies by sports stars who had made questionable life choices? They would much rather suspect the guy with taxidermy squirrels, even though the worst that man had ever done was give them ridiculous names, like Mr. Butternut Nutterton or some shit.

Even so, the bad ones always slip up somewhere. Despite his pristine home, Naomi had witnessed Pete Hartman grooming another child in the school yard, a fact she'd deliberately kept from the Wigginses.

He looked so innocent in his bed, eyes shut and mouth agape with just a bit of blood spilling from the corner. He looked like he might have been resting if not for the blood. An unfortunate side effect to squeezing the air out of one's lungs was the blood that seemed to track its way back up the airway. A positive side effect to squeezing the air from someone's lungs is when they die in a tragic fire, authorities don't usually do an autopsy on the lungs to determine if there's smoke damage. They died in a fire, after all.

She pulled herself from admiring his still form and looked into the flask that she held in her hand. A length of rubber tubing ran from his forearm into the flask, dripping blood into its mouth. Only half full. A glance at the clock told her she was pushing her luck. She closed the flask and placed it in the bottomless pit of storage she called a pocket. She removed the tubing and needle, also tucking it away to clean later, careful to not spill even a drop of blood. She placed a tissue to the tiny incision site of the needle and waited a moment for the blood to completely stop.

If there was one good thing these monsters could do, it was feed Naomi's annoying need for blood.

She stood wiping the bit of blood at the corner of his mouth with the tissue. She lit the relaxation candle he had next to his bed (she could only imagine the stress pedophiles dealt with) and held the tissue over the flame. It caught quickly and as she let it go, the fire sent it fluttering into the air to then land on the old shag carpeting. It caught a flame nearly on contact.

She lifted the corner of Pete's flat sheet and placed it into the candle, watching it smolder, then quickly blaze across the rest of the bedding to where he lay unmoving.

Done in by a stress relief candle. She hoped someone in the fire department would get an inappropriate chuckle out of this.

By the time the flames had spread from Mr. Hartman's room to the rest of the house, Naomi had made a place for herself on the opposite side of the street. Neighbors had noticed the smell and the growing smoke clouds and were gathering outside.

They didn't notice Naomi at all. No one pays attention to their shadow.

Naomi suddenly remembered the envelope Nora had given her. She pulled it out of her pocket and opened it. Inside were details for a job in the city. It would be a few days before she would need to be in the area, but she already dreaded traveling to the city. She didn't own a car and hardly had a home to call her own. Her fastest way of traveling was jumping through one shadow and hoping to come out the next near her desired location. Not only was it mildly unreliable, but it took a lot of energy. Energy wasn't something she had an abundance of. And the means of replenishing it were less than desirable.

She tucked the notes away into her pocket and felt for the flask that held Mr. Hartman's blood. It had a warmth to it that would fade over the coming hours. It had been days since she'd had anything to drink, and she was beginning to feel it. She was walking the line of recklessness if she didn't drink, but drinking the blood of vile people was just that—vile. The only alternative was hurting innocent people.

Naomi grimaced as she took a sip. It was just a taste, enough to keep her going, but not enough to bring her to full strength. She pocketed the flask. Time to go home.

Home is subjective. It's a feeling. A person. But it's probably a place for most. It's where you take your bra and pants off and hope no one needs you anytime soon.

The closest thing Naomi had to a home was a hole-in-the-wall bar on C Street. There were many bars on C Street, but the one she chose seemed to be the favorite of the Springfield lowlifes. That was likely why it felt like a home to her. It was called *Daisy's* by all the regulars even though the sign over the door read *Daisy's Dirty Delights*. It made the place sound more like a brothel than a bar with cheap drinks and decent burgers.

Daisy's was no bigger than a rest stop in the middle of nowhere. There was one disgusting bathroom shared by all the patrons, the sex workers on cold, rainy nights, and the staff, though most preferred to piss in the alley out back. At the front, a short bar curved around and connected to the wall, but it hardly left room for anyone to sit except the regulars—and the regulars kept to their sitting arrangements better than kindergarteners. At the back was a small stage where they entertained the idea of shows or karaoke, but no one came to Daisy's to see a show or sing drunkenly into a microphone. They came to buy or sell drugs, drink for cheap, and shoot the shit with the other pieces of shit around them who all had the same shit to shoot.

Naomi never made it to the bar. On her first night there, she'd left a particularly hard job and was trying to keep the tears from flowing down her cheeks. Her face had been dirty and bruised, as it had been nearly two months since she'd drunk. This was back when she thought she could die if she didn't drink. Instead, she'd learned the hard way that her body slowly deteriorated until she fell into madness and killed the first blood bag she could find—blood bag meaning *anything* containing blood.

She'd entered the bar and stalked to the back corner. She was too exhausted to bother blending into the shadows but found no one seemed to notice her. She felt relieved to find somewhere she could be invisible without trying.

Eventually, the bartender, a middle-aged man who kept in shape and had kind eyes, brought her a glass of water. He asked if he needed to call someone. When she didn't speak, he said he hoped the other guy looked worse than her. Naomi could only see the pulsating of his carotid in his neck. She ordered a bourbon—it was something she'd heard her dad order before—and hoped he wouldn't return.

Over time, the booth in the back corner became her home and the bartender, named Taylor, brought her a bourdon like clockwork.

And like that, Naomi became a regular.

Tonight, she'd been poring over her notebook for hours, planning out the next job with the details she'd received from Nora. This was one of those jobs she didn't make any money off as per her contract with The Den. She hated to plan these as they were never jobs she enjoyed, but it was too risky to walk into something blind. It was better for all parties if she sat down with her notebook and a sweaty bourbon to plan the job out.

It was the time of the night when the drunks started to fall asleep and Taylor began to call wives, kids, or cabs to carry them home. This meant the loud chatter was starting to quiet and people who worked the night shift would come in for a break.

Naomi hit a wall. Her brain was starting to buzz and her eyes grew tired of reading in the dim lighting.

Taylor came to her table holding a fresh bourbon and a glass of water. "Work got you down today, doll?"

"What have I said about calling me that?" she asked back.

"I know, but I love watching the way your nose wrinkles when I say it."

She rubbed her face, hiding the grin.

"Really looks like it was a long day," he observed. He ran a damp towel over the tabletop, though it was spotless already.

"It was good, actually. For what it could be," she said. "Do you ever have moments in your job where you feel like you did something really good?"

Taylor gestured over his shoulder to the smoky bar. "Every shot I serve fills me with purpose."

"Well, maybe not," she said. "I just do so much shitty stuff in my job. My whole life is filled with doing shitty stuff, and I don't know, if something good can come out of it, maybe it will be a little less shitty."

"Maybe one day you'll be less vague and let me understand what you're talking about, huh?" he asked.

Naomi rested her head on her fist and gazed at him coolly. "What happened to Stephany?"

He wrinkled *his* nose and picked up her old, watered-down bourbon.

"She was cute," she said.

"She was a little on the young side for me."

"What? Twenty-one?"

"Yeah… I don't know. She was a good waitress, but she got some gig off the internet and hardly comes in. I think she's headed for California or something soon." He leaned over the table a bit and pursed his lips.

"What?"

"She was really into cosplay, and… I don't know if I'm cool enough to get it," he said.

Naomi chuckled. It surprised them both.

"Those people are talented," she told him. "Imagine all the Halloween costumes she could make for your kids."

He shook his head and leaned farther over the table. He was doing that thing he liked to do right before saying something really gross that would make Naomi cringe. His blue eyes looked at her tenderly and his thin lips curved into a half smirk. It made the lines along his cheeks more prominent, but it was nearly unnoticeable under the thin beard. "Yeah, she isn't the one I think of when I think of having kids," he said.

Taylor could defuse even the tensest situations with one of his smiles. He was made to work in customer service and negotiate hostage situations, but he settled for listening to drunks cry about their problems. By the same talent, he effortlessly made his patrons swoon, so that even people who would have never been attracted to him sometimes questioned themselves.

In short, he couldn't manipulate shadows or scale walls like Naomi, but his powers were far more impressive. He was fucking charming. It's how he made good tips and how he made lasting impressions that kept his tiny, failing bar operating in an area of town that offered far better places to drink. It was how he put a tiny bit of good in an otherwise bleak world. And while Naomi wasn't an average person, she wasn't immune to his blue eyes and crooked smile. She sometimes forgot what light looked like while she was hiding in the shadows, but Taylor's glow was contagious.

Naomi's nose started to wrinkle.

Taylor pressed his palms into the tabletop, exposing his inner forearms to her, and shifted his weight from one hip to the other. "Come over," he said.

The longer he held this position, the more prevalent his brachial artery appeared, running the length of his forearm and under the cuffed sleeves of his shirt. Naomi could only watch it. She forced her eyes away and looked back at his smoldering gaze. "Get back to work, Taylor."

"We're closing soon and I'll have to kick you out," he pushed.

"And I'll find somewhere to go like I always do."

"I know of a somewhere," he said, his voice lower.

Naomi rolled her eyes. She shook her head and looked away, taking a moment to think. When she looked back to him, still deciding if she should take him up on his offer or not, she noticed someone enter the building.

It wasn't weird that someone entered the bar this late, but it was how she walked. A young blonde woman limped into the bar. One of her heels had broken off her thigh-high boots. It was the odd gait that drew Naomi's attention, but it was the girl's red and bloodied eye and nose that kept it.

Her smile faded and Taylor followed her gaze to the girl, who stumbled to the bathroom.

"Shit," he murmured. "Poor lady."

"Lady? She's got to be at most nineteen."

"Probably just another job."

They watched her disappear behind the bathroom door, trying to hide the tears that rolled down her cheeks.

"She shouldn't have to do that for a job," Naomi said.

"People put themselves in shitty situations to survive." Taylor looked at her and recognized the intent in her eyes. "Don't get involved, Naomi. You could make it worse."

"I don't see how it could be worse," she said. "If there is a pimp or a John out there who's doing that, maybe *someone* should do *something* about it."

"So, call the cops." He stood to his full height, collecting her old drink and towel again, knowing full well any chances of seducing her were completely off the table now.

"You and I both know where that will lead," she said.

"What else is there to do? Are you going to go vigilante?"

She raised an eyebrow at the thought.

He sighed heavily.

Naomi left the table.

"You can't save everyone, Naomi," Taylor told her as she walked past him and toward the back door.

She hesitated only a moment before pushing open the door and exiting into the chilly night air.

3

Amber thought herself mature for her age. Most nineteen-year-olds do. She'd graduated high school a year ahead of everyone else. It had little to do with intellectual excellence and more to do with being over school and everything that came with it. She didn't have time to waste on proms or dating. She had responsibilities no one understood.

Home was fine. It was filled with a loving mother and a doting father and Toby. Toby was short and stumpy and had round cheeks. He didn't speak much and when he did, no one understood what he was saying except for Amber, who always knew exactly what he needed. Toby was easy to please. A bottle and a raspberry on the belly usually kept the rose in his cheeks. He only cried when he woke and Amber wasn't there to snuggle him.

But home was where the comments started, the reminders that she could have been well into college on the path to becoming a lawyer or doctor or some other unrealistic expectation parents put on their kids. Amber just wanted Toby. She just wanted to gnaw on his chubby legs until he laughed so hard he puked. She wanted to watch him play soccer and basketball and grow up to have a hundred friends. But cleats are expensive and so are diapers.

When she found herself working nearly seventy-hour work weeks only to barely cover the expenses life brought, she jumped at the promise of a job where she made her own hours and could earn twice as much as she made working three other jobs.

She wasn't naïve. She knew what the job was and what it entailed. This wasn't even the first time she had to hide the marks from someone who got a little rough. But never in her career had she needed to learn how to stitch a busted eyebrow. This repair was far beyond the work of concealer and pressed powder.

She pulled her hair down and ran her small brush through it. It was matted in the back and there was nothing her tiny brush could do to help with it. She smoothed the front and parted it deep to the side, laying it over her cleaned but bleeding eyebrow. This should cover it until she could get home and then maybe she could find something to hold it closed.

Amber slipped out of the bathroom and moved toward the back of the bar, not making eye contact with anyone, not even the bartender who watched her from behind the bar. She quietly left through the back door that led into the alley, hoping no one would notice her.

Her hands became chilled as soon as she hit the night air. She cupped them over her mouth and breathed into them but stopped when the world started to shift. She pressed a hand on the brick wall of the bar to steady herself.

"Maybe you should sit for a bit?" She seemed to appear from the air, the woman in black, but the alley was dark and it was easy to go unseen back there.

"I'm okay," Amber said. She stood tall again and took a few steps away from her, only to stumble and hit the wall hard with her shoulder.

The woman came to her side. "I'm not asking. You don't have to sit in the piss, but just lean here for a minute and gather yourself."

Amber was too dizzy to argue and simply put her shoulder blades to the wall.

"Looks like it was a rough night."

"Just another night in capitalist America." Amber closed her eyes.

The woman feigned a grin and moved Amber's hair from her busted eyebrow, which now had a trail of blood down the side of her face.

Amber pulled away.

"Look, I promise not to lecture or even say anything if you let me clean that up. Walking through this polluted area with it exposed is the best way to get an infection."

"I don't need the help of a stranger with a guilty conscience," she said.

The woman shrugged at that. "Well, you're not completely off base. Maybe you can ease my conscience and at least let me put some ointment and a butterfly bandage on that."

Amber pushed herself to stand fully but found she was still far too dizzy. She leaned against the wall. "I guess I'm not going anywhere soon."

The woman reached into her pocket and pulled out a small first-aid kit. She pulled out an alcohol pad, a couple of butterfly bandages, and a packet of ointment. She closed the kit and put it back in her pocket.

Amber blamed her blurry vision and the dark lighting, but she couldn't make out even the slightest bulge in Naomi's pocket from the kit. "You got a name or do you prefer to be called 'stranger'?"

"Naomi."

"Naomi." Amber repeated to herself swallowing a lump as the blurred vision was beginning to make her stomach churn.

Naomi tucked the tools in between her fingers as she worked to clean the wound and the blood that dripped down the girl's cheek. "I know I said I wouldn't say anything, but you should really think about the company you keep."

"What's that supposed to mean?"

"If this was a friend, I would reconsider that friendship, is all."

Her eyes started to glaze a bit and she hid a sniffle. "It wasn't a friend."

"Who was it?"

"You should go back to not being nosy."

Naomi tucked the alcohol towelette back into the package it came from and opened the ointment. She applied it directly to the wound.

"Shouldn't you be wearing gloves?"

"I'm not worried."

"Why not? I could have some disease or something," Amber said.

"Your blood is clean," Naomi said.

"Yeah, right. You don't know that."

Naomi met her eyes briefly, then continued to attend to the wound. "You know, if there is someone around here hurting people, you should speak up. You could save someone else's life."

"Well, unless you're a sex worker I don't think you need to worry," Amber said. "Besides, the cops don't give a shit about us."

"So, it's a John," Naomi concluded.

Amber closed her eyes.

"Hey…" Naomi paused. "We all do shit we don't want to if it means taking care of people we care about. Trust me, I'm in no position to judge. But if you ignore the hostile parts of the job, you're only allowing those parts to hurt someone else."

Amber paused. "What if he already has?"

Naomi placed the butterfly bandage to Amber's eyebrow and tucked all the trash into her pockets. She watched as Amber's hard exterior cracked and tears started to fall down her cheeks. She waited patiently for her to continue.

"I love my job. It's so fucking stupid, but I do. I get to be in control and… I just really like it. But there is this one guy. This one shitty guy. Every job has shitty parts, right?"

Naomi nodded.

"This guy—fuck. He has a reputation, but you can't avoid him. He's such a dick and so fucking *mean*. He doesn't listen to our rules. And no one cares to do anything. You know what happens when a sex worker asks for help? They tell you to get a new job. Like it's that easy, you know?"

Again, Naomi nodded.

"So, what do we do? Suck it up and hope that when the guy finally kills someone it isn't you or someone you know. But he's getting worse. He's already put one friend of mine in the hospital and the other…" Amber covered her mouth for a moment to hide her quivering lip. "I don't know if the other will ever be normal again."

Naomi put a hand on her shoulder, and the touch caused Amber to crumble into Naomi's chest, sobbing heavily. She pulled her tight and let her cry for several moments.

After what seemed like eternity, Amber's cries began to stifle and she pulled back collecting herself.

Naomi handed her a tissue.

"Jesus, you have everything in your pockets," Amber said, wiping her face.

"Nearly," she replied.

"I'm sorry."

"Don't be," Naomi told her. "This guy. If you could wish him away, what would you wish for?"

"I wish the bastard would die."

"Is that what you would really like?"

For a moment, Amber's face lightened as though there was a chance for peace of mind. But it quickly left and her face scrunched into guilt. "No," she whimpered. "I hate him, but I could never live with myself if I knew he died because of me. He's a piece of shit, but I can't take a life."

"There are other options," Naomi said, crossing her arms.

"And you're the one to offer them?" she asked, skeptical.

"I'm a person with the means. Remember, you're not the only one with a shitty job. If you don't want him dead, would you settle for him just going away?"

Amber didn't speak. She swallowed a hard lump and simply nodded. "You could do that?"

Naomi nodded.

"It would make life easier for a lot of people out here."

"You would be helping all those people," Naomi told her. "Is this what you want?"

Amber nodded slightly.

Naomi pulled out the notebook from her pocket and pen. "What's his name? What does he drive? Tell me anything you can remember about him."

"It's, um, Hank… uh… Hopkins, Hodgins? No, Hopkins. Hank Hopkins. He drives an old Pontiac Impala, like a '95, I think, black. The inside is really torn up and a mess. Um, he's bald and has really dark eyebrows. He's like 5'9, maybe, but stout. I think he's either a retired cop or a vet or something. He has a tattoo on his forearm of some kind of insignia, but I don't know what." She tapped a hand to her forehead to think but was coming up blank. "I… don't know what else…"

"This is good." Naomi nodded. She looked back at Amber expectedly. "I don't work for free."

"Oh…" Amber's hands searched her pockets. "I don't have… I mean, I have a little, but…"

"What did you make tonight?"

Amber pulled a wad of cash from her purse. There were several twenties and a few ten- and five-dollar bills.

Naomi pulled a five from the wad and stuffed it into her pocket. She scribbled a number down on a notebook page and handed it to Amber. "Next time he calls, make up an excuse. Tell him everyone is busy but have him call this number. Tell your friends to call you and then direct him to this number. Make up something. If he enjoys beating women, he'll put the work into getting to one." She pocketed her notebook and looked at Amber.

"What should I tell people if they ask me?" Amber asked.

"Ask you what?"

"About this? About you?"

Naomi couldn't help but furrow her brow a bit. "Well, ideally, you wouldn't tell them anything because it would only come back to you, but I really don't care what you tell anyone. Just do what I said." She started to step away from Amber when she paused. "Can you walk? Are you better? Yeah? Good. Get some mace, take a self-defense class, and do what I said the moment he calls. Take care…uh?"

"Amber."

"Amber." Naomi nodded.

4

Taylor's lips pressed to the nape of Naomi's neck and she stirred. The knots in her stomach that she called reflexes caused her eyes to jolt open but feeling the familiar warmth of his breath on her neck, she relaxed. She pulled the pillow over her head and stretched under his sheets.

Taylor removed the pillow and met her eyes with a smile, which seemed to fade a bit. "Wow," he said.

"What?" Her voice was groggy and her eyes still murky.

"You looked almost disappointed to see me."

She rubbed her eyes and pushed up on her elbows. "I just thought I was somewhere else." She glanced at the mug in his hand.

"Somewhere better?" he asked.

Naomi thought back to the dream she'd been having. She didn't dream often, because she didn't sleep, and when she did sleep, she only dreamed about faces she struggled to remember. It made sleep difficult to come by. She was lucky that she didn't need much of it to function.

"So it was somewhere better," Taylor said.

"It's hard to find anywhere better than Tom Hardy," she said, though she was less than successful in her delivery.

"All that last night and you still dream about Tom Hardy?"

Naomi sat up, letting the sheets settle under her arms and taking the mug from his hand. She took the slightest of sips and half-heartedly shrugged.

Taylor chuckled.

"What time is it?" she asked, noticing he was fully dressed for work.

"After two; I need to head into the bar soon."

"Two?" She rubbed her eyes again.

"You went out hard. I mean, I'd like to think it was because of me, but..."

"I can't remember the last time I slept," she said.

Taylor brushed the mess she called hair from her face and settled his hand under her chin. Naomi felt her heart flutter but averted her eyes, trying to seem interested in her mug.

He took the hint and stepped back. "Well, take the day if you want. The bed, the apartment… Take that thing on the countertop while you're at it." He pointed to a pressure cooker that looked brand new.

"Why would I want that?" she asked.

"I don't know, but I don't want it. My mom sent it, but it's so clunky and annoying and has too many settings. I'll probably sell it online or something." He paused, looking it over, then reached for his coat and keys. "I know you probably won't be here when I get back because you never are. But if you are, maybe you could try some of the new recipes I'm trying out."

"Does Daisy's serve anything other than burgers?"

"Not yet, but I'm close to convincing the owner. I just need to come up with a good presentation of what we can offer, which is why I need someone to test them out."

"Why not Brad?"

"Brad has two talents in this world: he can cook anything and will eat anything. I could serve him a pickle stuffed with cream cheese and cigarette butts and he would tell me I should go on one of those cooking shows. Good man, but I need someone with a palette—or at least opinions." Taylor was looking into the mirror next to the door, smoothing his hair down and flattening the wrinkles of his shirt.

"You know I hate eating the meals you cook," Naomi said.

"Which is ridiculous, because I make amazing food." He furrowed his eyebrows.

Naomi frowned. The thought of eating anything caused her stomach to make an audible gurgle, which Taylor misheard as a credible reason to feed her.

He fixed the collar on his jacket and moved back to his bed. He kissed Naomi before she had the chance to turn away. "One day, I'll cook the most amazing meal that even you can't hate." He kissed her again and this time, she had to hide her grin. "I'll see you tonight, or whenever I do," he said, winking as he left Naomi to hold the barely touched tea in her hands.

She listened to the stillness of his studio apartment. It wasn't often she felt comfort, but she allowed herself just a moment to enjoy it.

She got up and dressed. She made Taylor's bed and went to the kitchen, where she dumped her untouched tea down the sink and got rid of the meal he'd left on the bar. In some other universe, she would eat the perfectly fried eggs and toast and feel warmth spread from her full belly to the far parts of her body. She would let Taylor kiss her without feeling a lump form in her throat and her stomach grow nauseous. Even if the sick feeling was self-induced, it served a purpose.

She was never very good at convincing herself, though.

Naomi looked the pressure cooker over. What on earth would she do with a pressure cooker? She didn't have a home to even plug one in, let alone the need to make food. And what else was there to do with it?

"It's not like I need a homemade bomb or anything," she thought aloud.

The notion lingered in the air and settled back into her mind, planting a subtle idea.

It would be a couple of days before Naomi put her plan for Hank into play, but as time passed by, she grew anxious. Soon she would need to leave for The Den's assignment. She would have preferred to put it off until she could help Amber, but personal preference wasn't a luxury she had. The more time that passed, the higher the likelihood of Amber calling her when she was unable to help. She would have just given her hope only to let her down, and who knew what Hank would do if every girl in the area turned him down. For someone as volatile as him, the result could be more than black eyes and broken bones.

The thought tied Naomi's stomach into knots.

She took no other work in the meantime. It was something that hurt her financially, but she made do. The benefit of being homeless and not needing to eat was the savings. Naomi wasn't overly optimistic, but she had to find the humor in the small, terrible things. Still her money acted to further her work at times. It paid for undrunk cups of coffee and bourbon so she could eavesdrop on the world's problems. It paid off informants when she hit a wall in research. Occasionally, it bought a meal for a hungry family. Naomi had little to no money, but every penny of it had a purpose.

When her phone rang, she hesitated to answer it. Three letters ran across the screen.

She gathered herself and answered. "Hi," she said.

She listened to the chatter on the other side of the line, knowing it would be a good while before she would get a moment to speak. "What did he say?" she asked. Another stream of endless talk. "But we can't. No, I can't. Because that isn't how this works."

She rubbed her forehead. "Do you have enough to pay the bills, the groceries, and the repairs? Then what's the problem? But I can't afford that. Can't you just settle for the simpler one?"

Naomi pulled her sunglasses over her eyes in hopes that no one near would notice her flushed cheeks.

She'd settled into the café in her usual spot by the window. She'd become as much of a regular at Java Joe's as she had at Daisy's, to the point where no one paid any attention to her and the barista knew her order and when to expect her. She hadn't made the same connections at Joe's as she had at Daisy's, but it was common practice to be left alone in a coffee shop.

"I don't understand this. I know, I know. I'm sorry. This is what you can do and aside from that... I'm sorry. Okay, okay. Love y—"

The call ended before she could get the words out.

Naomi closed her phone and set it aside. She breathed deeply, averting her eyes from the rest of the café with a hand on her brow. She had to calm herself.

"So, you *can* love," came a voice that belonged to a sweaty man standing to her right.

Naomi risked a glance and sighed heavily. "You're following me now?"

"I saw you in the window," Taylor said. "You looked upset and I thought I'd say hi."

"Hi." She waved weakly, keeping her eyes turned away.

"Hey, what's wrong?" he asked, reaching across the table, but she smacked his hand away.

She breathed deeply. "I'm sorry," she said. "There are people who are just really good about getting under my skin."

"Oh, so it was family on the phone."

"I didn't say that."

"You didn't have to. Everyone who has parents knows the double-edged sword of loving them."

Naomi felt normal for once and relaxed a bit. "You're sweaty."

"I was running. Some people do that," he said.

"Was someone chasing you?"

"Just my own mortality." He motioned for the barista to bring him two glasses of water before he took a seat across from Naomi at the booth. "Wanna talk about it?"

"Not really."

She fidgeted with the newspaper in front of her. She had it open to a small news story a few pages in. There was a yearbook photo of the local high school football coach and elementary school P.E. teacher next to a picture of a burning house. She hadn't left the page yet because she wanted to enjoy the details of the story—most particularly the "tragic loss of a local sports hero due to an unintentional mishap" part. Sexual assault was hardly a mishap, but she knew the paper referred to the candle and not Petey's dirty deeds.

"Naomi."

When he said her name, she found herself standing in the foyer of a small home tucked away from the rest of the world, staring at a room full of balloons, candles, and cake while she held onto her round belly for support.

"Naomi?"

When he said it the second time, she was simply a woman sitting across from an irrationally kind bartender who gave her far too much attention.

"I know we don't have anything clean or clear cut because I'm pretty sure you like it that way. But if anything, I want you to see me as a friend," he told her.

She pushed her glasses tighter now, trying to hide the welling tears. "You should really get a girlfriend," she told him.

He smiled as he shook his head. "That's what you tell me."

"My... my mom," she said, the words caught in her throat. "She just gets frustrated at times because of their living situation."

"Are they poor off?"

"No, more like secluded," she said.

Taylor tilted his head and waited for her to continue.

"I take care of them. Every penny I make, I send to my mom and dad. My dad's health has been bad and I told them not to worry about anything."

"Awfully kind of you."

"That's not how they see it," she said. "I do seclude them, but… but they don't understand, they couldn't understand why I have to."

"Maybe you could help me understand?"

Naomi let her eyes linger on Taylor. His gentle smile and soft eyes gave the impression of concern rather than curiosity, but she knew better.

"The short of it, Taylor, is because of my work there are people out there who would love to hurt my family. They're far better off hidden from the world."

He took the hint from her dry tone and dropped it, but not his grin. "Fair enough," he said, then frowned. "Hey, did you take my pressure cooker?"

Naomi smiled.

October 3, 1969

I had my first encounter tonight.

I haven't a fucking clue as to what it—they—were. It was both a ghost and a physical monster while simultaneously being nothing more than howling wind. It was as though I could see it one moment and the next I saw nothing, but I felt its unholy grip on my throat. Its grasp felt like a man's, but gnarled and skeletal as though bones alone dug into my skin. I could only thrash my arms about, hoping to hit something to defend myself.

I can't say who these things are... these ghouls of Cowden Street. I find it no coincidence that these monsters seem to patrol the same street as the Howling House. Cowden used to be the epicenter of Pickleberry in a time when it was nothing more than a trading route. Now the street is hardly used except for teenagers who want to test the town's hauntings.

In any case, I find myself gravely unprepared to handle them. I managed to get away this time with a few bumps and bruises. Considering how unprepared I was, I think it would be really ignorant of me to assume these ghouls are the greatest and strongest threat to Pickleberry. That can only mean I have no means of understanding what I'm truly up against.

I could use a friend, a partner, in a time like this. Steve Owens always seems annoyingly interested in the things I talk about. He's a man I've grown to count on through most of my life, which is why I find it so easy to tell him the stories of the town. But when I see the interest in his eyes grow, I feel guilty. I have no idea what I'm doing, and bringing him into the mix will only guarantee something bad happening to him. The guy has been through enough in his life. Pickleberry has all but chewed him up and spit him out. I can't be responsible for showing him the monsters behind the curtains.

The day I decided to save this town is the day I decided to walk alone. Margo is here. She'll always be here. She's far too good to waste her time with me, but as long as we live, she'll stand by and watch me tear myself apart, knowing it's my purpose. She never asks questions, but she's always there to tend to my wounds.

God don't make people like Margo anymore. If something happened to her, or that poor bastard Steve, I'd never be able to live with myself.

I'm better off alone at this.

Chuck

5

There had never been a time in Naomi's life when she knew how to dress up for evenings, even before becoming whatever monster she was now. She could manage a hair brush and a mascara wand, but she wasn't built for galas or dinner parties. Working as a henchman for The Den gave her a lot of useful skills, but glamor wasn't one of them.

In moments that required her to appear less drab, less monochromatic, it paid to be a regular at Daisy's, which attracted all kinds of interesting patrons. Icons like Ebony Dahlia. Dahlia had a flare for the macabre. In fact, she had a flare for life in general. She was the kind of beauty who entered a room demanding to be seen, whether it was in a ball gown or sweats with her five o'clock shadow shining through her tinted moisturizer. Dahlia was a master of catwalks, soap boxes, and anything she could turn into a stage. She had a talent for capturing the hearts of men whether they liked it or not, and she lived for helping their wives become the queens they were.

The first time she'd noticed her, Dahlia had told Naomi, "You know, a woman with bone structure like yours shouldn't waste her time in the dark corner of a place like this." Most people at Daisy's didn't notice Naomi, but Dahlia was always searching for a project.

"What should I do with this bone structure?"

"Find yourself a rich husband, girl!" Dahlia had made herself at home in Naomi's booth. "If I looked like you, I'd never work again."

Naomi had allowed Dahlia's large, manicured hand to touch her chin and shift her face from side to side.

"A cute bob and a little bit of liner and you're Joan Jett if she didn't have a dick," she said.

"Joan Jett has a dick?" It was a facetious question, but Naomi had gotten a murderer arrested that night and was feeling good enough to humor Dahlia.

"She sure do, don't you, Joanie?" Dahlia called over her shoulder at the punk who, if you squinted and dimmed the lights, could certainly have been the former guitarist of the Runaways.

The Joan lookalike had given the only response you expected from Joan Jett—she flipped them the bird before snatching up one of the shots Taylor was divvying out.

Dahlia waved her hand. "The real Joan probably has a bigger dick, but none of that matters because I'm going to teach you how to contour to the gods, my little brooding beauty."

In their time of knowing each other, Naomi had taught her how to quickly and efficiently fend off bigots and handsy onlookers, while Dahlia tried time and time again to convince Naomi to tame her mane. The most Dahlia managed was to convince Naomi to wear mascara on occasion, since it was a crime to neglect such full lashes.

They were an unlikely pair.

Now, Naomi stood in the doorway of a rundown apartment building in the downtown district and rang the buzzer. "Well," she said when her friend opened the door. "If it isn't the mysterious Ebony Dahlia, a work of classic art and dame to die for."

"I love a bitch who knows the proper way to greet a queen," she replied with a twinkle in her amber eyes. "And that's 'dame who died under mysterious circumstances,' but I'll let you off this once."

"I knew I wasn't getting it quite right."

"Let me guess: you need to steal some clothes?" Dahlia asked.

"You're the only person I know with gala gowns."

Dahlia rolled her eyes. "I'm the only bitch you know who wears the same size as you. Something black?"

"You know me so well." Naomi smiled.

Dahlia held the door open for Naomi and gestured for her to follow her up the stairs. Dahlia had a saunter that made every step she took appear as though she were waltzing through life. It made her footfalls on the steps light and delicate, whereas Naomi's boots caused thunderous echoes through the stairwell.

"What's the occasion this time?" Dahlia asked over her shoulder.

"I'd rather not say," Naomi replied.

"Could it possibly be a date with a certain bartender we both know?"

"I have no idea what you're talking about."

They reached Dahlia's apartment door that had been propped open by a shiny red high heel. Dahlia entered, kicking the shoe aside, and pointed lazily to the closet to her right. The loft wasn't large by any means, but Dahlia had a way of dressing things that made it look like a luxurious studio where a high-end fashion designer might spend hours and hours creating the next Paris runway look. In reality, it was just a man, with gorgeous cocoa skin and an astonishing talent with textiles, working her life away to present fabulous creations to the gay kids of her town.

Dahlia snapped open a velvet fan and lounged across her favorite chair, watching Naomi pick through the dresses. "You know, my granny had a saying: 'Piss or get off the pot,'" she said.

"Yeah, and…?"

"If you aren't going to husband up that man, step aside so some other deserving woman can." She let the fan flutter lightly, averting her gaze to sell the drama of the moment.

"You're more than welcome to him, Dahlia."

"Oh, not me, honey. I could spend all day gazing at the delicious sculpture gifted to us from God himself, but I don't think he could handle a queen like me."

"Your five o'clock shadow is showing, queen," Naomi said.

Dahlia snapped her fan shut.

"I'm sorry." Naomi covered her smile. "That was rude. Can you just help me pick out something and stop talking about Taylor?"

"You never told me the occasion."

"It's an event, like, I don't know, a gala, but not as extravagant. I just want to blend in."

"No one goes to a gala in hopes of blending in," Dahlia said.

Naomi shrugged. She pulled from the closet a shapeless smock made from flat cotton and held it to her body.

"Oh, honey! I use that to clean my apartment. Bless your heart. You are clueless, aren't you?"

Naomi pointedly gestured to her plain, black-on-black clothes.

"The one next to the feathered cocktail dress. No, not that one. The other one. The fuchsia one. That's not fuchsia. Do you even know what fuchsia is?"

Again, Naomi referred to her monochromatic outfit.

"The bright pink-purple one! Yes, next to that one." Dahlia pointed with the fan now.

Naomi pulled out a short, black dress with glittering tassels and sequins. She didn't even hold the dress near her body, and only gave Dahlia raised eyebrows.

"What? If I had thighs like yours, I would only wear dresses like that." She smirked.

"I was thinking less disco ball and more subtle."

"Less Tina Turner and more Dita Von Teese? I gotchu." Dahlia nodded. She moved to the closet, pushing Naomi aside and digging to the back. She pulled out a simple black dress with a sweetheart neckline and off-the-shoulder sleeves.

The dress dropped to just above the knee and had a slight slit. Naomi wondered if movement was possible but figured there were few things Dahlia couldn't stitch up.

"I haven't worn this in years. You could say I've evolved since this dress." Dahlia sighed heavily, pressing the dress to Naomi's frame.

Naomi didn't look at the dress against her body. She didn't even get a good look at the dress because now that she was standing so close to Dahlia, she could make out the purple and red marks hidden by her dark complexion. She placed her hand to her cheek and turned her face to look closer.

Dahlia pulled away.

"You gonna tell me about this or do I really have to ask?" Naomi asked.

"It's nothing. You know when the shows get slow, I do a few side jobs to cover the bills. This was one of those months and this guy gets a little rough, is all," she said.

"Was that agreed upon?"

"No, but when do I ever get a say in that stuff?"

"Dahlia." Naomi's eyes softened.

"It's nothing, I'll just keep away from him next time. Lesson learned." She shrugged and smoothed the dress over Naomi's body with shaking hands.

She pulled her arms around Dahlia. "What's his name? Is it Hank?" she asked.

"Yes," Dahlia mumbled through Naomi's chest, not at all surprised Naomi knew his name.

"Fuck," Naomi muttered and hugged Dahlia tighter.

"You're wrinkling the dress," Dahlia whimpered.

They pulled apart and Naomi apologized. She wiped the tears from Dahlia's face. "Is there anything I can do?"

"Will you just marry Taylor?" she asked through sniffles. "I've made the perfect dress for a fall wedding and none of my friends will get married so I can wear it."

Naomi hugged her again—with a grin this time.

Taylor had an effect on women. He blamed it on genetics and being raised by a single mom. His dad was a silver fox with a wandering eye and troublesome ways. Taylor was hardly a silver fox, but he knew that part of his life was coming close around the bend. He didn't have a say in the matter one way or another, so the best he could do was to smile politely when women commented on his baby blues. Or how he should be the face of Daisy's (something that never made much sense to him). Or how he was wasted behind a bar when he should be on the big screen with a smile like that. Taylor could only give his charming smile and pour them another fruity-tooty something or other.

If he were being honest (and he would never admit this because his mother raised him better), it was exhausting to deal with each night. He dreaded the nights a gaggle of drunk women wandered into his bar, but he swallowed his distaste and enjoyed the extra tips. He was secretly glad for Daisy's dirty reputation, as it tended to keep the clientele just as dirty.

That's why the night Naomi had wandered into his bar he was instantly interested. She was average. Nothing overtly attention-getting about her aside from the dark clothes and general atmosphere of doom and gloom about her. Oh, and of course the bruises and beat marks. But when she came in, she didn't give him a second glance. She barely gave him a first glance, for that matter.

Being ignored was a strange feeling. It was like being a mind reader and finally meeting someone who made things go quiet. For the first time in his life, Taylor had to work to get someone's attention, and if there was one thing Taylor was known for aside from looking good, it was his determination and hard work ethic.

"I'm leaving," she told him. It was midday and the bar was empty. Taylor was counting bottles of whiskey and writing on his clipboard when she'd entered and made a beeline to him.

"Like *leaving* leaving?" he asked.

She shrugged. "I've left before."

"You don't usually tell me."

She shrugged again.

He couldn't help but smile. "Do you know when you'll be back?"

Again, she shrugged.

"You have such a way with words," he said.

She rolled her eyes.

"Where are you going?"

"I ordered you a mail order bride and I have to pick her up from the airport." She gave him a half smirk, half frown and started to leave the bar.

"Daisy's could use a new waitress… I'll see you when I do!" he called after her.

October 14, 1969

I've lived in Pickleberry my whole life. My family goes back to the beginning of the town, back when it was just a minor stop on a trading route between major cities. The people in this town prefer small living to the city, which is why most of the families stay in the area. Even with the eventual increase of houses, businesses, and people, there was very little growth. Sure, the population went up a bit, but there are no shopping malls or chain restaurants. There is one grocery store on the town square, and it seems to do the job for most locals. Others will make the drive outside of town if need be.

All this is to say, I can't say I noticed anything weird going on until we started getting more outside attention. Pickleberry is mostly farmlands along the outer parts of the town, lots of vast open land that many developers would like to capitalize on. Yet we see nothing new. Any time I catch a man in a business suit handing out cards to old farmers too tired to tend to livestock or crops, I expect a luxury apartment or a strip mall to go up; you know, the like. But nothing happens. The farmers disappear from the town, packing up their trailers with as many memories as they can hold, and the land sits untouched. Who would buy land and do nothing with it?

It didn't matter, because the more land bought, the more I noticed things coming out. Ghouls and monsters in the trees. It's like we normal people are being outnumbered. This town may have been created by the average Joe, but it's slowly becoming something else entirely.

Maybe I should visit the historical society (otherwise known as Joanie). Maybe I'm missing something Pa didn't tell me. Or maybe he didn't know.

Chuck

6

Much of the outlying parts of St. Louis are suburbs where those who work in the city prefer to live, as it seems less like living in the city with the perfect mix of Missouri country and city convenience only a few short miles away. While downtown is considered a tourist trap for baseball or fans of archways, it offers very little in the way of hosting private affairs.

Fountain Grove was less a community than a communal gathering hole for people who thought themselves important. It rose like an oasis of awe-inspiring structures out of dense Missouri forest, its grounds surrounded by impressive gardens and, of course, fountains. There was rarely a weekend when there wasn't a gathering, but these events were never open to the general public.

In moments like this, Naomi was grateful for her ability to slip past people. Though she found it a little more difficult to do so in the middle of the day, she could hardly go in blind. She had to arrive early to scout out the area, even if it meant hiding in the trees with the squirrels and the cardinals.

Guests entered and exited the estate through a covered walkway lined with walls and archways. The combination of shadows and light created the perfect opportunity for Naomi, as long as her target was alone.

The name Nora had given her matched the name on the welcome sign above the entry. Although the dress Dahlia had loaned her was perfect for seduction, Naomi couldn't risk being seen at the party with the guy.

She pulled her phone from her pocket and searched. She'd already looked into the place and everything else to do with the job, but looking at her target's face was never comfortable.

"All right, Michael Robinson," she muttered to herself. "Who are you?" She pulled the flask from her pocket and gave it a little shake as the results of her search loaded. Finally, a picture of a young man with dark hair appeared. "All right, all right, young guy... business owner... investments... named Forbes up-and-coming CEO to watch… That's all?" Naomi frowned. "A rich dude with money to spend? Why does The Den even care?" She shook her head and pocketed her phone, giving the flask a shake again.

To preserve her energy, she'd taken the bus for four grueling hours to get here. Now she was thankful for doing so—with barely a few drops of blood left in her flask, she had just enough to keep her going through the night, provided nothing went wrong.

Preparation and the knot in her stomach aside, she could only finish off her flask and find somewhere to get ready for the evening.

Even if Naomi had a normal life, she found it difficult to believe she could ever enjoy a life like this. Sure, the endless supply of food and drinks served on silver platters would be nice, but the things that came along with it? Not so much.

Dahlia's magic worked too well, because despite being in a room filled with gorgeous women, Naomi attracted unwanted attention, even while draping her leather jacket over the stunning dress. The goal had been to lie low and skirt the rim of the party, listening, drifting, and blending in. Polite smiles and slipping into any shadow she could find was draining her, and after being at the event for nearly an hour, she began to hope for a natural disaster to end it.

She'd spotted Robinson early in the night. He was hard to miss, what with the introduction upon entry and the entourage that followed him. The hopes of getting him alone seemed slim to none, and Naomi found herself at the bar, considering actually drinking the champagne she'd been toting all night.

Maybe I can puke on the guy, then help him clean up. That happens in romantic comedies, right?

She rolled her eyes at the thought and poured the drink into the nearest potted plant before asking for another.

"He gave me his room key," whispered a blonde woman down the bar from Naomi. She was wearing a short and sparkling dress that barely contained much of anything underneath.

"Who?"

"Robinson!"

"What are you going to do?" her friend asked, shooting back a tequila and ordering one more.

"I don't know. He's cute and I bet he's staying in the nicest place. Do you think he's married?"

"Cherie, has that ever stopped you before?"

"No, I mean, like, do you think I have a chance? If I married a guy like that I'd never have to work again in my life." She refused a shot from her friend.

Her friend took the shot without wincing. "I'm going to say not to get your hopes up. You're hot, but guys like him live off taking home different girls all the time. Just go to his room and have fun."

"I don't know. I'm so nervous. I don't think I can wait until this thing is over."

"So, why wait?" Naomi asked.

The two women looked at her.

"I'm sorry." She grinned. "I didn't mean to eavesdrop, but why wait all night? There are a lot of women here and who's to say he won't change his mind later?"

"Gee, thanks." The blonde rolled her eyes.

"Why don't you mind your own business?" her friend asked.

"I know I shouldn't pry, but listen…" Naomi moved closer. She leaned against the bar with a charming smile. "You're in a room full of gorgeous people and this guy picked you out of everyone. That has to say something. So maybe he does want more? Why wait the whole night to find out? Be assertive. Walk up to him, whisper in his ear that you have an emergency that only he can help with, and he'll be putty in your hands. Guys like knowing women have problems only they can solve. Why do you think so many of them have opinions on birth control?"

The women shared a chuckle.

"Plus, he probably goes to, like, three or four of these events a month. He would love to be rescued. I don't know. I'm just a stranger, but if the richest guy in the room had his eyes on me, I wouldn't sit around and wait for things to progress naturally." She feigned a sip of her drink.

"She's right." The blonde's friend nodded, and Naomi could see the effects of the tequila on her face. "It's 2025; you shouldn't have to sit around and wait for him."

"That's so forward"—the blonde blushed—"and not like me."

"Sounds like you need some liquid courage," Naomi suggested.

Her friend jumped at the idea. "Yes, she does! Three more tequilas. You're doing one with us, lady!" She pointed to Naomi.

The bartender put the drinks in front of them and the friend passed them out. They held their shots up.

"To being that bitch and getting that bag," her friend cheered.

"To no more waiting tables at The Hill!" the blonde cheered.

"To luxurious destination weddings!" Naomi winked.

The friends shot back the tequila and while they winced, Naomi dumped her drink behind the bar and placed the lime in her mouth.

"Here I go," the blonde said, adjusting her tits and leaving the bar.

"You got this!" Her friend smacked her ass as she left and Naomi smiled, appreciative of friendship like theirs.

The blonde had a practiced strut, as though the path from the bar to Mr. Robinson had become a runway and she was a top model. When he saw her, he couldn't help but stare as the conversation went on around him unnoticed. The friend and Naomi watched as she flirted her way through the crowd and latched onto his arm.

Naomi excused herself. From the corner of her eye, she watched Robinson make an excuse and exit the party with the blonde.

She followed the couple outside, keeping her distance.

As they left the main building, the lights faded away. Though a few guests had taken to the gardens, seeking to escape the music and crowds and enjoy the clear skies and chilled night air, most were scattered about enough that Naomi wasn't concerned about them. They were far too caught up in their own partners to notice her or the couple she stalked.

Robinson and the blonde had almost made it to the parking lot by the time Naomi caught up with them. She waited for a good moment, but they were putting on such a good show, she felt like a voyeur.

As they reached the end of the structure, Naomi's phone vibrated.

Robinson's ears perked up. "Did you hear that?" he asked.

"It's probably someone in the gardens. Noise carries out here," said the blonde, pulling at his tie and kissing his neck.

Naomi ducked back, pulling her out her phone and looking at the number. She was about to ignore the call when she remembered Amber and Dahlia. She couldn't risk it.

"Hello?" she answered in a hushed voice.

"This Amber's girl?" The man's voice was hoarse. "She said she's busy, but she knew of someone new. This you?"

"Oh yes, yes, honey. This is Amber's girl. Uh… Ember." She grimaced at her own piss poor improvisation skills. She glanced over her shoulder to see where the couple were. "Yeah, I'm a little new to the business, but Amber told me you can treat me right." She made her voice sound a little airy but maintained a level of sultry desire. "Do you need some company tonight, baby?"

"Amber is sending me to Ember? You whores are really creative with your names."

"We all have our talents, baby. Why don't I show you some of mine?" She looked down the walkway to see Robinson coming near the final arch and stretch of shadow before reaching the light of the parking lot.

"Yeah, yeah, you should come over here."

"All right. Text your address to this number and I'll be there in an hour." Her stomach began to turn as Robinson inched farther and farther out of her window of opportunity.

"An hour? I can have some other girl here sooner than that."

"Listen, baby, you can't rush perfection. You can always call someone else, but I promise if you wait, you'll have a night you will never forget. What do you say?" she asked.

He was quiet for a moment, and Naomi's heart raced as she watched Robinson. She was about to hang up when he finally answered. "Yeah, fine. One hour."

The blonde ventured ahead of Robinson as he lingered in the shadow, likely taking in the view.

"Great." Naomi smiled as she hung up.

The blonde looked over her shoulder, grinning widely and running her hands over her hips. "Come on, handsome. I'm waiting on you," she teased, lifting her dress a bit higher up her thighs.

Michael Robinson's face was unchanging. He didn't react or smile. He just stood still.

"Michael? Come on, baby." She gestured for him to follow.

His face twisted and contorted. Limbs of smoke and shadow stretched around him as he reached a shaking hand to his chest.

"Michael? What is it?"

He choked and grunted before collapsing to the ground, leaving only a growing shadow and a set of glowing white eyes where his silhouette had been.

The blonde screamed and the shadow was gone.

7

Naomi appeared in the alley behind Daisy's with a bang like the firing of a flintlock.

She stumbled into the wall, so hard that the brick and mortar crumbled away. Teleporting from such a distance—as a shadow, no less—had fucked up her system. She fought to get her body under control. Her skin had darkened, blending like ink with the black of her dress so that it was hard to tell what was skin and what was fabric. Pressure on her forehead made her raise her hands to her face. With fingers that had lengthened by inches, she probed at the humps of horns forming under her skin.

What a horror show, she thought. *Get your shit together.* With a deep breath, and despite her churning stomach, she turned her skin to pale. From somewhere, she mustered the energy to push back the transformation. Her fingers returned to normal. The mounds on her forehead receded. When she grew lightheaded, she steadied herself on the wall and puked onto her shoes.

She searched her pockets for her flask. When she found it, she unscrewed the top and tried to drain its contents but couldn't manage even a drop. *Damn it.* She felt the hunter in her rise. A voice jerked her attention to the adjacent street—a young girl on her phone. She looked barely eighteen and had a scared look on her face. Clearly, a child who had gotten lost. Naomi could hear her heart racing in her chest, the blood rushing through her body. She felt her body tensing to leap out of the shadows.

"Get a hold of yourself." She smacked her head with the flat of one hand. "You don't have time for this. There's puke on your shoes."

She moved toward the back of the alley where the door for Daisy's was and went inside.

Taylor greeted her in surprise. "Naomi, you're back?" He looked her over. It was the first time he'd seen her in anything other than her usual black on black. "Oh…" He sighed.

"Can't talk. Puke on my shoes."

"Oh…" He grimaced.

Naomi stood in the bathroom barefoot and tried not to think about what caused the floor to be so sticky as she washed her shoes in the sink. Luckily, the puke washed off. The smell would probably linger for a while. She held them under the hand dryer for a bit until she decided she didn't have time to wait and slipped them on still slightly damp.

When she left the bathroom, Taylor was waiting.

"When did you get back?" he asked. "You look… you look really—" he began before she turned to look at him and he saw the weariness on her face. "You look really rough."

"Wow, thanks." She pushed past him.

"Is everything okay?"

"I can't really talk right now. I have to be somewhere," she told him.

"Oh? Like a date?"

Naomi heard the hurt in his voice and stopped in her tracks. She placed a hand to her chest because for a moment she thought she was having some kind of attack. She faced him for only a second. "No," she said. "Please don't do that again."

But before he could speak, she was gone.

Naomi didn't have it in her to teleport to Hank's place, but fortunately it was only a couple of blocks away. Outside his tiny house, she checked herself. She touched up any makeup she could, forcing a bit more of her energy into ensuring she looked human. She tried to tame her hair but knew it was pointless. She straightened her dress and checked her pockets for all her supplies. When she was set, she attempted to saunter across the street, but walking like a prized pony would never be one of her skills.

She knocked on Hank's door and within seconds, he opened it.

"You're late," he grunted. Amber's description of him had been perfect, right down the to the bald head and insignia on his arm.

"Sorry, baby. Like I said, you can't rush perfection." She grinned.

He looked her over. "Maybe you should've taken another hour."

Naomi allowed his remark to maintain character and stepped inside his home. He shut and locked the door behind them. She took a few steps inside. "So, what are you in the mood for tonight?" she asked, turning to face him.

Before she could react, he struck her face so forcefully that she stumbled back into his coffee table. It shattered beneath her. She moaned in pain, writhing in shards of glass and wood.

Hank leaned close, grabbing each side of her face with one large hand and hauling her upright. "When I give you a time, I expect you to be punctual. It's only polite, and if there is one thing I can't stand, IT'S IMPOLITE PEOPLE!" He slammed his fist into her jaw.

Naomi felt a tooth loosen.

He threw her on the ground. "Take your fucking clothes off!"

Through the blood and welling tears, while she struggled to breathe and push herself up, she could see he had a hand in his pants, stroking himself. The thought of young Amber enduring the same treatment caused a flame to ignite in her gut.

Impatient, Hank grabbed her by the throat. Then he saw Naomi's face. Her eyes had flashed from brown to glowing white. Her hand clenched the air as though she were holding firm to something invisible.

Hank's grasp loosened. He scrambled backward into his recliner, clenching his chest.

Naomi released her hold long enough to focus her energy into her legs and push up from the remains of the coffee table. She stumbled closer to him. "You rotten piece of shit," she spat. "I should just squeeze your heart to nothing right now." She raised her hand again, clutching air as Hank struggled to breathe. "But I made a promise to someone whose life is worth more than yours will ever be."

Hank tried to speak, but all that came out was a couple of labored rasps.

"Worthless, bald, fat fucking piece of shit. You think it's funny to hurt women—girls? Practically children!" Naomi squeezed tighter and tighter, her own words fueling her growing rage. "I want so badly to kill you, but where you're going they're going to do worse things to you. So, I suppose there is some justice in the end."

Struggling, he said, "You... got nuthin' to send me away for." Each word passed like sludge from his mouth.

"You may be right," she said. "But when you go around beating up young women and gay men, no one will even question that you have it in you to bomb pride rallies and youth homes."

His face was strained and distorted and beginning to turn red.

"It's funny what you can do with a pressure cooker, eh, Hanky? Depending on the ingredients, you can make dinner—or a homemade bomb." She leaned closer, allowing her clawed hand to dig into his shoulder while her hand clenched tighter. "One pressure cooker filled with nails and trash and a reputation like yours? Perfect recipe for twenty-five to life. Not that you're worth the waste of free healthcare, a bed, and three meals a day."

Hank hawked a mouthful of spit and blood into her eyes.

Naomi didn't even blink. She pressed harder on his shoulder and before she realized it, she'd completely closed the fist that held empty space in the air.

He let out a silent gasp and his whole body went still. His face was still etched with the despair of having his heart crushed.

His stillness brought Naomi's temperature down. Breathing heavily, she stumbled back onto the dirty carpet and rubble of furniture, holding her bleeding palm.

Silence reigned in the aftermath of what she'd done.

Regret should have filled her. Instead, her eyes homed in on the blood spilling down Hank's chin. Her clawed hand had begun to look more human as she reached up and wiped the mixture of blood and saliva away from her eyes.

She wasn't even aware that she was running her tongue over her palm until the taste of his blood sent an electric pulse to her fingertips. Her eyes rolled back in her head, and with energy she was unaware she had, she pulled herself across his lifeless body and grasped his face. A shaky finger touched the blood. The warmth caused her body to quiver.

She was at the end of the road. Her ability to control herself was fading, and if she walked away there was no telling who would fall victim to her hunger. What if she met Amber? Or worse, what if Taylor had followed her and his face was the first one she saw while in a hungered frenzy? The thought of harming Taylor was enough to ground her, if just for a moment.

"It's better this way," she told Hank. "Even if your blood is so wicked it tastes like sewage."

Uncontrollably, her blood-saturated finger made its way to her mouth and her eyes rolled back in her head once again. She leaned forward, dragging her tongue across his bloodied chin and up his cheek. Too frenzied to process the flavor this time, she latched onto his throat, ripping out his carotid and drinking until her stomach bloated.

Naomi tumbled from his lap as the taste of his wicked blood hit her senses. The combination of overeating on an empty stomach with the taste of shit and rotten garbage and soiled meat caused her to puke all over the carpet.

When she was done, she crumbled back into the mess from the coffee table. Her hunger was subsiding and her wounds were closing, but she'd vomited too much to regain her strength. Staying here wasn't an option. There was no telling who had heard the commotion.

Naomi composed herself as best she could. She checked her hands and her reflection for any sign of the monster, but aside from the gore, she looked normal.

The place was a mess. There seemed little point in framing Hank now. She had bigger problems–like the pile of DNA she'd left on the carpet and the slashed throat of the sick fuck who lay dead in the chair. She had only one choice now and no stress relief candles to blame it on.

She found some lighter fluid under the kitchen sink. She covered Hank, his chair, and the carpet in it. In the kitchen not far from his body, she plugged in the pressure cooker she'd tucked away in her pocket. Spraying the outlet with lighter fluid, she hoped there would be some connection between shoddy electrical outlets and a home fire. There was no point in leaving the explosive contents of the pressure cooker or the anti-LGBT propaganda she'd dug up. All that was left now was to throw the match.

But for some reason, she hesitated. Something in her compelled her to get rid of bad people. Maybe it was to balance the work she did for The Den, but deep down she knew it was something far more personal.

Naomi recalled being a child with a notebook hiding under trees, lost in the worlds she created in her drawings. She remembered being acutely aware of the immensity of the world and being overwhelmed by her minuscule existence in it. Should a child scribbling monsters and heroes into a worn-out spiral notebook be responsible for deciding whether a man should live or die?

Then she remembered Amber's busted eyebrow. Dahlia's bruised cheek. She lit the match and tossed it onto Hank's body.

The cold air was taking its toll on her body. She'd been through so much tonight that only autopilot allowed her to move at all. Her feet took her where they were most accustomed to traveling until, swaying and stumbling, she found herself in front of Daisy's.

The sign was no longer lit. Her body sagged. The closest thing she had to a home and now the doors were locked. She hadn't the energy to teleport inside, to sleep on the pool tables or clean up in the filthy bathroom. So she stood, her vision coming and going, hoping someone would just barrel down the street and take her out of her misery.

"Naomi?" A voice came from around the corner of the bar. "I just closed up. What are you doing back here?"

"T-Taylor," she stuttered, staggering toward him.

He hurried to meet her. "Jesus, Naomi," he said, finally seeing the blood and glass in the dim streetlights.

"I…"

She collapsed into his arms.

8

Glenn Beasley didn't need this shit. He'd specifically returned to his hometown after three tours and eight years of service in the Navy with the idea of living a quiet life with his family. How much bad shit could happen in a tiny town like Pickleberry? He'd figured it was busting teenagers with booze and driving them home. In his teenage days, that was most of what he did.

He'd left the service for his wife, Tamara, and their daughter, Allie. He couldn't blame them for anything, but Tamara had been wanting to get away from the life for years. After his final deployment, when he'd realized his little girl was latching on to all the other men in her life and forgetting about her own daddy, he'd agreed. Eight years was enough to look good on a resume and he had a lot of bridges that needed mending with his wife. He'd gone to school to get a bachelor's degree in criminal justice and settled in his hometown to be a deputy (later detective), where he was home for dinner and homework nearly every night and made it to every soccer game even if he was on duty.

It was a sweet gig being law enforcement in a town that mostly governed itself. Free cookies at the bakery and coffee at Dent Corner. Enough weird stories to fill novels or to put Allie to bed with. He had a nap at the intersection of Brad Street and H each day. And since parking at the edge of town caused drivers to slow down, he counted it as serving and protecting. Was it a waste of his degree? Maybe. Had he loosened his belt a few notches since leaving the Navy? Undisclosed. Was it worth it pulling up to Allie's school with the lights on and calling her out on the PA just to see how red her cheeks could get? Absolutely.

Things should have gotten better from there, but they hadn't.

Tamara felt she'd lost too much time running Glenn's life, time she would never get back. So, when she didn't meet him in the kitchen to have their usual cup of coffee before he left for work, he knew he'd lost her. He came home for lunch and found a note reminding him to pick up Allie from soccer practice. After that, Glenn only took his coffee at the station or on the go.

Now Glenn Beasley was a single father staring at the cold, stiff body of the local troublemaker, Skye Gibson, on the side of the main road leading to the high school.

The sun was barely over the fields when he'd gotten the call from dispatch. He thought he'd misheard it at first. Surely he would just be cleaning up a drunk teenager from the side of the road to be delivered into his bed. But the only bed Skye was going to be delivered to was a cold slab in the Leigh Memorial Hospital morgue.

To Glenn's left stood the newest addition to the Pickleberry Police Department, Jamie Shepard. To his right was the morning walker who had called in the body, Debbie Glendale. Jamie seemed a little green around the gills, while Debbie continued to jog in place while the trio stared at the body.

"Well, Deputy?" Debbie asked.

Glenn shook his head, barely glancing at her. "Hm?"

"What are you going to do about this?"

"Uh… I… uh…" he stuttered.

Debbie placed a finger to her neck and timed her pulse on her watch while she waited for his response.

"Oh, um, Jamie… call dispatch and—"

Jamie promptly puked in the ditch behind the group.

The corners of Debbie's lips turned downward and she stared at Glenn.

"I'll call dispatch," he said.

Fast approaching footsteps came from behind them and they all turned to watch as a woman the same age as Debbie power-walked past. She was wearing a tracksuit similar to Debbie's, only in different colors. She gave a friendly wave. "Morning, Deputy Beasley, Debbie, Jamie."

"Deputy Shepard," Jamie corrected in between spews.

The woman smiled, but her eyes grew wide when her gaze fell on the body. Her pace didn't falter as she walked past and on down the road, stealing looks over her shoulder at the scene.

"Jamie, when you're done puking, go to the squad car and set up a barrier," Glenn ordered. His radio was in his hand, but he wasn't exactly sure he remembered the codes for calling in a dead body.

"Great," said Debbie, counting the seconds on her watch. "Now I've been outpaced by Mary and I'm losing my fat-burning zone. Deputy, are you done with me?"

Glenn waved her on and she charged down the road, hoping to catch up with Mary. He wasn't thinking about statements or evidence. All of his training and instinct had left him. All he could hear was the choking cough of Jamie, who seemed to be forcing her last three meals out of her gut and into the ditch. "What the fuck am I supposed to do here?" he asked himself.

Jamie moved slowly, but she'd begun to pull the cones from the back of the squad car, occasionally coughing.

He lowered himself to look the kid over. Skye Gibson had been known to cause trouble with almost everyone in the town. To say he had enemies would be an understatement, but he couldn't imagine a person in his little town having enough indecency to do in the kid this way. He pressed the call button on his radio. "Dispatch?"

"Yes, Beasley?"

"Uh, I'm going to need an ambulance or… no… probably the coroner and maybe give the medical examiner a heads up?" He paused. "I… I just don't know. I've got a young male in his teens. Presumably, but pretty confidently, deceased, off of the east part of Cowden. He appears untouched except for the… the uh… well, the giant-ass hole in his chest."

"I'm sorry? I think you broke up for a minute there, Beasley. A what?"

"A hole. Right in the middle of his fucking chest." He inched forward, leaning uncertainly over the body. "I'm thinking his heart is missing."

Behind him, Jamie puked into a traffic cone.

9

"Naomi. Naomi, maybe you should get up. Naomi? It's been two days."

Naomi turned her back to Taylor and pulled the blankets over her head.

He glanced at his watch and rubbed her leg through the blanket. "I'll see you after I close tonight."

When she heard his steps fade to nothing, she pulled the blankets from her head. He wasn't wrong. She'd pushed herself so far beyond her usual limits that she could have slept for a week if Taylor wasn't there to remind her about the world outside. Two days was enough to feel a little clearer headed. She couldn't camp out in his life forever. She looked across the studio to his washer and dryer. He'd washed and hung up Dahlia's dress, but clean didn't hide the wear and tear. She dreaded returning the dress, knowing she would meet the full fury of a drag queen.

Naomi stood from the bed and dug through the pockets of her jacket. She pulled out several shirts and pants and helped herself to Taylor's washer. She couldn't remember the last time she'd washed her clothes—or herself, for that matter. The blood and puke that had been on her face was gone. Taylor had probably done his best, but there were smells that lingered in her nose.

Naomi showered while her clothes washed and dried. By the time they were finished, she'd cleaned up his studio. She dressed, gathered her belongings, and left, locking the door behind her.

Naomi recalled a winter wedding. She remembered wearing a simple white dress and feeling as though nothing in the world would be better than that moment.

She couldn't see his face, and the memory of his voice was distorted, like audio put through too many filters. She couldn't recall his accent or any specific words, only the amber tones and fluidity that made her insides turn to warm goo.

The memory faded. Naomi had made a promise. No more winter or fall weddings. No elegant, custom-designed dresses with the glowing painted face of the designer standing by for support, certainly not while standing before a dangerously charming bartender. She'd reached the pinnacle of existence in a previous life and now she had to shuffle through the muck until no one else needed her.

But Dahlia had left an inkling of something more in her mind.

"Oh, Avenging Gothic Princess of Crime and Punishment, you think you can slink from some piece of shit's shithole unnoticed, burn it to the ground, and go about your life?"

"I don't know what you've heard," Naomi said. "Must be some other brooding, dark-headed vigilante."

"No, no, you don't get to give me a destroyed dress and then slither out of an explanation that easily. Last time I checked, fake tricking didn't require gala-inspired dresses." Dahlia slurped at the iced caramel coffee that Naomi had presented as a bribe.

"I apologized for the dress. The gala got out of hand."

"That's not even what pisses me off," Dahlia admitted, tucking the dress under her arm and shifting the straw in her coffee. She leaned against the doorway of her building. She hadn't even offered to let Naomi in this time. "What pisses me off is you got that boy washing your laundry—*my* laundry—and he did it correctly?" She held the dress for Naomi to examine. "This bitch is torn to shit, but that man pressed it as if it's fresh off the rack. And he used the good shit. You can't smell that?"

Naomi didn't bother sniffing it. She rolled her eyes and waited for the rest.

"All that and you still won't lock that down?"

Naomi was speechless for the moment. "So you're going to casually accuse me of murder like nothing and *this* is what gets heat?"

"No one will miss that piece of shit. Even if you did kill him, who's to say? Not me. The world is better without him. But you're too damn smart to be this damn dumb."

"I didn't come for relationship advice, Dahlia. I love you and I'm sorry I ruined your dress." Naomi sighed.

"Oh, shut the fuck up." Dahlia shook her head. "Listen, girl, we all have our crosses to bear. But you're allowed to lean into happiness when it presents."

Naomi blew off the interaction. Her relationship with Dahlia was a toxic mixture of unexpected chemistry and being told she was wasting her good years when she should lock down a good-looking man.

But for the briefest moment, Dahlia had planted a seed of wonder. What would life look like if she left The Den and abandoned her misery for a second chance?

Naomi wasted the rest of the day avoiding both Daisy's and Java Joe's. Intentional self-isolation was the one means of coping she knew, but even she was getting tired of it.

She'd made it a point in life to keep people from coming too close. It was better that way. Better for her and much better for them. Still, without realizing it, she'd made a friend of a gorgeous, talented queen, the kind of friendship that called for tequila shots, pep talks, and ass smacks. More than that, she'd found someone walking this earth who cared about whether she lived or not, without it being about financial gain. To The Den she was just an employee, one who could be replaced in a moment despite the investments made to train her. They didn't care about her past life or her current one. They didn't care about the secrets she kept, unless those secrets gave them leverage over her.

Taylor had carried her home in the middle of the night while she was covered in blood and puke without once asking why. Taylor knew she had secrets, but he never pushed more out of her than she was willing to give. His kindness was beginning to creep under her skin and make her feel something she'd promised herself she would never feel again.

A fall wedding didn't seem so horrible. She remembered what it was like to have someone, a person who had her back. In her mind, she saw a face she couldn't quite make out. The details were fuzzy. Whoever that person was, their image had faded away. But now, when she thought of having someone, she was seeing Taylor.

That two days of sleep must have broken something in my head if I'm daydreaming like this. I'll never be normal. I'll never have that life again. No point in even thinking about it. It will only make it harder to face him.

She'd begun to accept that Taylor had become an important part of her life.

She wandered aimlessly around town until long after the sun had gone down, but eventually she found herself at the bar again.

Before her courage could wane, she went in. For the first time, she didn't go directly to her table in the back.

"Hey," she said to the cute bartender.

"Hey, you're up." He smiled.

"Yeah, maybe two days was enough. I was thinking…" She hesitated. "Maybe you could show me some of those new recipes tonight? I haven't got anything going on."

"I don't close tonight, for once. I'll be off in an hour."

"I can wait an hour."

"Bourbon?" he asked.

She nodded.

He poured her a shot and a glass of water.

She took both to her table and watched them sweat rings to the tabletop while Taylor worked the hour away, a ridiculous smile plastered to his face.

Naomi waited outside while Taylor wrapped up his shift. She felt the usual pang of hunger, but when she reached for her flask she remembered she'd never refilled it. She'd lost her cool at Hank's, and once again it had gotten deferred to the *maybe later* list. She would worry about that another time. She'd gone longer without feeding and there had to be some bad guy walking around from whom she could steal a few ounces.

She tucked the flask back into her pocket as Taylor came out. "Is this what normal people feel like? Leaving work before three in the morning?"

She shrugged.

They walked to his studio together and went in.

"You know, I've always wondered how you do that?" he asked.

"Do what?"

"Lock the place up after I'm gone," he said, closing the door behind them and tossing his keys aside. "You don't have a key."

I turn the lock's mechanisms because they're in the dark, she thought to herself. "Oh, um, fire escape," she lied.

"You take the fire escape?" He looked at the window. "Maybe I should give you a key."

"Nah." She waved him off, removing her jacket and laying it over the back of a lounge chair.

Taylor did the same and patted one of the bar stools for her to take a seat. "Welcome, welcome." He gestured grandly to the lackluster kitchen around him. "Before I share my delicacies with you, shall I treat you to a bottle of Sauvignon from… from somewhere in France…?"

"Aren't you supposed to be a bartender?"

"We don't serve a lot of wine at Daisy's." He uncorked the wine and poured Naomi a glass. "This wine pairs great with the first dish I have in mind: a basil risotto with a roasted chicken breast."

Naomi sniffed the wine, appearing interested. "You're going to roast me a chicken? At eleven o'clock at night?"

"Well, a breast," he said, eyes dropping.

"Don't look at my breasts."

"Sorry, they're just so nice."

She shook her head, suppressing an eye roll, but when she looked back to him she saw his eyes lingering down the front of her shirt. Her brows furrowed when he looped a finger around the leather strap that hung from her neck. It was long enough that whatever was at the end of it was lost between her breasts.

"I don't think I've ever gotten a good look at this," he said.

She felt the cool metal against her skin as he started to raise it but stopped him. "I forget about it sometimes," she said, tucking it down.

"Where did you get it?"

"It was a gift," she said simply, averting her eyes.

Taylor took the moment to let his gaze linger on her. Her collarbone, her neck, her face.

She feigned a sip of wine, hoping to distract him, her stomach fluttering.

"How is it?" he asked.

"Um… crisp?" She recalled the wine tastings her mother used to hold in the living room of her childhood home. Her mother always gave the impression of having refined taste.

"Excellent," he said. He began pulling out ingredients and utensils. Once everything was spread out on the table before him, he opened his arms wide and said, "I welcome you to Kirby's Kitchen!"

"Who's Kirby?"

"Me."

"Your name is Taylor Kirby?"

"You never knew that?"

Naomi feigned another sip of wine.

Taylor shook it off. "The name's a work in progress. This is the real magic." He pointed to the ingredients in front of him.

Naomi settled back on her stool and watched him prepare the meal, occasionally pretending to sip the wine.

Suddenly, he stopped.

"What?" she asked.

He slammed a cheese grater on the countertop and paused for effect. "Oh, grate. I seem to have misplaced my basil."

"Jesus Christ."

"Listen, I'm taking my thyme to prepare this meal for you," he said, sliding a jar of the green spice across the table. "The least you can do is appreciate the clever puns."

"You're a nerd." She rolled her eyes.

He shrugged. "I yam what I yam, Naomi."

She covered her face laughing, but when she looked back she was no longer looking at tall, dark-haired Taylor. Instead she saw a younger face, a familiar but fuzzy one with dusty blond hair, golden hazel eyes, and a smile that spread the whole width of his face. Even his laugh was different, like one she hadn't heard in a very long time and immediately felt guilty that she'd forgotten.

She pushed her wine glass back and her smile left her face.

"What's wrong?" Taylor asked.

"Um, I just need a moment," she said, leaving the bar and slipping into the bathroom.

She leaned heavily over the sink, breathing deeply. When she met her gaze in the mirror, she felt disgusted. "You're a fucking idiot," she said. "This was a mistake."

She recalled the excitement in Taylor's eyes and reconsidered. What was the harm in one meal? "It's just like any other night. No attachments." She shook her head at the image in the mirror. "No attachments," she repeated.

She left the bathroom with a better grasp on herself.

"Everything okay?" he asked.

"Guess I'm not used to wine," she said and took her seat at the bar.

The night continued with Taylor cooking and Naomi enjoying the conversation. She'd put on her mask now and was able to separate herself from the moment. When the meal was ready, he served it on two plates and insisted on waiting until

Naomi tried a bit of everything. Each bite turned her stomach a bit more, but she pushed through with an unaltered face. Once Taylor started to eat, she merely pushed her food around on her plate, hoping the conversation would distract from her lack of appetite.

"Is this one of those, 'I'm a girl so I can't eat in front of people' things?" he asked, finishing his plate.

"No."

"I never see you eat, and even now it's barely a bite here or there."

"What can I say? You're a terrible cook?" she suggested.

"Well, that's a blatant lie."

"I just don't have much of an appetite," she offered.

"I'll have to work on that," he said, frowning. "You know, Naomi, I'm not the kind of guy that has to know every detail about your life. And most of the time, I just accept that you come and go as you want and have a general sense of mystery about you."

"But?"

"But," he continued, "I notice things."

"Yeah?" she asked, feeling a lump form in her throat.

"Sleep all day, only up at night?"

"Like a bartender?" She'd known they couldn't avoid the topic forever.

"Close, but I don't think I've ever stood in the middle of the street covered in blood," he said. "If I didn't know better, I'd say you were some kind of day-walking vampire."

She crossed her arms. "Oh, really?"

"That or a vigilante."

"Which seems more probable, Taylor?"

He thought for only a moment. "Vigilante," he said. "I know your body. I know your strength and your innate desire to protect people. The girl, Amber, has been in every chance she can to talk about you."

Naomi tensed. "What does she say?"

"Just how great you are," he said, taking a drink of his beer. He'd given up on the wine a while ago. "Probably nothing at all to do with that fire at Hopkins's place."

She raised her eyebrow.

"That guy was an asshole. If there's any sense of justice in this world, it was evident when that fucker's house burned down with him sleeping inside." Then he paused. "But…"

"But," she repeated.

"I'm just saying, your secrets are safe with me."

She nodded thoughtfully. "I'm not a vigilante."

"Let's leave it at that, so I can say exactly that when I'm inevitably questioned." He grinned.

She shook her head, grinning back.

"That makes me kind of like Robin, right?"

"More like Alfred," she said.

He placed a hand to his wounded heart. "Ouch," he said, leaning forward a bit.

She leaned in as well. "It's a good thing," she said, meeting him in the middle with a delicate kiss.

October 30, 1969

We'd always been told to avoid the bar on the top of the hill as kids. Our thought was that our parents didn't want us around drunks and unsavory types. But the truth is there are more than just old men with demons in that place.

But there are always rumors, like the one that said that bar was full of vampires. Tonight I chased a skeezy motherfucker right to the doorstep of the old bar. He hesitated at the threshold, thinking I would respect some kind of boundary, but I'd already caught him trying to convince girls in the high school parking lot to visit the bar with him. There was no way in hell I was going to let him just walk off without some kind of intervention. In the unlikely (not completely improbable) chance this journal is used for evidence in some sort of assault case, I'll just explain that I wanted to have a chat with the fellow about his ill-intending ways.

When I crashed through the doors of the bar, I found him among company—the kind of company I would like to never keep.

The bar on the top of the hill isn't filled with vampires. It's damn near infested.

I can't fathom how they managed to fit so many cold and warm bodies into one room without making enough commotion to draw attention, but I guess I really don't want to know the logistics. I was pulled in without a fighting chance and taken to their leader, a Nordic-looking son of a bitch. He offered money for my skills and insights, something about a class war with the other unnaturals in the town. If I helped his kind get rid of all the other kinds, he promised to make me a very wealthy man.

Like I tell my kids, I suggested he just learn to play nice with others or move along. Mustering any kind of gall, I informed him I wouldn't tolerate turf wars in the town I called home, where my children slept, played, and inhabited.

The bastard laughed at me. He gave me a card with a phone number on it and sent me on my way. I think that was his way of offering help, but why would I ever take help from an organization named "The Den"?

If there's something I can take away from this, it's that The Den can never be trusted. They have the means to wipe this town from existence, but why haven't they? And their abilities and sadistic nature are far greater than my own.

Don't get involved with The Den. Even if they offered me the key to ridding every inch of this town of monsters, I wouldn't take it. Deep in my gut, I know that no good can come from The Den. And if I ever found myself in such a deep hole they were the only means of crawling out of, I'd fear for my family. Keys, tools, secrets. Whatever they could offer me, it doesn't come free.

Chuck

10

After Taylor had fallen asleep, Naomi left. After all she'd done in the past few days—her work for The Den, teleporting to Hopkins's and all that followed—it was no wonder she was half-sick with hunger. Add Taylor's meal on an empty stomach? Her growling stomach was a sign that she needed to stop playing pretend and get back to the real world. She'd enjoyed her vacation from reality, but if she wanted to continue to keep Taylor, Dahlia—hell, even the drunks at Daisy's—safe, she needed to leave.

She wandered the alleys and streets in the area looking for one guy, one bad egg, from whom she could steal some blood.

She found a junkie passed out behind a dumpster, but his blood was tainted.

There was a cop everyone knew to be dirty, but he was never alone long enough for Naomi to make a move.

Other than that, she only found a homeless man. He would have given it to her willingly—and therefore she couldn't take it.

Her pickings became slimmer as the day came and the world woke, making it impossible to corner someone. She didn't have the same advantage of the shadows during daylight, and after setting two fires in the area, she was walking on thin ice. By the time evening came, she was more exhausted than when she'd started. She gave up on her search and went to the only place she knew.

"Do you want me to fill that for you?" Taylor asked, bringing her the usual bourbon and water. He nodded to the flask she was turning in her hands.

She pulled herself from her tired thoughts and tucked the flask away. She shook her head and pretended to be interested in the glass of water.

"Dating a bartender comes with its perks, is all."

"Are we dating?"

He shrugged. "Or whatever you want to call this so you can feel more comfortable. I didn't know you even carried a flask."

"Surprised?"

"Yeah, a little. You never drink anything I serve you."

Naomi tried not to make a big deal and kept her attention on the drinks.

"I've got more recipes," he began. "If you're still as bored as you look come closing time?"

"I don't think that's a good idea."

"Come on. We're making kind of a habit out of this, and I more than kind of like it." He grinned. He was leaning like he usually did when he tried to convince her to come over. Palms pressed into the tabletop, forearms and brachial artery exposed.

Naomi had no control over her eyes as they trained on his arm. "I'm trying really hard to break bad habits," she said.

He wrinkled his nose and stood upright. "Well, you know where I live if you change your mind. Oh, Amber was looking for you earlier. She'll probably come back by later."

Naomi couldn't help but pinch the bridge of her nose. "That girl," she mumbled.

Taylor chuckled as he returned to the bar, slinging shots and smiles.

In terms of not making herself criminally liable, it was better to not see Amber, especially if she was seeking Naomi out. She was happy to have helped her, but any sort of celebration, even in the form of an innocent hug, would surely look incriminating, if not simply odd.

Just when she'd agreed with herself that it would be better to wander the city or even hide out in Taylor's studio, she noticed the Victorian ghost standing in the doorway. Or at least that was the look Naomi assumed Nora was going for, right down to the added layer of pancake powder on her face and black eyeshadow around her already sunken eyes. She wore a black dress, modern but vintage-esque, with a high lace collar. Her hair was a mess of curls stacked on the top of her head, and as she turned side to side looking about the bar, it tilted ever so slightly, surely throwing off her balance.

Nora drew attention. It was something she was very proud of. Even before she'd blossomed into her cold, gray skin, she'd turned heads. Maybe it was her unnaturally large eyes, high cheekbones, or wide smile. Or maybe it was how she seemed to glide into a room, never touching the floor, but dancing from one place to another.

So when Nora entered a room, she knew the pull she had. She knew how to hold the attention of men and women and how to use that attention to her benefit. She was aware that every gaze in the bar was locked on her, but she cared little about the gazes of men. They were bugs under her boots, bugs who scurried aside to make a path as she fluttered to Naomi's table.

"You weren't leaving, were you? I did make the trip all the way to this shithole just to find you." Nora dragged her hand over the back of the booth, her black nails like talons against the faded red leather.

Naomi settled back in her seat. She shook her head and tried to ignore Taylor's stares in her peripheral.

"Surprised to see me? I wanted to see how you live. What do you do while you're waiting to be unleashed like a poorly trained dog? I always imagined you sat in some bare apartment just waiting, but now that I see this place…" She looked around. "I've clearly overestimated your sense of self-worth."

Naomi tensed.

"And the lengths you go to to appear like one of these blood bags." A taloned finger tapped against the sweaty bourbon in front of her. "Bottom shelf, I bet." She laughed. "You could kill this entire bar in the flicker of a bulb and live like a queen among peasants. Yet you drink McCormick and pretend to be interested in… in…" She glanced to the television, one of many, above Naomi's head, where two grown men sparred in a Brazilian Jiu Jitsu match. "Whatever homoerotic torture porn this is? Is this a gay bar?" She looked around again.

"I know vampires are old, but you do know how telephones work, right?" Naomi asked. "What do you need?"

"Honestly? I just love seeing you squirm in person."

With an effort, Naomi maintained a blank face.

"You give the dead a bad name," Nora said. "Most people lighten up after biting the bullet, but I guess since you took lightning literally, you must have forgotten how to enjoy things." She pantomimed a lightning bolt striking the table and an explosion with her hands, giggling. "Get it? Lightning?"

"You're hilarious," Naomi said.

"Clearly, you're a waste of my efforts." Nora feigned wiping a tear. "We have a different kind of job for you. Nothing you've done before, but this will take a bit more sophistication and communication skills. I just wanted to make sure I didn't have to coach you through a business meeting."

"Business meeting?"

"You will be a representative for The Den tomorrow morning up North. This meeting is rather important for The Den, but more important for Rik."

"If the meeting is so important, perhaps Fredrik should go on his own," Naomi suggested.

"Oh, you know how pesky humans are about worms, being the early birds they are and all. No evening meetings could be made. You'll do fine. Just, you know, don't fuck it up." She grinned.

Naomi felt a heaviness pass over her chest and she exhaled. Her weariness and weight of carrying The Den's responsibilities settled in, darkening her features.

"Oh, Nay-Nay." Nora pouted. "You look terrible. Are you resting? Eating? You should feed before appearing tomorrow. We can't have you representing The Den looking like the dead." She smirked at the own irony of her statement

"I'll hunt tonight, don't worry," she assured her. She found Nora's humor exhausting.

"Hunt? Why waste the time? You're in a bar full of forgettables. You could toss a stone and hit at least three nobodies, as in *nobody will miss them*."

Naomi kept her face stoic. "I use this place to help my work," she said, hoping Nora would accept her excuse for not hunting in the only place that felt like home to her. "You'd be surprised the news you pick up from gossiping drunks. Gossip that could help The Den."

Nora shook her head with a chuckle that told Naomi she didn't buy it.

Somehow, without Naomi noticing, Taylor had approached the table. He replaced her bourbon on rocks with a fresh one and even topped off the untouched glass of water. In doing so, he couldn't keep himself from giving Naomi his usual flirty smirk before offering a polite nod to Nora. "Enjoy your night, ladies," he said, and Nora grinned back.

"Why not that one?" she asked Naomi.

"He's not my type."

"He seems it. Breathing, heart pumping blood and all."

"He probably has a wife or someone that would miss him," Naomi reasoned.

"I didn't see a ring. I did see the twinkle in his eye. It makes our job so much easier when they fall in love with us so willingly."

She laughed in a way that for a moment made Naomi flash back to the friends doing tequila shots at her last job. She felt sick to her stomach. "He's full of disease," she said.

"I didn't smell it. And I believe age has allowed me to fine tune my snoot for such things." She booped her own nose with a wrinkle and a grin.

Naomi swallowed a hard lump.

"Oh, barkeep," Nora said. She twisted in the seat and waved her hand delicately to Taylor.

"Don't," Naomi said, trying to keep her voice steady.

"Oh, don't be so drab, Novak. You're just a little shy about your abilities. You're still practically an infant. I don't mind offering a hand. It isn't like you've grown attached to this human, right?" She scrunched her face in a giggle, waving to Taylor once again. "Hello, handsome? Do you have a minute?"

Taylor smiled. He returned to their table slinging a rag over his shoulder. "For the most gorgeous ladies in the place? I can spare two minutes."

Naomi held her breath, keeping her gaze averted from Taylor.

"Oh, stop it." Nora giggled again, suddenly becoming a completely different person. "My friend here is a little shy. You see, she isn't very good at interacting with people. Somewhat socially inept, if you will."

Taylor sent a glance to Naomi and she closed her eyes.

"I'm kidding, of course." Nora held Taylor's forearm. "She would like to know what you're doing when you get off work?"

"Oh, really?" Taylor asked. He shifted his weight to one hip and placed a hand lightly on the other, speaking directly to Naomi. "I'm pretty sure your friend knows what I would like to do."

She kept her eyes closed, knowing if she opened them she wouldn't be able to stop the tears.

"Nay-Nay!" Nora reached across the table to lightly smack Naomi's hand. "Keeping secrets from your friends?" she teased. She turned her attention back to Taylor. Suddenly, her gaze was wide and unbreaking. "You know," she began, running her hand up his forearm. Her talon grazed from his sharp jaw to his chin, locking his gaze until all glimmer and light left his eyes. "I'm no stranger to a good time, and what is the saying? The more the merrier?" Her nail held his chin so fervently that it began to draw blood. "Perhaps we could all make this dreary night more entertaining together?"

"Taylor, please leave," Naomi finally said, but it was no use. His face was blank. He was already deep under Nora's spell.

"Taylor?" Nora repeated. "What do you say, Taylor? A bit of triple action might be exciting."

"Yes," he said, his voice monotone. "Yes, I would like that very much. Thank you."

"Excellent. Finish you shift and Naomi and I will wait for you." She pulled her nail from his chin. "Now go away," she ordered with a dismissive wave.

Taylor stood blinking for a moment before smirking at Naomi, not seeing the horror in her eyes. He played with the towel over his shoulder, then walked away, trying to hide the smile Naomi had grown to anticipate.

"I'm sure it will only be a few hours, but I'm certain one thing those witches never taught you was how to properly feed. They are witches, after all; we can't expect them to do anything well, can we? Someone has to teach you, or you could very well starve to death—and we wouldn't want that." Nora clicked her tongue. "Honestly, Novak, I don't know how you even survived this long. Drinking old, putrid blood from a rusty flask?" She shook her head. She looked at the blood on her fingernail, then offered it to Naomi.

Naomi turned away.

"You had your chance in his world," she said. "Now it's time to take your place in ours and do it as though you've known nothing else."

Naomi closed her eyes again, feeling a hot tear roll down her far cheek.

"I'm doing this for you, dear," Nora said, dragging the nail across her tongue and licking away Taylor's blood.

The cold night air and the unnatural silence of the forest settled into Naomi's bones. She found a sort of comfort in the cold. If her body was shivering and her skin chilled, then she knew she could still feel something. Even if she was miserable, the physical pain reminded her that life was still a thing. But when the gurgling pit in her gut spoke up, she was reminded how little she cared about being alive.

Optimism was something that escaped her. And while she felt some form of solace in the presence of the tall man sitting next to her, there was an omnipresent emptiness she would carry with her for the rest of her life.

"Are you cold?" he asked. His voice was a hiss and a spark and a collection of sounds that couldn't be translated and yet she understood it.

"No." She shivered.

"I suppose there is no warming the soul at a time like this." He reached a large hand to her head and caressed her mess of hair that hadn't been brushed in days. "We'll take care of that shortly." He sighed. "Witches are never considerate of others' schedules."

A rustle in the woods ahead caused her to look away. There had been noises the entirety of their wait, but Naomi didn't notice until he pulled her attention from her thoughts.

There was a heaviness, like oil, lingering on the air. It made it hard to breathe, but Naomi couldn't tell if it was the woods or something she carried with her.

She couldn't recall how they'd gotten to the clearing. The woods were dense; trekking among the trees would have been a challenge for anyone. Yet here the trees had formed a perfect circle around a large, aged oak that could have easily been the oldest thing in the forest.

Near the oak was a circle of stones. Nothing grew on this charred earth. It looked less like a firepit and more like a putrid place where life simply stopped.

The sounds of motion were becoming louder. They surrounded them now, coming from all sides.

Her companion sighed as though he were watching the intro to a show he'd seen dozens of times but couldn't skip.

Naomi had no energy left to feel surprised or scared of the unknown. The whole forest was a mess of the unknown. When someone—something—finally emerged from the tree line, she didn't even look up.

"He brings her to us, but she doesn't seem to have any life left to save," it said. It wasn't talking to Naomi or her friend. It was unclear entirely who it *was* talking to, until it split like a cell in mitosis and its new half responded.

"That should make for an easy trip through the shadows."

The two things, mere shadows really, with unclear forms and faces, split again, each half merging to form a third shadow taller than the others.

"Shadows are easier trekked when no light remains," the third figure agreed.

"It's about time." Naomi's friend sighed.

"Do you rush the setting of the sun too, fiend?" asked the third and tallest of the shadows.

"The setting of the sun is far more predictable than rotten forest witches," he replied.

The first two shadows hissed. Their ever-changing shapes began to form into something more solid and tangible, though still black as the shadows.

"Rotten forest witches we are. Rotten forest witches you have requested help from," said the third. Her body had taken on the shape of a woman, towering and intimidating. Her sisters were meek and slumped behind her, but this witch stood with shoulders back and eyes forward. She wasn't afraid of Naomi's companion, no matter how many faces he tried on her.

His hiss was that of an irritated sigh and it brought Naomi from her thoughts. Any other time, the sight of the three witches would have caused her to shriek in fear. Now she hoped they'd come to end her suffering, as unlikely as that was.

"I bring you a shell," he said. "A human devoid of all will to exist and yet she has pledged herself to me. A human at the end of her rope and still willing to give to me. Have you seen a more perfect offering of love?" He beamed.

"Methinks he knows not of love," a sister in the back hissed.

"Methinks he is incapable of it," the other returned.

"A pledge regardless," the tall one said. "So, we craft her for you and then what? What does a deceiver like you have to offer us?"

Naomi's gaze was off in the forest. She looked for shadows and shapes but saw none despite the constant sound of movement. She wasn't watching as her friend gestured grandly to the space around them.

"Black Bile?"

"Is he capable?"

"He cannot give what is not his, can he?"

The third hushed her sisters with a glance. "An interesting offer. Why would we want the place we already call home?"

"A home you share," he said.

"Just as the earth is shared," the third replied.

"Yes, but wouldn't both be better if you didn't have to share? Unlimited space. Your fill of shadows to command as your own." He grinned. "A beast would be no match against that type of power."

"And after that?"

"The city, sister? We could reclaim the city."

The third considered the offer. She looked Naomi over, lifting her chin with a gesture to investigate her face. "The void of her soul is darker than our skin," she said. "What horrors have happened to this woman?"

Naomi jerked her head away from the unseen force that held it and tucked her arms tighter around herself.

"I find life is generally dreary for humans," her friend said.

The third shook her head. "Methinks."

"Methinks, methinks," her sisters whispered.

"Methinks this darkness does not come from existence, but from something else." The first witch pinned her gaze on Naomi's friend.

He waved the suggestion off. "An unfounded accusation."

She didn't argue. No monster, creature, or deity would waste their time arguing the potency of a rattlesnake's venom with the snake itself.

"She won't be the same after," the third said.

"You promise?" Naomi asked, speaking for the first time.

Silence hung over the group.

"I would like her to be far more resilient," her friend said. "Adaptable. Maybe some traits of your kind, but a little bit of some others." He reached deep into a pocket in the inside of his trench coat and dug around. Eventually, he produced a small vial filled with a liquid Naomi couldn't make out in the dim light of the night.

He offered it to the third entity, who received it hesitantly.

"You bring your own blood?" she asked.

"Not mine. Well, not completely. Maybe a drop or two, but I don't think she would survive exposure to my blood." He laughed.

Naomi lifted her head to glance at him, wondering if she'd missed a joke—or something else. She didn't ask, though; instead, she settled her eyes on the grass that seemed untouched under the witches' feet.

"She will have to be broken," said the third. "In both body and mind."

"Not a problem," her friend said.

"I don't think you understand the process," the third began. "She—"

"You can talk to me," Naomi interrupted. "I'm here. I'm present in this too. This was just as much my idea as his."

Her friend gave an unnatural smile that caused the corners of his mouth to peel and crack.

"The process you are about to endure is beyond human comprehension," a sister in the back answered.

"Try me," Naomi said.

"Your spirit will be torn to pieces. The pain alone will make you wish for death. Any part of you that remains human will be a ploy, a façade, a means of blending in, but you won't be human anymore. Any family, friends, loves… you will never be a part of their lives again in the same way you are now. It would be better for you to entirely cut yourself off from them. Solitude will become your way of life in an existence bleak and null of light." She seemed unnerved by Naomi's lack of reaction. "Even I wouldn't accept this trade off, not for all the power in the world."

Naomi held the witch's gaze. Pools of white silk seemed to shimmer and flutter, but there was nothing behind her eyes except for the shadow that made up her body.

She envied the witch for that. She let her head tilt and her gaze shift to the large oak behind the sisters. A life void of love, full of loneliness, an outcast. Tears came to her eyes. "And in exchange, I'll be strong?" she asked, voice cracking. "I'll be useful?"

The sisters whispered among themselves.

"It is unlikely you will ever meet your full potential, but you will be feared. The depth of your abilities will expand to greater than either of you can comprehend."

"I have no doubt in her potential," her friend said.

Naomi felt his large hand on the back of her neck. She looked to his face. It was elderly and kind, but the edges were cracking. Despite this, she felt comfort looking at him. Whether it was his familiarity or his presence, she couldn't say. In any case, the dead, empty eyes and unnaturally large smile that didn't seem to fit his skin brought a smile to her lips.

"And this will help you?" she asked.

He nodded.

She looked back to the witches. "Physical pain would be a welcome distraction to my broken spirit. I agree to any and all terms or processes."

"This decision cannot be made drastically. Take the night—" the third began.

"I said I would do it," Naomi snapped.

The sisters whispered among themselves again.

"In exchange for the forest," Naomi's friend said. "When the time is right, of course."

"The empty promise of a hellion," scoffed the third. "But one we will collect upon."

She looked back to Naomi, stretching out her formless hand. The closer it came, the more definite its shape became, until she held out a hand with skin like charcoal.

Naomi shook it without hesitation. It was better to start the process and get it over with.

It would be seven grueling days before Naomi emerged from the forest.

On the sixth night of her stay, she was tied to the oak and left for dead. The witches had done their part. They'd beaten her body to its breaking point with no regard for human limitations and now had left it for the forest to decide whether she was worth the trouble.

A storm rolled in overnight and the witches returned, expecting to find her corpse tied to the tree. But the oak had been uprooted, struck by lightning in the storm. It smoldered on the wet grass.

Naomi was gone. In her place they found a creature curiously observing the forest, a figure as swift and silent as the shadows under their feet. Its body was an amorphous blend of branches and smoke, with horns sprouting where the head should be. Its mouth was a collection of gnashing teeth that shifted and jumped like the blade of a chainsaw.

When it noticed the witches, the creature sat upon the fallen oak and looked past them. "Did he not come?" it asked, taking great effort to form the sounds required for speech.

The sisters were split when they approached, but at the sight of the creature the two took shelter within the third, leaving her alone with the creature that was Naomi.

She shook her head and Naomi wept.

On the seventh day, Naomi emerged from the forest naked and disoriented. She didn't recognize the road she stood on, nor the houses across the field. On instinct, she reached deep into herself and disappeared before the emerging sun could touch her skin.

Life is a clusterfuck of train wrecks with brief commercial–like breaks of happiness in between (or whatever *Deadpool* said). Naomi had learned this early in life, when the train wrecks started happening with more frequency and a greater number of casualties. She'd trained herself to expect the wreck and skip through the commercials. It was easier to avoid happiness, to pretend that no such thing existed, than to deal with the consequences of getting too close.

In a moment of blindness, she'd forgotten the pain and lived a little. She ignored the screaming of brakes and alarms that could only mean one thing.

In the agonizing hours she waited with Nora, she could hear nothing but a train whistle ringing in her ears.

Not until Taylor lay sprawled on the bed they'd too often shared would the ringing stop.

He'd followed them like a zombie to the apartment and now he lay on the bed, flickering between consciousness and unconsciousness.

"I'm sure you have learned much of this on your own given you're still alive, but I do love a coachable moment." Nora grasped Naomi's shoulder's tightly before moving to Taylor's side.

"It really is pitiful, a creature like you reliant on a flask. Some might even call it embarrassing. The only conclusion I can draw is that you were never taught how to properly feed. You wouldn't intentionally embarrass The Den, right?" She stifled a rich giggle as she teased Naomi. "Now seems like a good time for a training session. With the benefits The Den has offered you and yours, you wouldn't risk appearing *disloyal* to us, would you?"

Nora had removed Taylor's shirt from his body and began working on removing his pants, jerking his body hard with each tug of his jeans.

"Why do men these days insist on painting on their pants? In my day, it took little effort to disrobe a man. Unbuckle his belt and they practically fell to the ground." She tossed away the jeans and settled on the bed next to him, putting on a show of being out of breath.

"I know I'm not the only one who noticed the predominate brachial artery." She dragged her finger lightly up his forearm. "Likely due to his impeccable physique and nights spent shaking cocktails. If I were to keep him as a pet, this would be my favorite source. It's intimate and yet tells others that he belongs to you."

She paused. "Naomi?"

Naomi was lost in images of their bodies moving on those wrinkled sheets. She didn't think she had the stomach contents to vomit. But seeing Taylor so helpless, she thought she might muster something. Even if it was just bile.

"Nay. Oh. Mee," Nora snapped her fingers with each syllable. "I am going out of my way to teach you something important. The least you can do is pay attention."

Naomi raised her eyes.

"This is ideal for keeping the human around." She wagged a finger to Naomi. "Arteries run the length of the body and are by far the best way to obtain maximum sustenance. There are several points you can feed from, but two stand out most notably. Here, the femoral artery." She ran a hand up Taylor's inner thigh as his head lolled away in protest, her black nail dragging along an invisible line she knew better than the layout of any city. "And here." She took the same hand and moved it tenderly, as a lover might, over the full length of his pelvic bone, hips, midsection, and chest, finally settling on his neck. "The carotid."

Naomi felt faint.

"Now, the question for you is: which do you choose?"

"Which will keep him alive?" she asked hoarsely. Her mouth was dry from her failed attempts to swallow down the lump in her throat.

"Alive?" Nora laughed. "We don't want to keep him alive. Living blood bags cause trouble. They tend to be the first ones to sharpen pitchforks and light torches for the forming mobs. The better question is: which will kill him the quickest?"

Naomi clenched her fist to hide the shaking. "And?"

Nora tapped her fingertip on his carotid artery, her grin broadening by the minute so that she looked less human and more like the monster she was.

Naomi took a deep breath. She motioned for Nora to move aside and took her place next to Taylor, who was having a bout of consciousness.

He twisted his head in her direction, bleary eyes trying to focus. "Naomi, I... I..." He tried to swallow but was so out of it he choked.

Naomi placed her hand over his mouth and turned his head away without a word. She traced the line Nora had drawn with her nail. A large, viable artery that pulsated from blood pumping to every inch of his body. She'd felt this before, in more heated moments, but now the flow was slower, more languid.

Nora crawled between Taylor's legs to watch.

Naomi leaned forward and for the briefest of moments hesitated. She wanted to apologize. She wanted to teleport them both from the room and hide him away in a cabin in the woods. She was good at that—hiding people she loved away. But there was an inkling of doubt in her mind. What if she wasn't as good as she thought? What if they found him and the others? Taylor would spend the rest of his life a toy for monsters far more sadistic than Nora. And the others? Naomi couldn't stand the thought.

With another breath, she pushed Taylor's face farther away and dug her teeth deep into the soft tissue of his neck.

He put up a brief fight before going still.

"Yes!" cried Nora, panting with the excitement of an animal making a kill.

Naomi drank until Taylor's heart grew still, then held her mouth in place, hoping to fool Nora.

But Nora was a primal beast. She couldn't be satisfied watching another feed. Instinct took over and she latched onto Taylor's thigh.

She was far less gentle than Naomi.

Naomi squeezed her eyes shut as tears slipped down her face. Even the train whistle couldn't drown out the sounds of Nora tearing Taylor's flesh.

When they'd had their fill, Naomi settled in the chair nearest the bed and stared at Taylor's body.

Nora sang a Spanish lullaby from the bathroom as she washed the blood from her face, chest, and hands. When she returned, she dropped a towel into Naomi's lap and placed a hand on her shoulder. "Congratulations, Novak. Fredrik will be very pleased to hear of your devotion. We may not be the same, but I feel as though we were almost sisters tonight. If it were possible for a mixed-blood and a vampire to ever have such a link…"

"What should we do with the body?" Naomi asked.

She waved dismissively. "Leave it." She spotted Naomi's flask on the table by the door and picked it up. Blood still flowed slowly from Taylor's wounds. When she'd filled the flask, she screwed the lid in place and tossed it into Naomi's lap. "I know how much you love your flask. I guess it can be convenient for someone like you." She sighed heavily and placed a hand on the doorknob. "We shouldn't linger. Clean yourself."

"I'm going to tidy up the place a bit first," she said, sitting up in the chair. "You know, fingerprints and all that."

Nora chuckled to herself as she opened the door and left.

When she heard the door click closed, Naomi whimpered but covered her mouth in the same moment. For a moment, she allowed herself to sob soundlessly into the towel Nora had given her. Then she gathered herself and took a breath.

She reached a hand to touch his foot but stopped. She twisted the towel in her hands and breathed once more. The ache remained, but the uncontrollable urge to act upon it passed like molasses, heavy and thick. She wiped crudely at her own face and hands, not caring if she missed streaks of blood. With shaking hands, she gathered the bloodied towel and the warm, heavy flask.

"I'll come back," she said. "I promise."

She stood, tucking both the towel and flask into her pocket. She left the studio.

The night air hit her head, and she felt energized. She couldn't recall the last time she'd felt this awake, every sense sharpened. Sounds pierced her ears and a smell caused her nose to sting. The odor when she left Taylor's studio was so overwhelming that she had to stifle a sneeze and cover her nose as she met Nora at the bottom of the stairs.

Nora was smoking a cigarette. As Naomi joined her, she flicked it to the ground. It struck a trail of liquid, and fire trailed up the wooden steps, straight to the door of Taylor's apartment.

"What are you doing?" Naomi asked.

"I hear there's an arsonist in this area. Cops will think this is just another attempt to cover a brutal murder like the others."

"Other people live in that building," Naomi said.

"Good. Maybe someone will smell the smoke before it burns the whole place to the ground."

Naomi watched the fire spread over the door, breaking the frosted glass and whooshing into the building.

"Here." Nora pulled a hotel key from her pocket. "We booked you a room in the hotel next door to the meeting place for tomorrow. You'll find all you need to know about the meeting waiting for you as well as some appropriate clothes. You should clean up and rest. You'll have to teleport there, but that shouldn't be a problem after that meal."

Naomi took the keycard. She could feel the fire growing hotter on her face.

"Maybe now you'll learn there's no room for anything else in your life," Nora said, her voice losing the chipper tone it had carried all night. "You belong to The Den and The Den alone. Never forget it. From what I hear, you have an awful lot to lose if you do."

11

The Leigh Memorial Hospital was built in the late 1960s, when the locals demanded a closer-to-home option for handling emergencies or birthing babies. Before then, the closest hospitals were nearly an hour away (two for a larger facility). When children fell from trees and broke arms, worried mothers had the option to drive the long distance or to resolve the issue with techniques farmers used on their livestock. When it came to delivering babies, most were born on the floorboards of minivans. There wasn't a mother in town who wanted a farmer's opinion on the topic.

The hospital began as more of a clinic, with a maternity ward, a nursery, and an emergency department. It was built next to the middle school, in the field originally intended for a football field. By keeping the building small, the council hoped to avoid angry townsfolk by still leaving room for the football field.

However, just a couple of years after it opened, a local organization put forth a great deal of money to develop the medical treatment available to the community. They expanded the labor and delivery wards, the emergency department, and even created space for primary care physicians and a walk-in clinic. The biggest development to the hospital was the blood bank. The consensus was that since Pickleberry was so far removed from the rest of the state, they needed a bountiful supply of blood to cope with emergencies or blood loss during child delivery. No one thought this was an odd idea.

Still more developments followed over the years to come, funded by anonymous investors. With the development of an intensive care unit, recovery wards, and even a hospice center, the community had everything it needed.

There was no reason to leave. And no reason to ask any questions.

It was in the hospice center of LMH that Steve Owens took his last breath. But just before he died, he received one final visitor.

It was another annoyingly sunny day in the Midwest. The birds had started their springtime songs as the flowers planted in the box below Steve's window were poking their heads from the soil. It was the time of year when the townsfolk, tired of rain, flooded outside to enjoy the sun before it was hidden by clouds for another seven days.

Steve lay with his head turned away from the window, eyes squeezed shut. That damned day shift nurse had once again ignored his requests to keep the window shut. His reputation as a grump ensured that no one would be around to check on him until lunchtime. He would just have to wait it out. It didn't matter how many times he smashed the call button. No one came.

Steve suspected the nurses were simply waiting for him to die so that they could give the bed to someone the community cared about. He wished they knew how much he shared their sentiment.

He hurt. Every inch of his being hurt. Disease had taken his body long ago and made him miserable, each day worse than the one before. In his current state, walking across a room was impossible. The mere act of holding his dick to take a piss brought so much agony, he often passed out in a pool of piss until someone found him. Now there was nothing to do but wait.

All he wanted was peace and quiet. No sun burning his eyes. No fucking birds carving their melodies into his brain. In silence he could slip from this world without the offense of Pickleberry's song of rebirth, instead of spending every waking moment waiting for the noise to stop at last.

After three weeks in that bed, he was growing impatient.

Steve squeezed his eyes so tight that tears trailed out the corners. He hadn't the strength to cover his ears, so he clenched his fists as hard as his muscles would allow. In this way, he hoped to expend the last of his energy and leave the bed like a gasp in the night.

The only sound that came from his bed was a plea. "Please," he croaked. "Come to me."

The room went silent. No birds, no cooling breeze in the curtains, no life outside the window. Even the blinding sun had dimmed, enough for him to notice through his eyelids.

Steve opened his eyes. His room was dark, and it took a moment for his eyes to adjust. "Is this hell?"

Hopeful, he looked to the window only to find it had been closed and the curtains pulled.

His weak heart sank. He'd lost track of time wishing for death and completely missed that it was lunchtime. Obviously, the nurse had returned.

"Took your fucking time, Lonnie," he growled, turning his head to the door and seeing no one. He scanned the room, but there was no one. "You must be some kind of deplorable heifer if you think it's funny to prank a dying man."

No answer.

He looked at the door again. "Lonnie?" he asked, this time with a tremor in his voice.

"No Lonnie here," said a voice near the window.

Steve turned his head. When his eyes fell on a face, he felt both relaxed and terrified. He thought he knew that face, but if this wasn't the afterlife, it couldn't be who he thought it was.

"Lonnie is two hundred pages deep in some panty-soaking romance novel. You know the ones, with the shirtless man on the cover holding a beautiful damsel as though she were a fuckable sack of potatoes?" The stranger smiled wide. "I'm not sure lunch will be on time today."

Steve tried to sit up but was too weak.

The stranger stopped him with an upheld hand. His nails were thick and rough, like the bark of a tree. "Don't overexert yourself for me," he said. He then gestured to the uncomfortable chair in the corner of the room. "May I?"

Steve nodded.

The stranger pulled the chair to his bedside and took a seat, leaning back and crossing one thin leg over the other. Steve couldn't make out much else from under his oversized trench coat, but he imagined the stranger had a body like a birch tree—tall and spindly, despite broad shoulders. While the skin on his hands were flesh-colored, they lacked life and had a gray tone. In fact, he was gray all the way to his jawline, where the skin turned supple and fresh, a mask that didn't match the rest of his body. The stranger rested his elbow on the arm of the chair and placed his jagged fingers under his chin.

"Do you know me?" he asked with a look that gave Steve chills.

"I know you're not Chuck, even if you look like him. But I know who you are," he said. "You're the demon."

"And that would be why you called me."

"I suppose I did call you." He sighed. "The reaper must be held up somewhere else."

"Reapers work for themselves and answer to no one's call. I always come when called."

Steve rested his head on the pillows, too exhausted to hold it up any longer.

The demon found the controls to the bed and raised it so that they could chat without Steve wasting any more energy.

"You're awful kind for a minion of hell," Steve gasped.

"I am far removed from the motherland, but I will accept your compliment." He leaned back, resting his chin on his fingers once again. "What is the pleasure, Mr. Owens?"

"I would like to tell you a story," he said.

The demon's head tilted.

"Strange, I know," he said, swallowing hard. "But perhaps to better understand why I called you here, you should hear it."

The demon raised his hand. "I need no rhyme or reason, but given you are a man who is about to gift me his last breath, I will listen."

"In my childhood, I shared a small house on the outskirts of town with six siblings and my mother and father. My father was a hard-working farmer and my mother a seamstress for those better off in town. My father was in the fields from sun up to sun down by himself so that us kids could go to school. My mother worked her fingers to the bone sewing beautiful clothes from scraps of fabric left over from her wealthy clients so us kids would look presentable for school. But when the later harvests came, and my father couldn't produce enough to feed us and make a profit, they left us. Just vanished. We were split among relatives and friends through the town like indentured servants.

"Both my brothers left town in hopes of greener pastures. The eldest was killed when he got involved with the wrong people as a means of making ends meet.

"My eldest sister, the oldest of us all, always tried to maintain contact with the rest of us to keep the family together. She died standing up to our uncle, trying to protect the little ones from his beatings. My younger brother killed him, got incarcerated, and was later killed in prison.

"Two of my sisters married and were dead in the first five years of wifehood, one to disease and the other by the hands of her husband, though it was never proven. The local law never gave two shits about my people and didn't even look into it."

"And the last of your siblings?" the demon asked.

"My baby sister died the last winter we were with my parents."

"A depressing story," the demon said.

Steve huffed. "In all my years in this fucking town, it has done nothing but take. My family, my home, over time my wife and children. It's like a poisonous well we have no choice but to drink from. I hate this fucking town." He hesitated, looking at the demon. "It even took you, Chuck, the one person I thought too strong and bull-headed to die."

The demon's eyes seemed to smile pitifully at him.

He looked away. "You're not Chuck, I know. Chuck made a name for himself in this town. They all thought he was crazy, but I think he was just able to look past the green lawns and picket fences to see the ghoulish faces pressed against the windows." He looked back at the demon. "That's how I know about you. Chuck knew about you."

"Did he?" the demon asked.

"Not a lot, I suppose. He read about you in some book. You were one among many in the book, but he seemed very interested in you."

"I'm flattered."

"You should count yourself lucky he died before you met him," Steve couldn't help but spit. "I'm sorry. I didn't call you here to defend him, but seeing his face makes me sentimental."

"Would you like me to change it? I believe I have your whole family in my wardrobe."

At this Steve chuckled, surprising the demon.

"You're as much a curse to Pickleberry as it is to itself."

The demon smiled.

"I know you like gifts," Steve said.

The demon's eyes narrowed.

"Chuck knew a lot about you," he said. "I don't know how to do this, but I would like to give you one. Well, it wouldn't be a gift so much as an exchange, if you accept. But I think you will."

The demon uncrossed his legs and leaned forward.

"This town has taken everything from me and now it won't let me leave. All these monsters and curses, it never stops no matter how much Chuck tried. Maybe he got it wrong. Maybe it wasn't the monsters but the town itself at the root cause of all this dismay. I ask two things of you, demon. End me and take this town and I shall give you my heart." He paused, licking his lips. "And my face."

The demon's thin hand moved to cover Steve's where it lay on the bed for a brief moment. Then he placed his hand on his own chest. An unnatural red light began to bleed out from under the coat.

"You would give these to me?" he asked. "An unadulterated offering to me on your deathbed is almost enough to warm my insides." His fingers undid the top button of his coat and then the one below, where glowing could be seen through his gray skin. "You see, where your chest holds an organ capable of love and good, mine only contains hellfire. To so willingly give me what I desire, what would make me complete…" He clasped the top of his coat tightly and squeezed his eyes shut. "Why, that could only be an act of love."

Steve's breathing was beginning to falter. The demon's words hardly registered, and he simply repeated. "You must take the town. You have to keep your promise."

The demon stood. He took Steve's shaking hand into his own and placed his other over his heart, feeling each passing beat grow weaker than the one before. "For a gift such as this, it will be my duty to uphold my promise to you."

Steve pulled his hand from the demon's and reached for his face. As his fingers brushed his chin, he uttered, "I'm sorry, Chuck."

November 14, 1969

Fucking demons.

It wasn't enough for there to be vamps and werewolves in this town among all the other unnaturals, but now we have demons. I wish I could say I'm surprised. If there were a gate to hell, Pickleberry *would* be the main entrance.

I've learned a lot in these past few months, some from hands-on evidence of these monsters. For example, shreds of Armani and Prada left in the woods after a full moon seem to point to werewolves among the wealthy class.

But most of what I've learned has been from sneaking around the historical society. The society head, Joanie, had taken such a liking to my interest in the town that she practically handed me a key to the whole archives. I would never tell Margo about my reluctant flirting, but I did what I had to do to find out about this town.

From the beginning, it was built on dirty deeds done for dirty devils, but for now I have to get this discovery down before I forget it.

Long before Pickleberry was anything, before this continent was anything, it used to be a gateway for darkness. I don't know why things changed, but it seemed over time the demons all left—except for one. This one seemed to have a different motive than the others. In everything I've read, demons are selfish beings, doing evil for its own sake. This guy seems to be the only one in existence who thinks his cause is good. I don't know much else about him yet, but I know there are boxes upon boxes in the archives I haven't even touched. I might have to bring Joanie some of Margo's lemon bars to see how much further I can get.

One thing is for certain: I am hopelessly, helplessly unprepared to fight the legions of hell. Maybe in my research I can find something, anything, that could help me.

After my truce with the vamps, I worry little about my family's safety, but I'm useless against a demon.

Chuck

12

When the alarm on Naomi's phone started to ring, she blinked for the first time in what felt like hours. The first part of her humanity left behind when she'd been turned was all her human functions. Food made her sick. Sleep seldom came, even when she begged for it. When properly fueled, her heightened abilities allowed her to go for extended periods of time without the need for rest. This meant she could potentially cross the world's largest desert with but a cat nap in the middle. After taking Taylor's blood last night, every atom in her body buzzed.

Unfortunately, she had nothing better to do once arriving at the hotel than clean herself, dress, and wait until she was needed—five hours watching for the sun to rise, her body vibrating with kinetic energy that demanded to be exerted.

She tried not to think of Taylor. But in this state, her mind jumped so frequently she had little control of it. She played the events like a movie with retakes and alternative endings, obsessing over every detail.

None of the obsessing changed things. No matter how many times she rewrote the script in her head, it was fan fiction. Taylor had suffered from the moment Naomi allowed him into her life. He'd felt every ounce of pain she and Nora had inflicted, and he'd died a slow, lonely death.

The alarm continued to ring.

Shadows observed. They followed and drifted, but they never harmed the ones they loved. Naomi aspired to be a shadow.

The office building was only a couple of blocks from her hotel. Naomi had no intention of returning there, so she tucked all of her belongings in the pockets of her jacket. She dismissed the driver who waited outside the hotel for her and walked through the misty morning. She needed to get into character. She couldn't wear last night on her face. Nora was testing her. If Naomi fucked this up, The Den would have no reason to keep her. She had people who counted on her.

Naomi paused, looking to the highest window, twenty stories up, of the building she was about to enter.

What would a fall from a height like that feel like?

When Naomi entered the building, the lobby was being remodeled. Basic white walls, tall windows, some of which were covered in plastic for protection during construction. Sections of the floor were taped off so that tiling could be replaced or repaired. In the corners, small-scale scaffolding, tools, and construction materials were laid about.

In the foreground sat a plump, cheery receptionist wearing a headset. She was on the telephone discussing the redecoration of the lobby when Naomi showed her the appointment card that had been left for her.

The woman's smile spread so wide her eyes disappeared as she mouthed "fourteenth floor" and pointed to the elevator around the corner.

Naomi followed the corner hallway to the elevator and took it to the fourteenth floor. The doors opened into an impeccably decorated waiting room with jade walls and navy carpeting. Directly in front of the elevator was a desk with yet another busy receptionist—this time, a younger fellow with sandy blond hair and dazzling blue eyes, talking on a headset and typing away at his computer. He gave Naomi a wide smile and pointed with his eyes to one of the charcoal waiting chairs.

Naomi took her seat, flattening the front of the black pencil skirt over her knees, and tucked one ankle behind the other.

Save for the receptionist, the room was empty. She took this time for one last pep talk, tucking the grief and anger into a box which she would allow herself to visit later. She'd effectively tied the strings of her mask into place when the elevator dinged. An older man exited, wearing a pair of nice jeans, a white-and-pale-blue-striped button-up shirt, and worn but shiny boots. Under one arm he held a binder with documents; his other hand held an aged and yellowed cowboy hat. He shuffled a few steps, moving as though each joint were attached with rickety bolts and hinges.

He stood a few feet from the receptionist, who offered a polite smile but didn't address him. The man sighed. His face was like polished leather from what Naomi assumed was hard-working days in the sun. His thin, white-and-yellow hair was combed back flat against his head but curled at the back of his neck. The longer he waited for the receptionist to speak to him, the more his white handlebar mustache danced on his face.

Naomi spoke up. "I get the feeling decor takes somewhat of a priority around here."

"You mean the gal downstairs?" he asked.

"She was talking about new curtains and from what I can tell, this guy has big plans for an accent wall and some impressive artwork," she said.

He shuffled his feet a bit. "I don't even know what an accent wall *is*." He shrugged, taking a seat next to Naomi. "Harold." He offered a hand.

She shook his hand. "Mr. Davis, correct? I'm Naomi Novak, representative with the Pickleberry Preservation Association."

"A fellow Berry." He grinned. "I've met with your bosses a few times. They seem interested in my land, but when a letter from someone in the city offering nearly twice shows up, I have to weigh all my options."

"I completely understand, sir. It's important that your expectations are being met in the deal, but I'm certain there's a sense of home with my association that you won't find in a tall building some two hours away."

"Three hours," he corrected. "For me, at least. The ol' Ford doesn't move like she used to, but she served me well on my farms for many years. Those rusty clunkers." He couldn't help but chuckle. "If I get it over fifty-five, it starts to shake so much I'm sure one day the motor will just shimmy right out onto the highway. So, it takes a little longer for us to get around, but I don't mind. The thing about Missouri, you never run out of beautiful things to look at." Without thinking, Harold reached for a pocket on his chest where Naomi could make out the outline of a watch. He stopped suddenly and instead rubbed his hand over his jeans.

"I'm sorry," Naomi said. "For your loss."

"I miss seeing her face enter rooms," he admitted. "When she passed, I missed the skip my heart made when I was surprised by her face."

"Now you get it when you check the time?"

"You'll never convince me digital is better than analog."

Naomi smiled.

The door of the office behind the receptionist opened, and out walked a well-dressed man with a phone pressed to his ear. He held a finger to both Naomi and Harold as they stood.

"Do you think he's talking to the decorator too?" Harold asked in a whisper.

Naomi suppressed a laugh by clearing her throat.

The man hung up and looked back to them with a blinding white smile. "Mr. David, and you must be the other guy or... uh, lady." He offered hands to shake. "I'm Robert Bittenbinder."

"Naomi Novak with the Pickleberry Preservation Association. Mr. *Davis* and I were just enjoying your lovely waiting room."

"This boring place? The whole building is due for an overhaul." Bittenbinder led them into the office. "I like to redo it about every three to five months, so that things stay fresh and invigorating. No one wants simple, boring things," he said, pointing to two chairs at a table in the back half of a pristine office.

Harold took the seat at the head of the table upon Naomi's insistence, and she took the one to his left. Robert fiddled around with papers on the table before taking the chair to his right and exhaling loudly as though his volume commanded the room.

"Mr. David—Davis? Davis. Mr. Davis, I can't tell you how excited we are to have you here and how we can't wait to share in this process with you. You have the lot out on I-44, right? We have big plans there—adult stores, tattoo shops, and strip clubs." Robert gave a crude grin.

"Uh, no, sir," he began.

"No? No, it's the old building off 65 in Buffalo, that's it," he said.

"Mr. Davis is the owner of the 100-acre plot in the town of Pickleberry," Naomi offered.

"I'm sure Mr. Davis can speak for himself, Ms. Novak."

"I'm certain he can, but with all due respect, if you took the time to learn about Mr. Davis and the family farm he has put up for sale, he wouldn't have to speak unnecessarily."

Robert rotated his chair with a coy smile, watching Naomi keep her composure and Harold's mustache twitch into a smile. "All right, touché." He nodded. "Well, in any case, I'm so glad you've traveled so far to hear my offer, Mr. Davis. And you, Ms.

Novak, to make a noble attempt at a counteroffer." He clicked his pen and opened a note pad before him. "In the spirit of good will—I *am* a gentleman, after all—I will let Ms. Novak begin with her offer." He gestured to her.

Naomi gave him an unamused but polite smile before turning to Harold. "Mr. Davis, as you know by now, I represent an organization with the same hometown roots as yourself. The Pickleberry Preservation Association always takes special care to ensure the community of Pickleberry is at the forefront of all business endeavors it takes part in. While we keep the good of the people of Pickleberry in mind at all times, we also seek to expand when and where we can. While plans haven't been drawn up for the land you offer, you can be assured that whatever they become will be put back into the community just as we have done over the years with investments in the hospital and local recreation opportunities for school-aged children. Your land will only be used to help preserve and maintain the sense of community found in Pickleberry.

"I know you've spoken recently with officials about price, and after more talks, I've been informed that I can offer you fifteen percent more than previously offered. While I'm sure this isn't as impressive as whatever Mr. Bittenbinder will offer, you can rest your bones knowing the land that your family made home will only be used for the community, and not for the profit of outside interests."

Harold's head tilted from side to side in consideration, but he offered no more.

"I think you could have dropped the word 'community' a few more times," Robert joked, nudging Harold with a loud laugh. "In all seriousness, we here at Overview Investments care about the community just as much as the next guy. We understand that each town has its own history and culture that they wish to keep intact, but that doesn't mean they should go without luxuries."

He leaned forward. "While Ms. Novak's offer does seem to ring true to your roots, there's something she can't offer you." He paused for dramatic effect. "I'm willing to offer triple what her Pickled Berries Preserves is offering, without even knowing the number. In fact—" He tore a piece of paper and folded it in half. "I'm going to write down a number off the top of my head that I'm certain will be far more generous." He scribbled something down and slid it to Harold.

Harold opened and read the paper.

Naomi watched his eyebrows join in an excited dance with his mustache.

He cleared his throat and set the paper back down. "It was a long drive up here," he said, flattening the crease of the paper. "If you'll humor an old man, I'd like to tell you a little about my land."

Naomi gave a polite nod, while Robert rotated his face away to hide a grimace.

"My great grandaddy bought that land when the town was still new. In those days, it was nothing more than a trading post with a few tents and huts here 'n' there. Over time, it became a popular spot to stop in between the towns, and the charm of the town caused people to stick around. My grandaddy was one of the first ones to buy up land because he had an eye for good soil. He made a modest fortune off the land and passed it down to my granddaddy, then to my dad, and finally to me. Farming is what we knew. It's what we Davises all grew up doin' and the only thing we were good at. Maybe it was the land. Maybe she's as fertile as a Catholic child bride and that was why she gave us so much. We were grateful for it. But when it came down to it, my late wife and I didn't share her fertility." He adjusted in his seat a bit.

"My only son was born on that land and he died on that land. I'll admit I don't want to see it turned into a strip mall with overpriced coffee shops, but I ain't got no one to pass it to, and I'm too old and tired to keep tending to the farm." A pang of guilt seemed to pass over his face and he spoke directly to Naomi. "Running a farm with no family help is expensive," he said. "I've created more debt trying to save the land than I have profited from it. I appreciate your people's desire to keep the land as it should be, but I spent my life taking care of that land. Maybe I ought to be a little selfish. With an offer like Mr. Bittenbinder's, I could live somewhere small where all I have to worry about is paying some kid to mow the grass. Somewhere south where the cold never hurts my bones."

If she'd had the option, Naomi would have walked out, allowing Harold to benefit as much as he could from his land. But she had far more at stake here. "It could mean the end of your legacy."

"I have no legacy left," he said. "Ain't hardly no one alive that comes to see me anymore. Pickleberry has had her fill of me, and maybe I should take the hint and move on." He shrugged. "Thank you for taking the time to travel up here, but I'm afraid Mr. Bittenbinder's deal is far too good to pass up."

"Excellent." Robert grinned.

"I have conditions," Harold began. "I don't want to drive through the town and see some kind of ugly skyscraper out there. What are your intentions with the land?"

"Oh, uh, community enrichment, of course. Like, uh, assisted living and youth recreation. Every town needs a place for teens to safely hang out and encourage community wellness," he said.

Naomi wanted to roll her eyes so badly she could feel them begin to twitch. "As promised, we could expand on important resources to the community, Mr. Davis. More departments for the hospital, making any kind of medical help available to townsfolk, without traveling several hours or more. Plus the job opportunities you would be offering for new graduates of Pickleberry High. You can really help the economy of the town, Mr. Davis," she said.

Harold's mustache twitched in thought. "I'm sorry, Ms. Naomi. This ain't a deal that comes by every day."

Naomi nodded. "I understand." She hoped she could tell The Den she gave it her all—and considering the night's events, she thought she'd performed phenomenally. But watching Harold pull the pocket watch from his chest pocket and squeeze it into his palm until his knuckles turned white made her think of Taylor's lifeless body, and she felt her mask slipping.

"Excellent, excellent," Robert said. He shuffled some papers around and put some in front of Harold. "No need to delay this. If you go ahead and sign these, Kurt outside can cut you a check and we will have you on your way."

Naomi started to stand when Robert stopped her.

"Ms. Novak, do you mind witnessing?" he asked as Harold signed with a shaking hand.

Naomi nodded, sitting.

The two men signed papers and shook hands. Before Harold could leave, Naomi shook his hand with a polite smile. "Congratulations, Harold."

"Thank you, dear," he said.

Naomi sensed a bit of reluctance in his joy.

"Just out here, Mr. Davis, and we will get you that check." Robert motioned out the door as Harold exited.

Naomi stayed seated while the reality of what had happened settled in. How would she explain this? They wouldn't believe she gave it her all, but how could she compete with such a large company when her instructions were clear on the budget? She was reaching for her phone when Robert chuckled.

"What a fucking idiot," he said, stacking the signed papers and tucking them under his arm.

"I'm sorry?"

"Old man doesn't know his grandpappy bought land full of black gold all those years ago. He could have been living it up. I should really thank you guys. You know, for lowballing him so hard he thinks he's getting a good deal from me. I'm going to make ten times what I bought that land for from oil alone, and then I'm going to build a fucking Starbucks on it." He laughed.

Naomi, the woman enslaved to work for a vampire den for the rest of her life, remembered that there were things more evil than murderous vampires—like businessmen. "A win for capitalist America," she said dryly.

"It is what it is, baby." Robert shrugged. "Take your time here. I know this will be a hard loss for your little community." He laughed again as he left the office.

Naomi pulled her phone out and dialed. It rang only once.

"Are we the owners of 100 acres?"

"No, he didn't go for it. We were grossly out bid," Naomi said.

"How disappointing, Nay-Nay. Couldn't get your head in the game?"

"I don't know what you expected from me, Nora. It isn't like I can glamor like your kind can."

"Maybe you should use your other skills? Kill him."

Naomi hesitated. "The farmer?"

"No, you idiot. The investor."

"What? Now?"

"Yes."

Click.

Naomi hung up her phone. *Fuck, fuck, fuck, fuck.* She had no knowledge of this building, of the security, or what to expect. She couldn't possibly wait until nightfall because the longer she waited, the closer Robert came to filing away the papers, making the sale official. It wouldn't matter if he was dead or not. Once those papers were filed, it was official. What options did she have?

She heard the elevator ding.

She hurried to leave the office, catching Robert just as he was stepping into the elevator. "Hold the door," she called.

Much to her surprise, he did so.

"Maybe on the ride down I could give you some tips for how to really sell it to these small-town losers," he said.

"I'm always open for advice to better my work." She tucked her hair behind her ear with a shy smile. "Honestly, this isn't my usual field of work. I was just brought in to fill in for someone else."

"Oh, really?" Robert pushed the button for the ground floor and turned to her, leaning against the wall of the elevator. He'd loosened his tie upon entering the elevator. With his half smirk and blond hair, it gave him a real *my daddy paid off a lot of people to hide the bad things I did in college* vibe. "You should leave your place and come work here. We're always looking for attractive young people to take under our wing. Someone with a bullshit 'for the greater good' routine as good as yours could go far here."

"Gosh, you really think so?" She grinned.

"Oh, yeah," he said, moving closer. "So, what kind of work do you do? Maybe I could watch sometime?"

"How about a demonstration?"

"Uh, what?"

Naomi moved her hands quickly, grasping an invisible rope, which she used to snare the elevator cables. Then she ripped them apart with such force the elevator rattled before free falling nearly thirteen stories.

When Naomi woke, there was a fireman standing inches from her face.

"Ma'am, don't move. Please," he said. "You've been badly injured and if you move it could make it worse. We have paramedics here for once we get you out, but just hang tight."

Her vision was blurred. It took her a moment to realize the firefighter was upside-down, or rather, she was. She reached a hand to touch her forehead, but gravity made it difficult. "What... the fuck...?" she managed. She raised her head a few inches, trying to see her surroundings.

There was little left of the elevator, only crushed metal and sparking electrical wires. The ceiling was several feet lower and there were holes where she was certain debris had fallen through.

As her grogginess wore off, she noticed pressure, then pain, in her abdomen. Awkwardly, she reached for her midsection. She stopped abruptly as her fingers felt something sharp and metallic extending from her gut. A rebar beam had torn through the ceiling and skewered her like a beast waiting to be roasted over an open fire. This wasn't exactly how she'd intended things to go. "Goddammit," she muttered, trying to get a grip on the metal.

"Ma'am, don't pull at that. We have to get this other guy out and then we'll be able to help you better."

Naomi's neck and arms were getting tired and she was losing her vision again. She let her head loll back and her arms drop to her sides, hovering above the ground. "Is he… is he dead?" she asked.

"Don't worry about that right now," the firefighter told her.

She turned her head toward Robert. He lay on his stomach, his face turned to her and his body buried by debris. For a moment, she thought he might just be unconscious, but when she squinted, she saw that the back of his head had caved in. She guessed the oozing goo that spilled from his nose and eyes and mouth was an amalgamation of brain matter, shattered skull bone, and blood.

The chances of a recovery seemed bleak.

In the flickering light, Naomi could make out the white of the papers under his shoulder, most of which were becoming saturated with his blood.

She turned her attention back to the rebar. It was thin, no bigger around than a quarter, and didn't extend much past her body, but her legs were numb and she couldn't simply stand from this position. She felt the crumpled walls and the debris between Robert and her. The metal edges were sharp and sliced deeply into her hands as she gripped them and dragged herself upward. Supernatural freak or not, it hurt like hell.

She screamed, pausing only once to catch her breath.

"Don't do that! Jesus Christ! Just don't move," the firefighter yelled.

Naomi took a deep breath and pulled herself free, so forcefully she slammed into the twisted wall of the elevator. In the cramped space, the best she could do was crawl, panting, through the rubble, past Robert's mangled body, grabbing all the papers in her hands. She emerged into the hallway leading to the lobby, where she unintentionally fell into the firefighter's arms.

"Fuck! Fuck! Where is the fucking medic for fucksake?!" he yelled, pressing a hand to her bleeding abdomen. "Why—wha—h—how? *How did you fucking do that?*"

She started to sit up, but he pulled her back down.

"I'm not kidding, lady. Don't move."

Naomi settled her head in his lap only long enough to allow the whites of her eyes to expand and encompass the entirety of her eyes. "If you want to walk away with your larynx intact, you'll let me go," she said. The skin around her eyes was darkening by the second as her face hollowed out.

He trembled under her body but released her, staring with wide, shocked eyes at the monster taking shape in his arms.

Naomi rolled over roughly, shaking the shadows from her face and pushing her feet under her. It took great effort, but with the help of the wall, she managed to stagger down the hallway, hiding the gaping hole in her stomach under her jacket.

"Ma'am, you need to stop and let me help you," said the paramedic who approached her.

She waved him off. "I'm fine, just a scratch. There's a man in the elevator who needs your help, and I think your guy is going into shock. You can come back for me."

The paramedic's attention fell on the firefighter, whose face was pale and trembling. "Jake? What the hell happened?"

Naomi slipped out while she could, lurching down the street until she couldn't keep her feet under her anymore. Her vision was beginning to come and go, and she knew if she passed out on the street she would be taken to a hospital. She hobbled across the sidewalk to lean against a rusty blue Ford pickup, then tumbled into the truck bed. Despite the midmorning light, the tall buildings covered the truck in shadow. She felt lucky to have stumbled upon this truck, where she didn't need to exert any energy to conceal herself in the shadows.

With the last of her strength, she pulled the flask from her jacket pocket. She would heal in due time after her forced meal the night before, but she was losing so much blood it would be hours before she could recover enough to walk. A small sip from the flask could get her on her way before the hour was up.

But she couldn't bring her shaking hands to even open the flask. Instead, she pressed it against her chest for comfort. Her grip on the signed papers was loosening by the minute, but as long as she had them, she felt her work was complete. This gave her just enough peace to allow her to pass out in the truck bed. Whatever troubles followed, she would have to deal with them once her body had recuperated.

It was a few hours before they let Harold leave the building. While he'd been nowhere near the elevator when it went down, they still insisted on checking him out and getting a statement. Not that he had much to offer.

After he was cleared to leave, he decided it was best to leave the city before something bad happened to him. He shuffled down the street to his rusted Ford, keeping his eyes on the emergency vehicles that came and went from the building. He was looking for bodies. He knew the rich jerk who had bought his land had been in the elevator, but he hadn't heard about the sweet girl who tried to outbid him. He hoped she was all right.

He climbed into the truck and slammed the door, looking at the check in his hands. He'd never seen so many zeros in his life, but looking at them broke his heart. He'd signed the papers, but after a fiasco such as this one, who was to say if this check would be worth anything other than something to hang on the wall and dream of what could have been.

He grumbled, started the old truck after a few turns of the ignition, put her into gear, and started down the road.

This had certainly been a rollercoaster of a day. He was so caught up in reliving the sale and its aftermath that he didn't notice the papers flying out from the back of his truck as he merged onto the highway.

Part Two

Homecoming

December 5, 1969

Pickleberry has a hold on people.

The families that stick around don't often have much choice in the matter. They're conditioned to think there's nothing better than what they have here. It's easy to think that when the news is full of shootings, rape, and corruption in any place that isn't here. This town has a mildly sustainable economy, so that as long as you keep your dreams simple, you can find whatever happiness means to you here.

But that happiness comes with a price.

This town has a way of chewing up and spitting out its people in differing degrees. Some of the people here suffer from premature baldness despite never having any genetics for it. Some get end-stage cancer. Others are targeted so badly their whole family is hurt, like poor old Steve Owens. Poor bastard never stood a chance against this town.

Steve had been the only one who believed me and willingly listened to my bullshit from day one. But even I couldn't stop his family's torment and the things that happened to him.

On the other end of the spectrum, there are those that leave Pickleberry, refusing to stifle their dreams. But those that leave never *really* leave. A part of the town follows them. It festers in their shadow, slowly degrading their sanity until they're too far gone to save. Years ago, a boy I graduated with dreamed of greener pastures, but he didn't even make it past the city limits.

Pickleberry knew his intentions, and she does *not* like to let go. Even if you manage to get away, she'll drag you back screaming. Or in a body bag.

Yet no one wants to acknowledge it. No one wants to see this town as anything other than idyllic perfection. Small towns are known for small minds but big hearts. The big-hearted people here keep the community going and without them, we would just have a mess of monsters playing dress up.

I just wish I could convince them to see past the veil. I wish they could understand that blind ignorance isn't better. But what do I know? I'm just the local lunatic.

Chuck

13

When Naomi awakened, the truck was rattling down the highway. She'd lost a lot of blood, and the chill air rushing over her caused her to shiver violently. For the moment she lay still—she was covered in blood and couldn't afford to draw any attention to herself. Hopefully, she would have an opportunity to bail out before the driver stopped and noticed her. Plus, when night fell, she would be able to hide in the shadows without spending too much of her dwindling energy.

She felt a droplet on her cheek. A few more drops of rain fell, and then a shower. *Typical,* thought Naomi. *Missouri's unpredictable weather.* Still, for the first time in a very long time, she thought she'd seen the face of fortune, though she didn't expect it to stick around.

The rain continued for nearly half an hour, heavy and constant. Naomi turned over in the truck bed gently, scrubbing the blood from her face and clothes as well as she could and grateful to see it wash down the truck bed and through the holes in the rusted corners at the bottom. By the time the rain settled to a drizzle, the sun had set. No better time to bail.

As the driver slowed to make a left turn, Naomi lifted her body over the edge of the truck and dropped, tucking and rolling into the ditch. She watched him drive off to ensure he hadn't noticed, breathing a sigh of relief when he hit the cross street and didn't hesitate in his course.

Naomi was soaked and chilled to the bone. She stood in the dark, dazed and weary. Though she had more stamina than she was used to, she'd taken quite a hit from the elevator.

The papers were long gone. They were in her hands when she passed out, so that had to mean the deal hadn't been completed. She felt sorry for Harold, who would surely try to cash the check only to have it bounce. The poor man was just looking for an out from all the heartbreaking memories. Now he was stuck.

Naomi looked around—and felt a sense of déjà vu.

Things were familiar yet somehow completely foreign, like a place she'd dreamed—only the dream was reoccurring and one she couldn't escape from.

She stepped stiffly from the ditch to the road Harold had turned onto. Standing there, she felt like she was standing in a memory, a memory where the hot sun danced on her neck as she trekked up the road in the summer for cold drinks from the local gas station.

She shook her head, assessing the field across from her. It spread out far until a tree line appeared. She pictured herself lying in that field on cloudy days, with a backpack of books, notebooks, pencils, jars, and snacks. Entire days hiding out in that field, working her way through all the books in her parents' tiny library, drawing monsters and magical creatures in her notebooks with short stories under each picture, and eating all the junk food in her house. The lingering voice of her mother yelling washed away any sense of warmth she might have found in the vision.

This was more than an elaborate dream.

She shuffled her feet to look at the house to her right, expecting to see an old farmhouse. A young girl with a toothy grin she considered to be a proximity friend lived in that farmhouse. Only the farmhouse wasn't there. Instead, there was a modern home with a brand new deck, and two large buildings in the back.

The sound of a car on the highway dragged her out of her revery. It was speeding in her direction. She shielded her eyes as the glare of the headlights washed over her and she saw the car swerve, despite being in the lane farthest from her.

As it passed, Naomi inspected her hands. She imagined she looked frightening. She wasn't using her abilities to blend into the night, and she hadn't exerted herself to hide her natural, less human features. Likely the driver saw what he thought was some horrifying monster or spirit on the road. Cue a rash of tall tales about a terrifying ghost woman asking for rides in the area.

She looked over her shoulder and saw that the car was already far up the road, probably hurrying to get away from her. It was then she noticed the street behind her. Something about that block of houses sparked a memory in her. She felt drawn to it.

Before losing herself down the road, she slipped fully into the shadows, hiding from any onlookers to remove her tattered and blood-stained clothes. She replaced them with whatever she managed to pull from her pocket and stumbled down the road. As she turned onto the street, she stopped to look at the first house.

It was like looking at the cover of a book she'd seen a million times in her childhood, but now as an adult. The feeling that welled in her gut was a mixture of blissful comfort and deep-seated tension. She thought she knew the house exactly, but the more she looked, the less she recognized it.

She shuffled to the end of the steep driveway. Where she expected a garage, there were large, clear windows revealing what looked like some kind of shop. The lights inside were dim, but that didn't stop her from working her way up the driveway and pressing her face against the glass. A counter connected two clear cases that held pastries or other baked goods near the back of the room. Behind the counter, a handwritten chalkboard hung high on the wall, with coffee machines below it. Seven small bistro tables filled the rest of the modest space.

She leaned back, confused. The house left a clear impression on her, but the shop seemed unfamiliar. She must have hit her head harder than she'd thought—until she noticed the dent near the corner of the house.

A dent. In bricks.

She raised her hands to feel at the rugged, chipped edges. The dent wasn't so big as to threaten the structure of the building, but it was noticeable. This made sense now as she looked back at the windows and read the words printed on them:

Dent Corner Café.

More than just a quirky structural feature, there was something about the dent that sent a shiver down her spine. Her chills were followed by memories of laughter—hearty, full-body, belly-aching laughter. Without knowing why, she found herself smiling.

This was more than déjà vu. It was clear she had a connection to this place.

She felt a sudden, desperate impulse to search. She'd lost something. She had no clue what it was, but the urge was so powerful that before she knew it, her feet had carried her up the stairs to the front door. Without thinking, she followed the shadows and slipped through the door as though it were a barrier that didn't apply to her kind.

Concealing herself in the shadows, she looked around.

The open floor plan showed her a grand entry decorated with scarlet rugs and velvet furniture in rich, bold tones. The space was well-lit, but the only occupant was a sizable woman sprawled snoring across a plush violet sofa, a Harlequin novel pressed to her large breast. She wore a pastel house dress that buttoned down the front, and thick, worn house shoes over fluffy pink socks. Her hair was wrapped up in a scarf, and aside from the awkward angle of her head tilted over the arm of the couch, she seemed comfortable. At first glance, Naomi thought she had a goatee. She wondered if the lamp was casting a shadow on her chin, but on second examination, she determined there was undeniably some hair around the woman's mouth.

The place seemed like a foreign land. Not a single thing was familiar to her. Still, she felt that drive to find… whatever she'd lost.

The sleeping, mustached woman didn't even stagger her breathing as Naomi walked from the door to the stairs, glancing into rooms and testing locked doors.

A groaning creak from the wood under her boots made her decide she was better off teleporting, despite the risks. She appeared at the top of the stairs, in full light, catching a glimpse of a teenage girl storming from one room to the next.

Naomi stepped back into the shadows of the empty room next to the stairs, her back finding the wall.

The girl banged on the door, crossed her arms, and thrust a hip to one side. When she got no response, she banged again. "Luke! I know you have my tablet! Give it back!"

Naomi flattened herself against the wall as a middle-aged woman emerged from another room. "I just got your sister to sleep. I swear if you wake her, you'll spend the rest of your teenage years cleaning out the dumpsters in your uncle's shop. Do you hear me? What is the problem?"

"Luke took my tablet again. I know it was him, because Ben has his own and Jonah never comes out of his room."

"Did you ask Audrey?"

Naomi closed the door without a sound and turned around. She was in a standard bedroom, with a queen-size bed pushed into one corner and a crib on the other side of the room. She glanced at the crib but didn't need to venture any closer; she could hear the steady breathing of the child inside. There was nothing in the dresser or nightstand, so she crossed the room to a door on the other side. It opened into a small bathroom. A shelf behind the toilet held towels, extra toilet paper rolls, and air fresheners, but nothing else. Naomi was about to open the opposite door when it opened on its own.

She slipped behind the door as a young woman entered.

"Why would I have your tablet, Deena?" she asked. "I don't even *use* a tablet. Tablets are just another way the tech corporations control our minds."

A voice came from the baby's room. Naomi recognized it as the middle-aged mom. "Audrey, why can't you use the other bathroom?"

"Ben came out of his cave for once and has moved his weirdness to the bathroom."

"I just put Sophie to sleep. Can't you wait until he's done?"

"Aunt Miriam, you and I both know Ben will be in there for an hour at the very least." She sighed.

Naomi pushed her back farther against the wall behind the door and held her breath.

"Sophie's been teething and hasn't been going down very easily. I'm not kidding. If you wake her—"

Naomi had to do something before Audrey tried to close the door. She raised her hands as though she were holding an invisible box. Smoke and shadow began to twist around each finger as her eyes glowed white. She gave them a little shake and suddenly, Sophie began to cry from the other room.

Miriam sighed. "I'm going to start shipping teenagers off to LMH to work as night shift janitors." Her footsteps left the doorway.

"Fine, I'll shower tomorrow." Then Audrey, too, was gone.

Naomi watched from the door crack as Deena banged against her brother's door. Finally, it opened and a scruffy teenage boy held out a pink tablet.

"Thank you!" Deena snatched it out of his hands and stormed away.

Doors closed; the hallway was finally quiet.

Naomi glanced out, considering where to search next. Another room, lights off, opened to her right. A kitchen, light slanting from the doorway into the hall, straight ahead. To her left, another dark room adjacent to a laundry chute. She was about to creep out of the bathroom when a shadow crossed the kitchen and another woman came into view, a stack of dishes in her hands.

She was middle-aged, with a tiny figure. Her hair was wrapped in a neat bun at the top of her head. She was a natural beauty, for sure. High cheekbones, perfect olive complexion, and green eyes set under dark, shaped eyebrows. She wore the weariness and the satisfaction of work accomplished in the day like a jeweled tiara.

Impatiently, Naomi watched as she washed the dishes, wrung out the wash cloth, and started to wipe down the counters. With the light on and the open doorway, there was no way Naomi could move without her noticing.

She considered the light fixture overhead. It was a simple hanging lamp, its cord woven through a chain that ran into shadow. With a flick of her finger, she cut the cord. In the darkness, the woman flipped the switch multiple times, cursing under her breath.

Another light, more distant, came on in the kitchen. The woman spoke in a language Naomi didn't recognize, and a male voice answered. Cabinet doors were opened and shut, and the man said, "Well, I can't remember the last time we bought light bulbs, Trina."

She sighed. "Write it on the list. I suppose this is a sign to just go to bed."

"Perhaps God is telling you to not worry yourself so much."

"When God owns a business in this town, he can talk to me about worries," she snapped. "I'm sorry, I'm just tired."

"Come to bed, my love," said the man.

Naomi heard them kiss and then the light went off. There was a shuffling of feet, the sound of a door shutting, and then nothing. The house seemed to settle in now. Lights were going out and she heard distant snores. She moved out of her hiding place and searched the first room, a large closet, then the next, an empty bedroom. The last room, by the laundry chute, was a closet full of cleaning products. Nothing of interest—and certainly not what she was looking for. Whatever that was. She leaned against the wall with a soft huff.

She was about to explore the rest of the house when she heard the stairs creak. After a few moments, the dozing book reader appeared. Her head scarf was disheveled and she was being escorted by a handsome man in scrubs. "I always seem to drift off when things start getting good," mumbled the woman.

"That's how you know the book is good. When it lulls you to sleep," the man told her, arm around her shoulder. "Why else would you read it before bedtime?"

"Oh, to have good dreams, George. Ohhh, such good dreams," she moaned.

George grimaced as he opened the unoccupied bedroom and guided the woman in. He reappeared moments later. "Good night, Mini," he whispered, pulling the door almost closed. Then he went to Miriam's room on the other side of the stairs.

Naomi listened. Snores from Mini, soft whispers from the couple with the baby. Finally, the house grew quiet. She began to wonder if she was really searching for a thing or just a reminder of how royally fucked up her life was in comparison to average families like this.

A quick peek in each room showed her a comfortable family, but not much else—Mini sleeping in a clutter of books and keepsakes; Luke with a controller in his hand, leaning from side to side with a racing game; Deena chatting softly on her recaptured tablet. A clean kitchen, and no dirty laundry.

She was beginning to feel discouraged. What had compelled her to come here? Was she starting to lose her mind after all the trauma of the last twenty-four hours?

She hadn't thought of Taylor since she'd awakened in the back of the truck, but the morning's actions—destroying property to kill a man and nearly killing herself in the process—maybe there was a part of her that hoped the elevator would have been the last of it.

She sighed. Now, alive and well, she forced herself to tuck Taylor safely away in a box at the back of her mind. If she let herself feel the weight of it, let the grief seep in, her mind would slip into a black hole. She couldn't afford to fall apart. There were people who needed her and if she fell apart, who would look out for them? Still, Taylor's face before he died appeared in the shadows on the countertop. When her eyes welled with tears, she made herself focus on her surroundings.

Another hallway led away from the kitchen. At the end was another room, dimly lit… She pushed the door open cautiously to find an empty bedroom. The place was a mess. Books and papers were stacked on the floor. The bed was unmade and the nightstands were cluttered with pens, gemstones, half-drunk glasses of water, and reading glasses. She opened the top drawer to see only underwear. The dresser behind the door was just as messy but held nothing important.

She examined the desk on the far wall near the window. Here she found an open notebook with scribbled notes that made no sense to her. However, scattered here and there on the page were glyphs she was certain she'd seen somewhere before. Her finger moved over the words on the page, but it was nonsense, the ramblings of a person with too many thoughts and little means of coordinating them. Intriguing, but frustrating. She kept looking.

Her eyes landed on a slate-colored book at the top of a stack nearby. On the cover were more glyphs and symbols, some of which she knew and others she recognized but couldn't place. Her finger traced the title:

The Lore of the Demon Eddow

She frowned. The name stuck in her mind like a melody she couldn't put words to. She picked up the book and tucked it under her arm, then turned and left the room.

She pulled the door closed behind her and pressed her back to it, listening to the stillness of the house.

A voice frightened her.

"Oh," he said, frozen in the hallway. He was a tall, lanky guy in his mid-to-late twenties, with olive skin and green eyes that seemed to shimmer even in the dark of the house. He had a mess of wet curls on his head, which he shook out like a shaggy dog, spraying Naomi with water. Under his arm was a worn novel and a toiletry bag, but as he stood motionless in the dark of the hallway, they seemed to slip a bit.

"You must be looking for Jonah," he said. "I'm Ben." He gave a small wave.

Naomi didn't move. No way he was talking to her.

"Hello?"

Naomi looked around and saw no one. She looked back at the man with a scowl.

"Yes, you." He stepped a bit closer, close enough for her to make out the square jaw and faint shadow of a beard on his face. "It's okay. This isn't the first time this has happened. Jonah's room is actually at the end of the hallway." He gestured over his shoulder.

Naomi pressed her back against the door, the color fading from her eyes until there was only white.

"Whoa, I didn't mean to scare you." His eyes dropped to the book tucked under her arm. "Is that my book?" he asked, reaching for it.

Naomi's breathing accelerated. Her efforts to blend with the shadows seemed pointless with this guy. Her skin darkened, but he didn't seem deterred.

"Oh, whoa, okay. I didn't realize you were one of those, but I really need that book. I don't mind if you hang around. Just don't hurt anyone." He reached for the book again.

Naomi grabbed his arm. She pulled him into his room and shut the door behind them.

He stumbled back onto the bed, looking a little alarmed. "You're a strong one," he said.

She faced him fully, looking at her pitch-black hands as though to confirm their color.

"Are you okay?" he asked.

"How can you see me?"

14

Glenn had quit smoking after his daughter was born. It was something Tamara had wanted him to do for years, but when he held Allie for the first time, the idea clicked. The first few months were rough, especially being in the Navy, but after a while he found a new normal. He thanked shore duty for that. Eventually, he found if he chewed enough gum to seal up the hole in the *Titanic*, he didn't miss smoking.

It had been years since he even looked at a cigarette. Living in a quiet town like Pickleberry, he had no reason to start smoking again. Allie made life easy, even if he was the only one there to make her meals, tuck her into bed, or attempt to put her hair into a ponytail. He was getting better at it. She was the most easy-going kid imaginable, and it made giving up addictive vices like smoking nothing to sweat about.

But now… Staring at two folders on his desk that held cases of victims who had been murdered and subsequently… disheartened? De-organed of the cardiac type? Had their fucking hearts torn out of their chests?

He was eyeballing the pack of Pall Malls Jamie had left on her desk when a voice snapped him back from his zoned-out thoughts.

"Looking a little green around the gills, Glenn." The sheriff stood at the entry of his office, a stained coffee mug in hand and the lingerings of a day-old Danish in his mustache.

Glenn sat up. "Sheriff Freeman." He cleared his throat, straightening the folders on his desk. "I didn't hear you come in."

"I've been here since around six. Figured I'd check into a few things before catching breakfast at Cotton's. Glad to see things have been quiet since I've been gone." He winked, taking a drink.

"Actually, sir…" Glenn took the folders into his hands. "I've been sitting on a few cases and I'm really stumped—"

"That Gibson boy spray paintin' walls again?" he asked. "Listen, if you got to put the kid in the tank for a few hours or even half a day, I doubt his parents would worry too much."

"No, sir, he hasn't been causing trouble."

"Allison Anderson's daughter selling the weed again?"

"No, I haven't heard from her in a long while." Glenn shook his head. "Sir, about the Gibson boy..." He stood, extending the folders to the sheriff, who was too busy brushing crumbs from his shirt to notice.

"What about him? You said he has been staying out of trouble?"

"Well, I suppose he has, but—"

"You're not letting him off easy, are you, Glenn? He'll never stay outta trouble if you give in to his puppy dog eyes." He wagged his finger.

"Well, sir, Skye Gibson ain't causing trouble because he's dead," he said, extending the folders again.

Sheriff Freeman paused mid-sip and looked over his shoulder to Glenn. He looked down at the folders Glenn held in his hand and then narrowed his gaze on Glenn's face. "Did you start growing that mustache while I was on vacation? A little scraggly, ain't it? Might take you a month to fill that in."

"Sir..." Glenn sighed, pushing the folders.

"All right, I heard you. What happened? Drunk driving? Tractor fall on him? We get about one of those a year." He took his time to set down the coffee and open the folders.

"We don't really know. Well, I mean, I think we know how he died, but I'm going to have to rule it as a homicide and I'm not even sure we have the paperwork for that here." He scratched at his neck, trying to keep Jamie's cigarettes out of his sight.

"Homicide? Whoa, there." The sheriff opened the folder but waved it around without looking at it. "People die, Glenn. I know you're a few years on the job and probably used to all the crime those places like San Diego had, but people don't get murdered in Pickleberry," he said. "It was probably an accident."

"They took his heart, Sheriff Freeman," he said. "And not two days ago we got a call for another victim. Same MO and everything."

Sheriff Freeman's bushy eyebrows furrowed over his gray eyes as they finally read the folder in his hands. By the time he got to the photos, his eyebrows were reaching toward the brim of his hat. He sighed, closed the folders, picked up his coffee, and handed the folders back to Glenn. "Well, it looks like you might get to finally use that degree, Detective Beasley."

Sheriff Freeman shook his head and ambled off to his office, closing the door behind him.

Glenn sat down hard in his chair, mulling over his next steps.

"Dispatch to Beasley," the radio on Glenn's desk called.

"Go, Dispatch," Glenn spoke into his handset.

"We got a call from Travis Miller off Farm Road 32."

"Yeah?"

"You know ole Travis? His dad owned all that land out there on 32 until he just up and left, leaving it to Travis and his siblings to deal with. Pretty sure they found him, like, a month later in Springfield at some bar, but he acted like he didn't even recognize his own kids. I don't know, man. I know farmin' ain't for everyone, but you got to be a real low-life to dump your responsibilities on your kids and then act like you don't even know who they are. That ain't never sat right with me."

"What did Travis want, Darrel?"

"Oh, well, he says he found a body layin' in his field."

"Shit."

"Yeah! It's not in great shape either. Well, the bottom half is a little fucked up, but I think the waist and above is good. Which should help y'all with tellin' who the guy is."

"What happened to the body?" Glenn was having trouble tracking Darrel's story.

"Long story short, Travis is worried he's gonna be in trouble, so he wanted me to tell you that if you're gonna come out to arrest him, just stay off the property, because he ain't got time for that right now."

"Why would I arrest him?"

"Well, he ran the fuckin' thing over with his tractor!"

"He what?"

"Yeah, that's how he found it. He said it sounded like he hit something big like a boulder or something, but when he got off the thing to look around there was blood and parts and bones jammed up in there. So, he wants to know if he's gonna be held liable, like tamperin' or some shit? I told him I don't know the law, I just make the call, you know?"

"I don't understand," said Glenn, shaking his head. "He found a body in his field? And ran it over with his tractor." He sighed.

"So, what will it be?"

"Huh?"

"I told Travis I'd ask you if he's gonna be in trouble or not."

"Did he put the body there?"

"I don't think so." Darrel was hesitant. "At least it didn't sound like he did. I think if he did he wouldn't have told me. He would have fed it to the hogs. I figured as much, because he said if you're gonna arrest him, he's just gonna do that anyway. Either way, I gotta call Travis back, because he may or may not be doing that right now."

"What?! What the fuck? Call Travis and tell him not to touch it and that he's not in trouble. Lord have mercy."

"All right, cool," Darrel said, and then Glenn heard him snap his fingers. "Oh, yeah, there was something I was forgettin' about the body…"

"Don't say it, don't say it, don't say it," pleaded Glenn under his breath.

"He says it's got a hole in its chest."

"Fuck." He sighed. "Copy," he said into the handset and tossed it on the table. His eyes fell on the cigarettes again. "Jamie? Mind if I get one of those?"

15

"What do you mean?" Ben asked.

"You can see me." Naomi stepped toward him but stopped, unsure. "You shouldn't be able to see me. No one has seen me yet and suddenly you can?"

"Oh, well, I've always been able to see shadow people."

"Huh?"

"Yeah." He rubbed his neck. "Ever since I was a kid. My parents always said I had night terrors. Pretty sure they were real, but when you say you see shadows of people in the corners of your room, no one wants to believe you. So they probably didn't see you because they don't want to. I will say I've never talked to one before, so this is pretty cool."

"I'm not a shadow person," she snapped. "I'm flesh and blood and more than you can comprehend." She shook her head, mumbling under her breath.

"Hey, it's okay. I won't tell anyone about you being here, but I'm going to have to ask you to return that book to me," he said, standing from the bed.

Naomi pulled the book from under her arm. "I can't tell if you're unrealistically brave or incredibly stupid," she told him.

"I'd like to think I'm the perfect balance of both," he smirked. "Honestly, I haven't been scared of your kind since I was, like, nine."

Naomi furrowed her brow. She reached for the door handle to leave when Ben grasped the book and stopped her. "Let go," she growled.

"As cool as this is, I can't just let you walk off with my stuff. I think I've been pretty understanding, considering you broke into my home and are stealing my stuff. But come on, now. Let me have the book back," he said, pulling hard.

Naomi pulled harder. "I need this book."

"*I* need this book," he growled back. "You wouldn't understand how rare it is. It took me two years to find it."

"And *you* wouldn't understand how important it is to me." Naomi pulled the book toward her. In the moment, she couldn't explain why the book was important. But she wasn't about to let him tell her she couldn't have it.

"All right, this is ridiculous. Let go of the book," he said.

"No."

"Let go of the book," he insisted, pulling harder.

Naomi's grip tightened and her eyes narrowed.

"Lady, let go of the book!" He tugged.

She dug her heels into the ground as he pulled her across the floor, closing the space between them.

"All right, you're acting less like a cryptid and more like a crazy chick, which is exactly Jonah's type. I caught you. Just let go and we can walk away," he said firmly.

Naomi's hold tightened so hard she could feel the book's cover tearing under her fingers.

"Let go or I'll tell Jonah you have to leave," Ben threatened.

Naomi rolled her eyes and pulled tighter.

"JONAH!" Ben called, giving the book one big pull as Naomi released it, her ears perking up.

"Imbecile," she huffed.

There was motion down the hallway. Naomi teleported to the street outside.

She fumed as she left Ben's street and headed up the main road. The town was mostly asleep by now and mist had begun to settle into the distance. Naomi paid no attention to the way it seemed to sway and weave around the town as though it had a mind of its own. She was too busy mumbling about Ben.

"Stupid fucking boy with his stupid fucking book. Stupid fucking book that I need. That could help me... help me understand? Answer questions?" She pressed her hands to the sides of her head and grimaced. "Why did I know that house, but not know it? I've been there. I know I have and yet I've never set foot in there. Why. Can't. I. Remember?" She gave her head a whack with each word.

She found herself standing at a four-way stop, with one gas station to her left and another across the intersection to her right. Something about the second one felt familiar.

"I used to buy frozen drinks from there in the summer," she recalled aloud. "In my childhood." She nodded, feeling her way through distant, fuzzy memories. "But I never had a childhood. Did I? Was I anything before… before? Yes, of course. I had to be, right? Right? There were others. Kids? Were there kids? Is this memory even real?" She rubbed her hand angrily over her face. "This town is fucking with me. Where the hell am I?"

She turned to face the street on her right. It was mostly a straight stretch with a slight decline that faded into mist, though she could make out the shapes of the tree line off in the distance.

"There," she said. "Why do I remember that?"

She walked down the silent street, past a small roadside park, a small medical clinic, a grocery store, and a post office around what she thought to be the town square. Beyond that, she found a high school with a small parking lot and a large, empty lot edged by the tree line.

Naomi faced the forest. It was the only thing in the town that she seemed to truly know. But looking at it left an unsettling pit in her stomach she couldn't explain. Was she delirious from the events of the night? Maybe losing Taylor was finally taking its toll. She wondered if now was the time to address the box she'd tucked away. She couldn't avoid it forever.

"I've never seen this place before," she told herself. She felt like reality was slipping away from her, and she needed something to ground her. And so she repeated, "I've never been here."

She couldn't bring herself to believe it.

Her shoulders dropped. All of the air she'd been holding in her lungs without realizing it fell out of her mouth in a gasp as the shadows cleared from her.

"In those woods I'll find a tree struck by lightning and burnt. But how do I know that?" She placed a shaky hand to her forehead.

For a long moment, she stared at the trees in bewildered anguish. Then she straightened her shoulders and sighed. "But there's no harm in strolling the forest at night."

And so, Naomi gave herself permission to get lost in the forest. But she was never lost. Though she had no memory of the place, she knew exactly where to go. After walking for what felt like hours, she came upon a tree, fallen and decomposing. It was home to thick, green moss, an array of insects, and even a family of mice. With no difficulty at all, she found the blackened bark and traced its path to the center of the decaying structure, where she could still see the remains of charring that could only have come from intense and concentrated heat.

She recalled the smell of burning flesh and the crack of lightning that caused it. It had been hot enough to burn through her core and fuse her skin to the tree. She remembered the sound of skin tearing and peeling as she pulled away from the tree. The bindings that had held her were nothing compared to the meld of skin and bark she had to separate.

She'd died tied to that tree. And like the budding life that flourished on and within it, she was given life anew. She'd thought she'd left it all behind. the tree, the town, the pain it gave her. But life still thrived where she'd died. Despite all hope and effort to leave this place behind her, it all had a way of pulling her back, and she realized it didn't matter how much fire she used. This town would always pull her back.

December 11, 1969

I suppose most people tend to avoid uncharted forests. But Pickleberry folks stayed out of the forest at the north end of town all together. I heard tell that back in the day the conservation department tried to map out some trails, but the rangers never came back. I wonder how many rangers it took before they gave up and started stocking brochures to scenic Ha Ha Tonka a few hours away.

Not that anyone in Pickleberry had an interest in exploring those woods. Not after all the stories their grandpappies told them, told to them by their grandpappies and so on. Stories about monsters, serial killers, and people who go in but don't come back out of those woods. My grandpappy told it to me and I'll sure as hell tell it to my grandbabies. The only difference is that I'll know exactly what's in those trees.

After my run-in with the vamps, I felt particularly immune to the curses of this town. They were watching me. Following me around town in their black cars, parking outside my home at all times. They didn't seem to want anything. Just to watch. If they felt comfortable enough to follow me down Main Street, I thought that they would surely follow me into the forest.

Only they didn't. Then, when I'd been lost in there for nearly two hours, I stumbled across someone I never expected. The city council. Having some meeting, or getting ready for one.

I was exhausted and disoriented. The air had confused me. Paths had changed without me making a turn. My compass gave me no help at all.

So it was comforting to come upon the city council members. Familiar faces and all that. Took a minute for my thoughts to catch up with me. A familiar face in the woods where people go missing? Why was the city council of Pickleberry the exception? What had I stumbled into? I expected the vamps to make an appearance, but when no one did, I got ready for a fight.

The council members were fast, but they didn't harm me. They seemed to laugh at my efforts and after whooping my ass, they sent me off with a guide and my tail tucked between my legs.

I suppose they had little concern of Pickleberry's local loon letting the town in on their secret gatherings.

When they dumped me at the spot where I'd entered, just off a side road nearest to my house, I spotted another black car, simply waiting. I gathered myself, cleaned off my pride, and flipped the car the bird. Then I limped home, wondering how I was going to explain this one to Margo.

I suppose this all goes to say: stay out of the woods. If vamps don't fuck with whatever's in there, it's probably something you should avoid, Chuck. Mind the borders. Keep whatever's in there, in there, and don't worry too much about what they're doing in there.

Chuck

16

The forest was heavy, the air so thick it filled the lungs with ooze. It weighed on Naomi's shoulders and thickened the clouds in her mind. Tears seeped from her eyes under its unnatural gravitational pull.

In the decaying center of the fallen tree, she saw Taylor, his face as charred as its seared heart.

She hoped someone had found him. That they'd smelled the smoke before the fire reached his bed and engulfed him. She hoped his body had been recognizable, so his mother could claim and bury him. The thought of Taylor's mother crying over his horribly disfigured body pulled her to her knees in heaving sobs.

Naomi was no stranger to loss. She knew that pain too closely. In what she could recall from before The Den, she thought she'd been through the worst of it. But this pain was unlike any other she'd felt, unnatural, soul-consuming remorse, so potent that for a long time she could only weep.

Gradually, her wailing drifted into silent remorse and reflection, and the stillness of the woods engulfed her. It struck her, after a while, that such stillness was unnatural. The quiet ran on, any previous evidence of life snuffed, nor even the whisper of air moving through the trees, like the forest was waiting for something to happen.

A howling scream shattered the night, neither human nor animal, but a mixture of the two. Like a hell-cat in a trap but clothed in human despair. Naomi leaped to her feet, the hairs on the back of her neck rising as she tried to pinpoint the source.

Another scream, this time a word, recognizable only to someone who knew the language—and not a language commonly known in Southwest Missouri.

Scuffling footsteps followed, accompanied by more shouting and howling. Naomi scrambled in the direction she thought it came from, but the noise seemed to be coming from all directions.

She quickly lost her bearings in the mess of non-existent trails and identical trees.

It wasn't until she found herself pinned to a tree with a hand to her throat that she realized she was being followed.

Nora pressed her lips to her ear with a snarling snicker. "My, my, what a surprise seeing you here."

Naomi felt her fists clench.

"Are those tears?" she asked, leaning back. "You wouldn't be mourning, would you?"

Naomi pulled Nora's hand from her throat and rubbed it. "It's the woods. It clouds my head and alters my… my being."

Nora crossed her arms. "I'd say that was a lazy excuse, but such is the prerogative of the Black Bile Woods."

"The Black Bile Woods," Naomi repeated.

"I didn't name it." Nora shrugged. "I find you being here odd, considering you're supposed to be dealing with our investment in the city. I guess for the time being, we could use the help." She motioned with a single taloned finger for Naomi to follow her.

Nora led her to a clearing. There a creature Naomi recognized as working for The Den lay in the dirt, holding a bloody hand to his abdominal area. He was breathing shallow, ragged breaths while another Den employee put pressure on a wound that looked already infected. Past the dying vampire was a group of other vamps pressing the face of a man into the dirt. At least, Naomi assumed he was a man from his appearance. He howled like a rabid wolf.

Among the trees across from them, a large, humanoid cat stalked, hissing and swatting at the group, waiting for a moment to attack.

Nora's arrival with Naomi was just enough of a distraction. The werecat struck, pinning the nearest vamp and crushing his head in her jaws before leaping away to engage another.

The captive roared, breaking away from the others' hold. Vampires scattered away from his slashing claws as he transformed into a towering werewolf.

"Don't just stand there, halfling!" Nora yelled at Naomi. "Do your thing!"

Dense shadows filled the spaces between trees, deepening as they crept into the clearing. They edged near the unsuspecting werecat and snaked around her large, padded feet. Her head snapped around and she lunged at Naomi, but the shadows held her. As Naomi raised her hands, the werecat found herself hovering in the air, twisting and writhing in pain.

"What is the end goal here?" she asked her employer.

"I have two dead employees," Nora spat. "What do you fucking think?" She was facing off with the werewolf. Though she was the faster of the two, she still made a great effort to avoid his grasp.

Naomi flung her hands to either side. With a loud crack, the werecat went still, her body falling to the ground like a marionette cut from its strings. Naomi turned toward the werewolf, clapping her hands together in front of her, parallel to the ground with palms together.

The werewolf slammed face-first into the ground, his snout pressed closed. He was much stronger than the werecat. He pressed his claws deep into the earth and with great strong arms began to raise his head.

Sweat broke out on Naomi's forehead as her palms started to come apart, fractions of an inch at a time. When they were an inch apart, the wolf was on all fours. Quickly, she pressed her palms into the dirt. The more he fought, the more the whites of her eyes overtook any inkling of color. The tips of her fingers turned black, the ink spreading farther up her hands the deeper they dug into the earth until it disappeared under the cuffs of her jacket.

Blood oozed from the wolf's snout as pressure from the shadows crushed bone and tissue. Still he resisted the shadows, his limbs shaking as his rage grew. Even with his snout crammed into the dirt, Naomi could hear his ravening howls and snarls. At any small waver in her hold, he gnashed and snapped, gaining ground in standing upright. She panted with exertion, her hands pressed so far into the dirt she felt like she would hit bedrock.

Then Nora thrust the heel of her boot into the back of his head, crushing his skull. He went limp.

Naomi fell forward into the dirt, her eyes and skin slowly shifting back to normal.

With an effort, Nora removed her boot from the back of the werewolf's head, twisting his head one way and then the other. The great beast transformed into a meek human with his neck left bent unnaturally, his wide, empty eyes locked on Naomi from under a matted mess of hair. Though she'd been on the same team as

Nora, Naomi had the inkling that, under different circumstances, it could just as easily have been her head crushed by Nora's boot.

Nora shook her foot to dislodge the bigger chunks of bone and brain matter. "What a waste." She shook her head. She dabbed at the blood on her cheeks and pushed aside the strands of hair that had fallen into her face, her eyes swiveling to Naomi. "You drank an entire human and are still weak as shit."

"I can't... I can't say I've ever fought a werewolf, Nora," she said, gathering herself.

"Do you have anything other than excuses?" Nora asked but waved the question away before Naomi could answer. She approached the dead vamp sprawled out next to the dead werecat. She sighed, then motioned to the others to carry him off. "Rik isn't going to like this."

"What happened here?" Naomi asked.

"We were attacked, obviously." She gestured to the dead bodies around them. "Cujo here dragged one of ours into the woods, where Whiskers was waiting to ambush us. Did you think this was some kind of bi-weekly Cryptids of Pickleberry meeting gone bad?" she asked.

"Pickleberry?"

"Yeah, Pickleberry," Nora said. "Don't you know where you are?"

"No," she admitted.

"Pfft, happy homecoming. No memory of the place where you were born and raised—twice, at that—and straight to the messy jobs. Here you stand in the very woods where you were made, and still nothing. Those witches sure did a number on you." She paused. "Though maybe it wasn't the witches?"

She shrugged off Naomi's plight and went to the spot where the injured vampire lay. His wound seemed to be festering more by the moment. "Carry our dead to the car. Can we move him?"

"With a bite like this, the sooner we treat him the better," said the vamp, applying pressure. "But I gotta admit, Lanora, it doesn't look good."

"Oh, an optimist! Get him the fuck out of here then." She waved him off. She rubbed her face and grumbled under her breath. "One hundred and eighteen years!" she exclaimed. "A hundred and eighteen years and not so much as a standoff with these mongrels. Now, suddenly, they've decided to act out?"

Naomi pushed herself to her feet and shook off her exhaustion. Nora motioned for her to follow and started off through the woods.

"You may have no memory of this place, but here are a few truths: none of us venture into Black Bile because it isn't our territory, just as these mutts keep to the woods when they look like the flea-infested savages they are. That is the only reason we managed these treaties," she said. She seemed to be mostly speaking to herself, with an occasional glance to Naomi. "But something has changed. Something caused them to venture out and attack us. And cats and wolves together? Not something I would have expected. Something is going on here." She paused for a moment, shaking her head. Then she looked at Naomi. "Did you save our investment?"

"The job? Uh, yeah, I crashed an elevator with the buyer inside and took the documents."

"Were you in the elevator?"

Naomi nodded.

Nora chuckled. "So, your schedule is clear." She nodded. "I want you to stick around this town. Something is happening, and I don't like it. Even the slightest shift in the balance, and utter chaos could unfold here. The Den has always liked this tiny place. It's treated us well for over a century, much like Tombstone did. For the most part, everyone has been contained to their niches—the werewolves, the werecats, Momo. Hell, even the ghouls. But now something has definitely shifted."

They reached the edge of the woods. "This isn't the first occurrence," said Nora, gesturing. Along the edge of the tree line lay a body illuminated by the moonlight. "They're becoming more frequent, even on the human side of things."

"One of yours?" Naomi asked.

She shook her head. "Human."

They approached the body. When Nora saw the gaping hole in its chest, she pushed her hands into the deep pockets of her high-waisted slacks. "Things like this don't happen in Pickleberry."

"What will Fredrik say?"

"Fredrik will know more when I know more," she told her. "Stick around, investigate all of this, and get back to me when you find out what the hell is happening. And stay out of the woods." She glanced over her shoulder, chewing on the corner of her lip.

When she looked back, Naomi's face held a subtle grin. "What is that?"

"I just enjoy seeing fear on you for once," Naomi said. "It makes you look almost human."

Nora's eyes darkened for a moment, as though she might be considering decapitating Naomi and taking the ass-chewing Fredrik would give her for it. Then she smiled, tucked her hair behind her ear, and stepped close to Naomi. Naomi felt her hand run up her midsection as she reached into the inner pocket of her jacket and pulled out her flask. She opened the spout and pressed the flask against Naomi's chest.

"You look tired, Novak. Why don't you have a drink?" she suggested with venomous sweetness. She dropped the smile and walked away, leaving Naomi holding the flask in the dark of the street.

Naomi held her breath. Even Taylor's blood had his musk. With shaky hands, she closed the flask and held it tight, hoping to find comfort in the only thing she had left of him.

Maybe that was the problem—holding onto him, holding onto the part of herself that wanted bonds and connections. She opened the flask and poured its contents into the grass at her feet.

She put the flask in her pocket and walked down the street, forcing herself to consider why someone would kill a person and take their heart.

17

The resources available to the Pickleberry PD were far from ideal. But when the worst crimes committed are drunk and disorderly, drunk driving, or being generally disorderly, there seemed little need to fund the department past a drunk tank, a couple of cruisers, and an air-conditioned office.

For this reason, Glenn had to dig deep into the supply closet to find a bulletin board and even push pins. When he set up the board and pinned up the pictures of the victims, now four of them, he was met with less enthusiasm than he expected from his fellow officers.

"Well, that's an eye sore." Jamie sighed. "Did you need to include the postmortems?"

"Yeah, Jamie, it seemed relevant."

"I just..." She shook her head and turned her chair away.

"What?"

"Well, it's just now I'm gonna have to eat lunch in my car. I can't eat looking at those pictures, and I hate eating lunch in my car because there is nowhere to set my Tupperware and I always dribble into my center console. Then it gets sticky and if I park on an ant hill, I'm just asking for a whole colony to move in."

Glenn scratched his mustache. "Why'd you join the department?"

Jamie turned to face him, but instead her eyes landed on the photo of mutilated Skye Gibson just over his shoulder. She scooted her rolling chair a couple of inches to the left until she could no longer see the picture.

"Well," she said. "I wasn't a very good student and the only jobs at LMH that don't require a lot of schooling were working in the blood banks and janitor. Well, blood banks, ehhh." She made a grimace and shuddered. "So, I did the janitor thing for a little while, until I found out that all janitors do is clean up the messes doctors leave behind and..." She made a series of noises similar to the office's old fax machine when the trays got jammed and shrugged. "No, thanks.

"I saw the opening for office jockey here and thought, I know the alphabet! I can file papers! But that doesn't pay much and then a deputy position opened a few months ago. I figured why not? Surely, that'd be a safe, clean job, right?" She leaned over to look at the picture of Skye again. "I've been proven wrong, I guess." With another sigh, she turned her back to him.

"You joined the department and didn't expect to see any action?" Glenn asked. "You were paying attention on career day when they talked about cops, right?"

"Yeah, and I've seen cop shows, but Glenn, this is Pickleberry." She gestured vaguely but didn't turn around.

He hated that she was right on that one.

"What in the Sam Hill is this doing here?" Sheriff Freeman asked, gesturing at the bulletin board.

"Case board, sir," Glenn replied. "I'm hoping it can help me keep my thoughts straight."

"You're blocking the coffee, Beasley," Freeman said, making a show of reaching behind the board for the coffee pot.

Glenn shifted the board forward just a bit. "I know this seems like a nuisance, but the sooner we solve these murders, the sooner we can put this board back into the supply closet next to the single set of riot gear. Then we can get on with our quiet, mundane lives in our quiet, mundane town."

"Well, until you solve this, I think I'll keep the coffee maker in my office. I don't think I can look at these pictures every morning and still drink my coffee," Freeman said.

"Me? You don't intend to help, sir?" Glenn asked.

"I'll sign whatever papers you need and back whatever decisions you make, but I've a thirty-something year record of zero murders under my watch. Sure, we've had a missing kid here and there, but we all know what happened to them." Freeman looked to Jamie for support.

"Some people can't handle the pressures of small town livin'," she agreed.

"Exactly right, Jamie, and so they move onto the next biggest thing. Springfield, probably, where there's a house fire at least once a week." He shook his head. "Three last week, if you read the papers."

"Yeah, but we've got four murders in the same amount of time." Glenn gestured to the board.

Freeman shrugged. "All right, if you want my opinion, I think drugs are to blame."

Glenn looked at the bulletin board and pointed the tip of his pen to the hole in the chest of the newest victim, a middle-aged woman who had no family to claim her. "Drugs?"

"Look at your victims, Beasley," Freeman gestured with his coffee mug. "Aside from the Gibson boy, who was already on a troubled path, do you recognize a single person up there? If this department has one job, it's to know the face of every resident in town. I don't know any of the three latest victims, and I've lived here my whole life. It's very likely we got some deranged meth head camping out in Pickleberry somewhere. He's enticing strangers into the area with good deals, or something of the kind, and when he gets them alone to sell his product, he kills them… does what he does with their hearts… and moves on. He's on drugs, so he isn't thinking right. That means he won't know why he's taking the hearts or even bother hiding the bodies."

Freeman slurped his coffee, pleased with his own theory, and headed to his office. "You're overthinking it, Beasley," he said, before closing the door for a mid-morning nap at his desk.

"I hate to disrespect the sheriff like this," Glenn said in a low voice to Jamie. "But I don't think it's that simple."

"What are you thinking?"

He studied the board, looking at each victim's face and their wounds while stroking the edge of his mustache. "All right, so he's right. I don't know these victims. They're not from Pickleberry or if they are, they're new or not part of the community enough for me to recognize them. But answer me this, Jamie: would you ever go out after dark? By yourself at the very least?"

"Oh, never! Everyone knows you should never go out after dark unless you're safely traveling with a group."

Glenn nodded. "I left Pickleberry, but I still remember my mama telling me that from the day I could comprehend it." He looked back to the board. "Don't walk alone at night, stay away from Cowden Street, stay out of Black Bile Woods. And under no circumstances are you to ever visit the bar on the hilltop or—"

"Howling House," Jamie finished his sentence with a nod. "Everyone knows this."

"Yeah, everyone who grew up here, because we heard the stories as kids." He tapped his pen to the board. "But if you don't live here…" He paused, waiting for Jamie pick up his thought

"If you don't live here," she said slowly. "You… wouldn't know?"

"Exactly." He nodded. "This lady was found near the woods. Everyone was killed in the middle of the night. They didn't know."

"What about Skye Gibson? His family has been in Pickleberry for generations."

"Even Gibson should have known better. But we all know he made his own path."

"Maybe the sheriff is right and it was drugs?" Jamie asked. "Why would strangers just wander into Pickleberry? There were always rumors about Skye…"

"Rumors without actual evidence mean nothing." He sighed. "Did we ever get the autopsies, toxicology, and all from the M.E.?"

She shook her head. "Still waiting."

"What's taking so long?"

"He may have to relearn how to do all that. It's been a while for him."

"Call him and give him a push," said Glenn. "While you're at it, make sure he's checking for foreign DNA." He waved off the face Jamie was giving him. "He's going to get annoyed, but I want to be thorough."

Jamie jotted down the notes on a pastel-colored to-do list with daisies and butterflies across the top. "Can this wait until after lunch?"

But Glenn wasn't listening. He was staring out the window.

At first he thought his eyes were failing him. The sun seemed to disappear from the sky. Next to the stop sign stood something strange, a shadow with nothing to cast it.

He couldn't blink, couldn't take his eyes off it for even a moment for fear of losing sight of it. But the longer he looked, the more he felt as though he were being sucked into a black hole. Some kind of appendages were taking shape. The size of a man when he'd first seen it, now it could easily be seven feet tall and growing, with limbs that looked as though they could reach clear across the street.

Smoke began to flow around it like a cape. Its shape shifted with each moment, but Glenn could see the shape of two large horns curling from its crown, just above a set of white eyes. As the seconds trickled by, the shadow began to appear less of a figure and more of an amorphous blob.

"Glenn?" Jamie snapped her fingers.

Glenn felt his heart jolt, and he looked at Jamie with tear-brimmed eyes. "Mmm?"

"After lunch," she repeated. "Dr. Horton probably won't even be back in the office until close to one."

"Yeah, yeah," he said. "That's fine."

He turned back to the window, trying to discreetly wipe away tears. Where the shadow had been stood a woman in all black. She appeared lost, looking one direction up the street, then the other. When her eyes found Glenn staring at her through the window, she shoved her hands in her pockets and stalked off.

Glenn didn't recognize her as a local, yet there was something about her that seemed familiar. But he was too rattled by what he'd seen moments before to chase her down. He leaned against the bulletin board and tried to steady his shaking hands.

"Glenn, I know you don't like coffee, but maybe you should switch," Jamie said, frowning at his odd behavior. "Those energy drinks are making you jittery."

He heaved a deep breath and let it out. "You're probably right, Jamie."

18

"I think I frightened the local law," Naomi said to Nora.

She was sitting with her phone pressed to her ear in the empty park, watching the swings sway despite the lack of wind or children playing. "It might be difficult to get anything out of him now."

"Why would you do something stupid like that?" Nora asked.

"I didn't mean to," she said. "Sometimes I can't control how people see me. Most of the time people don't seem to notice, but once in a while someone's eyes hit me at just the right time."

"Which one was it? The old guy, the young guy, or the girl?"

"Does it matter?"

"The sheriff would probably have told you to piss off. He doesn't have much patience for our kind. The little girl would be ideal because she's still new and full of newbie fear, which makes her far from reliable."

"I think it was the young guy."

"Detective Hottie?" Nora asked. "Mmm, what I wouldn't give to keep him in my back pocket as a blood bag." She sighed.

Naomi winced.

"Yeah," she went on. "He's not in on the supes yet, but he has enough pull to do something if you're not careful. You might have signed his death certificate, Novak."

"What do you mean?"

"Humans go one of two ways. They like to cut a deal, which are usually fairly generous, or they like to cause trouble—in which case we call you in to deal with them. In any case, play the field. See where he lands before confessing to being a part of the legion of evil."

"I'm not—"

"Convince me otherwise," Nora said.

Naomi sighed. "Maybe he won't recognize me." She changed the subject. "I couldn't get a good look at it, but he had a board set up with pictures. Possibly other victims? Either way, you were right about something going on."

"I usually am. Now, are we done?" Nora asked. "I've got things to deal with. Next time you call me, make sure you have something valuable to share with the group."

Naomi rolled her eyes as she hung up the phone and went back to watching the swings. "If you keep doing that, you're going to scare away the children," she called as they slowed to a stop. She heard a giggle, and a faint glimmer zipped from the swing set and off into nothingness. She sighed. "Fucking ghosts."

She had no clues to go on. Nothing more than what she'd seen on a second, more covert, peek through the window of the police station. Even that didn't offer much—whatever was happening was going to happen again.

With nothing useful on the murder board, Naomi racked her brain for other resources, running through the events of the night before. "Hmm," she said to herself. "The demon book." She wasn't sure if this was a valid excuse to pursue the book again, but stubbornness pushed any sense of logic from her mine.

In the daylight hours, she could pass as a patron of the café. Here she could order an Earl Grey and let it go cold as she waited for the man with the book to leave the house.

She did this for a couple of days, until the teenager behind the counter started giving her suspicious glares. Unfortunately, each time Ben left, he had the book tucked under his arm. If Naomi was to get her hands on it, she would have to do it when he was home.

There was only one problem: the last time she'd fed had been over a week ago. In that time, she'd pushed her abilities further than she ever had before. Teleporting long distances, crashing elevators, taking on werewolves; it was all taking a toll on her. She was starting to weaken, while her need for blood and sleep increased. She felt the empty flask through the front of her jacket and wondered if she'd made a mistake dumping its contents. Then Taylor's face came to mind, and she regretted not doing it sooner.

This wouldn't be the first time she'd pushed herself. All she needed was to get inside long enough to find the book, at whatever cost, and get out. Then she could simply avoid the house for the rest of her life.

She waited until it was dark and all of the lights in the windows went out. This time, she had the advantage of knowing the layout so she could jump directly to Ben's room. She would grab the book and get out.

It was wishful thinking—Ben slept with the book cradled in his arms, like an infant.

Naomi leaned over his sleeping body with a searing irritation. It called for every fiber of her willpower not to smash a pillow over his face. *What kind of paranoid child sleeps with a book like it holds all the answers to all the questions in the universe?*

She stepped back, forcing herself to relax. Even she had an inexplicable need for the book. It was hardly Ben's paranoia. Not everyone had a jacket with pockets that dumped into a shadow dimension like a Mary Poppins bag.

She moved carefully and soundlessly, shifting the book inch by inch from under his arm, taking a break any time his breathing altered. One more gentle pull, and it would free. Then he groaned, clutched it tighter, and rolled his body over on top of it.

Naomi had a silent tantrum. She pressed her back against the wall and lowered herself to the ground.

"Ow, ow, *owie*," he groaned. He rolled again, so that the hand with the book hung over the edge of the bed. She could see his grip loosening by the second.

Naomi inched forward. She grabbed the book when she felt it was just about to hit the floor, only to find Ben still had a hold of it. He made a grumpy noise, like he was starting to wake up.

Naomi weighed her options. Teleporting would probably take Ben with her, or at least part of him. Plus, she couldn't teleport as far with a passenger. Punching him in the face might knock him out, but it might also wake him fully up. She took the chance and teleported.

They both landed with a crash in the hallway outside his door.

Face planting on the hardwood floor snapped Ben fully awake. "What the hell?" He let go of the book to rub his face but then saw Naomi. "You?" he yelled, reaching for the book.

Naomi used her foot to shove him back and scrambled to her feet. An attempt to teleport only got her halfway down the hall.

"What the fuck?" Ben looked from the spot she'd been to where she was now.

Too dizzy to stand, she army crawled toward the stairs, clutching the book to her chest.

Ben pushed to his feet and leaped after her, but she teleported. She made it less than halfway down the stairs and tumbled the rest of the way, landing hard at the bottom. The book fell from her hands.

"Jesus." Ben grimaced from the top of the stairs. When he spotted the book, he hurried down the steps to grab it. Naomi reached for it at the same time. Her teleport carried them both to the middle of the street outside. She landed flat on her back with Ben on top of her. Her elbow cracked on impact with the concrete street, but she held tight to the book.

Ben rolled off her and pulled back. "Seriously, crazy lady, this is getting ridiculous. Let go of my book before I call the cops!"

"You think they'll come for a book-napper?" she growled, grappling. "I cannot stress to you the importance of this book. If you know what's good for you, you'll let me have it. I don't want to hurt you."

"What are you even saying?" He pushed to his knees, trying to use his height as an advantage. "This book cost me three months' pay and years of searching and waiting. I'm not going to give it up." He growled. "You're just going to have to let—it—go."

Naomi's grasp was weakening because of her broken bones, and her hands were beginning to lose sensation. She grimaced in pain. "This is your last—! LET GO!" Her eyes suddenly turned white. Two black voids took the place of her hands. Before either of them could react, the book had slipped into the void and vanished, leaving them holding only air.

They flew apart. Ben hit the ground hard but only took a moment to recover before sitting up. He searched for the book, but it was nowhere to be seen.

"Where is it?" He grazed his hands over the ground. The dim streetlights offered little help in his search.

Naomi pushed herself up, panting. "No, no, no!" She shook her head. She pulled her hands in front of her, one moving slower than the other. She grasped at the darkness, trying to recall the void, but nothing came. She tried again, and again, an interdimensional pocket check coming up empty.

"Where is it?" he asked, panicked.

"No, no, NO!" Naomi kept at it until she no longer had the strength to even open a portal.

"Where is it? What did you do with it?" he demanded, crawling toward her.

"I don't know!" she yelled back, punching the ground hard with her broken arm, then rolling to her side in pain.

"What do you mean, you don't know?" Ben was on his feet now, still looking around the pavement for the book. When his eyes came back to Naomi, still cradling her broken arm, he looked alarmed. "Whoa, whoa, are you okay? You look like you're about to pass out."

"Oh, piss off," she told him. With an effort, she managed to stand, swaying but upright. She turned to walk away but made it only a few steps before her legs gave out. She hit the ground hard, knees first and then her shoulder.

"I think you need to go to the hospital," he said.

She groaned, trying to push herself up and shaking her head.

"Come on," he pushed. "I need you better so you can bring back my book."

She scoffed.

Ben noticed the lights turning on in the windows of his house. "If people come out and see you lying in the middle of the street, they'll call an ambulance," he said. "You'll end up at the hospital whether you like it or not. Let me take you."

She growled, frustrated at her own legs. "The hospital is probably, like, an hour away."

"No, it's right up the road. It's small but has the biggest blood bank in the Midwest."

She paused. She looked at him fully for the first time, noticing his frizzy mess of curls and his wrinkled shirt stained with drool from sleep. "Blood bank?"

19

The residents of Pickleberry were grateful for the Leigh Memorial Hospital. Outside the convenience of first-rate medical care in their little town, LMH provided something even more valuable: stable employment.

Every year, a batch of hopeful high school graduates would be faced with the terrifying question of what they wanted to do with their futures. Most had family roots in the area and no desire to get away, but jobs were slim in a small town.

LMH had numerous departments, all growing and demanding more and more workers. This provided locals with an opportunity to leave and seek higher education, then return to their hometown and settle down as well-paid professionals—nurses or doctors, medical technicians, and all of the related administrative roles.

Over the decades, LMH had developed a reputation as a top-notch healthcare facility. This drew families from nearby towns—and an outside revenue stream. With hospital policy favoring local hires, this revenue streamed into Pickleberry pockets. Locals had money to spend! Money that kept the ice cream parlor open, allowed tiny cafés to find success, and even provided funds for monthly community festivals that enriched town life.

Gratitude for its benefits ran so deep in Pickleberry minds that LMH could ask nearly anything of its loyal and devoted staff.

But neither Naomi nor Ben were concerned about LMH's devotion to community growth.

Ben was there because he thought Naomi needed emergency services. Naomi cared only about the blood banks. They were hard to miss; they took up the entire wing adjacent to the emergency department. She gave it a calculating look as Ben led her past it to the emergency check-in counter.

The administrator took her information, then a triage nurse led her to a curtained off area to examine her injuries. After an efficient assessment, the nurse said, "Wait here. The doctor will see you shortly."

Naomi had no intention of seeing the doctor.

As soon as the nurse's footsteps faded away, she slipped into the corridor.

She was surprised she hadn't smelled the blood as soon as they entered the ER. The corridor reeked of it. While it caused her to perk up as a fresh pot of brewing coffee might, it also caused her queasy stomach to gurgle. The heavy, savory smell of metal and variety of good and vile blood enticed her. She could nearly taste it.

Fluorescent lights made it impossible for her to disappear, even if she'd had the strength, but Naomi didn't expect a lot of activity in the middle of the night. The ER waiting room would be the riskiest. She peeked around the corner. The administrator was shuffling paperwork. Ben, dazed and drowsy, was lost in thought as his eyes were locked in a gaze with nothing. Neither noticed her as she glided along the farthest wall and into the blood bank's vestibule.

It was empty. Presumably, they kept it minimally staffed at this hour. Even if there were a nighttime emergency, Naomi doubted it needed an entire team of medical professionals on standby.

She tried a few doors—offices, but few were left unlocked. A large donation center with swinging doors sat at the end of the corridor. Before it she found the processing lab, a small work area with a huge, glassed-in refrigeration room at the back. The doors to the lab were locked behind a key card entrance. She might have been able to teleport past the locked doors, but she worried she wouldn't be conscious when she landed on the other side. She peered through the small window at the top of the lab door. Behind the glass of the refrigerated room, she could see racks upon racks of red bags. She couldn't read any labels but gathered the room hosted LMH's supply of donated blood.

For a second, she wondered why the town needed such a massive supply of blood, but then she remembered that her employers owned a majority of the town. Vamps couldn't exactly pick off the townsfolk and expect no one to notice. And truth be told, Naomi couldn't be sure how many vamps called Pickleberry home.

Her hunger pushed such thoughts from her mind. Even if she could teleport into the room, this blood would be stagnant, like the reserve she usually kept in her flask. Not that she was one to be picky when it came to blood, but she knew it wouldn't have any of the flavor, tone, or dimension of Taylor's fresh, still-pumping blood. Grief struck her at the memory.

"You spoiled me," she whispered.

Voices coming down the hall made her perk up. She ducked into a nearby hallway, hoping they would enter the lab, but they passed the lab and went into the donation center. She crept out the door and peeked in. One man, one woman, both in scrubs but in different colors. Different departments? She withdrew, leaning against the wall to listen.

"Let me get you started, Larry," the woman said. Naomi heard shuffling that she assumed was them settling him into a station. "Just finishing up for the night?"

"Yeah," he said. "We had a patient pass, so there was extra paperwork. It was strange, though, Val. The guy was a hysterical mess up to the moment he left."

"Hardly strange for a dying man."

"It isn't uncommon for patients to express guilt on their deathbeds, true. But I'm telling you, Val, this guy must have done something mighty awful for how he was acting."

"Don't dwell on it. His time has passed and hopefully, someone will have good memories of him. What's going on in hospice that you haven't donated this month? You're never late to donate."

"New kids on the mid-shift. You know how it is. They don't want to do the hard stuff, or they don't know how, so it's a lot of picking up their slack. Let's get this over with. You know I don't look forward to being poked."

"You're good for now, Larry. I'll update your transcript before management starts getting on your case." A drawer opened and closed. "You just relax, take a bit of a snooze before heading home. I'll be back in ten."

Naomi heard a door close on the other side of the room.

She took the chance to glance through the doorway. Larry's chin had sunk into his chest. His eyes were closed. Heavy breaths gave way to soft snoring. Naomi eyed the attached bag slowly filling with blood.

If she wanted a taste of fresh and flowing blood, she would have to act fast—Val would return in a few minutes. She thought about grabbing the bag and bolting, but walking out slurping on a blood bag seemed likely to draw attention. Instead, she pulled the tube from the bag and put it in her mouth. She wondered whether Nora would be embarrassed or impressed to see her drinking blood from a human through a straw.

The flow of blood was slow but effective. It only took a minute for the pain to recede from her elbow and shoulder. After another minute, she gave it a bend and a twist. No more crunching. Full range of motion.

A soft sound from the back made her drop the tube. By the time the door from the nurse's office opened, she'd teleported soundlessly back into the hallway behind the swinging doors.

She heard Val cry out. "Larry!"

"What?" he said groggily. "What happened?"

Naomi peered through the thin crack of the doors, watching the interaction to ensure she was in the clear.

"You pulled your IV out of the bag while you were sleeping."

Larry leaned over his arm and looked at the blood that dripped from the IV tower, causing a pool to form on the floor next to his chair. "That's me?" he whispered. His eyes rolled into the back of his head, his face went white, and he passed out in the donation chair.

"Jesus Christ, Larry." Valerie sighed.

With Larry's blood fresh on her tongue, it was hard for Naomi to walk away. The taste, the tingling sensations sent to her fingertips and toes, reminded her that Nora was right. It was better to feed fresh. Larry's blood hardly curbed her craving; if anything, it amplified it. She needed something to kill her appetite.

She gazed through the frosted glass of the lab and to the collection of donated blood protected in a sterilized glass chamber. A couple of bags of stale, old blood would likely kill her cravings.

She was in and out of the lab in a moment, tucking cold bags of blood into her pocket to drink in a safer environment. She'd lingered too long already, considering she was supposed to be seen by a doctor at any time. She headed for the hospital exit.

Ben was at the reception desk, rubbing his face. "I told you I don't know her name," he said to the woman. "She had a broken arm and was pretty banged up. Have you even looked at her yet?"

"Sir," she replied, adjusting the glasses resting on the tip of her nose. "I don't know if you've noticed, but I'm not a doctor."

Ben gathered that she liked this shift because of the slow traffic. "But there's no one here," he said, gesturing to the waiting room. "Who else could they possibly be seeing right now?"

"I don't have to explain to you how the emergency department works."

Ben rubbed his eyes again. "I just want to know if she's okay."

"You said she had a broken arm?"

"Yeah."

"Well, she looks fine to me." Her eyes flicked behind him, then back to her computer.

He glanced over his shoulder to catch a glimpse of Naomi walking out the automatic doors and into the night. "Hey!" he called after her. "Wait!"

Ben sprinted after her, but when he got outside, he was met with an empty parking lot and a cold wind that reminded him he was wearing his sleeping clothes. He tucked his hands under his arms as he scanned the area for any sign of Naomi. Nothing but shadows and shapes shifting around in the dark. "All right, all right," he said, holding up his hands. "Your domain, I get it." With a sigh, he tucked his hands back under his arms and shuffled across the parking lot and up the main road to his own quiet street.

Naomi tailed him at a distance until he safely entered his home and was no longer a concern of hers.

August 10, 1989

I've let Steve in on too much. He has a natural passion for the strange stuff, and in all honesty, I'm tired of having my ass handed to me. Sure, I've learned a lot of tricks for fighting monsters, but I'm only one man against hundreds, maybe even thousands. There is honestly no telling how deep the dark tunnels of Pickleberry go—and who inhabits them.

Steve somehow knows more than I do about this. Or maybe he just picks up on things quicker than I do. It was his idea to start making weapons, weaponizing silver and holy water and nightshade and any other shit that works to fight this kind of nonsense. I guess his stint as a weapons maintenance tech gave him that advantage.

Margo used to not ask questions. Now that Steve seems to be in my shadow, she suspects I'm just using all this as an excuse to drink over at Bradley Keltner's garage. It annoys me to no end that she thinks I would throw away years of sobriety just to get shit-faced in someone's homemade bar, but can I really be mad at her? I've been at this for years now, and I've never given her even an inkling of what I do.

I can't bring myself to tell her. Over the years I've missed a lot: Jo's graduation, Caleb's games, even Margo getting her stories published in *The New Yorker*. But I can't let my guard down. Things happen when I'm not out on patrol.

The last time, bodies were found at the city line. No one in town talks about it because they consider that it happened in Dearborn and not here. Dearborn is such a shithole, everyone just expects bodies to be found there. But I know better. Four bodies, all missing their hearts? That's not just some random serial killer.

Same thing happened less than a decade ago on the border of Black Bile. No one wants to fuck with Black Bile, so once a reporter wrote up the story, it was handed off to die in the Historical Society's stacks with Joanie.

It seems more like witchcraft to me than a human crime, but the witches around here have always been craftier than that. So I don't know. Is there something new in the area that I don't know about? Or maybe something I've been keeping on the run with my patrols?

Either way you look at it, I have to be more vigilant. I gotta widen my patrols. Margo isn't going to like it, especially with Jo's wedding coming up. Maybe Steve can cover me for one day, so that all the good in my life won't fall to shambles.

Wishful thinking. I don't think I'm allowed to think wishfully anymore.

Chuck

20

The Ozarks are known for rolling hills that transform dramatically into rocky cliffs without warning. But no matter how long locals call the area home, they're no less awe-struck by the enchanting views. Layers of jagged and segmented rocks tell a story that could take days to decipher, but they never disappoint.

Some of the best views are only visible after a trek through densely packed forest. These spans of trees offer a vivid array of foliage at least twice a year and aid in the sudden formation of cliffs as a person could follow a twisting deer trail without noticing the dip in the earth until it was too late. Drop-offs like this are a good way of grounding a hiker in their surroundings—reminding them how trivial one step can be.

Past the rolling hills and dense forests, Missourians find vast fields that ebb and flow like golden waves. Here is where Midwest civilization began and continued to grow. In the vast countryside, folks could see the stars. They could hear the bugs and birds, and if they were lucky enough to own waterfront property, they might have their own little slice of peaceful heaven.

Missouri's lakes are no gulf shore, but there is a certain magic present in the combination of rolling hills, daring cliffs, and great bodies of water. These lakes are scattered across the state like an explosive sneeze from a toddler. In the most concentrated areas, the bodies of water are bordered by mansions hidden deep in the thick trees. In other places, the lakes splinter off into rivers. These rivers thin to spindly creeks scattered across almost every corner of the state, each offering its own version of enjoyment and unique personality to the towns they border, dissect, or slither through.

Some creeks offer fishing for small catch and sitting in tubes for several miles doing nothing but baking in the summer sun. But above all, no matter which town they travel through, they offer a place for locals to reconnect with the sounds of water and the wind through trees.

Pickleberry was no stranger to unique bodies of water. The town's local water hole could be called nothing more than a babbling stream that carried itself along the city line to the west, the back side of Black Bile Woods, and then connected into Pomme de Terre River farther past the forest and town. It was called Muddee River. Or at least that was what the Pickleberry folks knew it as even though the sign read "Maudie River." Muddee River just seemed to make more sense.

Contrary to what its name suggested, Muddee River wasn't at all muddy. In fact, it was likely the clearest stream in the state, though no one really went poking around Pickleberry to search for clean water. Though it was only a few miles long, it was a local hangout for teenagers, families or anyone who wanted to spend the day outside.

While Muddee River didn't offer large, sandy white shores, it did have isolated collections of sand, rock, and earth scattered along the waterside. They acted like cabanas for anyone who braved the chilly water for a piece of well-earned peace. A person would wade through waist-deep water, cooler and chairs in hand, to these tiny beaches or risk the drop off of a far less impressive, but still mildly treacherous, cliff. The payout was well worth it.

Settled into the nook and crannies of cliffs and drop-offs, Muddee offered ideal sites for teenagers to park their trucks on clear nights, climb into the bed, and listen to the calm water. Whether it be in the back of a truck bed or on a rocky patch of earth, most often than not, the banks of Muddee were a hot spot for reconnecting with what lay under a companion's clothes.

Glenn Beasley had fond memories of his own in the same spot involving the homecoming queen and some BPR stolen from his dad's garage fridge.

Those recollections fueled a deep despair when he found himself called to the river in his adulthood, but out of occupation rather than enjoyment. He stared at the two lifeless bodies in the back of a black Ford F-150.

Jamie clicked her tongue from a few feet behind him.

"Yes, Jamie?"

"Huh, oh, nothing." She tapped her fingers over her mouth and looked away. "You did call him, right?"

Glenn nodded. "Freeman is on his way." He removed his cap and wiped at the sweat that was forming under the band. "I don't want to call anyone in until he gets a look at this with his own eyes."

The river's rhythmic song was the only sound they heard. No wind rustling in the trees. No insect calls co-mingling with birds fluttering from branches or singing tunes. Everything was silent, except for the trickle of Muddee River.

Jamie cleared her throat, breaking the silence.

He sighed. "What is it, Jamie?"

"It's just, well, Dawson's needing to get home and he doesn't think he can wait for the sheriff," she said.

"Did you get his statement?"

"Yeah, but…"

"Yeah?"

"Just the flies… they're… well, what if they start to swarm? I can't… I can't see maggots," she said. "I'll lose yesterday's lunch if I see even one maggot, Beasley."

"Go tell Dawson he can go." He pinched the bridge of his nose. When he brought his gaze back up, he noticed someone looking over his shoulder. "I said—" He began turning, but instead of Jamie, he met Naomi. "Jesus, Mary, and Joseph!" he yelled, clutching his chest.

The woman didn't react. She simply looked at the bodies in the truck bed and ignored his heavy breathing.

Something about the woman unnerved him. He was certain she hadn't been there the moment before, but it was more than that. The black clothes, the jacket that hid any definitive form… she seemed almost a corpse. Her skin was dull and appeared to shift from one moment to the next. Her mess of brown hair cast her face in shadows, deepening the pockets around her eyes and the hollows of her cheeks. For some reason, she gave him the creeps.

But ever since seeing the shadow monster on the street, Glenn had been a little jumpy. Add that to the murders, and he thought he was right to be on edge.

He took a deep breath and gathered himself. "Ma'am, you shouldn't sneak up on people, especially those who carry guns. Not to mention that you can't be here. This is a crime scene."

The woman turned to give Glenn a once over. When she smirked, her features seemed less hollow and frightening, though not by much. "That's cute," she said. "You think you have authority over me." She turned her attention back to the bodies.

Glenn felt his cheeks heat and he stepped between her and the truck. "I'm an officer of the law."

She smirked again, taking a step forward, forcing Glenn to backpedal. "You seem awfully scared, Detective."

"Actually, I'm a… Wait, Detective?"

She nodded. "Sheriff Freeman mentioned the detective was already on site and I'm guessing it isn't the green-faced child breathing into the traffic cone behind the cruiser?"

"Sheriff Freeman?" Glenn repeated.

The crunching of gravel brought his attention to the sheriff's cruiser pulling up nearby. He stepped from his car with great effort, gave an encouraging smile to Jamie, and made his way in his own time toward them.

"Well, I see the whole town has turned out," he said, motioning over his shoulder to where a group of people had gathered to watch from the other side of the cruisers. Apparently, Dawson had called a few friends.

"Sheriff, this woman says—"

"You must be the professional that was recommended to me by Ole Freddy." Freeman offered a hand to the stranger.

"Yes, that's me." She nodded, shaking his hand, then offering her hand to Glenn. "Naomi Novak."

Glenn took it, surprised to find it warm and soft and not ice cold, like he'd imagined. "Novak? I graduated with a Novak."

"Interesting." She turned back to the crime scene. "I understand this isn't the first case?"

"This would be number… what is it, Glenn?" Freeman asked. "Five?"

"Six," Glenn answered.

"Six," Freeman relayed.

"Six." Naomi nodded.

"Sheriff, a word?" Glenn asked, pulling him a few paces away. "I'm sorry, but who is this lady and why is she here?"

"She's a professional," Freeman told him. "Listen, Glenn, I haven't lost faith in you or your ability to do your job, but people are starting to notice." He gestured to the growing crowd. "There are people in our town who have taken a personal interest in this case, and they offered some help."

"This Fred guy? Whoever he is."

"To name one. Don't you worry about him. But don't look at this like someone taking over. Instead, look at it like calling in reinforcements. Look at Ms. Novak as backup. Unless you think you're better off with just Jamie?"

"Oh, God, I caught a whiff on the breeze." Jamie could be heard behind the squad car making a series of sounds like she was possessed.

Glenn sighed heavily. He shook his head.

"Good. Now, get to work. The more people that turn up dead, the closer this town inches to anarchy. We've only got one set of riot gear, for Chrissake, Beasley." The sheriff tilted his hat to Naomi and meandered back to his cruiser, where he made a poor effort at dismissing the growing crowd before climbing in, making a four-point turn, and driving back down the gravel road.

"Jamie!" Glenn called. "When you're done puking, call it in."

Jamie's weak hand waved over the hood of the car.

Glenn returned to Naomi, hands resting on his belt. "Well, I suppose we're partners now."

"Are we?" she asked. "I'm not looking to shadow you. My employer has an intent interest in these crimes, so I'll need any information you have and any you may come across in the future. I would like to be clued in if more murders occur, but this isn't a symbiotic relationship."

"Meaning?"

"Meaning I don't have to tell you anything," she said.

Glenn stuck his tongue in the cheek of his mouth and listened to Jamie's pitiful pleas for the growing crowd to disband. "I suppose I don't have a say in that."

"No, you don't."

He shook his head as he pulled the tiny notebook from his chest pocket, ready to go over the notes he had on hand, but he looked up when a voice called to him from the crowd.

"Glenn! Glenn!" Ben was pushing past the gawking teenagers and local gossips, waving his hand high above the rest.

"You again?" asked Naomi.

At the same time, Glenn said, "This again?"

Naomi and Glenn shared furrowed glances.

"You know him?" asked Naomi.

"Yeah, I know him," he replied. "You know him?"

"He's a thorn in my side," Naomi growled. "Every time I think I've pulled him out, I find a sliver left behind."

"He's an annoying little shit, that's for sure," Glenn agreed. He handed the notebook to Naomi with a blank page. "Write down your number, and I'll get rid of him."

Glenn made a beeline to Ben, getting pulled into the crowd's questions. "Hi, folks, I have to say it isn't very neighborly of y'all to crowd about, putting your noses in the middle of someone else's tragedy. So, why don't you all go on home?"

"We've got a right to know, Glenn Beasley!" called a woman. "Y'all have gone on too long without tellin' us a thing. This stuff don't just happen in Pickleberry!"

The crowd joined in agreement with the woman.

"Tammy Jo, how are you doing, ma'am?" He didn't wait for a response. "Right now the department is investigating a series of unfortunate mishappenin's. The best you can do is go on about your business and let us do ours."

"You call holes in their chest a *mishappening*?" Dawson called from several people deep in the crowd.

The crowd's grumbles intensified.

"You willing to give more information about that, Glenn?" Ben asked, leaning to the side to look past Glenn at the bodies. "And your concerning new associate?"

There was commotion from the back of the crowd as people seemed to be pushed aside by an unseen force. A short woman wearing thick, black glasses appeared next to Ben, a cell phone in hand. "Wait, direct your response here," she told Glenn, focusing the camera phone on his face.

"Oh, hi, Ginger, you been working out? Usually you get stuck somewhere in the middle of the angry mob. Taking your vitamins too?"

"How charming for an officer of the law to berate a concerned citizen," she said.

He rolled his eyes. "I'm pretty sure decency goes out the window when you're related to the citizen."

Ginger growled and directed her camera to Ben. "Mr. Donowitz, you seem to know Deputy Beasley's new associate. Do you have any comments or concerns for *The Pickleberry Crier*?"

"Um, no." Ben pushed the camera out of his face.

"Ben, come on," Ginger whined. "I'm trying to build a story here."

"All right," Glenn called over the crowd. "Does anyone here even read *The Crier*?"

"What's that?"

"I get all my news from Ethan at KY3."

"Who reads a paper anymore?"

Glenn snatched up Ginger's phone. "Go home, Ginger. That goes for all of you! Go on home! I don't want to have to call Ebenezer to borrow a fire engine."

Ginger snapped her phone out of his hand. "You're not allowed to confiscate my stuff anymore, Glenn. I can pull Dad into this."

"Well, Dad also told you to stop calling me Deputy, when you know full well I'm a detective," he said. "And he can't tell me what I can and can't confiscate. Go on, Ginger." He shooed her off. "Get out of here before I have to call Dad to come get you."

Ginger extended her middle finger to him and followed the crowd that reluctantly dispersed, all except for Ben.

"You too, Ben. I don't have time for your crazy theories today," he said.

"I think I need to talk to you about your new partner," Ben said, looking past him once again.

He sighed. "She isn't my partner."

"Isn't it weird that she just showed up? Don't you know everyone in this town?"

Glenn stole a glance at Naomi, who stood with her hands in her pockets, watching the treetops. "I do," he agreed. "I do know everyone, She's... new."

"New to where?" Ben asked. "If she'd moved in somewhere, the whole town would be talking about it. Someone would have seen her and mentioned it to Freeman at Cotton's, just to get his blessing on the newcomer. Freeman mention her to you?"

"Well, kinda, but what difference does it make? I don't need to talk to you about this stuff." He started to walk off.

"I caught her in my house."

Glenn hesitated.

He lowered his voice. "She was sneaking around like she was looking for something and then she stole from me."

With a glance to Naomi, Glenn leaned closer to Ben. "You mean she crept through your house and none of the twenty-five residents who live there noticed her but you?"

"She's good," Ben whispered, making Glenn move closer. "She moved through my house like a shadow ninja. She was just walking around like no one in the world could see her. I think she can turn invisible."

"Oh, Jesus Christ! Go home, Ben." Glenn sighed, waving his hand at Ben and walking away.

"I'm telling you, Glenn!" Ben called. "She's not human. Her skin turns black and her eyes white. I saw her! She's like a walking shadow nightmare!"

Glenn felt his feet stop for a moment upon hearing this. He was looking at Naomi now and he swore for a moment her skin appeared as ink. But when he blinked, he only saw a woman waiting impatiently next to two dead bodies. He rubbed his eyes and stalked back to the truck.

Naomi pulled her hand from her pocket and handed back the notebook to him. "He isn't going anywhere."

"Some weirdos are more persistent than others. Just ignore him, he's harmless." He took the notebook back, thumbing through it to avoid making eye contact with her, not certain he would like what he saw.

"I looked through your notes. Hope you don't mind, but crowd control was taking too long," she said. "It seems like after six murders you should have a little more than that."

"Yeah? Well, I mean, I just… I'm not an… I'm still trying to get…" He rubbed his neck. At this rate, he would need to change his shirt from the amount of sweat he was excreting. "I do. I do have more, but it's back at the station. We got M.E. reports back this morning, but I got called out before I could look them over."

"Suspects?"

"Um, yes. Some of those. Back at the station also."

"And here? You have a CSU that investigates the scene for you?" she asked.

"No, that usually falls to me and Jamie. Well, mostly just me. I'm going to be frank," he said, finally mustering the courage to look her in the eye. "You're just a person," he whispered.

"Pardon me?"

"Nothing. Listen, this is a small town. We don't get murders. We barely get dead bodies and if we do, it's someone's great-great-grandpa whose time came or some kind of accident. In any matter, the case is usually pretty straight forward and we go back to drinking coffee at Cotton's or taking BB guns from kids shooting out car windows. This? This isn't what we're used to dealing with. And, well, I think I'm in a little over my head."

Naomi rested her hands in her jacket pockets again. "You think that's why they called me?"

Glenn nodded.

She sighed and looked at the dead bodies. "There's no incision mark."

He frowned.

"On the bodies." She pointed. "The male has a head wound and the female has strangulation marks. So, I'd guess the boy was knocked out first, then the girl strangled, before they came back to get the hearts. But there are no incisions for the hearts."

"So, they just took the hearts out?"

"Ripped them right out." She nodded. "Which I'd guess would mean it's some kind of feral beast with a specific taste for hearts."

"Which wouldn't seem likely," Glenn said.

She paused, remembering her night in Black Bile. She looked back to the body. "Sure, or someone barely human."

"A person couldn't do that."

Naomi looked back at him.

"Could they?"

She sighed. "Why don't I come to the station with you and see what you have before making wild assumptions?" she suggested.

Glenn nodded. "Let me get this called in and cleaned up."

As Glenn returned to the patrol car to do the job Jamie should have, he saw Naomi look to where Ben still stood a little way up the gravel road. She seemed to have a smug look on her face as she offered him a small wave.

Ben huffed and took off down the road.

21

The air in the Pickleberry Police Station was dense. Not only were the days becoming warmer with rising humidity, but the tension in the room was palpable. Then again, Naomi had that effect on people.

Jamie had outright refused to interact with her. Freeman took her presence as an opportunity to make himself scarce, remarking that Glenn had all the help he needed. Before that, he'd kept his distance, probably for good reason if he had any inkling as to who she worked with.

After twenty minutes of silently looking over Glenn's evidence board, Naomi heard Jamie's chair scrape back.

"Oh, would you look at that!" she said, making a grand gesture to the clock above the door. "Here it is past noon, and I forgot my lunch at home. I think I'll just head on over to Cotton's. Glenn, you want anything? No? Okay, cool." She slipped out of the station without waiting for Glenn to even acknowledge her.

"She's a nervous one," Naomi commented.

Glenn shook his head with a sigh, giving her a look like he was also getting tired of waiting for her to say something. "You know, I've been thinking," he said. "Novak isn't that common of a name. At least not around here."

Naomi twisted her torso to face him.

"And I just… didn't know if you would have been related to the only Novak I know or not."

"Unlikely," she told him. "It isn't my maiden name."

He nodded, but then a wrinkle formed in his nose. "See, that wouldn't be too weird. He stayed in the town for at least a year or two after school and then got married and left. And I swear something about you is familiar."

She turned back to the board. "Did you ever find them?" she asked.

"Who?"

"The hearts."

"Oh, no. Not a sign. I'm not sure what a person would want with just hearts."

"And if it were an animal, why not take the other organs and body parts too?" she agreed.

He nodded.

"And these are your suspects?" she asked, pointing to the pictures at the bottom. "A couple of teenagers and the mayor of Pickleberry?"

"Sheriff Freeman insisted on including the local troublemakers and known drug dealers and/or users. Jamie watches too many conspiracy videos online, hence the mayor. In her mind, the least suspicious person is the most likely culprit." He shook his head.

"Well, I guess she could be right at some point." She shrugged. "What does the mayor have that ties him to it?"

"Aside from a title? Nothing? He's accounted for on every night and… well, what motive would he have?"

Naomi shrugged. "And these guys? It seems like a big jump from busting windows and graffitiing bare walls to murder and mutilation. And in my experience, dealers don't tend to kill off potential clients."

"And none of the victims are known drug users or have really anything in common, for that matter," Glenn said.

"Well, that isn't entirely true." She pointed to Skye Gibson. "He was walking through the town at night, headed home from a friend's. These two as well." She moved her finger to the woman and man next to him, then to the girl she'd found with Nora near Black Bile. "She was looking for her cat near the woods." She recalled some scribbled details from Glenn's notebook.

"And the last two? Chad and Jenny?"

"Teenagers out after dark looking for somewhere to be alone. They were all going about their lives without incident, just at the wrong place, wrong time. How many people in this town actually go wandering around the town after dark?"

"No one, usually."

"Seems strange. Do you recognize them?"

"Yes and no," he said. "The boy, Chad, used to live in a little house off the square. His parents upped and moved a couple years ago. If I had to guess, Jenny was someone he met at his new school and they were just out there doing what teenagers do."

She nodded. "Victims of opportunity. No one else was out for the killer to get."

"So, that leaves us further from a legitimate suspect." Glenn sighed.

"I suppose, but it would also mean whoever is doing it doesn't care who they get. Kids coming home or making out in the dark, drunks stumbling home from a bar; anyone, really." She tapped her finger against her lip, then pointed it at Glenn. "If you cared about your citizens, you should put a curfew in place."

"Jesus Christ." He rubbed his face. "No one's going to listen to one of those, no matter how many bodies pile up. Do you know how difficult it was to mandate masks in public during COVID? I must have gotten at least three calls a day just to diffuse fist fights."

"Well, if anything, do it to cover your own ass. It's better to say you warned them than to have them accuse you of not putting in the effort."

Her hand went absently to her chest, where she pulled a medallion tied on a worn leather string from under her shirt. She twisted it mindlessly between her forefinger and thumb.

Glenn's eyes grew wide. "Brian Novak."

Naomi froze.

"I knew I recognized you," he said, pointing at the necklace. "Brian wore that smelly necklace every day of his life until he met you. I used to give him so much shit after games because it smelled worse than he did, and he still never took it off or changed the strap." He shook his head with a grin. "I figured it would take an act of God to get that thing off him."

Naomi tucked the medallion back into her shirt and pushed her hands into her jacket pockets, pretending to study the board.

"Man, he was a good one," Glenn went on. "I haven't seen him since we left for basic. I never saw him after that, though. What's he doing now? Did he get out?"

Naomi swallowed a lump. "He did," she answered. "He served his four and used the benefits to go to school."

"Oh, so does he work in Springfield or what?"

Naomi took a deep breath. She couldn't afford to lose her cool here, but there would be no getting around the topic as long as she was forced to work with Glenn. "He died," she said simply.

"Shit," he said. "I'm sorry. I had no clue."

She nodded, giving him only a glance before looking back to the board. "I don't think I can draw any more conclusions from what's here. We're going to have to do some leg work on our own. I'll do some digging and you should too. People are more likely to talk to a familiar face with a badge than me."

"Naomi." He stood. "I really am—"

"It was another life," she told him shortly and left the station with that.

She'd been hoping to seclude herself for a bit to collect her thoughts, but no such luck. Immediately upon exiting, she was ambushed by Ben, who had followed her and Glenn to the station, waiting for her to emerge.

She kept walking.

"So, what's your plan?" he asked, following close behind. "Weasel your way into the local law's good side and discredit legitimate claims against you? Then what? Huh?"

"I'd ask if you have anything better to do than follow me," she said. "But I know you don't."

"What's your game?" He grabbed her roughly by the arm and pulled her back. "Something like you coming to town can only mean bad things will follow."

She couldn't help but chuckle. "You have no idea." She pulled her arm away. "You know what I don't understand? You've seen what I can do and yet you still let me walk around with only mild harassment. Shouldn't you be running in the streets screaming and warning others?"

Ben moved to block her path and lowered his voice. "That's the thing," he said. "No one pays attention to any of that stuff around here. They've all got these perfect bubbles around their heads."

"Lucky me." She started past him, but he sidestepped in front of her.

"Right. It should be. But someone like you comes to town, robs my house, and suddenly people start turning up dead?"

She sighed. "You think I'm the killer and yet you're standing here talking with me?"

He inched back a bit. "Someone has to do something. I've followed the weird things in this town for years! Since my family moved here. The weirdest part? No one else notices them."

"People see what they want to see."

"Exactly!" He nodded, making a gesture from himself to her.

"And you think that's why you can see me?"

"I think the fact that I don't put my head in the sand is why I see you and the other weird things around here," he said. "Like the ghost children at the park. They run around all times of the day and night and no one notices them."

"Well, they're fairly harmless," she said.

"Yes, but I see them while others don't. I see them just as clear as I see any other child." He rubbed his face, exasperated. "Look, I don't know you. I don't know what you are, or who you are, or what you want, but I know I've been the only person in this place asking questions until you showed up. I hounded Beasley for autopsies on the first two bodies for days until he stopped answering my calls. But you, a stranger with no badge, just walks into town and he lets you stare at his evidence board?"

"What's your point?"

"My point is, you have your foot in a door I would like access to," he said. "And I *am* aware of some facts that could make your time here very difficult."

"If you think you can blackmail me—"

"All right, fine. I'll guilt trip you."

"It was a book," she said.

"A book that was almost a century old and rarer than you would even be able to understand!" he cried. Beads of sweat had formed on his forehead, and his eyes were wide and wild. He wiped his face once again, forcing himself to collect his composure. "All I'm saying is you owe me information and frankly, if you want to get anywhere here, you need me. Your weirdness may help you do whatever you do, but it also hurts you. I know who to talk to about the murders. Do you think anyone will talk to you? Brooding and tattoos? They'd probably call Glenn before even telling you hello."

Naomi crossed her arms. He presented a strong, manic case for himself. "I don't need a partner," she told him.

"No, but wouldn't it make life a little easier?"

The concept of an easy life seemed so foreign to her. "And the detective?"

"Detective?" he repeated. "Who? Beasley?"

She nodded.

"How much time do you want to spend explaining the ghosts in the park and the monsters in Black Bile to him?"

She sighed. "Fine," she reluctantly agreed. "You can help me with the townsfolk, but I'm not babysitting you."

"Why would you need to?"

She gave him a knowing look but didn't push the matter. "Let's go. You're going to tell me what you know, and I'll think about telling you what I know."

Ben followed Naomi around Pickleberry for nearly an hour, rambling about a dozen or more Pickleberry stories that circled around but never settled on anything good. When he started to forget entirely what they were talking about, he suggested they find somewhere to sit down and talk.

The park with ghost kids would be far too distracting, so they went to the Dent Corner Café. The café was empty. Audrey, who was supposed to be working the counter, was nowhere in sight. They seated themselves at a corner table.

"What was I even talking about?" he asked, running a hand through his curls and making them point in all directions.

"Knitting circles?" Naomi prompted him.

"Yes!" he snapped. "That's kind of a broad term, but if you find a gaggle of old ladies, you'll surely hear something worth remembering."

"Really? You think a group of old ladies holds the answer to these murders?"

"Well, it's better than anything you've offered."

She sighed because she didn't want to verbally agree with him. "Do you have any proof?" she asked.

He thought for a moment and then started to dig around in his pockets. He pulled a tiny notebook from his chest pocket and opened it, spilling loose pages over the tabletop. He flipped through each page, mumbling, and then his eyes lit up. "Oh! Oh, this one. I know this one is true because… well…" He tapped at his eye socket to suggest he'd seen something. "Several years ago, there was a man—Uh, Arnie, yeah, that's his name—who kidnapped kids from the park. He was a kind of weird guy. Everyone had seen him around, but no one knew anything about him. They just ignored him until the kids started to disappear. The rumor was he would have the kids follow him to the bridge on the north end of the park. There he would… well, he did really nasty things."

"Every town has a pedophile, I guess," Naomi said.

"Oh, no, I mean, I don't think he did that. But he would just, well, he'd cut off their eyelids so they would look at him when he talked. He used sticks and twine to make them, like, stands? So he could pose them and move them about. When they caught him, he screamed about just wanting friends."

"What happened?"

"The town lynched him. Right in the middle of the square. If you ask any granny here, he deserved what happened to him for hurting those kids, but I try to check every story with the local records as much as I can. There isn't much to offer in this town, but the Historical Society has a little old lady who loves lemon bars and conversation. If you compliment her coordinating cardigans and dresses enough, she'll let you look at pretty much anything. Well, there are two publications that date back that far. One is *The Pickleberry Crier*, which hardly anyone reads today. The other was a handwritten history of Pickleberry, penned by an unknown author."

"*The Crier*, huh?" she asked, remembering the name.

"It's all drivel. It has been since Pickleberry was founded. Your buddy Glenn's sister runs it now. She tells me she's going to change that, but so far she just writes about parades and who left their cans out the day after trash day. Back then, it fed the mob that lynched Arnie, calling him a lunatic and a menace to the town."

"He murdered kids," she said.

"I'm not defending him," said Ben. "But they never did an investigation. They just found the guy in his hideout, dragged him to the middle of town and—" He held up one hand like an imaginary noose and mimicked a head going limp. "Which yeah, he did it, but when you read this other guy's history of the town, it makes you wonder. He says Arnie wasn't all there. Feeble-minded, I guess. He was malleable. When they dragged him to the center of the town, he screamed and screamed about someone else. He said he didn't want to kill them, but some guy made him do it, and after he did he felt so guilty, he made a shrine to their bodies in his little hideout."

"He killed them in the park and took them elsewhere?"

"Down the creek," he said.

"Where the teen couple was found?"

"No, that's the river," he said. "The park has a small creek, which is more like an embankment. It's dry unless we get a good rain. It runs east away from the park and off into the woods. The bridge he took them to was part of that route, and he would carry them down the creek bed to just the mouth of the woods where he had some, like, hideout." He shook his head. "*The Crier* left out the details about the hideout."

"But what about the other guy? The unknown author?"

"He didn't say anything about the hideout, but as insightful as his work is, it's scattered. Ms. Joanie only has a page here or there."

"Joanie?" she asked.

Ben shrugged.

Audrey emerged from the back and came over to take their order. "Are you talking about ghosts again, Ben?" she asked.

"No, I'm talking about murders, Audrey," he huffed.

Audrey gave Naomi a once over, but her expression was so dull and flat, Naomi couldn't get a read on it. They ordered drinks—a creamy latte for Ben and Earl Grey tea for Naomi. Audrey took their order and delivered it without any further comments, then disappeared into the back room again.

"Anyways," he said, stirring his coffee. "All of this is to say that there are ghosts in the park, and the ladies at Knitta's Night still talk about the man that murdered kids."

Naomi stared, unsure where to start. "*Knitta's* Night?"

"Yeah, it's on Thursdays, because most of them have their grandkids on Fridays." He set the spoon aside and took a drink, then looked up at Naomi's "are you kidding me?" glare. He shrugged in response. "You said it yourself, this town has little to offer."

She leaned forward over the table. "So, nothing tells you more about this guy's death or his murders? Nothing else about the bodies or anything? Did they ever find them?"

"They found them, but that's all they wrote. No details about the scene or whatever. Both versions of the stories I have say they were mutilated, but not how," he said. "I know about the eyelids and the posed bodies because that's what people say. Plus, I can fact check the ghosts in the park. I can see them."

"Mutilated," she mused. "Just the eyelids?"

"Is this where you tell me something you know?"

"These victims, today's, they're missing their hearts," she said. "Some would call that mutilation."

"You think there's a connection between Arnie and what's going on now?"

She shrugged. "Would it be too crazy to think?"

"This was decades ago. Even if whoever made Arnie do it was still around, he'd be too old—or more than likely, dead," he said.

"That's assuming he's human." She tapped a finger to her chin. When she caught him frowning, she asked, "You see ghosts and me teleporting from your home, but *that's* a stretch?"

He shook out his curls in disbelief. "Okay, let's say you're right. He stopped years ago. There haven't been any more killings of kids or… whatever. Why would he just suddenly stop?"

"Ask The Zodiac or The Golden State Killer."

He gave her an exasperated look.

"I don't know the reason," she admitted. "But maybe if we knew more about those murders, the kids, we'd have a direction to go. Because right now as it stands, all we have is old lady gossip." She rested her face in her hands. "Do you know anyone that would know more about this story?"

"Well, there's always the knitting group."

"Fuck." She sighed.

"Or Ginger," he said.

"Ginger?"

"She runs *The Crier*. She has access to all the past publications and anything they might have on file, as well as her brother being in the PPD," he said. "I can get some stuff out of Glenn if I cover his meal at Cotton's, but that only goes so far. Ginger makes a mean moonshine I've heard Glenn has a weak spot for. Three drinks in and I'm sure he tells her anything she wants to hear."

"How do you know so much about his family?" she asked.

He rubbed his neck and took a drink of his coffee.

"Ah." Naomi nodded. "I forget how shallow the dating pool is in towns like this."

"It was like a fling, okay? I was new, and I think she was glad to find someone with no chance of being related."

She chuckled.

Her laughter startled Ben. He didn't think a sound so sweet could come from someone like her, and for the briefest of moments he felt the corner of his mouth turn up and his head tilt.

"If you don't remove that stupid look from your face, I'll remove it for you," she told him, her face settling into stone again.

"Yeah, sorry." He cleared his throat.

Naomi stood from the table, throwing some bills by her untouched tea.

"Where are you going?" he asked.

"You're going to help me find Ginger."

He groaned. "Please, God, no."

The Pickleberry Crier as a publication went back to the town's beginnings, but nowadays it existed as nothing more than a corner office downtown nestled between the post office and Cotton's, a narrow sliver of space that barely allowed two people to stand shoulder-to-shoulder. That generally wasn't an issue, as most of the time there was only Ginger typing away at her laptop. If there was anyone else in the office, it was her assistant, who showed up once a week to print and fold newspapers, or an older lady who came to ask why her paper was never delivered.

The tight space seemed smaller when Ben and Naomi were forced to stand an inch apart, hoping the rustling behind the desk was Ginger and not a large rat. When she popped her head up from the desk and saw them, she let out a shriek.

Her pasty skin flushed red. "Why the hell would you just walk into the office without saying a word?" she huffed.

"Most people have bells on their doors," Naomi pointed out.

"This isn't a pizza parlor. It's a publishing office," she snapped. Using her cat-eye glasses like a headband, she pushed her mess of red curls from her face, then settled her hands on her hips. "What could you possibly want, Ben?" she asked.

"Hi, Ginger." He waved. "This is Naomi—"

Naomi shoved his hand down. "I want to know what you know about a murder that occurred here," she said.

"You mean the teens out by Muddee River?" Ginger asked. "Nothing, thanks to Ben and Glenn."

"No, this would have been years ago," said Naomi. "The man's name was Arnie?"

Ginger cocked her jaw to the side and gave Ben a sideways glance. "I see you found someone else to eat up your ridiculous stories."

"I wouldn't say that," he said.

"I'm interested in the history of this town," Naomi said. "Even if it's just a story, I'd like to know more."

She narrowed her eyes. "Why?"

Naomi glanced to Ben, but he simply shrugged. "I'm a writer," she said. "I've been traveling all over the Midwest collecting stories of small-town crimes. For my book."

"That's why you were at the crime scene?" Ginger asked. "Must be some big writer if you have access to a crime scene. I'm related to a cop, run the town paper, and still can't get a decent interview."

"Well, my employer's… publisher… is close with Sheriff Freeman," Naomi said.

"A publisher and a sheriff. That's an odd combination," Ginger said. She leaned over the counter and started to look Naomi over with a critical eye.

Naomi frowned. "Do you know anything or am I wasting my time in this sad excuse for a publishing office?"

Ginger sat back, offended. "I don't have to tell you anything."

"You don't," Naomi agreed. "I just thought the *Town Crier* would be the best place to learn about the town." She sighed. "Ben did say I'd do better to visit the Historical Society if I wanted the dirt on Pickleberry." She tucked her hands into her pockets and looked at Ben. "Her name was Joanie, wasn't it?"

"Oh, yeah, yeah." Ben nodded.

Naomi pursed her lips. "I guess you were right." She turned back to Ginger. "Thanks for your time." She started to leave.

"Wait," said Ginger. "Wait. I'm sorry. No one cares about the newspaper except for old ladies who use it for their tiny dogs, or when some DIY mom wants to make a piñata. Nobody takes anything I write seriously. I mean, Ben was the only one who ever showed an interest…."

She shook her head, bringing herself back to topic. "There isn't a lot about Arnie. I tried to learn more about what happened, but everything I found was either biased or incomplete. I worked on it for a few years, but people don't want to remember what happened or consider that their version of the story isn't all there is to it." She drew a deep breath, thinking. "There *was* one old guy I talked to a few years ago who gave me some background, but he died last year."

"What did he tell you?" Naomi asked.

"I'm sure Ben has already told you most of it," she said. "Man kills kids, mutilates kids, man is lynched and dies screaming that he's innocent."

"And they found his cave full of kids without eyelids and shit?" Naomi asked.

"No eyelids? Is that what you told her?" she asked Ben.

"That's what *you* told *me*," he retorted.

"I just said mutilated," she said. "My guy told me it was less of a random act of mutilation and more like Arnie was collecting something from the bodies. He'd known Arnie as a boy. He said he had his troubles in school, that he was an outcast because of his mental capacity. But he wasn't violent or dangerous."

Ginger sighed. She opened a file cabinet next to her with the ring of keys that hung from the coiling bracelet on her wrist. She flipped through the folders near the back until she found the file she was looking for. She pulled out a sheet of paper with a few paragraphs scribbled across it.

Her eyes scanned the page. "Here," she said. "*There were many times I asked Arnie if he had made new friends. He was so painfully shy, but he must have desired companionship like anyone else. Most times he would claim he was too busy for friends and I would tell him that walking the town streets didn't constitute work so he ain't got no reason to not make a friend or two. Eventually, he confessed to have met a fellow who liked him. Someone who encouraged his collection of smooth rocks he picked from Muddee's banks. He said they were both collectors, but this man only collected items hard to get a hold of. In time, I would ask about this man and Arnie's talks would begin light and joyful. His face would light up when he talked about the way the man's chest shone like he had swallowed a lightbulb and it made him warm. I never knew what he meant by that, but Arnie always had a strange way of seeing things. But over time he said less and less, like he was afraid to talk about the guy. When I pushed, he just said the guy asked for him to help collect things, but he wouldn't tell me what, only that he didn't like it. I don't know what Arnie did to those kids, but he died screaming he was innocent and I believe him. I only wish there was more I could have done.*"

She looked back to Naomi and Ben with a shrug. "He wrote me this. He didn't like it when I recorded him." She let Naomi look the page over, with Ben craning over her shoulder.

Ben read the name at the bottom. "Gerald Winkler. Wasn't that Eunice Winkler's husband?"

"Wow," said Ginger. "You're almost as good of a detective as my brother."

"Ginger, I really wish you would stop discrediting the local law to the locals," came Glenn's voice from the doorway. He looked at the trio and furrowed his brow. "Are you following a lead, or did you just feel like visiting the world's worst journalist?"

"Eat shit," Ginger growled.

"Can I have this?" Naomi asked Ginger, pointing at the paper.

"I'll make you a copy," she said.

At Naomi's nod, Ben followed Ginger to the copy machine.

Naomi turned to Glenn. "Are you following me around the town?"

"Actually, I was here to voice my appreciation, or lack of, for a story my sister wrote about me. Little sisters never stop being a pain in your ass." He glanced over at Ginger, who grinned. He shook his head with a sigh. To Naomi, he said, "I didn't expect to find you here, but if you found something, maybe you could fill me in?"

Naomi could feel Ginger's and Ben's eyes on her neck as she shook her head. "Nothing new."

"Well, in that case, I'm glad to see you," he said. He reached for his back pocket.

Naomi took a step back. "What? Why?"

He pulled a wrinkled blue envelope from his back pocket. "I just... well, I don't know how to say this, and well, you know what they say about cards saying the things we can't...." He trailed off, hesitating, then thrust the envelope into Naomi's hand.

It was warm from his pocket and creased like he'd sat on it. She stared down at it without a word as he went on.

"Brian was my best friend in school. I didn't keep in contact like I should have, didn't know anything about his life after he left town. But the thought that I just slept through him dying? And I'm sorry. I'm rambling. I just... I'm really sorry for you losing him." He gave an awkward shrug. "That probably defeats the purpose of letting the card say it for me, but you should still open it."

Naomi made no motion to open the envelope. She simply pushed it into her pocket. "Don't mention it," she said evenly. With a gesture at Ben to follow her, she opened the door and walked out.

She heard Ginger say, "Smooth," and then the door closed behind her.

Naomi was already at the corner of the town square by the time Ben caught up with her. The questions burned away in his mind, but instead of asking what would surely be ignored, he just cleared his throat. "Any reason you didn't tell Beasley about the lead?"

When she looked at him, he could see a hint of red in her glossy eyes. "I don't think we have time to waste explaining we're chasing ghost stories," she said.

"That's probably for the best. He's kinda slow anyway." He looked at the letter in his hand. "Eunice Winkler is a regular at Knitta's Night," he told her.

"Gerald's wife?"

He nodded. "Maybe she knows more?"

"What day is today?"

"Wednesday."

"Fuck." She sighed, looking to the sky as it was starting to turn gold. "Maybe I should meet you at your home tomorrow?"

"Do you have anywhere to go? There are no hotels in this town."

She didn't answer, and he thought she suddenly looked bone-tired.

"Why don't you come over for dinner?" he suggested. "I have notebooks of lore about this town. Maybe something will stick out to you?"

"You and Ginger would have made the cutest curly-haired babies," she said.

"Okay, enough of that," he grumbled. He started off toward the street, hoping Naomi would follow.

When he glanced back, she was a couple of steps behind. A smirk played across her face.

January 5, 1990

Maybe I've been going about this all wrong. Maybe instead of trying to save the town from all the monsters, I should just accept it for what it is. Keep an eye out for troublemakers, but sit back a bit and enjoy my family. I've learned all I can. I've made weapons and truces.

Maybe it's time to step back a bit. These monsters are as common as the cows that get loose off 215. They can be a nuisance if you let them, but it's easy to corral them. To keep them where they belong. Jo is married and expecting her first kid already. It'll be the first grandkid for Margo and me. Maybe I should make more effort to be a grandpa than I ever did a dad. The family will never understand the sacrifices I've made.

All the nights spent patrolling the streets, all the hours spent in the workshop building weapons to protect us. Maybe it's time to put the tools and trade aside.

Maybe Pickleberry can survive after all.

Chuck

23

Ben's home was a bustling store front on Black Friday. Or at least it seemed that way when he led Naomi up the stairs into what was literally a fight over a TV.

Deena had Luke in some kind of hold that resembled a spider monkey clinging to a tree trunk and struggling to climb it. "You've had the TV for two hours! Mom and Dad bought you a TV for your room. Why are you even in the living room?"

He held the remote out of her reach. "I can't see the details of the game on that tiny thing. Urgh! I can't breathe!" Luke gasped as Deena's arm moved from his shoulders to his throat.

"If you two don't stop right now," shouted Miriam, "I'm throwing away every screen I bought in this house. DEENA! LUKE'S LIPS ARE TURNING BLUE!" She'd been in the middle of feeding Sophie, but now she put down the baby food and hurried to pry apart her teenagers.

Sophie's eyes welled and she began to wail.

In the same moment, a bulb shattered in the kitchen.

"Oh, Gabe," said Ben's mother, "get down from there." She held up a hand to help a middle-aged man, who was standing on the island. "We can't replace you as easily as that lightbulb. I told you to have Luke do that."

Gabe glanced to the grappling teenagers in the living room. Miriam was pulling at whatever stray limb she could grab. "He seems busy."

Naomi huffed where she and Ben stood at the top of the stairs. "Is it always like this?"

He'd been wondering if he should try to get a word in over the noise or try to slip them through the mess to his room, but at the sound of Naomi's voice, the room fell silent and all eyes turned to them.

"Is that a girl?" Jonah asked from the kitchen. He'd just picked out a piece of chicken from the skillet in front of him. He popped it into his mouth, looking Naomi over as he chewed. He gave her an approving nod. "Is he allowed to bring home girls?"

Deena and Luke had separated. Miriam stood between them. All three stared at the newcomer with eyebrows raised quizzically.

Even Sophie had stopped crying—she'd discovered the baby food jar left on her tray and was now using it as an edible fingerpainting medium.

Ben cleared his throat. "Family, this is Naomi."

There was a mild wave from his mother, but even she couldn't hide the surprise on her face.

"Do I look so horribly out of place?" Naomi whispered.

"I think they're more surprised to see me with a girl," he whispered back.

"Ginger was prettier," Deena said, her nose and lips curled at Naomi.

Miriam gave her a smack to the back of the head.

"Ow! What?"

Ben covered his face with his hand and then gestured for Naomi to follow him through the busy room. "We're just going to…" he mumbled. "Yeah, excuse me while I go die in my room."

When they reached the island in the kitchen, Trina seemed to snap out of her daze. "Naomi? It's so nice to meet you." She smiled, shaking her hand. "Since Ben won't introduce us, I'll do it for him. I'm Katrina, this is my husband Gabe, that's Miriam, and then Deena and Luke. Oh, and Sophie, of course." As she pointed, each face offered another smile.

The chicken thief waved his fork at her. "I'm Jonah," he said through another mouthful.

"Jonah, stop eating all the food," said Trina. "We have a guest. You will stay for dinner, right?" she asked, looking eagerly to Naomi.

She hesitated. "Oh, I'm not sure…"

"Mom, stop," said Ben, giving everyone—except his dad, who was back on the island screwing in a new lightbulb—a warning glare.

He took Naomi's shoulders and ushered her to his room. He closed the door behind him, breathing heavily. "I would apologize, but I don't think an apology would do much good."

"Don't apologize for your family," she told him simply. She sat on his bed and felt the tension in her feet and legs relax just a bit. She'd been walking for what felt like days, hardly stopping. Sitting on a comfortable bed was nice, even if the last memory she had of a real bed was one she tried to forget.

Ben's stomach gurgled.

"Have you eaten at all today?" she asked.

"It's fine," he said. "We've been running around a lot."

"I don't think about food because I don't eat it," she said without thinking. When she realized what she'd said, she paused, watching his face for a reaction. Nothing. She guessed after seeing everything she could do, not eating was no big deal. "You should eat."

He nodded. "Make yourself comfortable," he said, slipping out of the room.

Naomi listened to the hushed voices on the other side of the door, grinning to catch her name a time or two. Then she turned her attention to the rest of the room. Ben's desk was littered with papers and notebooks. She thumbed through scribbled notes that mentioned ghost houses, cheating wives, the ever-changing prices at the local grocery store, and the concerning growth rate of LMH. Beside each note was a woman's name—all the kind of name one expected to read on an outing roster for a nursing home.

Rumors from the knitting club, she surmised.

She picked up a notebook and flipped lazily through its pages until her eyes landed on a crude drawing of a tiny black yarn doll with red X's for eyes. She took the notebook to his bed and, pulling her shoes off, lay down on her stomach. When Ben returned, she was trying to decipher his handwriting, with little luck.

He had a slice of bread sticking from his mouth and a full plate in hand. The aromas danced through the room to Naomi's nose, and while her heart fluttered at the smells, her stomach didn't give so much as a little grumble.

"Smells good," she said.

"Tastes better," he replied.

"I'll take your word for it," she said, then looked back to the notebook. "You have the worst handwriting I've ever seen."

"That's a good thing. If my nosy cousins slipped in here and read through these, my parents would probably do an exorcism on me." He sat at the desk, pushing papers around to make room for his plate.

"What is this about?" she asked, showing him the drawing of the doll.

"Oh, that belonged to a demon. I had so many more notes about him, but they were all in that book you destroyed," he said with an edge of bitterness. "Or lost or whatever you did to it."

She stared at the doll, her brows furrowed in thought.

"Does it mean something to you?" he mumbled through a mouthful.

"No. I look at it and it's like déjà vu, but nothing comes to me." She sighed. "And the demon? This town is full of spooky shit, but what would a demon want with it?"

"He's an enigmatic type. He doesn't fit the usual demon trope. I don't even think he wants to do hell's work but just exist on his own. But he's old. He's been around for longer than most spooky shit. The book really went in depth on the theories about him and why he's so different, but they're all just theories. Anyone who claims to have an encounter with him can't remember anything, or they tell a story that's completely off base."

"What kinds of theories?"

"Well, most demons have a game they stick to, like habits. This guy's no different. He likes gifts. Giving them, getting them. He's also nearly impossible to recognize by the average person, because he likes to wear faces, like masks. I guess the only common thing about him is that he makes people miserable along the way. But if it benefited him, he did whatever he wanted. Most of the accounts in that book spoke about him making people do dirty deeds for the benefit of him, not hell." Ben shoved a forkful of food in his mouth.

"What was his name?"

He moved some food around in his mouth until he resembled a hamster. "It was on the book cover."

She frowned.

"Eddow?" he asked.

The name meant nothing to her. If she'd read it, she didn't recall.

"You know, I never asked why you came into my house."

"Huh?"

"Of all the houses on this street, why did you pick mine? How did you know to look here for the book?"

She thought. "I didn't. I don't even think I was looking for the book until I saw it." She looked the walls over as though she were seeing them differently. "I think I used to live here."

"No shit?"

"I think so," she said. "There's something very familiar about this house. Though I don't think it looked anything like this."

"Well, we built it up when my dad bought it, and of course the café was a garage. Did your family break the garage?"

"I think they may have," she mused.

He laughed. "I'd love to know the story behind that one."

"My dad was teaching my brother to drive. He was going to drive us to the gas station—" She stopped short. A minute ago she had no memory of the event, but as soon as the words came out of her mouth, she knew they were the truth. "Yeah, yeah," she went on, the words spilling out. "He was a showoff. He thought he was so grown up, driving Dad's station wagon, but he put it in Drive instead of Reverse and just floored it." Her finger traced the design on his comforter as she put the memory together. "My mother cried, but my dad laughed so hard he fell onto the grass." With a bemused smile, she looked at Ben. "I didn't know I knew that."

"Are there a lot of things you don't remember?"

"I'm not sure how to answer that," she said. "My childhood is foggy. I can only see glimpses of it. I know I had two parents and two siblings." She recalled what Nora had said. "I know we lived in Pickleberry. I guess it was here. So when I came here, I think I was just trying to piece it all together." She rubbed her eyes.

Ben turned back to his plate to scoop more food into his mouth.

When he turned back, Naomi had fallen asleep on top of his notebook.

He chewed slowly, trying to decide if it was better to sleep on his dirty floor or in his worn swivel chair.

24

People go their whole lives without knowing love like Naomi. It was true that when they met, she'd thought him a dumb boy who had taken too many hits on the football field. But as time passed, she began to wonder what a dumb boy was doing lurking around the tiny bookstore in downtown Pickleberry where she worked.

At first she wondered if maybe he was interested in the owner, an attractive, older woman with an air of mystery. But when he kept coming around even when the owner was gone, Naomi had to play with the idea of being the object of someone's desire. It felt silly and absurd.

"What's the best thing to read in here?" he asked one day.

It felt like a test. Was she about to be *Carrie*-d? Or was this genuine interest?

"How are you with the odd and disturbing?"

"I can handle it," he said.

"Child sacrifices?" she asked.

He hesitated but nodded.

"Murder, mutilation, and satanic cults?"

"Yeah, yeah, pfft, isn't everyone?"

She smiled at the tough guy front. "In that case, you should read Ray Bradbury." She pointed to a section on the shelf behind him.

"Does he write about murdering kids?"

She shrugged. "Nah, he writes about aliens and dystopian futures and Halloween. But he's my favorite and I recommend him to everyone."

He gathered one of each Bradbury title, an armful of books, and dropped them on the counter in front of her. "I'm Brian."

And as they say: the rest was history.

Despite their high school being small, their circles rarely crossed. Still, Brian turned up at the bookstore every evening after practice, reeking of sweat and body spray and asking her about books until she ran out of books to sell him.

When that happened, the only logical solution was to run away and get married. Brian had been recruited into the Navy and was leaving their tiny town with its tinier prospects. He was a vibrant dreamscape in the bleakness of her existence in Pickleberry. Naomi couldn't afford to let something like that slip away.

The life they created together in the southwest corner of the United States was a whole new concoction of strange and exciting. Anything outside of Missouri was a Martian landscape straight from Bradbury's tales. Whimsical and childish love grew and developed alongside the size of their family with their perfect Jessa.

The three bookworms cuddled in blankets with books and mugs of cocoa and coffee at any chance they could until Brian had his fill of the Navy. They stayed in the area for a year or two, getting all they could from Bradbury's wastelands, until the Midwest pulled them back with the promise of a forever home and affordable groceries. They settled in Springfield, a large enough town to offer opportunity for each of them.

Naomi took two pictures on the first day of school: one of a grinning kindergartener and the other of a scruffy freshman at the local university. It was an odd feeling sending off her husband and child to school on the same day, but reflecting back on cheesing faces, she couldn't recall if her heart had ever felt so full. Two shining, smiling beacons.

Recalling her early years of life, Naomi only saw an omnipresent darkness that followed her like a shadow. It hung over her head and stole any idea of love. She'd certainly never imagined a love like this, a husband dedicated to seeing her smile and a child who smothered her with hugs. The darkness seemed to leave once Brian stumbled into her store.

It wasn't until later, when she viewed their smiling faces framed on a podium surrounded by flowers and mourners, that she remembered the darkness.

Parents shouldn't bury their babies. That was twisted and backward and not how the story is supposed to be told.

Naomi buried her whole world—her Jessa and her Brian.

She shook hands and hugged weeping mourners, but she never allowed herself to feel the full weight of their loss until the crowds had left. She operated on autopilot, expressing gratitude for the support and comforting those who needed it.

After it was done, after all the people were gone and she was finally alone in the silence of her childhood bedroom, she felt their absence.

If only for a moment, she felt totally and utterly alone.

Her silent solitude was broken by her parents' hushed voices carrying from the living room.

"She can't afford that house on her own," her father said in a whisper he obviously thought she couldn't hear. "The medical bills alone wiped out any savings they had."

"I've always said that house is too big for her," added her mother.

"So, we agree?"

"Move in with us? We just got the space to ourselves and now we have to take on someone else?"

"Don't be selfish, Jo."

"What about us? Your meds are going up and your heart isn't getting any better. How much longer do you think you can work? So we gotta figure out how to keep you and me and *her* alive?"

"I don't want to burden you," Naomi said from the doorway. Midwestern and human obligation forced the words out of her mouth stiff and flat. She didn't want to burden anyone but the worms.

"You wouldn't burden us, dear," her father said. "Things are tight, but we'll make them work. You won't go back to that house alone."

She huffed, a dry sound of disbelief rather than humor. Her mother's glance to her father told Naomi she wasn't welcome in whatever conversation they needed to continue.

She returned to her room now no longer feeling solitude, but darkness, a shadow that grew within her own. The weight of the shadow caused her shoulders to slump and it became hard to breathe.

The despair pulled her tight like a frigid hug and chuckled in her ear.

"Seems like you could use a friend. Remember when you loved me? You were never alone when you loved me, little Nay."

The dark cloud that formed over Naomi darkened the room, and she was aware of little else. It screamed so loud in her ear that it drowned out the pity and platitudes and all the bickering about her future.

Its voice was a hiss and a crackle. The collection of sounds made no sense to human ears, and yet somehow she understood like it had been spoken to her since birth.

"Do you want to be strong, Naomi?" asked the voice.

Naomi's head barely moved in a nod. "I don't want to be a burden."

"I will make you strong. I will make you useful. After all, what are friends for?"

25

The sound of children's laughter woke Naomi.

It jolted her from sleep so suddenly she nearly leaped from the bed. She had a knot in her stomach, as though she'd overslept and failed to fulfill some important responsibility. On those rare occasions, it usually meant that her husband had snuck out of the room to let her sleep in. The sun would be higher in the sky than she was used to. She would shuffle slowly from the room following the aroma of pancakes and coffee. Wide smiles would greet her and the knot that filled her stomach would disappear.

Only this time when she woke up, nothing about the room was familiar. Despite the smell of eggs and toast in the air, she knew that none of the familiar faces she longed to see would be on the other side of the door. So, the knot stayed in her gut.

It wasn't until she heard Ben's snoring from the floor that she realized he was in the room. Her rustling made the bed creak and groan, and soon enough he was up doing the same.

"Ohhh, Lord." He took time to align his body before attempting to rise.

"You could have woken me," she told him. "It's your bed."

He waved her off, holding a hand to the base of his back. "It's nothing. You looked like you needed it more." He pushed himself into his swivel chair and relaxed into it. "You cry in your sleep."

Naomi didn't respond. It didn't surprise her, considering all her resurfacing feelings. She attempted to smooth the mess of her hair and pushed aside the blankets Ben had obviously placed over her. "How likely is it that Gerald's wife will confirm our suspicions?" she asked.

"Considering she's over eighty, it could go either way," he answered with a sigh. "And what are our suspicions?"

"That Arnie was working for someone, and that someone has something to do with the murders happening now." She stood from the bed, straightening out the blankets and tugging the wrinkles out of her clothes. "I don't want to spend the whole day here reading through all your sloppy notes, then another hour speaking to some old bag with dementia, only to learn something we already know. Especially when my gut is already telling me what to do."

"Do you talk so crudely about people because you don't want them to get close, or are you just a bitch?" he asked.

She paused, her eyebrows high on her forehead and speechless. "I don't recall asking for a psych eval."

He put his hands up. "All right, fine. What does your gut say?"

"We need to find Arnie's hideout."

"They probably destroyed it years ago."

"Okay, fine," she said, pulling on her boots and jacket. "We go for a walk and if we find nothing, we go talk to your knitting circle."

"It isn't *my* knitting circle," he said.

She put her hand up. "I'll be outside."

She opened his bedroom door to meet several faces staring at her. She adjusted the collar on her jacket and offered a polite smile but wasted no time leaving the house.

Ben met her outside nearly half an hour later. She gathered by his heated demeanor that he'd met some resistance on the way out. She was sure that standing on the street corner didn't help matters much.

"Your family must not approve," she said.

He shook his head. "Last month, Jonah brought home a girl with piercings on every inch of her face. She tried to burn the house down and they still asked her if she was Jewish and how many kids she wanted."

Naomi laughed.

"I had to answer a million questions about you before I was even able to make it to the door." He gave her a rueful look. "I'd like to give you a good excuse as to why I'm in my late twenties and still living with my family, but..."

"Don't worry about it," she said. "Maybe some future day we'll have time to exchange excuses, but none of that matters right now."

"Fair enough."

26

Despite the early hour, Pickleberry's streets were fairly busy. Many of the active residents liked to use the main roads for their early morning walks. They were able to get in more miles and see the goings-on in the town while doing so, without worrying too much about morning traffic.

For those who sought physical activity based less on personal motivation, an entire group of folks took to the park to get their doctor-mandated exercise. The park was the ideal place as the sun was low behind the trees, making perfect shade coverage in the hot days of summer, and hosted a path that was just one large circle with a curve here or there. An occasional incline offered enough of a challenge that those who frequented the place felt they worked hard enough to please the old docs at LMH, even if it was really the bare minimum of activity. After a lifetime of living, the bare minimum of activity was allowed.

This wasn't something either Naomi or Ben anticipated when they arrived at the park.

As they turned onto the main road, they passed several walkers, single or in pairs, trucking along the sidewalks. A woman zoomed by them, and Naomi huffed. "Is there a hurried middle-aged women's contest in town?"

"That's Debbie Glendale," said Ben. "She discovered the body of Skye Gibson, the first victim. I heard she barely broke stride and complained to the cops about ruining her pace."

"That's what she was concerned about?" Naomi asked.

"There's some stiff competition with the power-walkers in town. They all meet at Cotton's to compare notes on their paces, and anything else they might have noticed on their walks. You know, whose lawn needs mowing, and whose wife is madder than an evicted hornet because her husband *just* stumbled out of Jerry's garage bar."

Naomi watched them, the chattering gaggles of women and men who walked the loop. It seemed like such a privilege to worry about the state of someone's yard and not about who was harvesting the organs of murdered kids.

Ben broke her thought. "Oh, it's her."

"What? Who?"

He pointed to the pavilion in the center of the park. "Mrs. Winkler."

A group of chattering women crossed in front of them, giving Naomi's scruffy black ensemble strange looks. When they passed, she saw a silver-haired woman with purple-framed glasses and a sunshine yellow short-and-tee ensemble sitting in the pavilion, watching the trees.

"It would be a waste not to talk to her since she's here," he said. "I don't think Arnie's hideout is going anywhere."

She was reluctant to admit that he was right, so she just nodded in the woman's direction.

"Mrs. Winkler," called Ben as they crossed a stretch of green grass. She didn't respond. He called again, and then again, more loudly. "Mrs. Winkler!"

"Huh? What's that?" She turned her gaze from the trees and smiled. Her eyes appeared twice as large as normal behind her glasses. "Oh, Benny, dear. How are you? I didn't expect to see you." She looked at Naomi, tilting her head down and letting her glasses slide down the tip of her nose to study her with gray eyes. "Is this your girlfriend, dear?"

"Oh, no!" he said quickly. "She's a friend. I'm helping her with a project."

"My name is Naomi," she said. "Is it Mrs. Winkler?"

"Eunice, dear. Mrs. Winkler makes me feel like a widow."

"Well, aren't you?" asked Ben.

"That don't mean I wanna be reminded, Benjamin. Christ."

Naomi suppressed a smile. "I hear you have a lot of Pickleberry tales."

"I ought to. I've lived here long enough," she said.

"I wanted to hear what you know about Arnie and the kids that were killed," Naomi asked.

"Are you one of those murder tourists?"

"I'm sorry?" Naomi responded.

"Listen, if I thought it would bring some excitement to this town, I'd give the tours myself. It would sure as hell beat walking with these old biddies." Eunice gestured at the groups of women strolling along the walking path, chuckling so heartily that her belly shook.

Naomi settled herself on the bench next to her with an appreciative grin and leaned forward a bit. "I'm really just interested in Arnie," she said. "Maybe you could start there?"

Eunice's smile faded as her eyes drifted to the small bridge at the end of the park. "It really is bittersweet talking about that boy. I say boy. He was a fully grown man when he did what he did, but in my mind he was just a boy. I won't say he didn't know better, but I don't know."

Her eyes took on a faraway look. "He really was a good man," she said. "Yes, the murderer of children was a good man. No one ever got to see that side of him because it was all clouded by what he did. And those who knew that about him seemed to forget it. Are you from these parts, doll?"

"Not exactly," Naomi answered.

"Ain't no place like Pickleberry," Eunice said with a warm smile. "When the season changes, crops are harvested, and people are glad to be rid of the humidity from summer, they feel good again. But the days get shorter and the nights get longer and colder. We got a lot of big families who get stretched thin during the winter months. Not everyone can do holiday feasts or even put something under the tree for their youngun's." She realized she was rambling and recollected herself.

"This town is a community, and a community that gives when it can. The town will host food drives and toy collections. And Arnie, he… he would be the first one to tote boxes of canned goods to the church. He'd walk a mile to the other side of town just to collect a doll if he knew some little girl would get to open it on Christmas morning. Arnie operated better than the USPS." She chuckled at her own sentiment. "Every time he saw me it was, 'Y'all got any cans, Eunny?' I'd tell him to wander on off, that I gave my cans, and ain't no one wants cat food."

Her laugh turned into a shaky breath. She shook her head sadly. "Arnie was a good man, young lady," she said softly. "Not that we should just ignore the fact that he took little innocent souls. But it tore him up."

"And yet he did it multiple times?" Naomi asked.

She looked at Naomi, searching her face for something. When she couldn't find it, she leaned forward, rubbing one wrist, then the other. "Arnie didn't really have family. He kinda drifted from this house to that one, but we all looked after him in a way. He seemed to like our house more than most, probably because Gerry'd always send him off with two Cokes and a pocket full of cookies. And I didn't mind him. He could reach the cobwebs in the corners and always told me my hair looked like yellow cotton candy, good enough to eat. He'd laugh at any dumb joke that Gerald told. So, he was good company."

She paused as though piecing together the scene in her head. "It was probably two or maybe three in the morning. It was cold, just a couple o' weeks before winter, and the roads had started to ice a bit. We heard him fall up the porch stairs. When we opened the door, all we could see was him hidden in shadows, his sleeves soaking wet. I thought the poor soul had fallen into a puddle or something and had to be freezing, so I told Gerald to bring him inside. When we brought him into the light, we saw that his hands and his sleeves were red, just sopping in blood. More blood than I've ever seen in my life and that's saying a lot. I worked at LMH for decades and saw my share of accidents."

"Whose blood was it?" Naomi asked.

"Well, his blood, but I didn't know that at first. There was so much of it and he was still standing, even if he was a bit wobbly. I'd seen incidents like it before. Usually someone who'd had enough and was trying to just end it all."

"You think that's what he was trying to do?"

"I think he was trying very hard to end his life, but I don't know, couldn't? There was something that wouldn't let him do it. Gerald thought I was being dramatic, but the way he sobbed and pleaded, first for forgiveness and then for death. That wasn't a man that wanted to hurt anyone but himself."

"Why didn't you take him in or something?" she asked.

"I wanted to have him admitted to LMH. Even if it was just for the night, maybe we could've helped him. But the minute I mentioned it, he took off. There was no stoppin' him. The next time I saw him was just before they hung him."

Eunice's eyes were misty, but she didn't allow herself to cry. She looked back to the trees. "I know that boy—that man–was guilty of something, but I can't imagine him ever willingly harmin' anyone. Especially kids. I think there were people who were scared of him. He was simple-minded and a big guy. Dangerous? Never. A gentle giant more than anything. We all got demons we don't show, but to be condemned publicly by someone else's rash judgments? Arnie needed help, not to be strung up like that."

"You think he should have gone free?"

"O' course not. I think what happened to him is a reflection of this town's ignorance to acknowledge there are bigger things than ourselves out there." Eunice gave Naomi a sad smile. "Maybe my murder tour wouldn't be too interesting, after all."

"You've been very helpful, Eunice."

Her smile turned playful. "Ben always seems to find the most interesting women to run around with, but you are something else. That redhead was a chatty thing who berated me with questions. But—" She winked. "I'll save Ben's dignity."

Ben exhaled deeply and covered his face.

Naomi grinned.

Eunice patted Naomi's arm. "Arnie was a good man. Something happened to him that no one will ever understand. I just wish I could give him peace—in the afterlife and in this town. They call him a monster, but that ain't the man I knew."

Naomi stood from the bench. "I'm not sure how much we can help him now."

"You can't undo time," Eunice said. "Even if you came out with some guy confessin' to killin' all those kids, the town won't hear. Arnie got the ending he deserved just 'cause he made them uncomfortable. Proof don't count for nothin' against settled minds." She shrugged. "Besides, people were scared. Not many recall it or care to." She sighed and looked back out into the trees. "Maybe it'd bring him peace to know someone was looking into it."

When the silence grew long, Naomi knew they'd lost Eunice. Her gaze was distant and she imagined her thoughts were just as far gone. "We won't keep you any longer."

With a brief goodbye, they left her.

Naomi didn't speak as they walked to the bridge. She stopped when they reached its center, looking down the empty creek bed that wound off into the woods.

"What are you thinking?" Ben asked.

"I'm wondering if Eunice's words can be taken literally," she said.

"How so?"

"Your notes were full of talk about demons. It wouldn't be too much of a stretch for demons to do something completely fucked up. Eunice said Arnie had his demons, but what if she wasn't exaggerating? I think whatever we find at the end of this creek might have some demon work involved." She looked up. Ben had a white-knuckled grip on the railing. "This suddenly getting a little more intense than just seeing ghosts?"

"Well, I'm not completely surprised," he said. "Although I can't say I'm even remotely prepared to deal with demons if we were to find them."

Naomi nodded. Historically, she'd never brought other people into this part of her life. She dealt with the weird, the dark, the vamps, and the shadows all on her own. Sure, it had been nice to feel like she had a partner in all the crazy, and Ben's enthusiasm had been refreshing. But was it fair to involve him any further? "Maybe you should go back to your family," she suggested.

"And miss the demons?"

Naomi couldn't help but grin.

27

Demons have their purposes.

While there are those who never leave their lovely furnace, finding fulfillment in their hellish duties, others leave the tedious order of hell to do their work on earth.

Eddow was far cleverer than his brothers and sisters, who relied on ordinary temptation or despair to cow and corrupt the human spirit. He saw humans as a tool—a key to a doorway that offered abundant blessings for his kind. In order to use this tool, he first had to master it. To that end, he spent many years observing men and women. He learned the depth of their temptations—but also the depth of their love.

He found love to be among the most manipulable of man's desires. Even those who claimed no need had a weakness for it. It could make a human whole or utterly destroy them, depending on the application.

In his early years, he'd attempted to take what made humans whole. He tore lovers apart at such expedited rates he earned the name "Widow Maker." He expected to find fulfillment in this but instead, he found only disappointment. It might take years, but humans always found a replacement. Lovers moved on.

Through his experiments, he struggled to understand man's temptations. Lust, gluttony, pride—he found sin boring, toys for those with smaller goals than he. Sin broke the human heart, but humans healed too easily from a broken heart. He needed something more profound, more permanent. He needed to fragment them, to tear irreplaceable chunks from their hearts, to create wounds from which they could never recover.

It wasn't until he observed a pair of sixteen-year-olds that his perspective changed. When he snuffed out one of the young lives, an astounding tableau unfolded: the surviving lover huddled in the arms of friends and family, sobbing. But the lost child's mother… the mother cracked. She threw herself over the grave of the child and had to be carried away, so maddened it took four men to pull her from the headstone.

Eddow had never seen such pure and utter sorrow, such a hollowing, as that wailing, thrashing mother. He saw it. He saw the darkness fill her chest and encompass her whole being.

This woman might have other children at home. She could even have more children in the future. But no other child could ever replace the special warmth of that lost child in her soul. Nothing could replace the warmth that he'd ripped away.

A mother's love. He felt an immense curiosity about this bond.

At first, he enjoyed taking children. The wailing and misery were a melody to his ears. But he grew tired of the game. Children were so trusting, there was no thrill in it. Like a mouse showing its belly at the sight of a cat. He found it annoying.

But a thought occurred to him: Removing a child from a parent caused enormous pain, but what if he could break that bond altogether? Drive a mother's love away and harness the child's love for himself? A child so desperate for love might be willing to do *anything* for the one who showed them love—even taking on a monumental task without question.

A great demon could disrupt the bond without taking a life.

He wasn't completely successful on his first try, but once he learned the trick—to pull a parent's love from the child and step into their place—it was a high he'd never experienced before. One he would soon spend the rest of his existence chasing.

Eddow found it easier to corrupt an adult's bond—to foment resentment and drive a wedge between parent and child. For years, he found fulfillment in this work, and over the centuries he would fully shed the Widow Maker moniker and embrace others, given to him by humans who loved him so deeply their lives could only be fulfilled by devotion to him. Though the names changed over the ages, one seemed to reoccur every so often:

The Collector.

He didn't mind what they called him as long as he had their hearts. Their hearts filled him with what he assumed mothers felt, looking upon their squishy infants for the first time. And whether this was correct or not, he had the collection to prove it.

Naomi and Ben had walked about two miles up the creek when the air started to stink of body odor, stale food, and animal musk. They followed the scent for another half mile, until they found themselves staring at a hideout with a circular opening made from bent and tied branches. They covered their faces against the reek hanging heavy in the humid air.

"That's got to be man-made," said Naomi.

"It doesn't exactly smell like a forgotten crime scene," Ben mumbled through his hand.

"It smells like someone has been here recently," she agreed. "We have to go in."

Ben swallowed hard, which caused him to cough. "God, I can taste it."

"It's probably going to be disgusting," she warned.

"Uh-huh."

"You can stay out here."

He shook his head. "This is the most exciting thing that has happened to me since we moved to this town."

Naomi ventured closer to the hideout. The closer she got, the more her eyes watered. Her nose began to run.

"God, I regret eating breakfast." Ben's voice came out nasally, as he pinched his nose tightly.

"Just stay alert."

The opening was round and big enough for a person to fit through, but not comfortably. Naomi imagined whoever or whatever used the hideout was accustomed to climbing in, rather than entering upright. This meant she had to step in sideways and lower her head in after. Inside, the roof was low enough that she had to stoop.

The hideout was small, but every wall was lined with jars resting upon haphazard shelving made from objects likely found in the woods or by digging through people's garbage. Broken closet doors, banged up license plates, and discarded serving platters—all hanging from the walls by twine or fishing wire or stacked on poorly constructed supports. Naomi was careful not to bump into anything, sure the whole infrastructure would be compromised if she did.

Despite this, she wanted to touch each item and see what was inside.

"That's a lot of jars," Ben said as he climbed through the entry. He was probably a foot taller than Naomi, and the low ceiling forced him to hunch.

"It's *all* jars," she said. "Every inch of this place. No personal items, just jars."

Ben switched the hand he used to cover his mouth and reached for the closest one.

"Be careful," Naomi warned, nodding to the nearly invisible fishing wire supporting that row of shelves. If he bumped it, the whole row would likely fall on him.

He nodded and carefully took a jar from the shelf. He gave it a shake and then put it back, wiping his hand on his pants.

There were jars of every shape and size. They were covered in dust, making it hard to see the contents beyond a vague sense of color and texture—reddish brown and squishy, or pale and hard.

"There has to be hundreds of these things," Ben said.

"Or more." Naomi stepped toward the back of the den, where the roof was ever lower. There was a light source, faint but flickering, in a small cubby in the back corner.

"Do you think these are witch jars?" When Naomi didn't answer, he continued, "You know, hex jars? Made by witches who cursed people? They're usually made of contents of whoever the curse is meant to target, like hair, nails, or urine."

"I know what hex jars are. But the only witches I know of in this town don't use that type of magic." She pushed aside a ratty tarp serving as a curtain.

"What do you make of it?" he asked. "I kind of want to open one."

Naomi wasn't listening. She was staring at what appeared to be a small shrine. On a food platter or discarded cutting board stood a group of candles, melded firmly to its surface. Only one of the candles was lit, but by its light, Naomi could make out some etching on the wood—letters she'd seen before but couldn't recall their meaning. Behind the board, some faded papers had been displayed on the wall. They were scribblings done by what Naomi could only assume was a child: the standard family drawings, with a home, a mother and father, siblings, and a dog. And in the back, a tall, black figure with a red chest and branches for limbs. "It's an altar." She whispered to herself.

There were four pieces of art impaled on protruding branches. The one in the middle drew her attention. It was simply a heart, red and crudely colored on white construction paper. Something about it sparked a memory in her mind. She could see herself making the lines, carefully and lovingly. She could see the tip of her red crayon as it sped across the surface of the paper, filling the heart with color. And just outside the heart, she could see herself carefully writing the words, "love, Nay." In her mind, she watched a child hold up the picture and present it proudly… but to whom?

There was no one in the memory. Not even a blurred face she hoped to make out, only a void in front of her grinning face accepting her thoughtful art.

Her brow furrowed. She reached for the picture, but her eyes caught sight of something else: a small, black doll made of yarn and buttons, with red X's for eyes. She picked it up, and its weight seemed to break through her amnesia.

"Ben?" she called, her eyes still on the doll. "Do you recognize this?"

When Naomi finally looked up, she barely registered the open jar in his hand, his white face and sweaty skin. Her gaze took in the shadow that crept from the corner and took the form of a gangly man, his hands raised over Ben's head.

"Ben!" she shouted.

The man struck before Ben could react, knocking him into the nearby shelves. As he crumpled to the floor, the jars tumbled over and around him, shattering.

"They're not for you!" the man cried. He howled, raising his hands once again to strike at Ben.

Naomi took advantage of the darkness in the den. Shadows formed around her outstretched hand. She thrust them at the man with so much force he tumbled backward through the doorway.

When she rushed to Ben's side, he was pushing himself up, rubbing his head and waving her off. "I'm okay, I'm okay," he said, groaning.

She didn't wait for more but darted through the opening in pursuit.

Only she found no one. There were marks of disturbance in the creek bed, but no sign of their attacker.

A snapping twig made her spin back around—just in time to be struck hard in the jaw.

The man was thin and lacked finesse, but he'd laced his fingers together, swinging his fists and arms like a club. His blow knocked Naomi on her ass.

With the midday sun directly overhead, there weren't enough shadows for Naomi to use, but she had other skills. She leaped to her feet as he charged her again, this time catching his clubbed arms and breaking them.

He brushed off the pain.

Her eyes widened as he surged into motion, swinging his broken arms like a mace. Naomi dodged but wasn't able to pin him down.

It didn't matter how she attacked. Fueled by an unnatural rage, he countered or absorbed every blow she threw. There was something rooted deep in him that drove him to protect the altar regardless of any cost to himself.

This frightened Naomi. Even the toughest of tough guys fell to their knees if kicked hard enough in the balls, but not this guy. She could only hope to tire him out before she exhausted herself.

Finally, Naomi was able to wrap her legs around his and get him in a chokehold. He fought wildly to shake her off, but she held on. He dropped to his knees, clawing feebly at her arms.

Ben emerged from the den. "Naomi, stop!"

She didn't look up. "He's trying to kill us, Ben."

"It's—the jars—they're hearts.

November 26, 1993

Ignorance is bliss. If there was an honest slogan for this town, that would be it. That's how people live here. Until a few years ago, I hated it. Now I've learned that people have to. They have to shut out their fears and worries to have some sort of a normal existence in this place.

That's how I've been for the past few years. I ignored the rustling bushes when I knew it was too big to be an opossum or raccoon. I disregarded the beautiful woman luring drunk men into the bar at the top of the hill. I've ignored it all so I could watch my grandson play in the park without thinking too hard about the ghosts that run about him. I know about the dark and dirty deeds. But for the sake of my own sanity, I've forced myself to see only my grandson.

He's a good distraction. I'm far more worried about keeping him out of the streets and away from that pervert Jerry than I am about the ghosts.

It's been a few years since I pulled out this journal.

I wish I were writing here now to reflect on how great life has been since I put it away. Only if life was going as I hoped, I wouldn't have bothered even opening it again. But a few days ago, everything changed.

Jo unexpectedly went into labor. We rushed to meet her at LMH, but my sweet granddaughter arrived before we did. She barely gave her mom a moment to catch her breath—from what I heard, Richie almost needed a catcher's mitt. The thought of that little goob breaking into this world on her own terms, while Richie was yelling at Jo to hold it in and Jo was yellin' at him to fuck off, still makes me chuckle. An entry like that can only be a precursor for more trouble to come.

Grandkids have shown me a kind of love I never knew existed. I can't get enough of the little tots. After spending what feels like every waking moment with my grandson, I was eager to share that with his sister.

Imagine my shock when I entered the recovery room to greet the new addition and found an unfamiliar person in the room.

I shouldn't say person. What I saw looming over the side of the bed was nothing human. I didn't know what he was. It wasn't a vamp or a ghost or a ghoul. Nothing from distant memory fit his form. The only thing I knew was he didn't belong near my family.

He was tall and lumbering. Built like a tree, with a solid frame, skin textured like bark, and limbs like bundles of branches protruding out at his joints. I couldn't tell his full height, but he had to stoop in the hospital room.

His chest was hollow, like a rotten log, but as his eyes locked on my newborn granddaughter, the hollow space began to glow. Pulsating reds and yellows that intensified as he stared at the baby.

My innocent grandbaby. My Naomi.

When his jagged fingers reached for her, I felt my blood run cold. I must have made some sound at that, because he noticed me then. A look of surprise crossed his face, like he hadn't expected anyone to see him. But then he gave me the most horrifying grin I'd ever seen and disappeared.

I knew at that moment I had to pick up my trade again, my tools. I had to finish my weapons and make arrangements. I'd seen that look before. That ill intent, the greedy self-indulgence that would tear this town apart without a second thought. I can't protect my family by pretending these monsters don't exist. If I don't do something, if I don't try to protect my family, my Naomi, no one will.

My name is Chuck Paul Campbell. I was born and raised in Pickleberry and I have spent years devoting myself to this community, protecting them from monsters. If something happens to me, I hope this journal will help others learn the truth about this town and do what they must to protect it. I know people will likely think I'm a nut, but if I die trying to stop that monster, I need to know I tried to tell my truth.

Chuck

28

"Don't kill him!"

Naomi had her hand on the throat of the crazed man who had attacked them, but stopped, keeping Ben in her peripheral.

"Naomi!" cried Ben. "Don't kill him! There are *hearts* in these jars."

"All the more reason to—"

"Naomi, stop!"

Something in his voice made her finally look at him. All the blood had drained from his face. In one shaking hand he held an empty jar. The other held a purple heart.

They stared at each other while her muscles flexed with rage. "He needs to die, Ben."

"And you're not going to ask him about the jars? The hearts? The murders? Anything?!" he asked.

She forced herself to loosen her grip. In all her time working under The Den, she knew they didn't take prisoners unless there was a payout waiting. There was no dollar value on this zealot's life and she would be ridiculed for even hesitating to kill him. But she wanted to know just as much as Ben did. "You've got five minutes," she said, slamming her captive into the gravel but keeping her hand at his throat.

"Burn in hell," he grumbled.

"I've never met a collector that didn't want to talk about his collection." She pressed.

He winced and groaned. "It isn't my collection."

"Okay, fine. Who do you work for? What could they want with all this?" She squeezed harder. "Or do you have some master you stupidly feel the need to protect along with his plan?"

"It doesn't matter what I tell you," he rasped. "A deal has been made and the price is this town. My ancestors' devotion to the True One has come to fruition. Our task is complete and now your town will see the end."

"Humor me," she said. "You've been murdering the townsfolk. But the hearts? Why take their hearts?"

"We've killed for generations. A transient here. A stranger there. No one notices when the unwanted disappear. They're grateful, actually. It eases their guilty, privileged conscience."

"Teenagers? Locals? Those aren't unwanted."

"My master requested more and so I got more," he said. "He's the true collector. I am but a curator."

"You're giving yourself far too much credit. I guarantee your master doesn't even know your name," she said.

"My master knows my soul!"

He burst into sobs and Naomi recoiled. She wanted to feel disgusted by this pitiful being, but there was something truly heartbreaking in his weeping, like a fearful child only wanting to please an overbearing parent.

She softened her gaze, leaning in just enough for him to hear her voice, gentle and comforting. "Then tell me about him. Tell me about his love."

"He collects the hearts because he has so much love to give. It overflows from him and he has run out of cups to fill. But he has an endless hunger for it." He gave her a rictus of a smile, seemingly proud. "He knows I'm good. I'll provide vessels. I'll provide anything, if it fulfills his need."

He was panting in his fervor, and Naomi had to lean away from his rancid breath as he went on. "He'll complete his collection, and from it he promises to create a family of his own—one big enough to fill this town—and I'll have a place in it. I have no place here with these fools. I may be bound and trapped in a mortal's body, but my soul belongs in the comfort of his love. His reign and dominion."

He made an effort to sit up, grabbing tight to Naomi's shirt and pulling her close. "He will devour this town and everyone you love. There's nothing a fucking half-breed can do about it." He spat in her face and laughed wildly.

His laughter turned to wheezing as Naomi crushed his windpipe. When the wheezing subsided, she rose and turned to Ben, sniffling the stench out of her nose.

He still held the heart in his trembling hands. "Why did you do that?"

"He was a zealot with nothing but gospel to spill," she said. "He wasn't going to tell us anything else. We know all we need to now, and he won't kill anyone else."

"You should have brought him to Beasley."

"You heard him, Ben. Do you think anyone would have believed this lunatic's ramblings? They would think we sprang a psych patient from LMH. Besides, I don't work for Beasley. The people I work for don't operate on a law and order scale."

"What about the families? They'll never have closure."

She didn't have a good answer for that, so instead, she said, "You're holding a heart."

He looked at the blue-purple organ. "It belonged to someone. I couldn't leave it in the dirt."

Naomi appreciated his empathy but looked past him to the den of hearts. "We should burn it."

"Burn it?" he asked, his voice rising an octave. "There is so much we could learn here. All the relics and drawings. I've seen some of them before in my books. If I could come back with some of my books, I could do some research. Or at least take pictures. It could help us keep this from happening again. If nothing else, it could give us insight into the whole realm of demonology that no one knows about—where did you get that?"

Naomi had stuffed a cloth in the neck of a liquor bottle and was lighting it with her lighter. "My pocket," she told him.

"Wait—" He moved to stop her, but she was already throwing the Molotov cocktail into the altar.

They heard the bottle shatter inside. A split second later, a wave of pressure with the force of a jet engine crashed into them, throwing them backward several feet into the bushes. Flames shot up into the air, lingering only for a moment before being swallowed by a wave of nothing and disappearing so completely that not even an ember or the smell of smoke remained.

Naomi and Ben lay entangled in the brush for a stunned moment; then Naomi pushed Ben aside and got to her feet.

Ben gathered himself, breathing hard as he looked back at the altar. He still clutched the heart which, despite his death-grip, seemed unscathed. "What… the fuck?"

Naomi stomped over and climbed into the altar. The whole place looked untouched, except for the broken jars where Ben had fallen.

Ben followed. "It's protected by something," he said.

"You fucking think, Ben?" she snapped.

"I just—" He stepped back, hurt on his face.

She rubbed her face. Yelling at Ben was like kicking a puppy. "No, no, I'm sorry. I just…" She growled, pushing her hair from her face. "I can't destroy it."

"We could trash it. Break all the jars and smash the offerings," he suggested. "Whoever this guy worshipped will feel the hit."

"It's just broken glass," she said. "You heard the crazy guy. Whoever's collecting these means to use them. I can only guess it's for nothing good." She shook her head. "Deities rarely care about altars, though. They care about the idea behind them, but they draw no power from candles and hand-written letters. Burn one down and another zealot will make another." She growled again. "Fuck!"

"What? What is it?"

"I have to call it in," she said.

"You think Beasley will have a better idea? I don't think he'll understand any of this."

She closed her eyes in thought.

"You *are* going to fill him in, right?"

"I think your little detective already has a lot to handle right now," she said.

"Then what? Just tell him you never solved the case?"

"Filling in the humans of this town on shit they can't comprehend isn't even on my list. If you'll excuse me, I have to call my boss." She pressed her phone to her ear, her heart pounding in her throat.

Ben's lips were forming words, but she turned away as a familiar voice answered.

"You solved those murders yet?" Nora asked.

"Well, yes," Naomi said.

"Good! And?"

"The murders were committed by a crazed man. He's taken care of, but I have concerns."

"Concerns you can't handle?"

Naomi sighed. "I'm calling in a consultation, Nora. This seems bigger than me."

"What is it?" Nora asked. For a moment, Naomi thought she heard the same fear in Nora's voice as she had when they'd found that body outside Black Bile Woods.

"It's a shrine. Some kind of altar fashioned of branches and junk, but the inside is devoted to something I've never seen before.

Only—" She lowered her voice and stepped away from Ben. "I feel like I should recognize it. There are pictures I've seen before. It's like the worst case of déjà vu you can imagine, only the whole picture is blurry."

"What's in the shrine?"

"Hearts. Jars and jars filled with human hearts. Some of them look like they've been there for decades. Long enough to calcify. And some look only weeks, if not days, old." She glanced at Ben, who was still holding the heart.

When he saw her looking at it, he shuddered to realize it was still in his hands. He moved to the altar and put the organ on a shelf and rubbed his hands compulsively on his pants.

"Burn it, Naomi," Nora ordered.

"I tried," she said. "I threw a fucking Molotov into it. It sucked up the flames like a vacuum and blew me back a few yards. It's protected by something, and I don't think it's witchcraft."

Nora mumbled something.

"Sorry?"

"Shut the fuck up for a minute," Nora snapped. "Shit, shit, shit, fuck, shit, shit," she growled. "Huh? No, I've got it handled. It's the half-breed. Sir?" She cleared her throat.

Naomi was about to speak when a male voice came through the phone. "Naomi, is that you? It seems you've been having some troubles. This has become common for you as of late." The voice was deep and rich, with the scantest trace of an accent.

The casual inflection concerned Naomi. She mustered all her strength to remain calm. "Hello, Fredrik."

"Naomi," he said with a sigh.

"*Rik*, sorry. I'm sorry, it slipped."

"It's fine. You have quite the conundrum on your plate," he said. "The murderer?"

"Gone," she said.

"But there's more?"

"Mm-hmm."

"Pardon?"

"Yes," she answered.

"I see. I could sit here and listen to Nora fluster and fuss all day, but I can't recall if you've ever actually been to our headquarters?"

"Not that I can remember."

He chuckled. "And by what chance are you in not only the town of your birth but also the birthplace of our organization?"

Naomi furrowed her brow. "I'm sorry?"

"Why don't you come by?" he suggested. "Explain the situation in person. It's been so long since we've had words face to face."

"Oh, I, um—"

"I'll send you the details and dispatch my people to clean up at your location. Surely no one will go looking for a crazed murderer," he said. "Right?"

"Yeah, of course," she said.

"See you soon."

Naomi could hear the smile in his voice before he hung up. It sent a shiver down her spine.

"Are you okay?" Ben asked.

"What? Yeah, why?"

"You just look pale. Like, more than usual," he said. "What happened?"

Her phone pinged with a message. She frowned down at the map with a red pin.

"What?" he asked.

When she didn't answer, Ben snatched the phone out her hand.

His height was no advantage as Naomi forcefully reclaimed her phone.

Ben hunched over his knees, clutching the spot where she'd punched him in the gut. "The bar on the hill?" he panted.

29

Glenn stroked his mustache, deep in thought. Allie hated it, and Freeman and Jamie gave him hell about it, but he couldn't think properly without it. At this point in his life, he was turning into his dad: questionable facial hair, overgrown once-trendy haircut, and the beginnings of an impressive beer gut. But he wasn't thinking about getting a much needed haircut or the impending doom of going up a pant size.

Presently, his thoughts were lost in the faces on his investigation board.

"I don't think the county pays you enough to think that much, Beasley," Freeman commented. He was pouring his afternoon cup of coffee and watching Glenn's face run through an array of emotions. Beasley's changing face and Jamie's weak stomach were the only entertainment Freeman had in the office.

"Hmm?" Glenn asked. "Sorry, sir?"

"These murders really botherin' you that much? What's on your mind?" he asked.

"Aren't they on yours?"

Freeman chuckled and took a drink.

Glenn frowned. "What do you know about that bar up on the hill?"

Freeman choked a bit. "It's a legitimate and legal operation. We have no complaints and no need to snoop around, so I'd say it's law enforcement's dream."

Glenn's mustache twitched.

"You disagree?"

He sat back in his chair. "I've never been up there. What do they even do there?"

"Sell alcohol, I imagine," Freeman said.

"But I've never met a person who drinks there. I have to shut down Jerry's garage bar at least once a month for fist fights and operating without permits. I never even get noise complaints from that place on the hill. And unless Jamie is going up there in her own devotion to the job, no one here ever does any checking in," he said.

"Should we?"

"Checking the corners of this town is like checking a six-by-eight holding cell: eventually, you run out of places to look. I'm not saying I've checked everywhere, but I've never checked out that bar. Hell, we check out Cotton's regularly."

"I eat at Cotton's nearly every day, son," Freeman said.

"Still," Glenn insisted. "Sheriff, what if someone up there in that bar is behind these murders and we never bothered to check it out? What if it's right under my nose and I didn't notice?" He rubbed a hand through his hair.

Freeman sat his coffee down. With slow and solid steps, he moved to Glenn's desk. He placed a hand on his shoulder and squeezed, but it lacked enthusiasm. "Son, the only thing under your nose is that awful mustache. Now, what is really going on?"

Glenn sighed. "The kids in Allie's class are getting into her head," he said. "I think people are starting to get scared, and Allie's becoming a target because of my inability to solve this. Kids have no one to throw blame on or torture except for each other. She's been up through the night all week, and I feel like if I can't do something, she's just going to keep suffering."

"Take some time off," Freeman said.

"In the middle of an investigation?"

"Do it for Allison."

Glenn thought about it.

The sheriff returned to his coffee. "Allie will enjoy having her daddy around more, and the time away will be good for you." He looked back to Glenn to see him pull on his jacket and hat and secure his gun to his hip. "Where are you going?"

"I'm going to check out that bar."

"Glenn Beasley!" Freeman called after him, but Glenn was already out the door. "You damn idiot." He shook his head.

The bar at the top of the hill was a windowless brick rectangle sitting at the edge of a gravel parking lot. A road branched off from the back of the lot and went up a slight incline, but the focus of the property sat clear and present in the gravel pit.

There was nothing extraordinary about the building. No inviting decor or outdoor seating like most bars offered. There wasn't even a sign to indicate what the building was used for. The only reason Glenn knew it was a bar was because *everyone* knew it was a bar—local lore passed down over decades.

Still, this was the closest Glenn had ever been. He'd driven past it any number of times, but he'd never pulled into the lot. Now, standing next to his cruiser nursing a cigarette, he felt his hands shake just looking at it. The kid in him, taught to fear the place, was emerging. He could almost hear his mother's stern voice ordering him to stay away. It wasn't until the smoke from his cigarette started to burn his eyes that he remembered he was a thirty-something-year-old man and not some kid under his mother's foot.

"Well," he muttered, "I won't learn anything out here."

He put out the cigarette and approached the structure. The lack of windows was strange. Most bars were dark places, but this building looked like it was made to keep light out.

It lacked the expected grime too. The bricks were clean and well-maintained. Not the shithole cesspool he'd been conditioned to avoid.

A plain wooden door, painted burgundy to complement the brick, faced the main road. There was a small black mail slot next to the door. Glenn peeked in but nothing.

There were no building numbers, but above the door was a symbol. He couldn't guess what it meant, but when he raised his phone to take a picture, a rush of wind behind him made him jump out of his skin. "Jesus, Mary, and Joseph!"

Naomi was surprised to find the detective at the bar. "What are you doing here?" she asked.

He clutched at his chest, taking a deep breath. "You really have a talent for scaring the shit out of people."

"And you have a talent for putting your nose where it doesn't belong," she said.

"I'm a cop. I'm allowed to investigate. Do you have a reason for why I shouldn't be looking into this place?" he asked. "Maybe a lead?"

Naomi looked away for a moment. "There's nothing here. Nothing that would help you, at least."

"And you're here because…?"

She drew in a deep, slow breath, debating what to tell him. "The people who hired me to solve your murders are located here," she said. "As an officer of the law, you could go in and poke around, but I really don't think you'll like what you find."

"What will I find?" he persisted.

"Business men. So to speak, at least. Nothing but a bunch of money-wise individuals trying to protect their investments. They've put a lot of money into the community."

Glenn shifted weight from one hip to the other and cocked his head to the side. "You think I'm stupid?"

She shrugged. "Believe me if you want. I just feel that you could be putting your efforts to better use elsewhere."

Glenn looked at the picture on his phone before pocketing it and wiping the sweat from his mustache. "And where is that?" he asked, shaking his head. "'Cause I got nothing."

Naomi saw the desperation in his face, the dark circles under his eyes and the twitching of his eyebrows that had probably been furrowed for weeks. "You're a cop who actually does his job in a town where the murder rate went from zero to six overnight. I can't imagine any of this is easy to deal with," she said.

"Have you found anything? Anything at all?"

She wanted to tell him he wouldn't have to worry about the killings anymore, but how could she do that without raising more questions? She didn't have the time to sit him down and explain the hidden corruption of the town to him. At least not now. "Soon, I hope. I have to meet with my employer and maybe we can compare our notes after."

He looked the building over once again, and Naomi could see the reluctance in his face. Then he looked at her. "Have you opened the card?"

She'd forgotten about the card. She didn't want to open it but before she could think of an excuse, Glenn continued.

"I get it," he said. "It was a long time ago and you probably don't want to relive the moment. But it would mean a lot to me if you opened it."

She could read the anxiety on his face, but under that she saw sincerity. "If I open it now, will you leave and meet with me later?"

He nodded.

Slowly, she took the blue envelope out of her jacket pocket and turned it over in her hands.

He frowned. "You got some kind of bottomless pocket in that coat?"

She gave him a quick sardonic glance, huffing, but turned her eyes back to the card without answering. A long moment passed and then she pulled up the envelope flap and slipped the card out.

There were flowers and a bird on the front, with the word "Sympathy" overlaying the design. When she opened the card, a paper slipped out the bottom. She caught it before it fell and tucked it behind the card. Inside, a generic poem took thirty words to say what amounted to "Sorry for your loss." Below it, Glenn had scribbled: "I know sorry doesn't do anything, but Brian was like family and so are you. I am always here to help."

She feigned an appreciative smile and turned her attention to the paper he'd inserted. It was a photograph, faded and worn around the edges.

She recognized a teenaged Glenn, whose face hadn't changed except for the mustache. He had his arm over the shoulder of another boy about the same age. The longer she looked at the other person in the photo, the less his face made sense to her. It was like looking at the photo that came in a new picture frame. The more she tried to draw a connection to him, the less meaning he had to her.

She flipped the picture over but only found the year "2010" written on the back. She tucked the card into her pocket but continued to look at the picture, her frown deepening as she tried to make sense of it. Why had Glenn given it to her?

Finally, he cleared his throat. "I'm sorry," he said. "That obviously wasn't a good idea."

When she looked up, his brow was furrowed in regret. She shook her head, putting the photo in her pocket. "No, no," she said. "It's fine. Thank you."

Glenn relaxed but was still watching her as if he might want to say more.

She tucked her hands into her pockets and held his stare. "We had a deal," she reminded him.

"All right," he said. He looked back at the door for a moment, swiping a thumb over the corner of his mustache, then met her gaze. "I'll take your word on this place. If there was something going on here, you'd let me know." He shuffled off to his cruiser.

Naomi watched him drive off down the main road. With a breath, she straightened her jacket and ran a hand over her hair, then entered the bar.

The door opened to a small lobby. It wasn't an inviting space. A muscular man sat on a stool next to thick, black curtains, ready to turn away any innocent visitors before they were subjected to things no one should ever see. Naomi hoped since it was the middle of the day, she wouldn't be walking into an orgy or a bloodfest, but the odds were slim.

The man didn't speak. He merely gave her a once-over, glancing at the tattoo she exposed on her forearm, and went back to his novel, which featured a rugged man with his shirt flying open in the wind and a half-naked woman clinging to his waist.

Naomi entered through the curtain and found a nearly empty room. A lounge to her right was furnished with plush chairs and couches centered around an oversized coffee table. To her left stood a large high-top table, without any chairs. She could only imagine what usually covered those surfaces. The bar beyond was small. The wall behind it was lined with glasses and candles, but no bottles. There was a door on either side.

She'd never stepped into The Den before. She'd expected the headquarters of a powerful organization to be larger, more impressive. Not some hole-in-the-wall decorated with too many shades of red.

"Did you crawl here?" Nora asked as Naomi stepped away from the curtain. A young vampire was attempting to serve her something red and gelatinous. "Do you know how many shitty drinks I've had to suffer through waiting for you?"

"I'm here to see Rik, not you."

"It's so cute when you talk like that. Like an equal. Like watching a toddler throw out orders." Nora feigned a chuckle. She picked up her drink, scowled, and glared at the bartender, who cowered under her gaze. Without a word, she slammed the drink against the bar, shattering the glass. She turned her attention back to Naomi. "Rik has better things to do than deal with you." she said. She pulled the rag from the apron at the bartender's waist and wiped her hands. "Tell me exactly how you failed this time?"

"I got the murderer," Naomi said. "There will be no more murders in town, at least not from him. But there are bigger problems, and I have more questions than answers. I think something big is coming here."

"Like a Starbucks?" Nora teased.

"If you won't listen, why am I even here?" Naomi snapped. "I could be out there doing something." She shook her head and headed toward the exit when a voice stopped her.

"You're here because I asked you to come," Rik said. He'd entered so quickly it appeared as though he simply formed from nothing. "If you have something you think I should know, by all means, share it."

She turned slowly to face him.

He was as imposing as she remembered. Ridiculously tall and lean. Not a strand of silver in his icy blond hair, which was pulled back with a piece of leather at the nape of his neck. Chilling eyes that lacked the usual yellows and reds and grays most vampires formed after being turned. With his sharp jaw hidden under a short, manicured, light brown beard, he resembled the hipster Vikings of the modern day. Except that, unlike those posers, he'd actually once been a Norseman.

He adjusted the cuffs on his pressed velvet jacket, chuckling at her hesitation. "I know it's been a while, Mrs. Novak, but there's no reason to act like a stranger. Surely Nora has been treating you well since you've come to work for me?"

It was an empty question. Rik didn't care how Nora treated Naomi.

"Of course." She nodded.

"And the work is treating you well? As well as we compensate you, I should hope it is." He raised an eyebrow. "How *is* the family?"

"Taken care of," she answered simply.

"Good, good." He tucked his hands behind his back. "And what have you found?"

"An altar, in the dried creek bed near the woods."

"That's not strange at all. A new deity is born every day, it seems," he said.

"It was full of human hearts. What seems like decades-worth of hearts, maybe even longer. The zealot collecting them told us—"

"*Us?*" Nora asked.

"Me. Told me that he'd been collecting them for generations. Some kind of familial cult," she explained, trying—and failing—to steady her racing heart.

"Also not unusual. Have you met the people of this town?"

"Inbreds," Nora scoffed.

Rik allowed a smile.

"He said he was collecting the hearts for his master and that his master wanted to create a family with them," Naomi said.

Rik's smile faded.

"He said we were too late and a deal had been made."

Naomi saw the fear on Nora's face again. She was beginning to recognize it easily, but with Rik she could only see the corners of his mouth turn down ever so slightly.

"I… I don't know if this is important, but I think I knew him," she said. "There was a drawing. It sounds ridiculous, but I think I made it, as a kid. And there was something else…" She dug through her pockets and produced the black yarn doll with red X's for eyes.

Nora and Rik exchanged looks.

"He really did a number on you," Nora said.

Naomi frowned. "What? Who?"

There was a sudden commotion from the curtain behind her. They all turned as the doorman entered, dragging Ben by the neck of his shirt like a troublesome puppy.

Her eyes grew wide. She couldn't decide if it was rage or fear that caused words to fail her.

"And what have we here?" Rik asked. "Reginald, did this man try to break in?"

Reginald nodded. He tossed Ben between Naomi and her bosses.

"An A+ performance as usual, Reginald. Thank you."

The doorman pulled his novel from his large back pocket and returned to his post.

"Well, my dear boy, you must be lost," said Rik. "No one comes here of their own free will unless they have business with me. And given I've never met you before, I'd say you're just another one of the nosey townsfolk. We love the people of this town, but the nosey ones have a special place. Don't they, Lanora?"

"Nosey townsfolk taste the best." She grinned.

"Naomi, I'm sure it has been a while since you've fed. Why don't you join us? We've treated you like an outsider for so long, but maybe if we broke bread together it would help our relationship.”

“More like breaking necks,” Nora said.

“Lanora,” he scolded mildly, chuckling.

Ben’s face jerked toward Naomi. She stared back, paralyzed.

“Dear boy,” said Rik. Against his will, Ben looked up into his icy eyes.

“He looks exotic,” Nora commented. “I bet he tastes better than the bland Caucasian buffets of this town.” She was inching her way to Rik’s side, her eyes glowing.

The look in Nora’s eyes made Naomi sick. She still saw that unearthly glimmer in her nightmares, hovering over Taylor’s semi-conscious body. She wasn’t sure where she mustered the courage or strength, but before she could stop herself, she put herself between Ben and Rik. “You can’t!”

Nora and Rik shared a hearty laugh.

“I said you can’t,” she said. She raised her chin.

“We heard you,” Rik said. He feigned wiping a tear from his eye. “We just can’t imagine why.”

“Because he’s mine,” she said.

Their laughter subsided slowly and Rik adjusted his jacket once again. “You’ve evolved.”

“No more flasks?” Nora asked.

“It’s demeaning,” she said. “You’re right, Nora. I shouldn’t degrade myself with poorly-aged subpar blood. But I don’t have the conviction to drink as you do.”

“A killer who can’t stomach killing,” Nora sneered. “There’s a punchline missing somewhere.”

“I’ve found a way around it,” she said. “This is my blood bag.” She gestured to Ben, whose face was completely cold and unreadable. “After your lesson, I found this was the best for me. I should have done it with Tay—the bartender,” she said, swallowing hard. “Lesson learned. But he’s mine. While I’m not your equal, I know you have a code and you’ll respect that.” She was speaking to Rik, as she could see Nora’s face twisting in annoyance.

“What utter bullshit,” Nora said. “I know you have a soft spot for humans and this is probably just another one you’re fucking. Rik, this is a piss-poor attempt at keeping us from killing him. I’d think it’s a little late for that. No one stumbles into this place and leaves.” She leaned forward, swiftly grabbing Ben’s chin and turning his head to examine his neck. "He isn't even marked, Rik."

"His mark isn't obviously visible," Naomi said.

"Bullshit," Nora insisted.

"She's right, Mrs. Novak. If he isn't visibly marked, any vampire can simply feed on him with no way of knowing his ownership. It's this kind of laziness that leads to conflicts within a clan, like in 1886. You recall, Nora?"

"Months' worth of trials and I still feel as though we put an innocent vamp to death." Nora sighed.

"Naomi," Rik said. "You have to be obvious with your markings. I know you're still young, but really."

"Why don't you just mark him now to save everyone trouble?" Nora asked.

"What?" Naomi asked.

"She's right," said Rik. "Do it now, with two *highly reputable* witnesses, and be done with it. Then you and your blood bag can be on your way."

Naomi looked at Ben. He swallowed but bravely held her gaze.

"I suppose Nora was always right about you," said Rik. "What were you calling her? *Worthless half-breed that should have been left to burn in Black Bile?*"

She chuckled. "That was it exactly."

He waved his hand to dismiss her. "Just get out of here, Naomi. Leave the human."

Naomi clenched her jaw. "I said he's mine."

She lowered herself to Ben's side. He recoiled from her touch and she was forced to grasp him by the nape of his neck, rendering him motionless. She latched to his neck, telling herself she would only have one drink and no more. But when his blood touched her tongue, it was so delicious she couldn't stop. She took several long gulps.

Ben whimpered. A moment later, she felt tear drops on the fingers that held tight to his neck. She let him go, and he slumped to the floor. His blood was already sending sensations to the tips of her fingers and toes. Her head buzzed pleasantly. Nevertheless, her stomach churned.

"She *has* evolved," Nora said. "Last time she did that, she sobbed like an infant afterward."

"I expected more," Rik admitted. "But enough is enough for now. Gather your human and leave, Naomi. Lanora and I will discuss what you've told us. When we have a plan, you'll hear from us." He turned away, shaking his head as though he were disappointed. "Just another boring day, I suppose," he remarked to Nora.

Naomi looked to where Ben shuddered on the floor, his head in his hands. Maybe there was something in his blood that made her feel courageous. Or maybe the pressure of the last few weeks had broken the floodgates, but suddenly words were spilling from her mouth.

"My life is a game to you, isn't it?" she asked. "Just another form of entertainment, and if I don't perform as expected, it was a waste? I do all your dirty work. I've killed, tortured, haggled, conned, and devoted countless hours to you. For what? To be called *worthless*? A half-breed? An embarrassment to your kind? We aren't the same kind!"

She found herself rising to her full height, her fists clenching at her sides. The whites of her eyes spread until it overtook the golden brown. "I'm grateful every day that I suffer through life that at least I'm not some cold monster like you, who can't even stand a little sunlight without catching fire. You play as though you're so powerful. But if I'm so weak, why am I the one doing all of your heavy lifting?"

The shadows in the corners of the room began to swell and expand. Naomi's hair began to rise and twine about her face and neck.

Nora shifted nervously. Rik merely listened with an even face.

"I don't need you," Naomi spat. "*You* need *me*!" She raised her finger to him and her skin began to turn black, beginning at her fingertips and bleeding quickly up her arms and into her face. "I have no reason to be your lackey. What would you do if I wasn't? Kill me? I fucking beg you! You'd be doing me a favor just to put me out of my fucking misery. But you're so fucking pathetic and reliant on me, you could never do it."

The shadows had completely filled the room. Naomi's lower half dissolved into the darkness, an amorphous fog that moved on its own.

Nora moved close to Rik, whose face remained unfazed.

Naomi's skin roiled like oil, making it hard to distinguish her features from the shadows. The darkness had become an extension of her limbs. She pointed jagged, uneven fingers at Rik, with such conviction that he swallowed, taking a small step back.

"You have nothing over me," she said, her voice echoing in the emptiness. "You will no longer control me."

Slowly the shadows drifted back into the corners where they belonged. Naomi's form returned. Her shaking fingers still pointed at him, but now on human hands. Her hair settled around her face and her skin returned to porcelain. The golden brown returned to her eyes.

She reached for Ben. He tried to shrug away from her, but she hauled him to his feet and dragged him out of The Den without another word.

Nora exhaled in Rik's ear. "Should I have her killed?"

Rik shook his head. "Lanora, my dear, I have a new job for you."

"Yes, Rik?"

"I want you to find Mrs. Novak's family."

30

Naomi got Ben into his bed and pulled the blanket to his chest. When she attempted to push the hair from his face, he turned away. She settled her hand on his shoulder, but he shoved it away.

"Ben."

He rolled onto his side, putting his back to her.

"Please, let me explain."

He pulled his blanket over his head.

"They would have killed you," she said.

"Get out," he said, his voice muffled.

"I can't just leave you."

"I said get the fuck out!" He emerged from the blanket just long enough to yell at her.

Naomi's hand hovered over his back, but she pulled it back. She left by teleportation, reappearing on the street outside. The sun was setting now and families were beginning to return home, but no one noticed her.

For a long moment, she watched the top floor of Ben's home, her heart thudding dully in her chest. Despite the balm of the evening, she pulled her jacket tighter around her hunched shoulders as she walked away.

She was a drifter in her own hometown, without a bed, without an ally, and now without employment. She was free to roam the world now. Free to leave the town, the state, or even the country. But something stopped her.

Maybe it was unfinished business, or maybe it was a curiosity to see how the Murders of Pickleberry mystery played out, but Naomi found herself back at the shrine. The zealot's body was gone. Who had collected it she couldn't say, but there was a very low chance the man had simply walked off.

The inside was undisturbed. Shattered jars still covered the floor, with hearts strewn among the pieces—all except for the one Ben had been carrying, which he'd placed carefully on the shelf next to the others. To Naomi, the hearts in their jars were just organs that offered no answers to her most pressing questions. But Ben had cared, and she wondered if maybe she should too.

In truth, she was more interested in the pictures at the back. They still clung to the walls like cheap wallpaper. Most of them meant nothing to her, but looking at the scribbled heart tied her stomach in knots. She'd made that drawing, as a child. She was certain of this.

But she couldn't for the life of her remember who she'd given it to. She played the memory over and over in her head like an old film. She pictured giving it to her siblings first. When that didn't fit, she tried to imagine presenting it to her mother and father.

But at the thought of their faces, the enormity of her actions started to settle in. There would be consequences to her actions at The Den. She slid down onto the dirt floor, her back pressed against a makeshift shelf that rattled as her shoulders shook with sobs.

She hated the work she'd done for The Den. But there had been a reason she'd done it. She'd made an agreement. She was created and molded for The Den in exchange for a comfortable salary to ease the burden she put on her family. But now where was she? The likelihood of someone like her just happening onto another job, especially one using her current skillset, was basically nonexistent. And now her family had to suffer for her mouth and her temper.

Leaving aside her family concerns, she faced the realization that she'd also lost a reliable and valuable companion. Someone who possibly could have been a friend, despite the lack of normalcy in her life. And for what? Freedom?

Did she even know what to do with freedom anymore? There was no cute bartender waiting at the end of this. No curly-haired weirdo eager to share the town's secrets. No husband and dimple-cheeked gremlin greeting her with open arms. Only a family whose life dangled dangerously close over a pit of sharp vamp fangs. Even if they were hidden away, she couldn't expect to hide them forever.

She cried until her eyes burned from the tears and she wanted nothing more than to just fall asleep. But Ben's blood was too fresh in her system. Her mind buzzed. Her skin crawled with electricity. With nowhere to go, she raised her eyes to stare at the crude drawing on the wall across from her, a heart no less tangled and unlovely than her own. Who had kept it all these years?

She stayed there until her limbs began to stiffen and she knew the blood buzz had worn off. The sun was rising on a new day.

The police lot was empty when Glenn Beasley pulled in. As he parked his cruiser, he saw a shadow in the station window—a shadow that moved in a way no human shadow did. A shadow that definitely wasn't Sheriff Freeman or Jamie.

Glenn nearly forgot to pull his keys from the ignition as he jumped out and ran to the door. It was locked, but when he gave it a pull, the shadow moved sharply and disappeared.

"Hey!" he shouted, fumbling with the keys to unlock the door. "Hey, I see you, punk! Don't move!" When he finally got the door open, he entered with his gun drawn. He saw nothing and no one. Freeman's office was closed and locked. The supply closet was clearly visible and offered nothing. The main room was clear. He was about to put his gun away, when he heard a tap on the glass entry door behind him.

He turned sharply to see Naomi on the outside of the station.

"Hi, sorry," she said. "I didn't mean to startle you." Her eyes were red and her hands trembled at her sides.

He breathed deeply, holstering his pistol. "Hi, hey," he said. "Are you okay?"

She nodded. "Are you?"

"Thought I saw something in the station."

She didn't comment. "There's something I have to show you."

Naomi refused to answer any questions Glenn posed until he stood in front of the altar, by then at a loss for words.

"What... what exactly am I looking at?" he finally managed.

"I wish I knew." She gestured for him to follow her inside the den. "Brace yourself," she warned as she entered the opening.

Nodding, he followed, ducking low to avoid hitting his head. When he stood upright, he gasped.

"Are these…?"

"Hearts," she answered.

"From the…?"

"The victims."

"But there are so many."

"Apparently, they've been collecting for years." She crossed her arms and stepped aside, letting him take in the scene.

"They?"

"There was a man here yesterday when we discovered it. I subdued him, but I can't say where he is now," she said.

"Can't or won't?" he asked.

She didn't answer.

He gestured to their surroundings. "I know you're under no obligation to tell me, but given the circumstances, I think I'm allowed to ask some questions."

"I have limited answers," she said.

"All right. What is this?"

"I think it's a collection. A shrine too."

"Whose collection and a shrine to who?"

She shrugged.

"And the guy?"

"He was a nut that spouted some cult-like prophecy nonsense but offered no useful leads." She rubbed her pendant over her lip for comfort.

"Some of these hearts are hard, like rocks," he said.

She nodded. "They've calcified. I think it's something in the jars. They could be decades old."

"So we have a serial killer," he said. "One that's been around for a while."

"Or more than one. The guy implied that his ancestors followed the same tradition," she explained.

Glenn removed his hat and ran a hand through his hair. "I don't even know what code to use to call this in," he said. "Yesterday? Did you find this before or after I ran into you?" She started to answer when he interrupted. "You were telling your bosses first."

"Listen," she said. "For your own safety, don't go to the building on the hill. There's nothing good for you there."

"You're only leaving me with more questions."

"That's something I'll have to live with. I'm not sure I want to tell you more. For your own sake." Her eyes drifted as she pressed the pendant to her lips.

Glenn could see she was lost in thought. "The people will have questions."

"You'll think of something."

Glenn replaced his hat and moved past her. "Maybe I should call this in," he said. Then he hesitated. "Are you too busy for coffee?"

Naomi's shoulders sank as she thought of the only coffee place she knew in town. Her breath seemed stuck in her lungs.

"The coffee at the station isn't gourmet," he went on, "but I think it's better than the stuff they sell over at the Donowitz place."

She exhaled and nodded.

31

The station was quiet, except for the clock ticking closer and closer to mid-morning. This only mildly bothered Glenn, who was used to being the only one who showed up on time. He had a book binder full of pictures, notes, and evidence from the cases he'd worked and was going through missing persons cases, while Naomi stared at the steam rising from her untouched coffee. "I'm going to have to call the M.E.," he said, mostly to himself.

His voice pulled Naomi's gaze up to his.

"There were what… *hundreds* of hearts in there? It'll probably be months before he gets through them all, lazy fucker," he grumbled.

Naomi's brows went up.

"No one is ever in a hurry to do anything around here," he explained.

"I've noticed." She looked around the empty station.

"The sheriff is likely at the diner eating breakfast. Jamie tends to roll in whenever she likes. It's annoying, but most of the time it doesn't matter."

She nodded.

"I just… I'm trying to figure out how and why you went from completely blocking me out to handing me everything," he said.

"Things changed. I'm off the case, I guess," she added. "Since I'm not working on anything, I have no reason to stick around. Why shouldn't I tell you?"

"I just get the feeling you're not telling me everything."

Naomi looked back to her coffee, considering. "You've lived here your whole life?"

"Most of it," he confirmed.

"You never noticed anything weird?"

"Like what?"

"Just anything."

He mulled. "The mayor's house is in the middle of the woods, yet all my life I've been told to avoid the woods. The house out on Cowden has a reputation for being bad, but like most everything else, it gets chalked up to rumor. The knitting circles and walking groups tell a new story every day. I can't waste my time checking them all out."

"You never noticed the strange sounds from the woods?"

"Animals?"

"The screaming from the house on Cowden?" she pressed.

"It's old. The wind catches a hole right and…" He shrugged. "Screaming."

"Playground equipment that moves on its own in the park?"

"Wind?"

She gave him a skeptical look. "The wind moving merry-go-rounds?"

"And gravity?"

"Okay, Detective, tell me why this town needs a hospital that size?" she asked.

"The nearest hospitals are hours away and women got tired of giving birth to babies in mini vans." He seemed confident in this answer, but he wavered a little when he looked into Naomi's eyes.

"And the massive blood bank? It's bigger than the maternity ward or any other department in the hospital."

"Well," he mused, "accidents happen and, you know, childbirth can have problems with bleeding. It never hurts to keep blood on hand."

"You think every hospital has a blood bank that big?"

"It's a precaution. People from other towns come here because we're closer than other hospitals."

"Oh, so you must get a lot of emergencies where the victim experiences massive blood loss. Like really traumatic ones and pretty frequently?" she asked.

"Wellllll," Glenn began. But he knew the ER department saw about as much action as he did. He thought about other weird things that happened in Pickleberry, the things that sounded too big to be a deer or bunny that stalked along the forest's edge.

His mustache twitched. "You don't think this was just a serial killer."

"I think it's a piece of something much, much bigger," she replied. "Something you'd think I was crazy for even mentioning."

"Just say it," he insisted.

Her hands closed around the coffee mug and squeezed. "I tried to destroy the altar. The man who attacked us there made the hearts seem very important to someone with no good intentions. I thought it was better if they were gone, just in case."

He frowned. "That's evidence, but okay."

"Well, clearly it didn't work," she said. "Whatever is using those hearts isn't just some man with an obsession. I told my employers, and I saw fear on their faces." She leaned forward. "My employers aren't the kind to be scared, Glenn. I think you're facing something big."

"Wait, what do you mean, *me*? You're not seeing this through?" he asked.

"If I were sticking around, I wouldn't have told you any of this," she said. "I can't stay in this town. I left once, but it pulled me back. This time I'm going to make sure I never come back. But I can't leave without at least giving you an idea of what to expect. I know I'm being vague, but just… keep your eyes open. If things seem strange, they probably are."

Glenn sat back in his chair. There were so many thoughts and questions racing around his head, but all he could manage was a nod. "All right."

"All right?" she repeated.

"All right." He nodded. "None of this makes sense, but at the same time nothing about it surprises me at all. I'll just have to adjust. What else can I do?"

Naomi breathed a sigh. Uneasy or relieved, he couldn't tell.

"I'll take care of the altar and the hearts," he said. "I'm the one who should be doing that anyway."

She nodded.

He scratched at the back of his neck. "Listen," he said. "About that card…"

She couldn't hide her eye roll.

"Grief is weird. I don't know exactly when he died, but that pain doesn't just go away. I get it. You don't want to go back down that path. You don't want to undo any healing you've done. The way you looked at that picture—"

He raised his hand when she opened her mouth to cut him off, and she looked away.

"You can keep it in your pocket and never look at it again for the rest of your life," he said. "Just promise me you won't throw it away."

Naomi looked back up.

She removed the picture from her pocket and looked at the two young faces smiling at the camera. "Do I know him?"

"That's me," he said. "I know I look a little different, but—"

"No," she said and pointed to the young man next to him.

Glenn frowned. He wondered if she was joking, but the pure confusion on her face convinced him she wasn't. He suddenly felt sad. "You don't recognize him? That's Brian."

Naomi shook her head, gazing uncertainly at the photo. One hand lifted to worry at the medallion. Then she cleared her throat. "Yeah, of course. I see it now. He just looks so young." She forced a smile.

Glenn couldn't decide if he believed her, but he didn't want to press it either way. "It's been a while," he said.

She nodded. "It's just when I recall his face—"

"You don't have to give me an explanation."

"I won't toss it," she reassured him.

"I believe you."

She fell silent and shoved her hands in her pockets. "Take care, Glenn Beasley. This fucked up town is in your hands now."

She left Glenn at the station.

His mind was no doubt racing, considering all the information she'd dumped on him. But all Naomi could think about was the photo tucked away in her pocket.

She didn't know who that man was, but he wasn't her husband.

32

As much as she wanted to, Naomi wouldn't leave Pickleberry so easily. She'd spent days aimlessly wandering the town, hoping at some point to work up the gall to just proverbially pack her shit and leave, but it never came. And after night after night of standing in front of Ben's house, she couldn't act ignorant as to why she'd stuck around.

She was worried about the idiot. There was no chance of getting involved in his life again, just how she'd wanted it, but the thought of leaving him unwatched didn't sit well. Even if she'd marked him, his days were numbered. He'd become known by The Den, and even if for some reason they decided to respect their codes for someone who didn't even qualify to live by them, they would likely wait for his wounds to heal and take him in.

Naomi wondered who else would be pulled in if Ben was taken. There was a lot of blood in his house, and he couldn't disappear without going unnoticed.

She tried to push away any thoughts of his protection or future, but still they lingered. They explained why she stood in the shadow of the one broken streetlight, watching his home.

She had to pull herself away. She could spend the rest of her life camped outside his house, but it wouldn't help him. She had to disconnect herself. She had to do what she should have done with Taylor and cut the cord when things became too familiar. Considering what had happened to Taylor, she should count herself lucky at how things had turned out with Ben.

Naomi's phone buzzed.

It had been buzzing for hours now and she couldn't bring herself to look at it. There wasn't a soul in the world she wanted to talk to.

After a series of vibrations, she risked a glance. Several missed calls and text messages, but one voicemail.

She held the phone to her ear and the sound of Nora's sick giggle caused her to swallow hard.

"Hello, Novak. Come. Come see what I've found."

The text messages were a series of taunts. A collection of "hahas" or emojis indicating a joke Naomi must have missed the punchline to. The most recent message was different. It wasn't especially ominous—just an address—but somehow she knew she couldn't ignore it. She didn't recognize the street name, but the attached Google map showed it wasn't far from where she was.

What was there? She racked her memory. In her mind, she saw a stretch of houses that went past Ben's and circled down the cul-de-sac. Just beyond lay an open lot. Nothing there but tall grass surrounded by a barbed wire fence.

It took her less than ten minutes to walk to where she remembered the lot, only now instead of barbed wire and grass, she found a tall, wrought iron gate set between brick stanchions, with more wrought iron fencing stretching off to either side—the kind of fencing used not to keep livestock in, but rather to keep strays out. On the other side, elegant gardens surrounded elegant homes with white plaster molding. The people who lived here likely didn't want to be bothered by outsiders.

She wasn't expecting to see a gated community in the middle of the suburban Pickleberry, but the sigil on the gate—similar to the one tattooed on her forearm—told her Rik had some part in this. The Den had their bloody fingers in everyone's pot in this town. It shouldn't surprise her in the least that they had a secluded, elite community among the commoners.

She eyed the security cameras mounted to the gatehouse. They knew she was here; no point in hiding. She hoisted herself over the gate and looked around, then followed the map on her phone till she found the address.

A spacious house stood amid a lush garden. A paved walkway wound through the garden and skirted a koi pond, where several orange-and-white fish, illuminated by the moonlight, circled each other with graceful ease. She crouched to watch their tranquil motion, imagining what such a brief and carefree existence might be like.

Shouting pulled her from her thoughts. She looked up, frowning at the tall, lean man charging at her across the lawn. She couldn't make out his face, but a mess of dark hair sprouted from his head, and she could tell by his voice that he was older.

"Hey, you little shit!" he bellowed, swinging his arms. "This is private property and unless you live in one of these complexes, you're going to have to leave."

Naomi stood. She'd found an elusive moment of peace and now it was interrupted by some snooty rich guy who thought he owned the town because an egotistical vamp had put him in a fancy house.

"Now, you listen to me," he went on, stepping toward her. "You better get your ass out of here or I'm going to kick it over that fence." He stopped short, squinting at her face. "Nay?"

There was something strangely familiar about him, but the person who came to mind looked nothing like the man who stood before her. She shielded her eyes from the house lights to get a better look. "Dad?"

"Naomi! What are you doing out here? Did your mom finally call you?" He closed the space between them and embraced her tightly for the first time in her memory. "Are you okay? You seem tense."

Her words jumbled one over the other as she tried to hold back her tears. "I just... I can't... It's really you?" she asked. "Last time I saw you, you were..."

"Sick? Sick and tired," he said. "I feel the best I've felt in my life. No pain, no meds, no sickness. And look—" He ran his hands through his thick hair. "My hair grew back. Can you believe that? In my fifties?" He chuckled. "I think I'm giving Brad Pitt a run for his money these days."

She wiped a tear, taking him in. His tall stature was no longer weighed down with pain and illness. His skin glowed in the lights. His eyes, one blue and one green, glistened behind a wide smile. "I just don't understand."

"When you moved us to the farmhouse, there was a man who showed up. He said he'd been sent to start treatments, something about you arranging for the best doctors or something. I don't know. Anyway, he gives us his snake oil and by the next week, I'm walking without a cane, dropping weight, and breathing without hacking. He even encouraged your mom to try it. She looks at least twenty years younger, but don't tell her I said that."

"Who was he? Did you get a name?" she asked. "The snake oil man?"

"Oh, I can't remember. Maybe your mom does. I remember him being insanely big, not big big, you know. But, like, big. Tall, like a tree. Like a really tall tree," he said.

She nodded. "I just... I can't believe you're here. Why are you here?" The elation of seeing her dad in such great shape was passing and the fear started to settle in. The work she'd done, the measures she'd taken to keep her parents safely tucked away were all undone. Aside from a couple of siblings who had long since grown distant from her, her parents were the only thing she had left in this world. Now they lived unprotected in a town full of monsters. In a neighborhood possibly inhabited by them.

"How long does it take to take out a bag of garbage, Richie?" came a voice from the door behind them.

Naomi recognized it automatically and a chill went over her body.

"Jo!" he called to her. "Come look who it is!"

"Is he here already?" she asked, hurrying to her husband's side. When she saw Naomi, her excitement disappeared. "Oh, hello, Naomi," she said.

Joanne was a tiny fraction of a person next to her husband, comparable to a garden gnome. The last time Naomi had seen her she'd had wide hips, thinning hair, and dull skin. Now her frame was thin and her hair shone even in the dim light. Her skin was smooth and perfect, as though she'd shed the outer layer like a snake to reveal fresh and glowing skin underneath.

"I didn't know you'd called her," her dad said.

"I didn't," she responded plainly.

"Oh," Naomi said.

"Well, it happened so fast and you never answer your phone anyway," her mother said. "I figured we would settle in and then give you a call."

"Settle in?" Naomi asked.

"We sold the farmhouse, dear."

"What? Why would you do that?"

"Well, someone showed up and offered to buy it. At first we thought he was crazy, but then he offered us free residency at an exclusive complex. He told us we'd won a sweepstakes," she said. "So, a chunk of money in our pocket from the house and moving out of the middle nowhere and back to civilization for free? How could we pass it up, Naomi?"

"I didn't even know we'd entered a sweepstakes." Her dad grinned.

"I'm sorry, I don't understand. You just left the house and moved here?" Naomi asked. "Why? What was wrong with the farmhouse?"

"It just became dull," Jo said.

"There were acres of land there. Your gardens, animals, all of it. I made sure it had everything you needed. Entertainment, groceries delivered. You didn't need anything else," she said.

"You kept us so isolated from the world, Naomi. You can hardly blame us for wanting to go out, especially since your dad is feeling up to it now. I don't expect you to get it. You travel the world for work and never visit," she said.

"Naomi," said her dad, "we know you meant well, but your mom is kinda right. We were alone out there. The man who bought the home told us this town was small but had a strong community. That's the exact kind of thing we wanted."

Naomi looked to each of her parents, bewildered. It was like they'd been trained to recognize her and say all the appropriate things but had no inkling who she really was. Or who they themselves were. "You don't remember this town, do you?"

The pair shared frowns and uncertain glances.

"Why would we?" Jo asked.

"Oh!" Richie cut in. "Jo, do you remember the name of the man who came out to the house after we moved in? He gave me the treatments?"

"The tall one?"

"Mm-hmm."

She thought it over. "Oh, Eddie or something of the sort. You know who might know? That man who bought our house. He seemed to know all about the area. He should be here soon. He sent me a message that he was dropping by to see how we were settling into the neighborhood. What a fine gentleman." Her voice had a smitten quality that made Naomi's stomach turn.

"You are far too kind, Mrs. Dodds," said a voice near the house.

A shiver ran up Naomi's spine. It was impossible to tell if Rik had been standing there for ages or had appeared on the spot.

"Mr. Larsson," gushed Jo. "It's so nice of you to check in on us. Everything here is just wonderful."

"Call me Rik," he said with a smile.

When he took her mother's hand and pressed it to his lips, Naomi felt the blood drain from her face.

He let her hand fall with the grace of a lord. "As the owner of this complex, I like to keep in touch. I hope you're enjoying the new place?"

"What's not to love?" Richie grinned. "Naomi, why don't you come in and see it?"

"Um…" Naomi cleared her throat, her eyes resting briefly on Rik.

"Richie, we have company," Jo said. To Rik, she added, "Our daughter dropped by without calling ahead."

"She's right." Naomi nodded. "I'm sure you guys are tired from moving and adjusting anyway. Why don't I just come by some other time?"

"I can't stay either," said Rik. "I have another appointment to keep."

"Well, it was a pleasure seeing you again, Rik." Jo grinned and skipped inside with the spring of a giddy schoolgirl.

Richie hugged his daughter. "Naomi, you come by whenever you can. We know you work hard for us." He nodded his goodbye to Rik and followed his wife inside the house.

Rik inhaled deeply and exhaled the night air like he was enjoying the scent of Naomi's real-life nightmare. "I have nothing over you?" he asked. "I find it very disrespectful to call your parents nothing."

Naomi didn't speak. She could feel her heart pounding in her throat.

"I'll forgive you for the outburst. This is a high stress job. One is allowed. But if it were to happen again…" He grimaced and let that thought hang in the air before continuing. "Why don't you figure out how to destroy that altar? And soon. You messed with his collection, and I imagine he won't be too happy about that. Whatever he's planning, it's very likely he'll push it forward a bit."

"Who?" she asked. "Whose collection?"

He shook his head. "This would be so much easier if he hadn't wiped your memory all those years ago."

"You won't even give me a hint?" she snapped. "You're setting me up to fail."

"Dear Mrs. Novak, I could tell you his name, what he looks like, who he is, and what he did to you, but you won't even be able to hear it until he wants you to. Use that brain of yours. Or your human's brain. He seemed unusually in tune with things. Either way, I would resist any rebellious urges you may have from here on out."

Rik was gone before she could open her mouth to speak. She was glad to be rid of him, but in the silence of the evening listening to the water of the koi pond, she felt more alone than she ever had in her life. Alone, helpless, and a complete and utter failure.

She walked away from the complex.

Her head was buzzing with schemes, but no matter how she played them out, there was no getting her parents away. They were in The Den's grasp and there was nothing she could do about it. They were the only thing that kept her going. Now that losing them was a real possibility, she would do Rik's work like a dutiful employee.

She considered how to destroy the altar. Having dragged Glenn into it only made it more difficult. She needed to tell him to stop. Don't disturb it. Don't bring anyone in. Just don't do anything.

It was late enough she didn't expect anyone to be out, let alone at work. A chat with Glenn could wait until tomorrow, and she needed time to think. She kept walking, down empty streets and past darkened homes, her pendant pressed to her lips as her thoughts sloshed around in her brain like soup.

She was so distracted, it caught her off guard when her shoulder smacked into something hard, something so tall and immovable it spun her off balance and off the sidewalk into the street, where she landed on her ass.

"What the fuck?"

"That's how you're going to greet me?"

She'd been about to get up, but at that voice, her whole body froze.

"I know it's been a while, but that wounded even my heart," he said. "Well, if I had one." He chuckled, but there was no hint of camaraderie or enjoyment, just the rattle of a snake's tail.

Naomi didn't look at him. The hairs on her neck and arms stood up, and a wave of nausea passed over her. She hoped if she didn't look at him, he would disappear.

"You look so pitiful on the pavement. Let me help you up, my love." He extended a hand.

It didn't appear quite human—more like a giant, clawed hand had put on a poorly fitting human-skin glove, without bothering to make it look natural. The flesh looked supple at the tips, but the life and color faded at the wrists. Under the edges of his sleeves, she could make out dry, scaly skin that reminded her of the tree she'd been tied to in Black Bile Woods. She pushed the hand away.

"You must have trouble remembering me. I can understand that," he said.

His voice chilled her to the bone and yet somehow lit her chest aflame with a rage she couldn't understand. Finally, she looked up.

He towered over her height by several feet. His figure was hidden by an oversized trench coat and thick, black pants. He could be built like a tree trunk under that coat, or like a scrawny weasel.

But when her eyes came to his face, her heart leaped into her throat. Tears of love and joy welled in her eyes. Then the illusion crumbled. Sorrow and horror swept over her. The fiery rage rushed back, flushing her cheeks and causing every muscle in her body to tense.

"Do you like it?" he asked, caressing the edges of his face with long, gangly fingers. "I picked it just for you. When this face became available years ago, I just knew I had to add it to my collection. I've had it tucked away waiting, wondering if or when I would ever use it. It fits me well, yes?"

She swallowed. "No, you're too tall."

"Well, I don't particularly enjoy embodying the flaws of the faces I wear. I enjoy seeing over counter tops." He giggled to himself.

Naomi pushed herself to her feet but added distance between them. "I think you're exaggerating a bit."

"It takes a special person to see past such flaws and to love someone so purely. I always admired that about you, Naomi. Your love truly knew no bounds."

"I can't imagine I ever loved you."

"Ow! Did that hurt? Saying that to his face?" He gave a playful clap and giggled once more.

"I don't know you," she said, but without much conviction.

"Oh, but I think you do," he said. "I think deep, deep down you remember everything. You just don't want to. You're carting around amnesia like a dirty security blanket, and it is quite pitiful."

"What do you want?" she asked sharply. The idea of having history with this man—this thing that stared at her with cold, dead eyes from behind the impossibly vibrant skin of a man, but that was certainly no man at all—the idea of being linked to him in even the slightest way filled with her with a whirlwind of emotions that were hard to pin down. Fear, if she were to guess the root of the growing pit in her stomach. Fear camouflaging the denial and dread and self-loathing that any connection with this thing would bring.

"Do I need a reason to visit?" he asked. "Well, I suppose I do, as it seems someone has been messing with my collection. I really don't like that." His tone told her he was angry, but the unearthly grin plastered on his face made her unsure. "You know how much I love my collections, don't you? You helped me with my favorite collection of all. Too bad nothing came of it."

She kept her expression flat and said nothing.

"Wow, you really don't remember. Okay, okay, I'm going to help you." He waved his hand and from her pocket, the black yarn doll emerged. It floated through the air to his large hand, where he caressed it delicately.

"Don't worry, Nay. I'm not mad at you. I know that even if you really wanted to hurt me and my collection, you wouldn't be able to." He wrinkled his nose playfully. "My collector, on the other hand? Well, zealots are a dime a dozen. Don't fret that either." He held up the doll. "I know you have questions, but probably very little desire to ask me. I know the effect I have on people. So when one of those pesky questions pops into your brain, here's want I want you to do. Are you ready?" He held his hand open and the doll floated to her, landing weightlessly in her hand. "Ask the doll. That's all! Just ask the doll. It is yours, after all. Maybe next time we chat, you'll have a little more to say. I have some big changes in mind for this little town. I would love to get the dream team back together."

Before she could react, he was gone.

She looked at the doll and frowned. Her head was fuzzy now and she felt faint.

It took her entire focus to walk, but she made her way as quickly as she could to Ben's doorstep. She was hoping he would be the one to answer it, but he wasn't.

"Oh, it's you." Audrey scowled.

"Is Ben in?"

"Ben doesn't want to talk to you, stalker," she said.

"Just get him, please."

"I don't think so," Audrey replied.

Naomi slammed her palm on the frame of the doorway. "Listen, you intolerable teenage drone. Do I look like I want to play games with you? I have no time for this. Get your cousin now, before I break the door off."

Audrey stepped back. "Uncle Gabe!" she called, but instead, it was Ben who stepped forward.

"It's all right," he said. "I'll handle it."

Audrey left without protest.

"What do you want?" asked Ben.

Naomi pressed the doll to the screen of the door that separated them. "You know the altar we found?"

"What about it?"

"I met the deity it's devoted to. Only I don't think it's a deity. I think it's something worse, and I know him."

"Why do you say that?" he asked, crossing his arms.

"Because he's wearing my husband's face."

December 3, 1993

In my time learning about monsters, I've amassed quite the collection of questionable literature. Much of it gives Margo the creeps, but it all has its purpose. I had to travel to find a lot of them, and it's a library that would make any oddity collector proud. The majority were more fictional than factual, and only a handful provided any practical applications, but I read them all.

When I saw that thing hovering over my granddaughter, something struck me. The hollowed, glowing chest was something I recalled from my readings. It took nearly all day to dig through the books, but when I found what I was looking for, I knew exactly what I was dealing with.

This was far more than a monster. More than a shadow in the night that terrified children. He was a demon. The book called him Eddow, along with many other names.

He left hell early in creation. I can't be sure why, but my guess is he didn't like the monotony of it. He seemed to like Earth and had an odd love for humans.

I feel as though he's looking for something. The book calls him a collector, but it's mostly speculation. A few theories about how he might colonize Earth, or take control of mankind, or bridge hell with our world somehow. Given his interest in my granddaughter, I have my own speculations about what he might be looking for, and I don't like the looks of it at all.

Even newly born, Naomi possessed an interest in him. That concerns me more. If my Naomi is what this demon seeks, that means he'll latch himself onto her and groom her to be whatever it is he needs.

What would he do to accomplish his goals? Would he steal her away while she was young enough to mold to his own ends? Or invade her mind with force or demonic sway? If he could isolate her from those who might protect her from his influence, he could solidify himself as a god to her.

Here's what worries me most of all. The book tells how he keeps a collection of faces he wears as masks when he wants to interact with humans. He would use the face of a deceased loved one to tempt a person, or worse, drive them mad. But when it came to his image, the book could only speculate based on the accounts of less-than-reliable people. Lunatics in nuthouses and the like.

But when I saw him, he looked exactly like the lunatics described. I saw no mask, but his pure form. I've always been able to see things others can't, but if he knew this... If he knew I saw his true form? It probably would end badly for me. Or for Margo, or Jo, or who knows who else.

I think I should make my last preparations. My next moves may be my last and I have to ensure I've done everything in my power to stop him before he catches on.

If something happens to me, I leave Steve Owens in charge of hiding this journal and anything else that damned demon bastard might want to get his hands on. I've forbidden him from carrying on any of this work. I'm sure he'll be pissed, as he already feels I keep him out of the loop too much. Maybe one day he'll understand why I do this. My writings and notes will be tucked away wherever he chooses, but my weapon will not be his responsibility.

It feels strange to think my last days may be just on the road ahead of me. I guess I always knew that I wouldn't die an old man in a warm bed, but now I gotta wonder. Did I do enough? Did I love Margo enough? Does she know it? I've failed in a lot of places in my life in the name of safety for this ungrateful town, and I don't know if it will account for anything in the end.

But if I can keep my Naomi free of harm, at least I will have died knowing she could grow up to have a normal existence, and that will be enough.

As for tonight, I think I'll finally crack open that bottle of Johnny Walker my Pa gave me all those years ago.

Chuck

33

Ben sat at his desk, slowly swiveling in his chair as he examined the doll. The squeaking of his chair filled the silence between Naomi and him, until he caught a glance of Naomi's grimacing face and slowed to a stop.

"You found this at the altar?" he asked.

"I must have pocketed it before the zealot attacked you and forgotten about it," she said. "But he seemed to know about it."

"And he is… your husband?"

"No, he's just wearing his face."

"Like a mask?"

Naomi nodded.

"So, you know him?"

"He knows me for sure. I feel like I should know him, but…" She trailed off with a desperate shrug. "When I think back, it's a blur. A literal blur in my memories. I see myself as a child interacting with someone or something, but I can't tell who or what it is. Just blurred colors and pixels, like a bad photoshop job."

"I recognize the doll," he said. "It was mentioned in the book you destroyed."

"I didn't destroy it," she said.

"Whatever you did, we don't have it now."

She raised her hands in acquiescence. It wasn't worth the fight.

"It belonged to the demon Eddow," he went on. "We talked about him before, but in passing. I never thought a demon would bother with a place like this."

"A small, unsuspecting town?" she asked. "Kind of ideal, right?"

"I guess, but if he had ill intentions against people, wouldn't he go somewhere bigger?"

"I don't know." She shrugged, gesturing around the room. "You're the one with demonology and theology books all over the place."

"And *you're* the actual monster."

Naomi hunched forward over her knees.

"I'm sorry." He sighed. "I didn't mean…."

"No, I deserved that," she said. "I mean, you knew I wasn't exactly normal, but I should've told you. I should've warned you about the bad stuff. I just hoped you'd stay away."

"I should have," he admitted. "Curiosity kills cats and myself, admittedly. Got any other dark secrets? Do you have to kidnap and sacrifice babies too?"

"Jesus," she said.

"I'm trying to keep an open mind."

"It doesn't have to be *that* open. But…"

"But?"

"There are gaps in my memory. I know that when I became what I am, there was a space of time before I came to work for The Den, but I can't recall any of it. I remember being made. I remember the pain, the fear, and then it felt like the following week I was off on jobs."

Ben leaned forward in his chair, curiosity—and something else, something softer—in his eyes. "And when you say *being made?*"

"They call me a half-breed, but I don't think that's accurate. I'm more of a patchwork—human in shape because I was once a human, but with attributes of vamps, demons, and whatever else the witches decided to toss into the mix. There's so much I can't remember, but when I was in the woods, some of it came back. I remember the witches. The things they did to me, the things they taught me…" She looked to her hands. "It's the reason I am what I am now. I asked to be made into something useful and they gave me what I asked for."

"No offense," said Ben, "but why would you ask for that?"

Naomi held his gaze. Her memory was obscured, like it was stuck behind a wall in her mind. There were faces in her mind, but they lacked features. "I lost everything," she said at last. "I had all I wanted and I lost it. After that, the only thing I had left was my parents. I've never been close to them. I actually think they hated me growing up, but they're all I have left and I'd become a burden on them. My dad was sick and we were so bad off. I needed to become useful to help them. So I became this… I remember how. I remember the ceremony and the lightning, the woods catching fire and walking through the fire, but I don't remember who or what brought me into the woods."

"Do you think it was Eddow?"

"I think there's a good chance, but why can't I remember him?" she asked. "And when I saw him just now, it felt like he *wanted* me to remember."

"What did he say?"

"He gave me the doll. He said… *ask the doll.*"

"That's it?"

She nodded.

"Well, did you?" he asked.

"Did I what?"

"Ask the doll?"

She scoffed.

He handed Naomi the doll. "How is this any crazier than anything else we just talked about?"

Naomi let the doll settle into her palm. It was so small and light, but it made her skin crawl. She looked at Ben. "What am I supposed to ask a doll?"

"Ask it who took you to the witches."

She sighed. "Doll?" she began, staring at the yarn doll that sat peacefully in her palm. "Doll, who brought me to be made?"

There was no reaction from the doll. No movement or sound, just two red X's staring back at her.

"This is stupid," she said. But when she looked back up, she saw a tree line. She was looking into the darkness of the forest, her heart pounding in her throat. She rubbed her hands on her pants and swallowed hard. A voice broke the silence, and she jumped.

"Hey," it said.

Naomi looked to her left. The person standing next to her was so tall she had to crane her neck. He was awkwardly built, with aged skin and the look of a man who had done a lot and seen even more. But the kindly smile on his face put her at ease.

"It'll be all right, my love," he said. "I'll be here with you. This is for the best. When you leave these woods, you'll be a changed woman. Changed for the good. All that heartache will be behind you and I will be here for you just like I always have."

Naomi felt his hand take hers, and when she looked at it she saw the doll again.

"Naomi?" Ben asked.

"It was my grandpa," she said.

"Your grandpa did this to you?"

She shook her head, frowning hard. "He's been dead since I was a baby."

Ben sat back abruptly and rubbed his curls. "I really wish you hadn't destroyed my book."

"Who knows how much of my life he's meddled with," she said. "What do you remember? Maybe there's something, some clue that will give us an idea of what he's trying to do or how to stop it?"

He shook his head. "He's a collector, we know that. He likes being among humans or at least he prefers it, especially children because they're more impressionable." He rubbed his temples. "We know the altar is his, so he must love being treated like a deity. The center of attention, but maybe more than that? Maybe if he prefers humans, there's something about them that he likes. A trait? Or how they see him?" He sighed. "I don't know. Demonology isn't exactly an exact science. It's stories interpreted by guys who stare at ancient tablets or listen to stories from crazy people. Even if I had the book, I'm not sure how helpful it would be. But at least it would offer us *something*."

"Okay, okay, I get it. You miss your book."

"I'm just saying, without the book, asking that doll is the best option we have to learn more about Eddow. But it seems like we need to know what to ask to get the right memories. How do you know what to ask if you're missing the information to begin with?" He tapped his hand against his knee, then snapped his fingers. "You need an outside source," he said. "Like your family. Where did you say they live?"

"Hang on, let me try again," she snapped. She adjusted in her seat and glared at the doll. "Doll, show me what Eddow wants."

There was a pause as both of them waited in silence for something.

"Anything?"

Naomi snapped her eyes shut and squeezed the doll in her palm. "Doll, show me where Eddow is."

She opened her eyes and looked around the room, expecting to see something spectacular, but there was only Ben's face, sweating with anticipation.

She grumbled and tossed it aside. "It doesn't work."

"We're not asking the right questions."

"Obviously."

"Naomi, I'm picking up that you don't want to see your family and I get it, but we need more information," Ben said firmly.

She sighed. "I know. I'm just so hesitant to pull them into anything."

"Where are they?"

"Down the street, actually."

"And you never mentioned it?"

"Oh, no, this is new," she said. "My employers, you know the ones who asked me to hurt you? They didn't like my outburst, and so they found my family, who I'd hidden away, and brought them into the center of this nightmare town."

Ben thought for a moment. "I know that worries you, but maybe they can help."

"How?"

"You can ask them about your childhood. Maybe there's something that stands out?"

The thought of facing her parents filled her with dread. "I don't think I have it in me."

"I'll go with you."

"What? No," she said firmly. "I can't let you put yourself in danger again."

He gave her a pointed look. "Yeah, well, you can't really stop me either, and we both know what happened the last time you didn't include me."

"That was a shitty attempt at a guilt trip," she said.

"Yeah, but it worked, right?"

She rubbed at her face to hide her smile.

"I think we should regroup," he suggested. "Maybe start fresh between us?"

She nodded. "Yeah, okay. Uh… I'm Naomi. I work for a vampiric organization known as The Den. I don't know exactly what my title would be other than vamp bitch or, I don't know, henchman? Henchwoman? I'm mysterious and strange, and people usually avert their eyes when they see me."

"And before all that?"

"Huh?"

"Who were you before that?"

Naomi swallowed a knot. "A mom," she said. "And a wife and the luckiest woman in existence. I wrote stupid short stories about dogs and purple cakes and tried to bake said purple cakes, but I was never a good cook." The thought made her smile.

"I've never seen that smile," Ben said.

She felt a tear roll down her cheek but didn't wipe it away. "And you?"

Ben cocked his head, thinking. "I'm Ben. I read too many old books and take notes on literally anything. My family is from Jerusalem and they all live here because it's just easier. I was a forever student at the community college in Springfield, but that was probably two semesters ago and now I don't know. I used to work at the bookstore in town, but the owner hasn't been around much. So I read and I write about demons and all the strange things I see in this town."

"And your ability to see? You could see me clearly in the shadows when we first met. No one can do that."

"I couldn't tell you," he said. "I've always been sensitive, I guess."

"A natural seer." She nodded. "You're a rarity in my world."

"I'm an oddity in mine."

Naomi offered her hand to him. "Nice to meet you, Ben."

"And you, Naomi."

"Now, next time I tell you to stay away, do it."

"No promises," he said.

She grinned. "Fair enough."

34

Glenn had Jamie meet him at the bridge instead of the sheriff's office for her 8:00 a.m. start time. When he led her into the creek bed, carrying a stack of large plastic containers, she started to wonder if he'd lost his mind.

"You're not going to murder me and stuff me into one of those bins, are you, Beasley?" she asked.

Glenn grunted in annoyance. "Keep moving."

When they reached the shrine, he set down the bins and wiped the sweat from his mustache.

She peered into the dark entrance with a look like he was crazy if he expected her to go inside. "I'm sorry, Glenn! I know I've been a really crappy worker, but my heart isn't in law. You know that. But if you let me live, I promise I'll do better! I'll be the best deputy you've got, I promise! Just don't murder me and chop my body into pieces!"

"Jamie, I'm not going to kill you," he said. "We need to process this crime scene so the M.E. can do his job."

He ducked through the opening, then turned and poked his head out. "Hand me that bin and grab the lantern." He took a bin from her and vanished inside. "Now, I have to warn you, Jamie, this might be a bit disturbing. There are a lot of—"

But she'd already stepped inside. She lifted the lantern and stared. "Are… are those… h-h-hearts?"

"Yeah, as I was saying—" But before Glenn could finish his sentence, the air whooshed out of Jamie's lungs and her body thudded to the ground.

"Jesus Christ." He sighed, tossing the bin down.

Ben offered his bed to Naomi, but when she hesitantly informed him that his blood was keeping her at optimum operating levels and that she didn't need to sleep, he asked no more.

She spent the night reading his journals and notes. Though he'd left most of his notes about Eddow in the book itself, Naomi hoped she would find something useful in the rest. Unfortunately, as the sun rose, she knew little more than when he'd fallen asleep.

When he finally stirred an hour later, she was staring out the window.

"How do you manage to sit in one spot for so long?" he asked.

"Practice, I suppose," she said. "I'm concerned for the detective."

"Who?" he mumbled, ruffling his curls out of his face.

"Beasley. I told him."

"You told him? Why would you do that?"

"I thought I was leaving," she said. "I didn't want to leave him empty-handed. I didn't tell him everything, like I have with you. He just knows about the altar. You think he'll move the hearts?"

"There's a good chance he will," Ben said. He stood from his bed, stretching tall and adjusting his clothes.

Noami's gaze was still on the horizon, her eyebrows drawn.

"Call him, if you're so worried," he said. "I should probably shower anyway." He grabbed an armful of clothes and left the room.

Naomi pulled her phone from her jacket and dialed his number. It rang for several moments before she gave up and hung up. "It's probably too early," she told herself. "He's fine. He's still alive and unharmed." She set the phone down on the windowsill. "Probably." She clenched her fists, looking at the phone. When she picked it back up to call him again, it rang in her hand. "Glenn?" she asked, relieved.

"I missed your call," he said. "I'm out here moving these organs. I *had* help, but well… anyway, what's going on?"

"You're moving them?" she asked, breathing more easily. "Where to?"

"Why? I thought you were leaving town?"

"Things have changed, I guess."

"Oh, well, that's kind of a relief, honestly," he said. "I was starting to feel like I was a little over my head with this stuff. We're moving them to the Leigh Memorial Hospital. The M.E. will examine there. I'm not sure what he'll do with them after, but at least the hospital is better than the middle of nowhere."

"No, don't move them!" she said, suddenly panicked.

"What? Why?"

She didn't answer, her mind racing through the possibilities. "If we move them, he'll be pissed," she whispered to herself.

"Who?" he asked.

"But if he's planning something big with them and we can't destroy them, maybe we can hide them?"

"What the fuck is going on?"

"Okay, okay. Yes, move them."

"You mean like I intended to?"

"Yes, yes," she said, hoping she was making the right decision.

Silence stretched across the line.

"Detective?" she asked.

"Naomi," he said. "There's a lot you're not telling me, isn't there?"

"Would it make you feel better if it was for your own safety?"

"Not really."

"I can't tell you right now, because I don't even know what to tell you," she said. "When I know more, I'll let you know. I promise, okay?"

"All right," he said. "Just get me informed as soon as you can." He hung up.

Naomi pocketed her phone. When she withdrew her hand, she found she'd somehow pulled out the photo Glenn had given her. She wanted to shove it back to the bottom of her endless pocket, but something compelled her not to.

She stared at the stranger in the image. It wasn't Brian. She could remember Brian's face as easily as she could recall Taylor's.

Couldn't she?

Her eyes drifted to the wall as she tried to recall their time together, but everything was blending together as one. Her younger years felt like a story told to her secondhand. She knew the characters and the names. She knew most of the events, but the face of the man she'd been married to didn't match the face in this picture.

She furrowed her brow in confusion. Why was it when she saw Eddow in the street, she'd instantly identified his face as her husband's, but here, staring at an image she'd been told was his, she couldn't recognize him? If she dissected both faces, they found the same structures. Same jawline, full cheekbones, and up-turned nose. Even the shape of the smile was identical. But if she were given this picture and asked if it matched Eddow, she would have said no. The contradiction made her feel delusional.

Worse, the more she tried to make sense of it, the more out of focus her memory became. When she thought of Brian, she saw Taylor's face. When she saw Taylor's face, the details had gone grainy, like the reception in her brain was fading.

"Who is that?" Ben asked, looking over her shoulder. He'd returned from his shower and was still putting off a large amount of heat, which warmed Naomi's back.

She glanced at him, then back to the picture. "Glenn," she said.

"And the other guy?" he asked.

"I have no clue," she said with a shrug. She tucked the picture back into her pocket.

Ben leaned in for a look. "How much can you fit into that?"

"As much as I want," she said. "It's a void of nothingness. Like a black hole. I put the thing in and when I want it I call on the shadows to bring it to me. It comes in handy, but at times the shadows give me things even when I don't ask."

"Huh," he said. "So, you just send things into the shadows and when you call upon them, they come back? Can you do that with anything?"

"Well, I have to put it there. My teleportation works similarly. All the shadows are connected, and it's like opening a doorway in one to go to another." She gestured to her pocket. "This? This is like a closet, I guess."

He pulled socks onto his feet and leaned back on the bed. "So, when the book disappeared, did it go there?"

She rotated the chair to face him. "In a way," she said. "It isn't my pocket, so it's a little out of my realm."

"So, the portals, or uh, doorways, only work in your realm?"

"Well, no. It's like public land. All that inhabits the shadow realms exists there. It isn't the nicest place to hang out. But I pass through so quickly that no one notices me."

"But you could summon the book? Call upon the shadows to return it? Or whatever you do?" he asked, pulling on his shoes.

She considered it. "I don't know how deep it is. I'd have to keep the door open for a while," she said.

"But it's doable?" he asked.

"Naomi?"

"Yeah, Ben?"

"Why are we in this field?"

Across from Ben's home and Highway 215, one of the main roads that ran through Pickleberry, was a large, open field. In Naomi's childhood, she recalled spending her time in the field hiding from her family. In the expansion of Pickleberry, the field had remained untouched. No houses or shopping malls had popped up. The only residents were a few cows scattered off in the distance from Naomi and Ben. This made it the best location to host an experiment.

"Because I have no idea what is going to come out and I didn't think your bedroom or the middle of the street was a great place," she replied.

She stood rubbing her hands together and breathing deeply.

"What do I need to do?" he asked.

She paused. She reached into her pocket and pulled out a large, powerful flashlight. She tested it on herself, squinting, and then tossed it to Ben. "Stand here," she said, pointing next to her. "If anything starts to come through the portal, I want you to shine the light at it."

"And it will stop them?"

"It's a flashlight, not a laser. It'll slow them down while I close the portal. This could be really dangerous," she explained. "The things that could come through this portal could cause who knows what kind of trouble. And I'm not exactly sure that I can stop it."

"If we had that book, we could have all the answers we need," Ben said. "Unless you think there is a way to learn about Eddow without it or just talking to your parents. Maybe this is worth the risk?"

Naomi undid the buttons on the sleeves of her jacket and rolled them up. She rubbed her hands together again. "I would like to thank you for the blood. This wouldn't be possible without it," she said.

"Uh, you're welcome," he replied, holding the flashlight like a claymore, ready to attack.

Naomi held her hands before her with her eyes closed. She breathed in deeply and when she opened her eyes with an exhale, they were white. Her fingers spread wide, reaching for the openness before her.

Nothing happened for a long moment, but when Ben looked at Naomi to see what she was doing, he noticed her tattoos shifting and moving over her skin. They moved like vines from her forearms to her hands and seemed to drip from her fingers like ink and into the open air. They drifted like ferrofluid pulled by a magnet several feet in front of her and then started to form a swirling pool that grew in size until the edges began to cloud.

Ben heard thunder and looked to the sky. The sun seemed to dim, but there wasn't a cloud in sight. With a second rumble of thunder, he realized it came from within the swirling black pool in front of them. The blackness and shadows started to split, creating a void in the air a couple yards in length. The opening of the void was defined, but looking in, Ben saw nothing. No shapes or figures, just black.

"How will you know when you've found it?" he asked.

"Shut up," she mumbled, sweat forming on her brow. Her fingers began to shake as she grasped the air and her face matched their struggle. "I… I've got it," she gasped. "I can feel it." Her fingers curled as though she held something and she started to pull her arms toward her chest, but she moved so slowly a person wouldn't notice the shift at first, but only feel the air grow heavier as thunder rumbled again.

Ben watched the portal with wide eyes and waited. He saw nothing but black until he caught a glimpse of dull gray in the dark. "I see it," he whispered.

"Keep your voice low," she muttered. "We don't need to draw attention." Her arms were shaking as she pulled, her muscles growing tired. It felt like she was trying to move a freight train.

Ben shifted his weight nervously from foot to foot, the dry grass under his feet crunching lightly.

Naomi gasped lightly as her arms froze.

Ben bit his tongue.

Her eyes grew wide and terrified. "Light! Ben, light!" she shouted.

Ben fumbled with the light, startled, and couldn't find the button to turn it on. Once he was finally able to turn it on, he nearly dropped the flashlight as the beam landed on something that caused his skin to crawl.

There was no doubt it was a face that peered through the opening to the pair, though it had no certain features at first glance. It had no eyes or other facial features, but it tracked Ben and Naomi with an alert attention. It was just a mass of shapes and shadows that blended completely with the hole until he shone his light on it. When the light hit its skin, it recoiled.

Ben was given enough time to make out hollow shells where eyes would have been and a large, gaping mouth that grew by the moment. Shadow dripped from its lower jaw to top like oil ascending. The longer Ben watched, the larger the mouth grew, until a howling reached his ears. The sound moved like a doppler, in waves that increased in intensity the longer it carried on. As the sounds intensified, it shifted and the pair realized it was angry and coming right for them. It disappeared for a moment, appearing in bounds like a cheetah in gallop.

"They're coming!"

Naomi pulled her arms toward her chest faster, but she was still far too slow. "Keep the light on it!" Her hands shook and the tension started to travel to her legs, which also started to buckle. "It's so very close…"

"So is whatever that thing is!" The light shook in Ben's hands, but he kept it directed on the thing that charged in their direction. There was motion on the right side of the portal, and Ben was certain it was another creature. He flashed his light quickly, hoping to get an understanding of how close it was, when he noticed it was large, flat, rectangular and gray, a stark contrast to the blackness of the void.

"I see it!" he shouted, settling his light on the cover of the book that grew nearer and nearer. When he was able to read the title, he felt his hands start to sweat. The book was near enough now that he considered reaching into the portal and yanking it out. As the echoing sound of the creature's galloping feet started to reach him, he suddenly became too terrified to move. He watched the book with wide eyes until it reached the very opening of the portal.

"The shadows, Ben! Shine on the shadows!" Naomi shouted through gritted teeth, pulling even harder toward her chest.

There was a howl, something so hollow and unearthly it caused Ben's stomach to drop. It shifted from one to many and behind the book, he could see the shadows shifting and moving. The light that covered the book moved and shifted as Ben noticed clawed hands grasping at the cover of it. When the light touched the shadows, they hissed and withdrew, but only for more to reach out again.

Soon the book, which was nearly out of the portal, became covered by shadow. A clawed hand grasped from the left and another from the right. This stopped Naomi from pulling and in turn began to move her across the field, her feet catching on the tall grass.

"Shit!" Ben grasped her arm, holding her back, but kept the light steady ahead of them.

"It's hiding… behind… the book," she grunted. She leaned into Ben's hold, who had to move his grasp around her waist. She regained her stance and found new strength in her arms.

Her teeth were gritted so hard she thought they might shatter, but she pulled despite the muscles in her arms screaming from fatigue.

Any small shadow that attempted to move toward the opening cowered from Ben's light, but the large set of claws held tight, inky skin sizzling from Ben's light.

Naomi fought to regain control of the book. She thought she had it and put all her strength into pulling, even letting loose a scream as it felt as though every muscle in her body was tearing. Only there was a jolt that ripped her forward. Her eyes, their normal brown, shot open wide and horrified.

"Ben, light, Ben, light, light." Her voice was a near whisper, but Ben had the light placed on the portal. "Ben, Ben…" Her voice merely air without sound passing over her lips now.

"I'm shining the light!" He struggled to hold tight to her waist and keep the light steady.

"Ben, Ben," she gasped. Naomi was no longer pulling against something. Her hands were extended before her but limp, as though someone were holding her by the wrist. "Run!" she screamed.

There was a deep, guttural growl that almost resembled a laugh as Naomi struggled to free her hands, pulling and pushing against Ben.

Ben stumbled backward and fell several feet behind Naomi. He attempted to stand, but when he witnessed what was coming through the portal, he could only sit in the grass, paralyzed by fear.

A figure void of features, no eyes to see, no mouth to grin, pushed through the portal. Its head came first, followed by two large, pitch black hands that grasped the edges of the portal as it crawled through.

Naomi brought her hands back in front of her, palms together, as she tried to close the portal and quickly.

She wasn't fast enough. When she snapped the portal closed, the shadow had been half way through and was severed at what would have been the waist. It hit the ground, dispelling in a cloud, but reformed into a full figure as the black vapors rose. It stretched and adjusted to its new form, opening its mouth to let out a howl but only expelling smoke and toxic fumes.

Ben choked on the fumes. They made it difficult for him to find the strength to stand.

"Goddammit, Ben, run!" Naomi yelled again.

The shape of the shadow shifted, shortening its torso and arms, redirecting the shadows to its legs. It swung a leg back and brought it into contact with Naomi, who flew backward.

The air had been knocked from her lungs and she struggled to get enough strength to stand. She hunched over, taking deep breaths, trying to regain control and focus her attention on the shadow. She raised her hands to it, trying to control the shadows that made up its body, but it did no good. The shadow didn't hesitate and started toward Ben, who was still in shock.

Naomi's tattoos shifted and traveled up her left forearm under the sleeve of her jacket. They crawled down her right forearm and blackened her fist, extending from her knuckles to form a blade. She charged forward, putting herself between Ben and the shadow.

The shadow wasn't bothered by her. It flung limbs, each growing and receding as it redirected its composition to whatever part of its body needed to attack Naomi. With each hack and slash, the limb would erupt in smoke only to rejoin in another location on its body, ready to strike again.

Naomi was hardly able to keep up with the attacks but she pressed on, moving faster than even she knew she was capable of. She shifted and adjusted her tattoos as they needed, forming a shield when struck, or two blades when one wouldn't do. She leaped through portals as fast as they appeared, jumping behind the shadow only for the shadow to be facing her, ready to counter.

The embodiment of the shadow didn't follow rules. It would be everywhere and nowhere at once. The consciousness at the center of it knew her next moves before she did, and there was little she could do to divert it.

She was panting on the ground, regrouping, when the shadow landed a blow to her ribs. She felt them crunch but didn't focus on it. She only focused on the fact that Ben was still sitting on his ass watching the fight.

"Ben, get the fuck out of here, *please*," she gasped, struggling to stand.

The whimper in her voice brought him out from his fear. He shook it off and grabbed hold of the flashlight. He flashed it at the shadow. It did little aside from disorienting the monster, but it worked long enough for Ben to get its attention.

"Over here, you fuckfaced cloud of smoke!"

It moved toward him, trying to shield itself from the flashing light but growing more annoyed with each flash.

When the shadow was just a few feet in front of Ben, he leaped, arms spread wide, and wrapped them around the solid yet changing form of the shadow. It buckled, traveling backward into the portal Naomi had opened and disappearing into the void.

Its shape slipped from Ben's hold, disappearing and leaving him to levitate in the void. Before Ben could comprehend the danger he was in and meet the insurmountable wave of shapes and shadows ready to devour him, he felt something take hold of his ankle and rip him from the portal.

He landed hard in the grass, staring at the bright blue sky that hosted a blinding sun, listening only to his panting and the silence of the world around him.

Naomi collapsed to the ground, breathing heavily. Her tattoos shifted back to their place on her skin and her whole body shook.

The two didn't speak. The fight had started and been over so quickly that they were trying to process whether they'd died or not.

Ben pushed up on his forearms. "Are you okay?" he asked.

She tried to push up but was still too weak. "Is it gone?" She settled into the grass.

"I don't see it."

"Are you sure? If even a shred of that thing survives, it could manifest," she warned him.

"It's gone, Naomi. Are you okay?"

"I'll be okay." She waved him off.

"Do you need blood?"

Naomi swallowed hard. She controlled her breathing in the moment and pushed herself upright. Her hands, arms, and legs shook, but she tried to control them as she managed her breathing. "Never, *never* offer me that," she said. "I'll never drink from you again, Ben."

Ben moved to her side, crawling through the grass and pushing to his feet.

She refused his support, but he gave it to her anyway. He didn't mention the book and wouldn't mention it again after what he'd witnessed. Given that Pickleberry had a magnetic attraction for bad things, he thought they'd gotten off pretty easy.

It was likely the pounding of their racing hearts in their ears that deafened them to the world around them. That or the desire to move on from their failed attempt and regroup somewhere less itchy, but the two left the field. Ben supported Naomi under her arms and didn't take notice of anything else.

If Naomi had the strength, she would have set fire to the whole field just to be sure it was clear. She was good at that—setting fires to cover her ass. But now she couldn't even force her legs to work properly, let alone light a match. She trusted Ben's intuition and let him carry her from the field, paying no mind to whatever was moving in the grass behind them.

35

The joy of using a moving company is the opportunity to sit back and let someone else do all the work. Jo and Richard didn't pack a single box. They'd simply packed two very large suitcases while movers did the rest of the work. They were living in the lap of luxury.

The downside of using a moving company is the headache of waiting for said moving company to arrive. Jo and Richard had left their home before the moving company had arrived, so as far as they knew, their goods could still be sitting in their former home collecting dust.

Jo had warned Richie to not get too comfortable with someone else doing the work. As any head of household, she knew exactly what to expect when someone else did the work she was so used to doing herself. She'd warned Richie not to leave anything behind that they might miss in a week or more, but he thought she was being dramatic.

That would be why Jo was blissfully watering her rex begonias and painted nettles while Richie paced the outside of the house, bored out of his mind. "It wouldn't have taken too much room to pack one book," she told him.

"Our things should arrive today, Jo, and when they do, I'll be too busy unpacking to remember what it felt like to be bored," he told her. He stopped abruptly in his pacing, clutching his ribs. He gave Jo a sly glance and hid the grimace on his face. "I'm going to go sit down," he said, closing the front door and leaving her on their doorstep peacefully watering her plants.

Jo was humming a tune, the tune of being right, when she heard steps approaching the gate of their living complex. She'd gathered there weren't many people living in the complex as she hadn't noticed anyone come and go. So, the sound of people approaching the gate perked her ears up as she was eager to socialize with new neighbors. She felt her hopes fall short when her eyes landed upon Naomi accompanied by a strange young man.

"Oh, hello, dear," she called, but it was hardly loud enough to reach them.

Naomi waved and pointed to the gate.

"I'm in the middle of watering my begonias," her mother said with a sigh, but she put the watering can aside and opened the gate anyway. She gave Naomi a once over. "Nay, you're filthy. Do you ever shower?" She looked to Ben and did the same to him, noting the grass stains and grass clinging to his shirt. "Another poor boy?"

She didn't wait for a response but returned to her begonias. "Your father is inside," she said.

Naomi glanced at Ben and half frowned reassuring his confused and offended face. "Thanks, Mom. I'm glad to see you too," she said.

Jo hummed her tune, admiring the leaves of her nettles.

Naomi entered the home with Ben close behind. It was nearly empty except for a navy blue couch and matching lounge chair and a couple of bar chairs at the bar attached to the kitchen. The space was open and large, with ceilings that reached near cathedral height. The living room was bright and cozy, the far wall covered with empty shelves and cabinets and a fireplace at the wall near the windows and door. The dining room was lackluster, but the floors were new hardwood that Naomi knew her mother likely enjoyed. The kitchen was crafted as though it had her mother in mind, and Naomi felt a smidge of happiness knowing the joy she would get from it.

Her father was hunched over the bar, a cup of coffee and newspaper in front of him. He looked up when she entered and his eyes lit up. "My Nay-Nay!" He grinned, his arms wide. He embraced her tightly. "And this is?"

"Hi, Dad," she said. "This is Ben." She gestured through his tight hug.

"Ben? Short for Benjamin, I bet. A good Christian name." He shook his hand.

"Oh, well, not quite," Ben said.

"Jewish?"

Ben nodded.

"I thought you had a bit of a Jew look to you," he said, nodding to himself.

"Dad!"

"What? I didn't assume it… oh, oh, well. Everyone is so easily offended nowadays. You know I meant no harm, right, Benny?"

Ben nodded.

"'Atta boy." He gave Ben a strong smack on the arm and returned to his coffee and paper. "I'd offer you coffee, but we only have one other cup. If only one of you wanted some, then…"

"No, thank you," Naomi told him.

"I'll take a cup," Ben said and as Richie turned to clean out Jo's pink mug, he looked to Naomi, who was subtly shaking her head. "You know what? I think I'll pass," he told Richie.

"Suit yourself. It isn't very good anyway. So"—he opened his arms wide to gesture to the house—"what do you think of the new *casa*?"

"It's nice. Smaller than the farmhouse," she pointed out.

"But location, location, lo-ca-tion, Naomi!" he said. "Come on, I'll give you the tour." He started to leave the bar when she stopped him.

"Actually, we have some questions for you," she said.

"Are you getting married again?"

Naomi went tense and wore her discomfort clearly.

"What? We never see you and then you show up with a new guy. It's probably been months since you visited us at the farmhouse, so I just assumed you were busy with a new life and a new guy and here is a new guy, so… am I wrong?" he asked.

"Drastically," she said sternly.

"Good, no offense, Ben. I'm sure you're a good guy, but I really liked the other one." He shrugged and took a sip of his coffee.

"You make it sound like I had a choice," she said, and Ben heard the sadness in the undertones of her voice.

"Oh, Jesus, Naomi, you know I don't think that," he said, disgruntled. He shook his paper once, twice, and then fidgeted with his coffee cup. "For the love of…" he grumbled, scratching at a dry patch of skin behind his ear.

"Dad, I just wanted to ask you about my childhood," she said, desperate to move past it.

"Your childhood? You don't remember it?"

"I just want a different perspective. I think there are some things I don't remember or I'm not remembering correctly. Did anything stand out?"

He thought for a moment. "I don't know, Nay. You were always so reclusive to us. We never knew what you were doing or thinking. I guess withdrawn was more like it. When you started to write those stories, I figured you were just an avid daydreamer lost in another world. You were always creating characters and talking to them."

"I talked to them aloud?"

"Well, just the one mostly. What was his name… Ted…Teddy?"

"Eddie?" she asked.

"Yeah, yeah, that sounds right." He nodded. "You had full conversations with him as though he was sitting right in front of you. Hate to say it, but you were a strange kid." He shook his head, taking another sip of his coffee and giving another bout of scratching to his ear.

Naomi pulled the doll from her pocket and showed it to her dad. "Does this look familiar at all?"

He took it in his hand and studied it for a long while.

"It's probably nothing," she said, reaching for it.

"No, no, I remember this. You used to carry this around, but I have no idea where or how you got it as a kid. We didn't give it to you and if I'm not mistaken, it was your grandpa's," he said. He put the doll on the counter and shivered.

"Grandpa's?" she asked.

"Yeah, I always thought maybe Lucas found it in his stuff they stored away and then you took a liking to it, but Lucas would have never let you take it if he found it, so I don't know." He frowned. "Your grandpa had the weirdest shit," he said.

"How so?"

"I don't know. He seemed to collect strange things. Books about creepy shit, bones, and relics, and just weird shit. That must have been genetic, because you used to do the same thing now that I remember it," he said. Then he chuckled. "Honestly, Nay, we were pretty convinced you were going to be a serial killer because we would find animal organs in your bedroom. But look at you now." He smiled, then looked her over with quizzical eyebrows. "You're doing okay, right?"

"Oh, yeah, sure." She nodded, avoiding Ben's eyes.

He laughed again. "You know, if your grandpa hadn't died *after* you were born, I would've thought you were his reincarnated spirit, because there is a lot about you that reminds me of him. There has to be some spiritual bond or something at least, if a person were to believe in that," he said.

"Why is that?"

"I don't know. You couldn't have a memory of him because you were too young, but you used to just stare at his picture like you'd known him your whole life. Your eyes just lit up. I never understood it, but your mother was glad for some kind of bond."

He frowned, looking past Ben and Naomi to stare out the front window at Jo still admiring her plants. "Honestly, I'm a bit glad you never met him. He was a nut." He lowered his voice and scratched. "He used to fill your brother's head with stories about some town where monsters ran everything. Werewolves in the forest and vampires living on blood donations. He had a good imagination, I'll give him that, but it always worried me with Lucas." He paused. "Have you spoken to Lucas at all?"

"No, I haven't," she said simply but leaned in. "Grandpa talked about this stuff?"

"Yeah… yeah, and the stories got weirder up to his death. They said heart attack, but I always wondered if his mind just slipped and…" He stopped. "I shouldn't be talking to you about this," he said.

Naomi gave Ben a glance, who returned the same look. "Do you remember where he lived?" she asked.

"Some place called Pickleberry."

The pair shared another glance.

"Dad, do you know where you are?"

He thought for a moment. "You know, it never occurred to me to ask." He chuckled.

"This is Pickleberry," she said.

He frowned. "Huh, small world."

"Do you not remember living here?"

"Huh, here? I've never lived here before."

"We grew up in the house on the corner," she said, gesturing toward the direction of Ben's house.

He thought for a long while, lost in another scratching fit, and then chuckled. "So, you can't remember your childhood, but you can remember living here? Maybe you should have your brain checked, Naomi. I've never lived here and I would remember living in a house with a café for a garage," he said.

Naomi felt like it was a worthless battle and simply sighed. "What was Grandpa's name?" she asked.

"Come on, Nay. You don't even remember his name?"

She shrugged.

"Chuck Campbell," he said. He frowned and shook his head at her, but Naomi watched his face grimace and the palm of his hand press into his forehead.

"Dad?"

"I'm okay. I just get these random headaches. Since the treatment, I think my tolerance for caffeine is a little sensitive. I should switch to decaf," he told her, rubbing his forehead and then running his hand through his hair. When he lowered his hand, there was a clump of hair in it. "That's strange." He shrugged and dusted the hair to the floor, looking back at his newspaper.

"Maybe you should see a doctor, just in case?" Naomi asked, voice shaking.

"With that and the itching, it would probably be a good idea," Ben agreed.

"Oh, it's just a couple patches of eczema, is all." He waved off their concerns. He lifted the sleeve of his henley and showed them a dry patch. "Got one here and behind my head. Probably from all the traveling and trying to settle into a new place."

"I don't think that's eczema," Ben mumbled.

The dry patch of skin on Richie's forearm was dark and flaky, like a thin layer of bark that was beginning to peel from the trunk. The patch behind his ear was thicker, like that of an aged oak, and Richie's extended scratching had only amplified the rough condition.

Naomi let her wide eyes speak.

"Yeah, I'll set up my PCM at LMH soon. I just would like to have a place to sit that doesn't make my sciatica act up like it does with this loaner furniture," he told her. "I'm fine." He grinned.

Naomi watched his face. His laugh lines were exaggerated by his wide and warm grin. She felt the lump form in her throat but swallowed hard. "Okay, well, it was good catching up," she said. "Thanks for answering all my silly questions. Ben and I actually have a lot of work to do." She collected the doll and started for the door, ushering Ben to follow.

"So soon? Well, all right. You always were such a hard-working, busy lady," he said. "We'll see you two later! I love you, Naomi," he called from behind her.

Naomi stopped so abruptly she felt Ben smack into her back. "What did you say?"

"I love you? Don't act like this is the first time I've said it to you."

Naomi nodded and hurried out the door, barely telling her mother goodbye.

"You won't even stay to help us unpack?" Jo called after her.

"I'll come back to help," she reassured her.

"We'll see, then."

"Okay, Mom, love you," she said but got no response.

She walked fast out the gate and Ben had to nearly sprint to catch up.

"Hey, hey, what was that about?" he asked.

"Something isn't right," she said.

"What? Your dad's weird headache and hair and skin thing or the fact that he said 'I love you'?"

"All of it. I know it makes me sound like an angsty, love-deprived child, but I never remember my parents telling me they loved me. I mean, you saw my mom." She nodded over her shoulder to her mom. "I'm telling you, Ben, something isn't right here. What if Eddow has something to do with it? I wish my grandpa was still here."

"Your grandpa?"

"They thought he was crazy, but they said the same thing about me. Maybe he was the only one who was actually sane?" she wondered aloud. "I saw Brian's face when I ran into Eddow. What if all those years, he was wearing my grandpa's face?"

"Your family could play it off if you mentioned it growing up," he agreed.

"Child sees a picture every day and turns it into an imaginary friend."

"Or child has a spiritual connection with the ghost of deceased grandpa, if they're the type to believe that," he added.

"Either way, it wasn't my grandpa, but if Eddow wanted his face I feel like he had his reasons."

"Guess it's time to find out where Chuck Campbell lived."

"Guess so." She nodded.

36

Ben managed to find Chuck Campbell's home in a few Google searches. Even if Chuck didn't have much of a digital footprint, most of the records were public. Naomi's grandpa, like most everyone else, was at the whim of the digital age, whether he partook of it or not.

"Hmm," he said, looking at a map.

"What?"

"This street"—he pointed to one that was on the outline of the city—"I've heard of it before."

"Well, it *is* a small city," she said.

"Yeah, but I think there's something about it. A lore or something? I can't remember," he said.

"We don't really have the time to sit around, Ben. If there is something there, we'll just have to deal with it when we get there."

Ben was reluctant, but he followed her through the streets and toward the outer edge of the city.

"Why don't you own a car?" Naomi asked later as they neared the park again and the connecting street.

"Why don't you?"

"Teleportation?"

"So, why can't we just teleport?" he asked.

"It would probably be a good idea to conserve my energy, considering I used most of it trying and failing at retrieving your book," she said.

Ben took the hint and didn't speak.

They followed the road that ran behind the park and crossed the other main, Highway H, where the atmosphere seemed to shift. The houses of Pickleberry were mostly well-kept and modest, but once they passed the high school and neared the edge of Black Bile, the houses seemed less loved. It started with older houses here and there and soon enough, the conditions of the homes shifted from less than ideal to distressed to outright decaying and decrepit. Many of them looked as though they'd been completely abandoned and were mere bones and guts of their former selves.

"For a town so small, it's hard to imagine they even had space for a skid row," Naomi said.

"Skid row has people. You know, life and presence. This place?" Ben shivered, looking at the empty houses. "It's like a ghost town contained within a completely normal town. I don't like the looks of this place at all."

Naomi didn't say anything. She just pressed on, quickening her pace a bit. Ben, though he had a longer stride than her, had to skip a bit to keep up, but his eyes were on the houses that surrounded them.

It seemed that the farther they went down the street, the darker it became even though it was barely midday. A fog started to settle around the houses. They traveled the road, watching the fog inch in their direction. Then they met it at a cross street, and the day seemed to shift completely to night.

"Cowden Street," she said, reading the street sign. She paused to look at it as the name lingered in her brain.

Ben didn't notice that she'd stopped and was several paces ahead of her. She wasn't looking at the sign anymore. Now she was looking at an old house that stood out from the others. It was worn down but seemed to be maintained enough to remain standing. The porch was decayed, but there were boards that appeared to have been replaced, only they were intentionally weathered and tattered to match the rest of the old appearance of the house.

By the looks of it, Naomi could tell its bones were ancient—centuries older than most houses in Pickleberry—but there were bits that didn't seem to match. A shingle that seemed intentionally loose. Windows spattered with mud and green mold as though it was meant to block out curious eyes. The new but curved boards that made up the steps leading up the porch. Even the yard seemed too intentionally maintained. The grass grew wild and free to the sides, but down the middle seemed to be sloppily whacked short to show the old stepping stones that led to the house.

Then there was to consider that most of the houses in the area were relics, fragmented structures of what used to be homes. One could look right into the rooms and see the peeling wooden walls that had been placed decades before. What was once walls no longer fit the criteria as Naomi could see the slow movement of fog passing though the crack of broken boards.

This house was sound. It had walls and a roof and a door secured with a padlock. Padlocks were meant to keep something out. Who would need to be kept out of an abandoned house?

"What do you know about this house?" she asked Ben.

"Just an old house? Unless…" He began looking around at the other houses. "This could be the Howling House," he said.

"Howling House?"

The wind moved around them. It made the leaves fly across the yard behind the barely standing fence, and the house seemed to creak and groan.

They watched the house, thinking nothing of the wind, until there was a moan—a groaning so sorrowful Naomi had to physically hold her chest. It was low and soft, lingering on the wind, but when the wind passed, it grew louder and more remorseful until it faded to nothing. Naomi swore she heard sobbing at the tail end of the howl. She pondered the padlock again. What was it meant to contain?

"You know nothing about this house?" she asked.

"It's haunted?" he guessed. "I've heard it mentioned before, and it's usually as a warning to stay away."

She stared at the house.

"Something the matter?" he asked.

"When this is all over," she started as her eyes scanned the windows and every opening of the house, "we should look into this place."

"You think something's going on?"

"I think it's worth looking into." She peered at the sky above that was starting to cloud over. "We don't have the time now." She pressed on down the street, leaving Ben to examine the house for a moment and then sprint to catch up.

"So, what? That house gave you the creeps, but none of these others do?" he asked.

"They're all devastating," she said, looking them over. "It looks like this was once a beautiful neighborhood and something happened here. A long time ago, it looks like from the architecture, but I don't feel sadness when I look at this avenue of haunted houses."

"I feel anger," Ben said with a shiver.

She nodded. "Anger and resentment. Whatever happened here, someone felt as though these people deserved it, even if others might disagree. That house…" She glanced over her shoulder as they began to put distance between themselves and the Howling House. "That house feels… it feels like a prison and I feel torment there."

"The howling was sorrowful," Ben agreed.

"You may be a touch of an empath," she told him.

"Like you?"

"I'd call myself conditioned," she said. "When you see it every day, you learn to recognize it."

"Hmm." Ben thought about this as they continued down the street.

They were quiet in their walk as the fog seemed to steal their desire to speak. The air had a chill to it and soon, it seemed like the sound of their footsteps wasn't the only thing echoing around them.

"Do you hear…?" Ben asked.

She nodded before he finished and looked past him to the houses behind him and then to the ones behind herself. "I see nothing, but I hear it," she said.

"I see shapes," he said, looking past her.

"Where?"

He nodded to a house that sat a little closer to the road than the others.

"Behind it?"

"In the windows," he said. "And the one behind it."

"Can you see how many?"

He shook his head at first, squinting. "I can't—" He quickly looked over his shoulder to the houses behind him.

"Ben?"

"There are more. They're not in the houses. They're watching us."

"Are they close?"

"Not yet," he said. "They're not moving, just watching us. I don't think they like us being here."

Naomi hunkered down a bit. "If we're lucky, we can pass through without trouble. Keep your eyes open, but don't speak unless they're coming our way. Move fast, but calmly, Ben," she said.

Ben's face went white as his eyes darted frantically to either side of the road.

Naomi patted her chest as though she remembered something. She reached into the front of her shirt and gave her medallion a gentle kiss. She removed it from her neck and turned to Ben, placing it over his head, barely stopping in her walk.

"What is this?" he asked.

"It'll protect you, but I want it back," she told him. "Just trust me and keep moving."

Ben nodded, holding the jewel in his hand.

Naomi didn't have the heart to tell him it was just a piece of metal on a smelly bit of leather that would do little against the things that stalked them. She'd hoped it would act as a placebo to get him moving and, if anything, keep his nerves steady.

They worked through the center of the dilapidated suburb, hoping the longer they traveled unbothered would mean they could make it through without conflict. Only the farther they went, the more tense Ben became.

He had his lips pursed closed, but that didn't stop the whines and whimpers from escaping from him.

"Ben," Naomi hushed him.

"They're moving," he whispered.

"Just keep moving forward."

He whined.

He started to slow down and Naomi had to grasp him by the arm, pulling him along behind her. "Their faces, their faces are so horrific," he uttered in a whisper. "Decrepit... decaying... Ghosts? No. Ghouls?" he was mumbling to himself when Naomi shushed him.

"Are they charging?" she asked.

"No, not yet, but they look angry. They're getting so close."

"Where are they exactly?"

"Both sides, they're coming from the houses." He looked about frantically again. "They're behind us as well. Oh God, their limbs are... Naomi—"

"Are they in front of us?" She stopped him.

"No. They seem to not enter the tree tunnel ahead."

"Then we get to the tree tunnel," she told him, pushing him ahead of her a bit.

Ben stumbled over his feet and fell to his knees. He was too panicked to stand and only managed to travel several more feet half crawling and half trying to stand. Only he didn't have the chance to gain much ground. The feeling of fingers, icy and thin, grasped the nape of his neck paralyzing him.

Naomi saw Ben's body fly backward, causing him to hit the ground hard, but nothing near him to cause it. She rushed to him but met something solid, something strong that knocked her back several feet and forced her to gasp to catch her breath.

There was nothing around them, but Ben's eyes still moved in a frenzy. In the fog and the creeping darkness, Naomi was beginning to see less and less of him, but his panicked face stood out.

She heard the feet encircling them. Some were shuffling, while others seemed to move quite fast but then stopped just short of her. In other moments, she heard the whooshing of things that moved unseen at lightning speed past her. Still she saw nothing but Ben.

She spread her fingers and allowed herself to feel the shadows moving and drifting around her. The shadows clung to her skin, turning it pitch black as the form of a human figure drifted away. Her face was clouded in amorphous shadow where there was once hair and the whites of her eyes bled, filling her whole eye with white. Her limbs were exaggerated, changing in length and size but more so frightening when she extended them around her. She grasped for the shadows, feeling her whole being fill the space around her and Ben and in the between, she felt things unnatural and moving.

These unnatural, unseen things, the things Ben watched frozen in terror, moved upon him but hesitated to attack. Naomi couldn't see what they looked like; she could only feel the spaces they occupied.

But Ben could see them. He could see their faces that lacked structure and features. Some had wide, toothless grins that occupied the full space of where a face would have been. Others had no mouth at all, but sockets where eyes or noses should be that were sunken deep within hollowed shapes. Some moved in jerky, hesitant motions, while others were so swift his eyes couldn't keep up.

None touched him, but they seemed interested in him, as if confused by his presence, unable to determine what he was. Ben only felt terror-filled anticipation, wondering at what moment they would break and devour him. But it never came. Before they were given a chance to risk coming close to him, he saw them being picked off one by one. One flew in one direction, two or three flew in the other. When their attention was taken from him, the circle they'd formed around him broke.

Ben met the towering shadow that had tossed the ghouls aside. It reached a hand for him and he cowered away. The fear of the monsters he'd encountered in Naomi's portal was too fresh to him. He felt grossly unprepared to take them on a second time, especially in the darkness, where they seemed to thrive.

He felt the shadow grasp his forearm and started to scream, but a voice came to him. It echoed in a manner that made it difficult for him to understand, as though he were listening to the after echoes of a rock tumbling down a well, each softer than the one before. The shadow pulled him to his feet and gave him a firm shove toward the tree tunnel.

He didn't pause to see why the shadow was helping him. He only pushed to his feet and sprinted as hard as he could until the fog cleared, the howling cries of ghouls were long behind him, and the sun seemed to return. He was several yards into the tree tunnel when he stopped. Though it was shaded by the overhanging branches, he felt as though standing in the tunnel and looking into the fog was like observing where day met night. His eyes took several moments to adjust, but he could see nothing looking into the fog. He could only hear the howls and cries that he hoped didn't belong to Naomi.

Silence fell. The last echoing cry lingered in the air and drifted into the distance. But Ben heard nothing except ringing silence in his ears.

He held his breath to listen. It made his head spin to do so and eventually, he was forced to take a breath for fear of passing out in the road. But there was nothing ahead of him. No sounds. No shifting shadows in the fog. Even the fog seemed to slowly dissipate, allowing his line of vision to go farther than a few feet ahead of him. He was stuck in the limbo of wondering if he should carry on but equally filled with dread at the idea of continuing with this mess on his own.

He considered the option of going home and forgetting about all of this, though it was unlikely he could forget. He knew going home meant living blissfully ignorant to the horrors that were about to befall Pickleberry, as it didn't seem like Pickleberry could sort out its own problems.

After what felt like an eternity of waiting, he took a final deep breath and stood upright. He wiped his sweaty hands on his pants and tucked Naomi's medallion into his shirt. He gave one last look into the fog and then through the tree tunnel and down Cowden, where their destination awaited. He walked away with the fog and the horrors of Cowden behind him.

"You're just going to leave me?"

He stopped so abruptly that he nearly fell forward, but he managed to shift his momentum enough to turn to Naomi as she limped from the fog. He hurried to meet her but didn't dare cross the line of fog. When she'd crossed over, he pulled her into an embrace.

"Ah, easy…" She winced, pushing him off and holding a hand to her side.

"Sorry." He looked her over but found no visible wound. "You're okay?"

"I'll be fine," she assured him.

"Did you kill them all?"

"God, no. After a while they started to run away, but it took a few rounds first," she said. She held his arm for support while she steadied herself. She removed her hand from her side and Ben noticed the blood.

"You should sit down," he said.

She stood upright and wiped the blood on her pants. "It's nothing." She started to walk but felt Ben pull her by the shoulders to the ground. "Stop, I'll be healed in a moment," she told him.

"Then you can sit for the moment."

She scoffed but rested instead, hanging her head between her knees. She wanted to have some quick, witty comeback but just breathed, letting her head bob and her muscles relax.

She was on her feet five minutes later, ushering Ben down the road. "I imagine when it gets dark, those ghouls have a little more freedom," she said. "We should keep moving."

Ben nodded, glancing over his shoulder into the fog.

They were less than half a mile from their destination. It was a meander down one hill, up another, and down one more where at the bottom of the hill they were met with a valley harboring the remains of a couple of homes. They didn't look to be in as bad of shape as the houses previously encountered, but they'd clearly been unoccupied for a few years at least. The first house sat away from the road but offered them nothing interesting. It was where the road came to a T that they found what they were looking for.

This home was a trailer that had been planted in concrete and with additions built on to look more like a typical home. There was a tall porch on the side they approached that overlooked the wild yard. To the left of the house was a vacant lot that reached behind the house and went farther than they could see. The house looked worn down and had obviously been empty for a long time.

In the center of the yard in front of the porch were the remains of a flowerbed, with a man-made fish pond on the other side of it. Both were overgrown and left in such disrepair nothing could thrive but frogs and weeds. A whole mess of both greeted Naomi and Ben as they walked carefully up the unsteady steps of the porch.

Ben cupped his hands to the window and looked in. "I'm a little surprised it isn't empty," he said.

"Guess no one wanted to live here," Naomi replied. She was looking through the sliding glass door into the living room and kitchen behind it. There was still furniture scattered around the place, but nothing of personal value. There were no pictures on the walls, no books on the shelves or blankets thrown over the couches.

"How long did your grandma stay here?" he asked.

Naomi tried to recall. "Until she died. I was, like, thirteen or something, I think."

"Wonder if it's locked?" Ben nodded to the door handle.

Naomi gave the glass door a pull, but it didn't budge. She disappeared suddenly and reappeared on the other side of the door, unlocking it and sliding it open for Ben. "The floor is weak, so be careful," she warned him as she headed for the kitchen.

"I'll take this side," he told her, heading to the left and down the hall toward the bedrooms.

Naomi entered the kitchen and pulled open a drawer here or there but found nothing. The cabinets were bare, along with the drawers. The kitchen sink had a constant drip but when she turned on the faucet, nothing came out. The sink was rusting and the countertops were cracked and broken. The place looked as though it hadn't been touched since before her grandma had passed away.

The living room offered even less as it held nothing but smelly, moldy couches and dirty carpet. She looked over the bare book shelves, ran her hand over the smooth walls, and examined the laminated floor, but found nothing. Or at least nothing that looked interesting. There were no hidden compartments or panels. It was just an old, sad house.

There was a crash from one of the back bedrooms and Naomi hurried to find Ben sprawled on the floor.

"What happened?" she asked.

"Remember when you said the floors were weak?" He was trying to push himself up, but his foot was stuck in the floor.

Naomi pried back the boards as he pulled his foot loose.

"I've got to stop making you save me," he said.

"You'll grow out of being a damsel in distress someday," she said. She helped him to his feet. "Does it hurt?"

"No, it's fine," he said. He had a picture in his hand: a scribbled drawing on a piece of yellowed paper. "This is all I could find. But it's just a scribble." He started to set it aside when Naomi grabbed it.

"This looks like the scribblings in the altar," she said.

"You think it's yours?"

"I don't know. Do you remember every picture you drew as a kid?" she asked.

He shrugged.

"Someone had to have left it here," she said.

"Didn't you have a brother?"

Naomi thought. "You think it was just left behind?"

"What's the alternative? Eddow was here and left a child's drawing behind?"

She frowned. "It does seem less likely," she admitted. She dropped the drawing on the ground. "I think the house is a bust."

"I saw a garage as we walked up," he said.

They left through the sliding glass door and headed toward the back of the house. There was an open gravel lot that would have been a driveway between the house and the garage, but the garage was less of a garage and more of a glorified shed. It was hand-built and in rough shape but still standing. The large doors at the front of it were chained and locked close with a combination lock.

They approached cautiously.

Ben looked the lock over while Naomi examined the doors and the sides of the building.

He lifted the lock to look at the back. "The combination is written here. Twenty, twenty-two, thirty-seven," he read aloud and continued to mumble under his breath as he put the combination in.

Naomi noticed the hooks that the lock was attached to. It sat offset from the rest of the door, as though there was something more than just welded metal underneath it. "Ben, wait!" She tried to stop him, but it was too late.

Her warning caused him to turn his face to her as he tugged on the lock to open it. Only instead of opening the whole lock, the metal underneath shifted and pulled down, revealing a mechanism that sprayed liquid. It was pointed directly at his eyes, but when he turned away it put enough distance between him and the lock that it just grazed the front of his shirt.

He stepped back enough for the rest of the liquid to fall to the ground, but when his shirt started to smolder and melt away like it was made of plastic, he began to panic.

Naomi pulled at his shirt, ripping off the sections that burned and threatened to singe his skin underneath. She tossed them to the ground and watched the smoking and curled remains of the polyester-and-cotton blend.

"Thanks," he told her.

"This lock is sitting out from the rest of the door. The combination was a ploy to trigger this," she said.

"Booby traps are a good indicator we're on the right track."

"That or an overly paranoid man."

"So, what? The lock doesn't work?"

"No, it'd be a different combination." She held her chin in thought. "Try three, nineteen, seven," she said, "but stand to the side when you do it and be ready to move."

Ben nodded. He positioned his body away from the direction of the lock as he input the combination. He pulled gently and the lock lowered again, shooting out another stream of acid, but hitting no one.

"Hmm," Naomi thought. "I wish I could remember their wedding anniversary."

"Do you think his birthday is too obvious?"

"Maybe, but I wouldn't know it anyway," she said.

"What about yours?"

She frowned. "Try eight, twenty-one, nine."

He twisted the lock from one way to the other and pulled, safely out of the way, only to have another stream of acid shoot out, but with less velocity this time. He barely pulled his hands back in time. "Was that yours?" he asked.

"My brother's."

"Give me yours," he said, ready.

"Eleven, twenty-two, nine."

Ben entered it and pulled sharply before dropping the lock, expecting another round of acid, but instead was surprised to see the lock hanging open.

Naomi wasn't sure how to feel. She'd never known her grandpa. Why would he have such an attachment to her? She removed the lock and opened the doors slowly. There were no more traps on the other side of the door. Just a mess of books, rusted tools covering a dusty workbench, and spiderwebs. Lots and lots of spiderwebs.

Ben looked a bit green.

"Don't like spiders?" she asked him.

"Most of the world doesn't like spiders," he assured her. "Don't you?"

She looked at a brown spider with a round belly that clung from the web near the door. "They're just orb weavers."

"A spider is a spider," he said.

"Ben…" She rolled her eyes. "Help me look through these boxes."

Ben moved hesitantly but began pulling boxes from the stacks along the far wall. "Do we have any idea what we're looking for?" he asked.

"Anything that sticks out, I guess. If he knew something about what happens in this town, it's a good start. So maybe anything pertaining to that," she suggested.

The answer didn't give Ben any direction and instead, he spent the next several hours searching through broken tools and long forgotten heirlooms.

Naomi became fed up with the boxes and as Ben began to look for hidden compartments in the workbench, she took to running her hands along the walls for panels or abnormalities.

After what felt like a full day of searching, they came up empty.

"I'm starting to think your grandpa didn't know anything. Maybe we should regroup?" Ben asked.

"How?"

"I don't know. Brainstorm a bunch of questions to ask the doll? We could sit there for a while, but there are only so many things you can find out from it, right?"

"Do we have that kind of time to waste?"

"We're looking through boxes of old clothes and rusty tools and… and junk? Do you think we're using our time wisely right now?" he asked.

Naomi sighed heavily. She searched her mind, thinking of all the structures on the property, but her memory of the place was cloudy. "There's the house, this garage… Grandma used to have a garden, but we saw what happened to that. Where else would there be—?" She stopped suddenly.

"What?"

Without speaking, she left the garage with Ben on her heels. She went around the corner of the garage, which overlooked about an acre of open field. In the middle of the field was a small shack that didn't even look large enough to house an adult.

"That?" Ben asked.

"The well house. It's the only place left. Unless you have a better idea?"

He looked back to the garage, thinking of all the untouched boxes and spiders, and shook his head.

They started for the well house, climbing a rickety fence and crossing the open field. The sun was starting to near the horizon now, making it partially visible through the trees. The dimming light added an eerie effect to the well house, which looked to be held together with rotten wood and duct tape. It seemed to sway and rock in the subtle wind.

When Naomi pulled the door open, it fell off the hinges. She exchanged looks with Ben, who then ducked low to look in.

"Wait," she told him. "If the garage was rigged and we found nothing, this will more than likely be rigged."

He nodded.

She dug in her pocket for a flashlight and shone it into the darkness of the damp and moldy well house. There was a steady drip from one of the pipes that ran above the main structure of the well. The corners were full of cobwebs and spiders unseen, but she couldn't see anything obvious.

"No tripwires, mechanisms, or anything," she said.

"No more acid?"

"Doesn't appear to be any." She pocketed the light. "Doesn't mean it's completely clear, though. Maybe I should go this time?"

Ben gestured for her to lead the way.

Naomi dipped low, looking around the corners of the entrance and seeing nothing. She crawled through the entrance, careful to not touch the sides, and looked around closer. When she was inside, she noticed padding that ran along the edge of the opening. Attached to the padding was wiring that led to a device pressed against the entrance wall. She looked closer and saw on the top edge of the opening a line of small nozzles that pointed downward.

"Looks like we could have caught an acid shower or something," she said.

Ben didn't move his head past the opening but looked in.

Naomi pulled the wires from the device that had a small light on the top. When she removed the wires, the light went off. She tentatively touched the padding, waiting for something to happen, but nothing came.

"Doesn't seem like enough room for two in there," Ben said.

"Lucky for you," she said. "Keep your eyes open for anything I can't see."

Naomi ran her hands over the walls and crevices. She searched around the pipes and even destroyed spiderwebs looking for something, anything, but she came up empty. She shuffled around, her legs tucked underneath her and her head hunched forward, trying to examine every inch of the small area until she ended up in the same spot she'd started in.

She sighed deeply, wiping her dirty hands on her pants. "Maybe this is a dead lead," she said.

Ben stood up straight, resting his hand on the roof of the well house and looking around desperately. There was a tree line ahead of him. Not part of Black Bile, but just a small cluster of trees that created the property lines in the area. It stretched to his left and followed up to the road where they'd come from. To the right of his vision, he saw the rest of the broken fence that ran parallel to the road. Across the road was an old trailer that he hoped was empty based on appearances alone, and to the left of that was an ancient house. It was no more than a structure now that reminded him of the houses they'd passed farther up Cowden, where the ghouls had attacked. Only it didn't look to be inhabited by monsters. It just looked old and abandoned.

"Wait," he heard Naomi say from within. He ducked low, looking in the well house to see her pulling back the dirt under one of the pipes. The dirt was wet and soggy as it was directly underneath the dripping pipe. There was something the same tone of dark brown as the dirt that covered it a few inches deep. As she dug away, she found the corners and revealed a cigar box. She had to dig out the sides, dirt encrusting under her nails as she did, until finally the box came free enough to remove fully from the dirt. She slumped back in the effort to pull it and handed it directly to Ben.

He stepped back, box in hand, to give her space to crawl out and once she was free, he lowered himself next to her.

Naomi wiped the packed dirt from her hands to her pants as Ben removed the caked mud from the edges of the box to open it. When he finally got it clean enough to open, they found only damp letters in which the ink had bled.

Naomi continued to wipe her hands on her pants as Ben thumbed through the letters.

Each was a sealed envelope that seemed delicate in his hands, but all had the same word written on the envelope. "They're all for you," he said.

37

Naomi fell back on her haunches as she read the letter that was on the top of the pile. It seemed to be the most recent of the bunch and the thinnest, but the only letter without her name on it. Inside was a single page of scribblings that simply said:

"If you've made it this far, you'd be glad to know that you don't have further to go. I can't say what you are seeking here, but I can say you won't find it on this property.

"Sharing secrets can help lessen the load. So if you're looking for the secrets of Chuck Campbell you'll have to look outside of your tunnel of vision to find it.

"Because even those who come from dirt can be more valuable than the most precious of gems."

"Is that a riddle?" Ben asked.

"A poor attempt." She looked at the writing on the envelope and the others in the box and Ben's hands. "This writing is different," she said. "My grandpa didn't write this one. I think it's implying someone else helped him."

"You wouldn't happen to know any old family friends, would you?"

"Off the top of my head?" She shook her head, then looked back at the letter. "'*Even those who come from dirt…*' What do you suppose that means? The earth?" she asked.

"Or poverty? *Dirt poor?*" he suggested. His eyes moved to the old house across the road. "Look out of our tunnel of vision, we haven't got much further to go… Do you think a house like that always looked so disheveled?"

Naomi looked in the direction he was staring and had to stand to get a better look at it. "No windows or doors or driveway," she said. "I don't imagine so."

"Wouldn't hurt to look," Ben said.

She nodded.

They followed Cowden Street, walking alongside the Campbell property for less than a stone's throw from where they'd been sitting in the mud. The house seemed to grow in height as they approached it, or maybe that was just the feeling they got with the sun fading and the darkness seeping into the corners of the open and exposed house. There was no glass in the windows. There was no front door or porch leading to it. The house seemed as though it had been planted there, incomplete and out of place. But it was lived in. There were worn marks in the wood of the front door where it likely saw most of the traffic, but for the most part it was like someone had started to build the house and then given up halfway through.

Ben allowed Naomi to approach first as she had the better sight in the dark. Even with her flashlight, he felt blind looking through the opening where window panes would have been.

Naomi held tight to the door frame as she leaned in, looking. There was a general sense of uneasiness in the place. Even with all she'd faced in her work, this seemingly empty place gave her the creeps.

"It's overwhelmingly sad," Ben commented.

"You feel it too?"

"It's covering the walls like cheap wallpaper."

"Whoever lived here didn't live well. The floors are weak all over. Step lightly," she warned.

She looked to the open area that could have been a kitchen or a living room, but the lack of plumbing made it difficult to say. Directly in front of her was a set of very narrow stairs leading to the top floor. Looking up, she saw the rotten and weak wood that supported the upstairs.

"Maybe avoid the upstairs for now," she said. She stepped inside with Ben close behind. There were no cabinets over the countertops but a few cabinets below them. There was no sink or stove, but on the floor were outlines of where a large stove might have been. She looked into the cabinets, reaching and letting her fingers feel the wood. She knocked lightly, listening for hollow spots where she expected solid and solid spots where there should be nothing.

Ben kept his hands to himself. He ran his flashlight over every inch of the home as though he expected the light to find something for him. He was uneasy here and it was starting to make him queasy. He found himself leaning heavily on the walls as he searched.

"Are you okay?" Naomi asked.

He waved her off but before he could speak, they heard rustling from upstairs.

Ben shone his light up the stairs. "Could be a rat," he said.

"Could be another ghoul."

"More likely a rat."

"I should go first." She stepped on the first step and it dipped under her weight, threatening to break. "One at a time and step to the sides," she told him.

Ben followed her up the stairs, taking his time to test their strength. At the top, he found Naomi standing in the middle of the room, her hands out as though she were balancing on a high wire.

"Stay to the wall, it's weaker in the middle," she said. She moved slowly to the far wall, feeling for compartments or hollow spots. The rest of the room was empty and left little for her to search.

Ben pressed a hand against the wall to steady himself. The queasiness in his stomach was getting worse and standing at the top of the stairs didn't help. The wood where his hand sat started to give under his weight. As he expected to fall in through the wall, he instead felt the floor go out from under him. He tumbled to the ground, landing in the middle of the room, not moving.

Naomi turned sharply but didn't move. "Are you okay?" she asked. "Move slowly."

He shifted his weight, trying to lie on his back, but found his foot stuck. "Yeah, yeah, I'm okay." He looked at his foot. "I think I'm stuck, though."

Naomi moved around the edge of the room to his foot and helped him remove it from the split boards.

"At least I'm good at finding the weak spots," he said, but she didn't respond.

"There's something under here." She pulled the boards back and reached into the hole. She removed a leatherbound book tied shut with a strap and handed it to Ben. She returned to the hole before he could respond and removed another item from its depths. It had a charcoal cover with black lettering and without a second look, Naomi handed it to Ben.

"Is that... is this?" His hands trembled.

"I got your book back," she said.

"I can't believe it! There are, like, less than a handful of these in the world."

Naomi saw tears in the corners of his eyes but didn't spend long focusing on it. "There is something else in here," she said, reaching into the hole. She bent low, stretching farther with the wood nearly reaching her shoulder.

Ben opened the book and flipped through the pages. They were filled with handwritten notes and drawings in the margins, many of which were nearly identical to the notes he'd made in his own copy. He felt his chest swell and had to take a moment to prevent himself from crying. He looked back to Naomi to express his gratitude, only to find his feelings of bliss quickly vanquished.

In the last rays of golden daylight, he saw the movement in the window above Naomi's head. He wasn't given a chance to warn her as the sight of red, glowing eyes stole his ability to speak.

The gasp that escaped his mouth was enough to get her attention and when she turned to the window, she was met by a creature leaping toward them, taloned hands outstretched. Her feet met its chest as she kicked it overhead, where it rolled across the splintering floor, landing in the beam of Ben's flashlight.

"What the fuck is that?!" Ben exclaimed. He clutched the books to his chest and crawled backward from the snarling and sniveling creature that was attempting to recover from the hard landing.

Its skin was blotched red and black, and it looked sticky. It exuded an odor of burning flesh and rotten carcasses, and it moved in quick, flashing movements as though they were snapshots in a flipbook. Its face morphed from small, no indication of anything but red eyes, to a gaping hole of nothing but jagged teeth pointing in every direction. When it moved back to its feet, it twisted as though its body operated on two separate planes. The top half twisted completely around, followed by the bottom half, until it was crouching to the ground like a puma ready to pounce.

Its body pulled back to spring forward, but as it became airborne there was a crack of thunder next to Ben's right ear. He cowered down, thinking he'd been struck by lightning, and felt a splintering, stabbing pain in his ear. When he opened his eyes again there was no monster, just the illuminated outline of where it had been and a pile of ash on the floor.

He looked to Naomi, who held a smoldering pistol outstretched. It was old, something that would have been used in nineteenth-century southern Arizona. The barrel was steel, but the handle was black painted-wood with sigils carved into it, from what he could see around Naomi's hand. He wanted to admire her find, but the pain in his ear caused his head to feel as though it were splitting.

"Move!" she yelled. There were two more monsters crawling through the windows, but with the ringing in his ears, he hadn't noticed them.

Naomi raised the gun to fire at one monster, but it moved too quickly and she lost it in the motion. The other climbed to the ceiling above before dropping on top of them. Naomi lost the gun during this, her hands busy with wrestling the monster away from Ben.

While they struggled, the other monster drew its attention to Ben and charged him. Ben managed to roll out the way, but the monster turned so quickly it was nearly on top of him. It gnashed its serrated teeth, but it was soon ripped away by a developing shadow before it had the chance to reach him.

Naomi could barely stand when she flung the monster from Ben and to the opposite wall. It struck the wall so hard the whole house shook. The floor creaked under her feet, but it supported her enough for her to focus energy into her tattoos that shifted from her upper arms to her knuckles, forming a black blade. She moved quickly, but the monster was faster as it was in front of her one moment and then on the ceiling the next. It reared back, building up momentum before leaping for her with such power they collided and fell through the floor.

Naomi took the worst of the fall, feeling wood stab into her back, limiting her movement. She managed to roll to her front and was attempting to crawl away when she felt claws dig into her back. They were in her shoulders and in the meat of her back, digging deeper and deeper by the second. The weight of the creature made it impossible for her to move.

It was reaching one bloody claw over its head to strike a deathblow when Ben fired the pistol from the top of the stairs. The monster was struck by lightning and faded to nothing, raining ash over Naomi's motionless body.

Ben hurried down the stairs so quickly he didn't pay attention to the weak steps and tumbled down them, managing to catch himself enough to land next to her. He pulled her body into his lap.

"There's… there's… more…" she gasped. Her breathing gurgled as blood filled her punctured lungs.

"No, no, they're gone." He had both of the books and the pistol on the ground next to him and was trying to keep her awake. "What do I do? Naomi? Tell me what to do," he pleaded, looking at her broken body.

The pendant dangled from his neck and in her direct line of view. It shook with his cries. But a smile began to form over her lips. She reached for it, but her breath stopped before she could touch it and she fell motionless.

"No, no!" He shook her body. "No, no, Naomi. No, goddammit, no," he sobbed. He panicked, looking around for something—anything—to help, but he only had one thought. He pushed the sleeve of his shirt back and bit hard into his wrist. He bit and tore at it, shredding the skin until he managed enough of a flow of blood to hold over her mouth. He let it fill her mouth, but it only dribbled out at the corners and down her chin.

Defeated, he pressed his forehead to hers and wept.

38

The Black Bile Woods were still. In the silence, the air hung heavy. Even on a usual night there was an unsettling feeling to the woods. This was a natural self-defense in a way, as the eerie aura tended to keep the people out while the unnaturals in the town thrived on the strangeness. But on this night all things, all monsters and ghouls and witches and werecats and wolves and cryptids, were hushed. They were silent and tucked away in corners and burrows, hidden, for at the very center of the woods stood something far more fearsome than themselves.

He'd been there before, seemingly decades ago. He hadn't taken the time to observe the woods then. He'd been in Black Bile on a mission with a beloved and his attention was on that alone. Now he allowed himself to really take in the forest: the dim, dark shadows. The dull, musty odor that threatened to offend his nose. And the utter quietness that would drive a sane man mad.

He appeared to blend in with the trees that surrounded him. Here in the woods, he had no reason to wear a mask. He could be himself, for there were none to look upon him. And any who might glance upon him would only see a strange tree, tall, gnarled, and decaying.

But he liked the woods. He liked blending in without feeling like he was lost in the crowd. If there was one thing he adored, it was the attraction he drew. And even here, the snakes that hid under brush and timber watched him closely.

Something moved. He could hear four feet over the ground churning up the dirt, then the shaking of trees as the thing jumped from tree to tree. When the thing appeared in front of him, it leaped from the trees and landed heavily, leaving a crater in its wake. It took some coordination and balance, but the thing moved to two feet and walked hunched forward with heavy, staggering footfalls.

"My child," he cooed. "My love, my gift, my beauty, and my prize. Such devotion you have shown me." His smile grew wide in adoration. "Only one left?" he asked, looking at his child.

"The others have fallen," it hissed, but no motion was made on its face, just the widening and narrowing of red eyes. "She has found it." It was unable to stand still, keeping its hands or body in constant motion as though the motion helped it maintain balance. "She called upon thunder and lightning and we fell as stars die."

He didn't speak. He simply watched the creature move and shake. "I have always loved these woods," he said finally. He looked out through the small clearing in which he stood and let his eyes land upon a fallen and burnt tree trunk. "I think I'll burn them down one day. It has become polluted." He nodded. "Like this town." He looked at the creature.

"And your protégé?"

"I am afraid Naomi has forgotten what it means to love." A waft of sadness came over his dark and gnarled face. "If I can't remind her, well…" He trailed off, lingering in the thought of his own statement. "If she has her grandfather's toy, we haven't much time, have we?"

"Will you call upon the legion?"

"No, I must collect a gift first. An army needs a general," he said and smirked.

The dark had fully settled around them. The only light visible came from the flashlight that had been forgotten upstairs. It offered enough light for Ben to make out the vague features of Naomi's face, but his eyes were too cloudy to really see anything. He'd been holding her body long enough for his legs to go numb, but he ignored the pins and needles. He ignored the excruciating pain in his ear and the blood that had tricked down his jaw and dried on his neck. None of it mattered because now he had no idea how to save the town and the only person who could help him had just died saving his life yet again.

Ben removed the medallion from his neck and put it over hers. He didn't understand the importance of it, only that she'd wanted it back. As he smoothed it over her chest, he felt the gut-wrenching sorrow return and once more began to sob over her body.

There was a sound that stopped his sobbing, a faint buzzing in a rhythmic pattern. He realized that it was coming from her pocket. By some miracle, he was able to locate the noise in the void of her pocket only to find her phone lit up with a call from a private number.

He swallowed hard and answered it without a second thought. "Hello?"

"Oh? Is this a new lover? I wonder if you taste better than the last one," said the woman.

"Who is this?"

"Oh! Oh, oh, oh, this is the blood bag. The pet. Dear boy, why are you answering your master's private phone?"

Ben swallowed hard. Even if he didn't know who the woman was, he knew where she was from. As he tried to form words, he found them caught in his throat. "She's… she's dead," he managed.

"Excuse me?"

Ben sobbed.

"For Christ sake. I'm going to have to put pants on for this, aren't I?"

Ben let the phone slip from his hand as he was overcome with emotion again.

The phone went blank as the call ended.

Ben stared at it, cradling Naomi's head under his chin. "Who would I call? Who would help?" he whimpered. He thought through all of the people he knew and all of the people he'd met. "Beasley!" he gasped. "Beasley, Beasley," he murmured, reaching for the phone, but when he had it in his fingers, a voice caused him to jump and drop it.

"I have no doubt the good deputy could give you a hand with the body, but maybe I would be a little more useful," said the man in the doorway.

He was a tall shadow of a man and when he stepped closer, Ben could make out a beard and a ponytail that led him to recall Rik from their dramatic meeting in The Den.

"I'm not sure you can do anything good," he said through sniffles.

"She's a pain in the ass, but she's also an asset I would not like to replace," he commented. "Unless you think you're better off drowning her with your blood and reviving her with your tears?"

Ben shook his head.

"Good, because you're looking a little white and we will need that blood," he said. He stepped forward, allowing Ben to get a better look at him despite the darkness. He pulled a black case from the inner pocket of his jacket and knelt next to Naomi's body. He gestured for Ben to lay her out on the ground as he unzipped the case and pulled out a very large syringe and a small bottle of clear liquid.

"What is that? Some kind of elixir?" Ben asked.

"Adrenaline. It works on the strange and boring alike," he said, filling the syringe. "No offense," he added but hardly meant it. "What an utter disappointment she has been." He sighed.

"Why bother to save her, then?"

"And how many shadow-bending hybrids do you know?" he asked. "A rare commodity is one you don't want to lose. That's just good business. Besides, I am contractually obligated to keep her alive." He gave a heavy sigh, as though it pained him to admit Naomi's value. "Life is a series of doorways, boy. Individually and collectively. And at the end of it all, there is only one doorway we have to worry about. Don't you think a door like that would require a special key?"

Ben didn't speak. He didn't know what to say and held his head in thought.

"Either way..." He paused, tapping the bubbles from the syringe and looking longingly at Ben.

"What?"

"My payment."

"Oh, I—I don't—" Ben looked about.

Rik reached over Naomi's body, grabbing Ben's wrist, and ran his tongue over the wound that still bled openly. His eyes fluttered a bit and he sighed heavily. "I've always loved a good AB, but I absolutely adore an AB+. AB is like a cold, refreshing drink when lost in the desert. AB+ is that plus a garnish of lemon."

Ben pulled his arm back, mildly disturbed.

Rik chuckled and raised the syringe over his head before plunging it into Naomi's chest hard and injecting the contents.

It was barely a minute later when Naomi's body tensed so suddenly it shot her up several feet before she fell back to the floor with a loud thud. She gasped and wheezed, choking on the blood in her throat.

Ben helped her to sit upright.

"Make sure she feeds," Rik said, putting the supplies away. "She'll resist, but she must. She'll be so ravenous she stands a good chance of killing you. So be careful, I suppose." He put the case in his jacket and stood, dusting off his suit.

"F-f-fu… fuck… y… yo…"

"Oh, you're welcome, my dear Mrs. Novak." He grinned. "If I could make a suggestion? If your intentions are to save this town, you would do it much better at full strength. Allowing your tank to run to empty and then being rescued is not setting yourself up for success. And for the sake of everyone in this town and my investments, success is very much desired," he said.

Naomi was still catching her breath but had thoughts forming quickly.

"Why can't you do it?" Ben asked.

"Pardon?"

"You're so concerned with the town and your investment, but you've done little to nothing to save it."

"Oh, did Mommy and Daddy do all your homework in school?"

Ben didn't speak.

"This is far more Naomi's problem than anyone else's, and I really despise cleaning up after others. However," he began with a sigh, "with that being said, The Den stands ready for whatever trouble you two unearth. I did show up and revive her, didn't I? We are nothing if not good to our employees." He grinned again.

Naomi tried to spit, but it lacked luster.

"Charming," he said. "Ensure she feeds and for fuck's sake, don't go back down Cowden. Any idiot in this town will tell you that is a bad idea." He rolled his eyes and strolled off, disappearing into the night.

Naomi pushed herself from Ben's arms. She felt as though she were clinging to life by a thread and wished that instead of mending that connection, they would have just severed it. Her back was still full of punctures and the pain it caused was nearly unbearable, but she felt less useless on the ground that she did in Ben's hold. Despite her wishes, a bit of Ben's blood had made it down her throat. It wasn't enough to help her recover from the attack, but it was enough to give her a taste and now she fought the cravings.

"Here." He offered his wrist to her, but she wouldn't even risk a glance. "Naomi, you have to."

She shoved him away, but it did little as she was still very weak.

"Okay, look at it this way. I'm already bleeding and if you don't drink it, I'll just bleed all over the floor," he said. He pushed his wrist toward her again.

Her skin was turning black around her eyes and the corners of her mouth. When she caught the scent of his blood, her eyes became white and before he had a moment to realize it, she was latched to his arm. Her eyes were wide and wild as she fed and it wasn't until Ben was unable to sit upright that they finally became normal. When she grasped enough of herself to realize Ben wasn't looking good, it was nearly too late.

He slumped over, his eyes dazed and glazed over, as Naomi pulled his face into her hands.

"Hey, hey," she said, giving him light taps to the cheeks. "Are you okay?"

His head lolled a bit, but he formed weak sentences. "Yeah, yeah… I'm good…" he managed, but when he made the effort to sit up, he only slipped back to the floor.

Naomi gathered the books and the gun, tucking them into her pockets. She didn't bother with the flashlight left on the upper level, and she pulled Ben to his feet. He swayed before her, but before he could tumble over, she ducked low, putting her shoulder in his midsection, and lifted him from the ground.

She carried him from the house and teleported before reaching the street. Where her feet meant to touch the pavement of Cowden instead, they touched the pavement of Bradly, just in front of Ben's home. The street was dead, as she expected, and though there was a light on in the café, no one stood in the window to watch them appear. She looked to his house, teleporting from the street into his bedroom. They landed silently despite the busy noises from outside his room. She lowered him to the bed and removed his shoes, forcing him to get comfortable.

"Are you mad at me?" Ben asked. He'd noticed she was tense and wordless. Though it wasn't abnormal for Naomi, there was a distance that appeared between the two.

"Of course not," she answered, pulling his blankets over him.

He pushed them away. "Yes, you are," he said. "I had to let you feed. There was no other option."

"Ben, it's fine. You know I never wanted to do that, but I understand. Just lie down and rest. when everyone goes to sleep,

I'll get you something to eat," she told him. She pushed him down, but he mustered his strength to sit upright again.

"No, you're hiding something. What's wrong? You have to tell me. I just gave you, like, eighty percent of my blood, and I think I'm deaf in my right ear."

She sat on the bed near his feet and sighed. "You should've let me die. If I'd died, I wouldn't have any reason to be in this mess."

"Isn't that a little selfish?"

She shrugged. "It's terribly depressing, I know," she admitted. "But my contracts, my obligations to The Den, my family, all of it… None of it would matter if I was dead and if I died in a fight or by some other means not of my own, then fine. What else could I do? I went out fighting, obeying and doing what I was told. That'd be it. The end of it all."

Ben leaned forward as much as he could manage before feeling woozy. "Between the two of us, you're the only one who has even an inkling of ability to save this stupid little town. And I know your relationship with your family is complicated and you don't really have any ties here, but I do. I love my family very much and if I just gave up, knowing the end is on the horizon, I… Well, I don't think I'd be able to live with myself," he said.

"I have no right to convince someone like you that life is worth living, though you know taking it yourself isn't the choice. But Naomi, your life matters to me. It matters beyond keeping my family alive. And I know you don't want to hear that and have the guilt of my attachment on your conscience, so if it makes you feel better, just stay alive until we can save this stupid town. All right? Anything after that is between you and your own guilt because you know I'd never want you to go."

She didn't look at him.

"Hey," he prodded her.

She turned her glistening eyes his way.

"You can't die until the town is saved, got it? Simple as that. All right?"

She nodded and pushed him back to his pillow. "Get some rest," she told him.

39

"You know, I think if you had a hobby you'd be less stressed," she told him.

Jamie had been sitting at her desk watching Glenn reluctantly and slowly remove each picture and note from his evidence board and place them into a white box. She was relaxed, enjoying a cup of chocolate pudding that she'd packed for lunch, her legs resting on her desk.

"You don't think the stress has anything to do with my line of work?" he asked, not bothering to look at her as his eyes were still on the photo of Skye Gibson.

"We have the same job, Beasley. I'm not nearly as stressed out as you are."

Glenn gave her a scowl.

She shrugged. "What? It's true, and do you know why?"

"You let me do all the work?" He went back to the evidence board, pulling the last notes from it and tucking them into the box.

"That is presumptuous," she said.

"Your word-a-day calendar seems to be paying off."

"I know, right? But no! I have a hobby. Do you know what helps me to relax?"

"Sleeping at your desk?"

"Bird watching!"

He feigned an interested smile and nodded.

"I've got a whole mess of bird feeders going, and I see the most interesting birds in my back yard. Did you know I saw a gray catbird the other day? I didn't even know we had any in this region. And he came right up to my window. He was so curious and alert and adorable even if he did poop on my patio furniture." Her face was animated as she recalled meeting the bird, and Glenn could only fake so much interest before tuning her out.

"And you know what? Bird watching has changed me. It helps me relax and unwind. More than that, it's made me more social. I've gotten into collecting little bird figurines. I've got a list goin' of birds I've seen and then I like to collect the figurines. I haven't found the catbird yet, but there is this man I met who seems to be quite the collector himself, who offered to help me out. And just like, that I'm making friends and connections all because of birds!"

"Fascinating." Glenn sighed.

"I'm just saying, if you put effort into a hobby maybe you'd meet someone. Make some friends and be less stressed about the nonsense that goes on in this town." She licked her spoon and turned her attention back to her pudding, not catching his glare.

"*Nonsense?*" he asked. "People have died!"

"No need to get defensive. People die, Beasley."

"And you're supposed to care because it's your job. You know, I've bitten my tongue for a while now, but why are you even here? I know there aren't many jobs in this town, but receptionists at LMH would probably pay about the same as here and you would actually get to sit around all day. Why are you even in this job if you don't want to help people?" he demanded.

"There are less than five thousand people in this town," she retorted. "How many problems can they actually have?"

"Well, six of them were murdered in less than a month, for starters."

She shrugged.

Glenn wanted to smack his head against the evidence box in front of him. Instead, he shoved the lid down harder with a growl. "Go home, Jamie. Take some time off and think about what you're doing here and if you can come up with an answer that involves any of your actual job requirements, maybe you'll keep your job," he told her.

"Are you firing me? You can't fire me," she said.

"I'm telling you to go home and consider how important this job is to you. Maybe time away will be good for you. Take the rest of the week and get back to me," he insisted. "Until then, I don't want to see you back in the station." He lifted the box from his desk and went to the storage room to tuck it away. When he returned, she'd gone, leaving her nearly finished pudding sitting on the top of her desk next to her badge and gun.

When Ben opened his eyes, he watched the blades of the ceiling fan rotate slowly. His head hurt and his throat was dry. The discomfort, paired with the slowly rotating fan blade, made him feel as though he'd escaped from some kind of medical experiment and was waiting to see the after effects.

When he turned his head to the nightstand, he found two bottles of water along with a sleeve of crackers, a power bar, and an orange. There was even a bottle of ibuprofen waiting for him on the occasion he needed it. He thought for a moment that his mother had seen him a mess and left him the care package but when he heard the creaking of his office chair, he remembered who had put him to bed the night before. He managed to raise his head just enough to make eye contact with her. Her hair was pushed behind her ears, her feet were pulled underneath her in the chair, and the leather-bound notebook lay open in her hands.

"How do you feel?" she asked.

"My ear is ringing still. It feels like my body spent the whole night refilling itself with blood," he said. He had to roll to his side to push it upright.

"Not exactly sure that's how it works, but I get it." She nodded.

Ben took the water from his night stand and struggled a bit to open it. When he had, he took only a sip before leaning back to press his back against his headboard. "Anything good?" he asked, nodding to the book in her hands. He had the palm of his hand pressed against his ear and rubbed it in a circular motion, trying to keep the concern off his face.

She looked it over. "My grandpa was an avid note taker," she said. "And he was also Pickleberry's resident monster hunter, it seems."

"Huh," he said, thinking aloud. "Wonder if he was elected?"

"I don't think anyone knew about it. From the looks of it, he tried to keep it that way. There is a lot in this journal you'd love to learn."

"Maybe when my head isn't spinning."

Naomi closed the book. "I'm sorry."

"For?"

"I should've stopped sooner. You wouldn't be in such bad shape if I'd stopped."

"Don't—don't worry about it," he said.

"I left the book for you," she said, looking at the charcoal book. "I can't even bring myself to look at it."

Ben sat forward, looking at the book. "I can do it."

She tossed it over his bed and looked back to the journal.

"Your grandpa knew a lot," Ben said.

"He knew more than both of us do," she agreed. "He had a run in with the, or rather a, zealot too, at the same altar."

"And?"

"He knew as much as we did. He couldn't destroy it either, but when he started researching into it and Eddow, things were a little sparse. I thought maybe he just kept his notes in the book, but then it stops. Just like that, like mid thought," she said.

"That can't be good."

"When I look at the dates, they're all around that time I was born, and then he died shortly after that."

"You think Eddow caught on?"

"I think he had a reason to be nervous; otherwise, what would one human be to him? Compared to everything else in this town, or even this world. What is one human who knows too much but really is nothing special?" she asked.

"You think he was onto something?"

"I think we found it." She looked at the desk where the gun she'd used to kill the demons the night before sat.

"A demon-killing gun," Ben said.

"'*Like the mighty gods of old, this pistol calls upon lightning and thunder to strike down enemies,*'" she read from the journal.

"Some kind of legendary tale out of mythology. What did he call it?"

"It doesn't have a name."

"All the good demon-killing weapons have a name: Legend, The Legend, Legendary, Lendario," he pondered.

"There are other words, like thunder and lightning." She read the passage again. "Stormfront?"

"As a Jew, I can't endorse that name."

Naomi thought and when she realized what he'd meant, she dismissed the name with a scrunched nose.

"The gun is covered in markings. The gun isn't the storm, but it controls it, directs it?" Ben said.

"Stormrider," she said.

"Stormrider," he repeated thoughtfully. "Yeah, it fits."

She nodded, looking at the gun again. "There's only one problem," she said. "There are no more bullets."

"I imagine something like this doesn't take anything we can buy," he said.

"*'My devotion to understanding this demon goes beyond how to manage it. The only way I can manage it is to kill it and the only way to kill it lies in two parts. First, the conductor and the power. The gun, the pistol I've crafted and inscribed with power is useless without ammunition of equal power. And the means to power the weapon is something I will take to my grave,'*" Naomi read. "He doesn't write more about it and if he even intended to, he just stops. Unless there is something in the book, we have nothing to go on."

Ben began to thumb through the book but stopped suddenly. "What if he meant it literally?"

She looked at him, confused.

"What if he took it to his grave? Where was he buried?" he asked.

"The old cemetery, like everyone else."

"I know this sounds crazy, but what if—"

"He had it buried with him?"

He shrugged. "It would mean desecrating a grave to get it, and few people would do that. There aren't many grave robbers nowadays."

Naomi thought about it. She didn't want to jump to digging up family members, but if she'd died and needed to hide something, she might do the same. She looked the journal back over, wondering if there was some other clue. "I suppose it wouldn't be completely asinine to do that," she said. "But what if we're wrong?"

"Your grandpa sent us on a chase for a box of letters, a couple of books, and a gun. Why is this so crazy?"

She agreed but hesitated. "Let's let the idea simmer. You rest, and we'll read through the rest of these. Maybe there is more to learn."

Ben opened the book. It was strange having it back in his grasp. Though it was identical to his own copy of the book, it still felt foreign. And the notes scribbled in the margins and on scraps of paper didn't help. Though the handwriting was different, many of the notes were similar to what he remembered in his own copy. However, there was a point in his own copy of the book where he'd stopped because the combination of his over analyzing every page and researching never reached past that point.

That was where he opened the book first. Even with all of the notes from Naomi's grandpa, he figured he knew all he needed to know from the first half of the book. And he was right. In the second half, there were chapters devoted to Eddow's intentions, conclusions drawn by what researchers could understand about him. But when Ben read past what was written in the book, he found that Naomi's grandpa had theories of his own.

He found many of them far more likely than those printed in the book. But as he read further, he felt the hairs on his neck stand on end and any weakness left his body as he was suddenly alert and awake.

"Naomi?"

She lifted her head from the journal.

"I think your grandpa might have been onto something for us." He leaned forward, speed reading through the book but trying to condense what he was reading.

"What? What is it?"

"Your grandpa thinks because of Eddow's dislike for hell, but his superiority to others, he would want to create his own version of hell. He says he would have a loyal following, but he would have to have a means of summoning them. And vessels?"

"The hearts," Naomi said.

"When he summons his following, he would be unstoppable," he said.

"So he has the hearts and the place. No one would suspect a quiet place like Pickleberry. What is he waiting for?"

"He seems to think that Eddow is missing something. He needs something to help him summon his... his army? But this doesn't really make sense. It says he needs a person who walks both worlds." Ben frowned at the book for a long moment before his eyes opened wide.

"What?" she asked.

He held a note stuck to the page. It had her name on it.

She swallowed. "In his journal, he talks about seeing him for the first time. He saw his true form and when he saw Eddow, he was standing over me as an infant. He talks about protecting me, but I thought it was just for the sake of protecting my family or a baby," she said.

"Apparently not."

"But that doesn't make sense. If Eddow was the one who brought me to the woods to be made, why didn't he use me then?"

"Maybe you had to be made before he could?" he asked.

"Then why doesn't he use me now? I've been working for years, and he could've come at any time."

Ben shook his head. "Maybe you needed to come to him or maybe he wasn't done collecting. I don't know, but it fits. You kind of walk on both sides. Once human and now…" He hesitated. "Not," he said. "Maybe you know enough to use the doll now?"

Naomi closed the journal. She tucked her hand into the pocket of her jacket that hung from the back of her chair. She pulled out the tiny yarn doll and looked at it. "Any suggestions?" she asked.

"Ask who Eddow is looking for."

"Doll," she said. "Can you show me who Eddow is looking for?"

She stared at the doll and then the blank space on Ben's wall next to the window, waiting for the vision to come. "Nothing."

"It's not a crystal ball," he said. "It can only show you your memories, even if you don't remember them. You have to center the questions around you."

She nodded and thought about it. "Doll, will you show me when I met Eddow?"

The room went white, and she found herself staring at a high ceiling with florescent lighting. She felt warmth and comfort, as though her whole body were embraced, and when she looked to the faces that were gazing upon her, she realized she was an infant snuggled in her mother's hold. From behind her mother, she saw a face she couldn't quite make out as her vision was blurred and the memory was foggy. But she recognized her mother and her father. This person wasn't her grandma or grandpa, but whoever they were, they were very interested in Naomi.

She blinked and found herself staring at Ben's wall.

"Well?"

"Grandpa was right," she said. "Eddow has been interested in me since I was a baby."

Ben sighed.

"Doll," she said. "Show me when I left Pickleberry."

She was sitting in a car, the warm sun on her face and the wind blowing in through the windows, causing her hair to fly around her face. A hand was holding hers. It was warm and callused, yet gentle. She wore a thin silver band on her ring finger and a smile on her face, but when she looked to whoever was holding her hand, she only found herself looking at the wall yet again.

"Well?" Ben said.

Naomi didn't move. She was grasping for the warmth on her face and the gentle touch, like she'd been pulled too soon from a dream and was determined to return.

"Naomi?"

She shook her head, looking at him, a bit flustered. "There are holes in my memories."

"I wonder how much of your life he has tinkered with?" he asked.

"It's hard to say anymore. I barely remember much before The Den. I know I had a family... have a family, I mean. But the details are foggy." She looked at the doll once again. "Doll, show me everything," she said.

"That's a bit broad," Ben said.

She nodded. "Doll, will you show me my life?"

She saw herself as a child sitting at a table with her grandpa, scribbling on pages of colored paper, and then the next moment, she was overlooking a dead animal, her hands deep in its insides, digging around. Her grandpa towered over her shoulder, watching. She saw various moments of herself killing and gutting animals, all to remove the hearts and present them to her beaming grandpa. All of this escalated to her seeing herself standing over a bleeding kid, her hand holding a rock over her head. She grew fearful of what she was about to see, but her grandpa stopped her. He embraced her as she cried.

Things seemed muddled after this. She didn't see her grandpa any longer. Instead, she saw herself through adolescence, awkward and alone. For much of her youth, she found herself alone, hidden under trees with books and notepads until suddenly, she wasn't. There was someone else. Someone who met her at her locker and held her hand on the way to her classes. Someone who stole kisses outside of the principal's office because he thought it was funny to make her squirm with anxiety. In all of these memories, she never saw his face. Or more like, she couldn't. There was something blocking her from seeing it. A cloud or blurred vision. In any sense, when she saw herself holding his hand in the car with the warm sun on her face, she knew who it was.

Her memories with her husband flashed by too quickly. They were married and then in a blink, she had a daughter. She felt her stomach turn as she knew what to expect after that. The treatments, the sleepless nights, the endless tears. The question of the existence of any kind of benevolent being. Before she knew it she was broken, sitting in the tiny bedroom that had once been in the downstairs portion of Ben's house, back when the house was just one story. She felt the heartache and despair and when she felt the guilt of being a burden to her family, she wished to simply no longer be. But then she saw his face.

Her grandpa appeared to her as a dream in the dreariness of her nightmare, but he stood so disturbingly tall he barely fit in her room. Still, he comforted her. He told her it would be okay and he promised her he could make it better. "After all, what are friends for?"

She stood in the forest surrounded by creatures that looked unlike anything she could have dreamed up. Their eyes were milky white, swirling pools that seemed to see everything at once while never looking directly at anything. While they exchanged words they were amorphous shadows, shifting from one shape to another without dropping a sentence. Naomi thought they might have been clouds of black smoke, never taking a full form.

As their time together passed, they became less ambiguous and developed a form that Naomi couldn't pinpoint. They looked far less like the shapely clouds of smoke and shadow and now appeared squat and short. They moved in motions, shifting from one posture to the next, as though it were easier for them to move this way. It was like their limbs were stiff and deformed from years of misuse and this was the only way they knew how to move. If a greater distance needed to be covered, they would hop and skip as it seemed faster. Naomi thought them funny little things, but she would never chance a giggle as she was likely to meet their prior, more terrifying form.

They scurried around the fire, the three of them. They called orders to each other, but Naomi understood none of it. And when they finished, they handed her a cup from which she drank without hesitation, hoping it was poison. When she finished it, the first creature struck her hard enough to send her off her seat and into the dirt. The others did the same, cackling and hooting about, and this continued for what seemed like an eternity. All until Naomi learned to avoid their strikes. When she grew angry enough to rise through the beatings to end the creatures, they spit in the fire.

The smoke turned black and Naomi collapsed.

The creatures retreated into the darkness of the woods, the flashes of lightning illuminating Naomi, foreshadowing her creation. She relived the sensation of her body igniting. She remembered what it felt like to have her insides cooked and her skin singed to a crisp.

She saw herself emerging from the woods alone, her skin covered in tattoos and black from ash. She stood in the middle of the road, looking her fingers over as her head buzzed. She didn't expect to be alone. She expected to be comforted and safe, but when she emerged, unsure of who or where she was, she reacted on instinct and hid in a realm new, yet somehow familiar to her.

For a time, the light disappeared and she only knew shadow. She lived in a place where only shadows dwelled and she wasn't alone. Creatures inhabited the unknown realm with her, but she found they mostly ignored her, for they were demented and twisted on their own. She thought them like sea creatures of the deepest ocean in that they were strange, deformed, and managed to find their way in the dark without sight. They coexisted in a space both vast and compressed all at once.

Naomi became a dweller in her own time. Looking back at her memories, she didn't recognize the thing she'd become. With no one to communicate with and no reason to be human, she spent her time slipping away from anything that resembled humanity.

When her grandpa found her, he came from the darkness like a beacon of light. The creatures of the deep seemed to avoid him whether they had a reason to or not. But she'd lost so much of herself in that place that she didn't recognize him. She was feral—a primal bump in the dark that had forgotten how to speak, how to walk upright, and how to be anything at all.

His voice called to her and for a split second, he could see the scared little girl behind the inked skin and enormous white eyes that now covered most of her face.

"My Nay," he said, spindly fingers reaching for her. "You've seen too much. Let me cleanse your mind from all the muck that serves you no purpose."

When she took his hand, she viewed her life in glimpses, each one showing her less and less a creature and more a passing human.

The pair traveled the world together. She watched as they would spend days on end with no sleep or food, mindlessly searching for something. In moments when they weren't looking, she watched herself kill and desecrate innocent lives with her grandfather over her shoulder, always beaming. Sometimes, before she would drain the life from an innocent, she would watch her grandfather play cruel games with their victims. In some ways, it seemed as though he were testing their endurance, like they were lab rats and he enjoyed the educational opportunity. In others, he was disappointed and just seemed to torture the ones who didn't measure up to whatever standard he had. Other times, he simply allowed Naomi to feed endlessly. There was no discretion as to her victims. If her grandpa ordered her to feed, she would feed without regard to whether she was draining a grown man or an unsuspecting child.

But she did it carelessly. She obeyed and when she dropped a body and wiped her chin, she would look at him, basking in his proud smile.

Naomi squeezed her eyes tight, hoping to move past the memories.

"Someday," he would tell her. "Someday I will have my Eden and when I do, you'll be right there with me."

She never spoke. She never offered a voice unless directed to and when finally he grew exasperated by all their work, he asked her, "Are we working for nothing?"

"No," she answered. "Never."

"I need more, Naomi. Our work may be relentless, but it is nowhere near done. My children are fragile. Though they will answer my call, they are but plaster and not fit for service. And my love, my *love*, she is lost." He choked on his words, but that piqued Naomi's curiosity and his demeanor shifted.

"I will have my Eden," he told her firmly. "But perhaps now isn't the time. I am weary. And I have an agreement to fulfill. If you are to be of any use to your family, I suppose it would be best if you didn't carry the weight of this expedition."

Naomi saw herself walking into The Den. She shook Rik's hand and when she looked at her grandpa, he was no longer smiling. He merely waved his hand to her, forcing her to leave his side, and then he disappeared.

She relived all the horrible memories of the work she'd done for Rik, but she had no control over what she saw. The last thing she recalled was sitting in a bar gazing at the handsome bartender behind the counter, and then she was staring at the wall of Ben's room.

Her head felt light as her eyes rolled back and she leaned so far back in the chair that it tipped over.

"Naomi!" Ben called. He jumped from the bed, pausing only for a moment from dizziness before moving to her side.

Her head lolled from side to side as she tried to regain control of herself.

"Hey, hey, you're okay. You're okay, right?" he asked.

Naomi's hand pressed to her forehead. "What have I done?" she groaned. "We were right. He wanted a weapon to do his dirty deeds and it's me."

Part Three

How to Unmake the Maker

40

The Pickleberry Cemetery was located down H Highway past the high school, nestled in a small cubby outlined by Black Bile Woods. It was a tiny thing with a little church in the middle of two plots of land. The first plot sat at the bottom of a steep hill. This area had the most attention and care as it acted as the face of the cemetery. The graves were clean and orderly, spaced out respectfully and carefully to please those who paid a little more when burying their loved ones.

The plot of land up the hill was far less loved. While the groundskeeper still mowed the grass regularly, he took less care to trim the weeds around the stones or to power wash their faces. This area was covered almost entirely by trees, which caused the grass to grow thinner than the lower level of the graveyard. The operators of the graveyard also took less care to ensure the graves were properly spaced here. It wasn't uncommon for a funeral to be put on a temporary hold because the grave digger went too close to a neighboring plot, causing a casket to fall through the dirt into the new hole. Eventually, the operators learned to dig the holes days in advance to prepare for this mishap. But they never learned to allow more space between graves.

On this evening, the bells of the church had just stopped ringing, allowing the dull echoes to reverberate around the graveyard as a small group of people could be seen dispersing from their graveside ceremony. There were only half a dozen people in the group, two of whom were employed by the funeral home. The workers escorted the other dry-eyed attendants from the grave and to their cars.

"That has to be the least sorrowful burial I've ever seen," Ben said to Naomi.

They were tucked in the tree line of Black Bile. Not far enough to worry about trouble, but enough to go unnoticed by those who were attending and closing the service at the center of the graveyard. Still, any distance within the tree line caused Naomi to keep a listening ear and a watchful eye into the woods behind them.

"Poor soul must not have anyone," Naomi said.

They watched as the attendees climbed into their cars and drove down the hill and out of the graveyard. The workers returned to the church.

"Now?" Ben asked.

"They shouldn't stick around for long," Naomi told him, shaking her head. "I can't imagine they have a reason to hang around this church all day."

Sure enough, it was less than half an hour later when the workers emerged from the church, climbed into the same car, and left the graveyard.

"Okay, let's go," Ben said.

"Wait!" Naomi stopped him, nodding to the grave where they'd seen the small group.

A tall man stood in front of the fresh grave. He seemed to be admiring the stone.

"Oh shit, is that—?" Ben asked.

"Eddow." Naomi nodded. "Why would he be here?"

The two sat in silence as they watched Eddow wave his hand over the grave. The dirt that had been piled over the grave shifted and moved as though he turned back time. It formed a pile on the far side and when his hand passed over it completely, he stepped into the hole. His long limbs made it easy to do so, but for a moment he disappeared from their view.

"What the fuck?" Ben whispered.

"Shush."

Eddow emerged, clinging something to his chest. He held it with the same tenderness a mother would a newborn. When he rose from the grave, he waved his hand half-heartedly and the dirt filled the hole once again. He cradled the thing he'd retrieved from the grave and Naomi could have sworn she saw him kiss it.

He held the object out in front of him, and Naomi was able to see that it was a heart. The heart began to twist and shift in his hands. It started to sprout spindle-like thorns that continued to grow and grow, reaching out around his hand until it appeared as though a circulatory system was forming in the air before him. The system grew to be fully formed and then covered itself with bones and muscular tissues. It stopped somewhere between muscles and skin as the outside of the thing stayed red and sticky. Whatever it was, it was large, larger than Eddow by several feet, and broad. The monster's height alone wasn't the only thing that contributed to its magnitude, and it seemed to be nothing but solid muscle.

"It's like a titan," Ben gasped.

"It's a fucking beast," Naomi said at a loss of breath.

When the Titan's face formed, he resembled Eddow in the red eyes and branch-like head covering, but he seemed disoriented and confused when he looked himself over.

They couldn't hear what Eddow said, but Naomi could see him smile as he offered his hand to the Titan. The Titan took his hand into his own, making it appear tiny in comparison, and together they disappeared in the tree line of Black Bile on the distant side of the cemetery, far from Naomi and Ben.

The air over Ben and Naomi grew heavier, and they heard rustling from behind them. It was the unsettled scuffles of creatures large and small that had been silently watching the pair until Eddow entered. The thick air caused Ben's head to spin, and Naomi struggled to breathe. In wordless agreement, they left the tree line of the woods and sprawled over the grass of the cemetery, gathering themselves.

Naomi tucked her head between her legs, trying to regain her breath.

Ben rubbed his face so hard his vision blurred and his skin turned red. "So he harvests at graveyards now," he said.

"But only that grave. There has to be something about it," she said, looking back around the graveyard. "Come on." She motioned for Ben to follow.

They crept across the graveyard, more concerned about the monsters that seemed to follow them from Black Bile's tree line rather than the cemetery workers. They moved to the grave Eddow had unearthed and looked at the stone.

"Steve Owens. A Kind Man Cursed by Misfortune," Naomi read.

"Who puts that on a gravestone?" Ben frowned. "Aren't these things supposed to be, like, optimistic?"

"Why do I know that name?" she asked. "Steve Owens… My grandpa's journals! Steve was a friend of his. He was the only person Grandpa confided in and the one who hid all the notes we found." She looked sad. "Why would he make a deal with Eddow?"

"You think he made a deal? After being a friend of your grandpa's and all?"

"Grandpa left him out of a lot of stuff; maybe he didn't know everything. And if not, then why this grave? We're standing on land full of hearts for the taking. Why didn't Eddow collect them all?"

"Because he likes gifts," he said. "He never collected the others. The zealot did. So that means…"

"Steve would have had to give it to him—or someone else did," she said.

They were silent for a moment, and Naomi caught Ben doing the sign of the cross from the corner of her eye.

"You're not Catholic?"

"I'm uncomfortable," he said.

"Let's go," she told him. "We probably shouldn't hang around for too long. Let's find my grandpa's grave."

They split up, searching each row carefully. This took more time than anticipated as many of the headstones were so faded it was difficult to read them. After nearly an hour of searching, Ben found it and called for Naomi.

Neither of them made the first move as they stood looking at the faded headstone.

"Can you do the same trick he did?" Ben asked.

"In a way—yes. There are shadows below the dirt. I just push the shadows up," she said.

"Well?"

"I'm digging up my grandpa's grave, man. I'm not exactly excited about it."

He nodded, but when he noticed the dark settling in and the movement of things unknown past the tree line of Black Bile inching closer, he prodded her a bit. "I get that, but we probably shouldn't be here for too much longer."

She nodded. She motioned her hands as though she were gathering a pile of dirt in between them and lifted, causing the full mountain of packed dirt to rise from the ground and settle next to them. She motioned her hands to open the lid of her grandpa's casket, and they were struck with such an overpowering smell that she lost focus and the lid slammed closed.

"Oh, God…" Ben leaned over his knees, hacking and coughing.

Naomi covered her mouth. "We should've expected that," she said through her fingers.

"Expected? Sure. Be prepared for? No. No way. No one could ever be prepared for that," he said. He heaved, but nothing came.

"All right, all right," she said. "We have to get through this."

She pulled the front of her shirt over her nose and Ben did the same, though it didn't do much good. She motioned again as the casket lid opened and she was faced with the desiccated corpse of her grandfather. She swallowed hard and remained in place frozen.

Ben looked at her, hopeful he wouldn't have to be the one to jump in the hole, but when he saw her wide eyes frozen, he knew better. "I got it," he told her. He crawled down, carefully placing his feet along the edge of the casket. He didn't want to risk stepping on something inside the casket, so he took care to keep his feet along the edge. But they slipped and he felt himself falling toward the skeletal face of Chuck Campbell.

Naomi gasped.

Ben froze in the moment, hoping it was all a nightmare, but when he pulled away he could feel the stickiness of deteriorated and rotten flesh stick to his own skin so clearly that there was no way it was a dream. Through shallow breaths, he was able to keep his puking at bay and focused on searching around the casket for anything. His hands pressed over the body, feeling the bone underneath, but nothing stood out. He had to lift the body from one side to the other, searching underneath it, until he finally found a small box at the bottom, under Chuck's feet. He sat back, looking the box over. It was sealed on all sides, making it look more like a block of wood, but when he shook it, he heard rattling.

"Hey." He showed the box to Naomi and when she was ready, he tossed it to her. He then stood up, trying to stay to the edges again, and reached for Naomi's hand.

She helped pull him up and once he was on solid ground, trying to breathe in the clean air, she closed the casket and re-covered it. "Thanks for that," she told him, searching her pocket for some kind of cloth so he could clean himself.

He shook his head and waved his hand but found it difficult to form words through the urge to puke. He took the kerchief from her and wiped his face. "Don't mention it," he said when words finally came.

She looked the box over. It was entirely seamless and offered no clear way to open it. "It's a puzzle box," she said.

They heard footsteps in the woods nearing them.

"We shouldn't stick around to solve it," he told her.

She agreed, and they hurried out of the graveyard and toward the main part of town. When they reached Highway 215, Ben started toward his house while Naomi turned in the other direction.

"Where are we going?" he asked.

"You're going home," she said. "I'm going to The Den."

"So, we're both going to The Den."

"You're not coming."

"What else can they do? And you marked me, right? I'm going with you. Besides, after what we saw in the graveyard and that old house, I'm not sure I'm afraid of vamps anymore."

"Just go home. Take the box, get cleaned up, and let me deal with this," she told him. "I know you can handle it, but we're seriously outmanned and running out of time. You figure this out, and I'll see what I can do for reinforcements."

He was reluctant but agreed. He took the puzzle box and headed home.

Naomi gathered her thoughts as she headed toward The Den. She was there in moments and this time, she found a few cars outside of the building but paid them no mind as she entered. She nodded to the guard with a new romance novel in hand and headed straight into the main area.

There was more life this time as the sun had set long ago and the vamps were coming alive, so to speak. They began to gather in the main bar area, dealing cards and ordering drinks, warming up for some action that would likely occur that night.

Naomi met several sets of eyes when she entered. Many of them looked interested in her at first, but when they caught a better look, they merely shrugged her off and went back to their poker games.

Nora was leaning over the bar, holding the bartender's face in her claws as she affectionately berated him—something she enjoyed doing. But when she caught sight of Naomi, she shoved his face away. "Oh, look who made it," she said. "Here we thought we might have to go back to the market for a replacement." She grinned.

"You'd never get that lucky," Naomi said. "Where's Rik?"

"Occupied."

"Tell him the demon Eddow is about to overrun this town if he doesn't become unoccupied," she said.

Nora's face went flat and shaky. Naomi had only seen that fear after they'd encountered the deranged beasts in the Black Bile. She cleared her throat and entered Rik's office. A moment later she returned, holding the door open for Naomi.

Rik sat at his desk when she entered. In front of him lay a tray of assorted blood-related delicacies. At a glance, Naomi spotted something gelatinous, a deep red soup that still bubbled, and near the back, several lines of red powder. She was certain he'd set out this platter with plans relating to whatever was to occur that night. The annoyed furrow of his eyebrows upon looking at her confirmed this.

"What a pleasure it is, Mrs. Novak."

"Ehh, doubt that."

"Any time I don't have to revive you from near death is a pleasure," he assured her.

"We have a problem," she said.

"Per the usual." He nodded. "You've found your demon?"

"And then some. The altar of hearts is his, and he means to use them to raise an army. There were hundreds of hearts there and who knows how many more he has collected elsewhere," she said.

"And you know this how?"

"I watched him raise something in the graveyard that was bigger than him. If he were to recreate hundreds of those, this town wouldn't stand a chance."

Rik leaned forward.

"If this town goes, there goes your investment," she said.

He slammed his hand on the top of his desk. "Leave it to a demon to null a contract!" He sighed.

Naomi crossed her arms, not even wanting to know what kind of deals Rik had made with Eddow. "The hearts have been moved and tucked away, but the place isn't exactly secure. I think as long as he doesn't find out where they are, we're okay. Or at least, we've bought ourselves enough time to make a plan or something."

"And do you have a plan?" he asked.

"We have the beginnings of a plan. We have a weapon."

"Oh, a weapon." He feigned enthusiasm.

"It's better than nothing, but I think we might have time to gain more," she said.

"What makes you think that?"

"He's looking for something, and I think it's me. I ran into him and he seemed happy to see me, but now that he has his beast, I feel it's only a matter of time before he does whatever he plans to," she explained.

Rik laughed and Nora joined in.

She rolled her eyes. "What is it now?"

"You? He had you for years. Why wouldn't he just put whatever plan he had in action years ago?" he asked.

She merely shrugged. "He's looking for someone. Someone who walks between worlds, human and yours."

This caused Rik and Nora to laugh louder.

"You know, it would be more helpful if you just told me why this is so funny," she said.

"You still think you're human?" Nora croaked, hiding a snort. "You still think after all of this, you're human?"

"You don't walk between anything, darling," Rik told her.

"Except for your own delusions," Nora choked out.

"If he needs someone of both worlds, it wouldn't be so obvious. It would probably be a human who doesn't even realize they are," he said.

Naomi frowned. She thought and when the realization hit her she couldn't hide the terror on her face. "Someone who can see?"

"Oh, oh, no," Rik crooned. "Is it your pet human? If you were smart, you'd kill him before the demon has a chance to."

Nora cackled so hard she found it difficult to stand. "It won't be quick if he does it."

"Regardless of whatever you choose, we have an investment to protect," Rik told her. "If and when you are faced with the demon, we will do our best to aid. But we know the best solution here."

Naomi nodded, at a loss for words, and started for the door when Nora calmed her laughing enough to call after her. "For the sake of this town, you have to kill that boy, dearie!"

41

"You know what always drove me nuts? Nuts! I mean it. People think that nuts are all natural and the perfect snack for avian kind, but really you can't go throwing around just any kind of nut. Sure most of them are fine, but people will see birds flying around their back yards and think, 'Oh, I wish I had some feed for them,' go to their pantry, and find the first thing, which is usually salted peanuts or some kind of chip. I know they seem harmless, but when we really think about how salt isn't even great for us in large amounts, we have to imagine the impact it has on a tiny bird body. An excessive amount of salt could kill them, and most people don't think about that.

"They don't think about anything but themselves and how cute it would be to see a bird on their window sill. I wish people took more time and consideration to learn these things. Even a quick internet search would tell them what is okay and isn't okay to give them, but no one ever puts in the extra effort. I think people are just selfish. You know what I mean?"

Jamie caught her breath, taking a long drink of her coffee, but her eyes held the same intensity as she stared unblinking at the tall man who sat across from her.

"I couldn't have said it better myself, my love," he said.

Her eyes lit up gleefully. "No one understands me and my hobbies like you, Jake— uh, Eddie. Sorry, I keep doing that; you just look so much like someone I used to know."

He brushed off her apology with a wave and grin. "I get that a lot. I must have one of those faces. But I am no stranger to the odd hobby or two," he assured her.

"I don't think bird watching is very odd, but I don't think I would have ever gotten into collecting without your help," she said.

"Collecting is a bit of a passion of mine." He grinned.

"That's so neat. Aside from the birds, I don't think I collect much," she said thoughtfully.

"I would surely call you a collector of words," he told her.

"I definitely have the gift of gab, if that's what you're meanin'." She giggled. "But between you and me, there are people who take the whole collecting thing a little far."

"Oh?"

"Yeah, I've seen those hoarder shows, where people save anything from old cans to newspapers to socks. Blek, just clean your house, for crying out loud." She shuddered.

Eddie wrinkled his nose in a kind laugh that caused her eyes to stare dreamily. "You're so funny," he said. His eyes grew curious. "Tell me, have you, as an officer of the law, ever stumbled upon someone's collection that really struck you? Maybe some old lady with a doll collection?"

"Well, yes, actually that exact thing. When Mrs. Nelson passed, no one had seen her for days and we had to do a wellness check. We found her body, but as soon as we opened the door to her house it was just crawling… well, not crawling because that would be terrifying… but just covered with dolls. Every inch of it. I had nightmares for days."

"I find dolls to be misunderstood. Someone took the time and love to craft something so life-like and yet so much better than life. Their skin is softer, their eyes wider, and the hair always holds curl and yet somewhere along the way, someone thought they were terrifying. I imagine Mrs. Nelson's collection was something marvelous."

Jamie sighed. "You always see the good, Eddie. I didn't even realize good people like you were real." Her face scrunched a bit. "I made generalizations about people being so horrible, but my experience is tainted. I mostly spend my time at work and my boss is an asshole. I guess my old boss, now. I'm a timid person—a gentle soul, if you will—and he has me do the absolute worst things. Setting up crime scenes for dead bodies, staring at their dead faces while I eat lunch, and don't get me started on the hearts. The human hearts!" She rubbed her face and neck as though her skin crawled.

"Hearts?" Eddie asked.

"Huh? Oh, yeah! You want to know about weird collections? We found a weird hovel or hole or nest or I don't even know what to call it in the creek bed near the park. It was filled to the brim with human hearts. In jars and cups and boxes and ugh, I don't even want to think about it," she said.

Eddie's face seemed to crack a bit, and he was grateful Jamie had her attention turned away as the rage heated his core and made his mask slip from his face.

"Human hearts in jars," he whispered, his beady eyes wandering the edges of the room. "That is a strange and eclectic collection.,"

"Eddie? You okay? You seem a bit… uh… unwell?"

Eddow didn't look to her. His eyes were off in the distance as though he were watching something, but he reached across Jamie's kitchen table and placed his rough hand to her chin.

Jamie felt her heart flutter and her cheeks flush. She leaned forward toward him in anticipation of something more when his grasp lowered to her neck and he grabbed hold.

"Eddie?"

His hold was gentle at first, and she wondered if he'd been lost in thought and not noticed his grasp had slipped. But then she saw the tremble of his face, the swift shifting of his eyes as though he were unable to focus on one thing, and his grip tightened.

"Eddie, you're hurting me," she whimpered.

Eddow rose from the table but never released his hold on her neck. This pulled her across the table, spilling their drinks over the numerous bird guides Jamie had spread over the surface of the table. He pulled her across the table as though she were a mere rag doll and the more she whimpered and cried, the tighter his grip grew.

"Those are mine. Those gifts were collected for me, my *fucking* hearts and those *fucking fuckers* think they can just disturb them? Observe them? *Touch them?*"

His grip was so tight that Jamie was starting to lose consciousness when he finally lifted her into the air, bringing her face to his.

Eddow attempted to regain his composure with a breathe. "Come, my dear, let us go check on my collection."

And with that they were gone, leaving only the soiled books covering Jamie's table and floor.

"So, what did they tell you?"

"We have to kill Eddow, Ben."

They returned to the field near Ben's house where they'd opened the portal the first time. It offered the best place for them to talk without ears listening in.

"We can't rely on the gun because we don't have a surplus of bullets. Even without him raising an army, Eddow's friend is sure to give quite the fight. Look, if I'm being honest, I would rather you not be there at all," she said.

"Well, that's too bad," he replied.

She sighed. "Ben… I really feel like it would be better for you to stay away."

"After all of this, you think I'll just let you do it on your own?"

She bit her tongue hard. Would telling him the reason why she didn't want him around make a difference? From the short time of knowing him, she figured he would probably find it was more reason to stick around. Naomi didn't know exactly what Eddow wanted with Ben. But with the memories of her time with Eddow fresh in her mind, she knew Ben's future in his hands didn't look promising. If he didn't measure up to Eddow's expectations, he was as good as dead anyway.

She looked away.

"What's going on?" he asked.

"Forget it," she said. "Did you get that box opened?"

"No. There are no notes about it in the letters or books."

He tossed her the box, and she held it for less than a minute before she had it open, pushing a panel on the side and popping open the top.

Ben watched, surprised.

"I like puzzles," she said. "It runs in the family, apparently."

Inside the box were six bullets with symbols carved over the surface, along with a letter. Naomi glanced over the letter, realizing what it was from the start. "Here, this is for you." She handed it to Ben.

He looked it over. "This is to make more."

She examined the bullets and pulled the gun from her pocket, reloading it. "As I was saying before, we can't rely on the gun," she said. "We only have six chances and we can't waste even one. We shouldn't waste any on his friend, but I have no idea what we're up against."

"How do we know these will even work on him?" he asked.

Naomi stopped. "What else do we have?"

Ben sighed. "And our plan?"

"The Den will help when we call upon them. He doesn't know that we moved the hearts, so maybe that will buy us some time, but when he finds out he won't be happy about it. And I don't know how long it will be after that. One thing is for sure: I have no idea how this will end."

"Are you worried about the town?"

"We don't have time to evacuate everyone, and do you think they would believe us?" she asked.

He shook his head. "And our families?"

"Maybe we should try to convince them to leave, but I'm not hopeful my family would move because of me again."

"And with the festival tonight, there is no way my family will leave," he said.

"Festival?"

"They do them, like, once a month. It's like a craft fair. My aunts make all kinds of things for it and the café picks up a lot of business. Missing out would be like business suicide," he explained.

"And then just trying to explain... all of this?"

He nodded.

"So, the plan is to hope he doesn't find out about the hearts and where they are. In the meantime? Maybe we should look into a better place to keep them?" she asked.

"Do you think it would be possible to get them out of Pickleberry?"

"Not on our own. This is the shittiest plan ever." She sighed.

"It's like you said, what else do we have?"

Naomi watched him. She watched the tension on his otherwise carefree face and for a split moment, she found herself immeasurably grateful for him.

Before she could even give him a simple thank you, there was an explosion in the distance. It was loud and ground-shaking, causing both of them to hit the ground. When they recovered, they spotted a pillar of smoke for only a moment before it was completely gone as though nothing had happened.

"Was that—?"

"It had to be."

Naomi took his hand, and they disappeared from the spot.

42

Jo had had a cozy kitchen at the farmhouse. She'd had just enough counter space and ample lighting over the stove. She adorned the walls with portraits of chickens and bunnies and coordinated her hand towels with her curtains, alternating between red and navy blue. When she worked through all of the clean red towels, she knew it was time to wash her red curtains, which meant the navy curtains were pulled out from the linen closet.

Her window sill was full of potted succulents and figurines she'd collected from the grandkids over the years. Though none of them visited, she still looked at them every day. Naomi had even sent her a hanging shelf when Richie mentioned she was running out of room on the sill. Richie installed the shelf and the collection of plants and figurines grew.

But the window wasn't above the sink; it was on the opposite wall of the kitchen. This left Jo awkwardly craning her neck to admire her collection or simply staring at the boring wall in front of the sink. Her mind wandered during these times. She had a lush garden with a bird bath and a variety of wildflowers that drew in the butterflies. If she had a window over the sink, she would be able to admire nature while she worked.

Richie had offered to put in a window for her, but Jo was adamant Naomi would pitch a fit over any renovations to her home. Naomi encouraged her parents to do whatever they wanted to make the farmhouse their home, but Jo didn't want to bother her to ask.

Richie didn't want to bother either of them, so he settled on building shelves and reading Stephen King novels.

Despite the garden, the spacious kitchen, the fireplace, and three acres of land, Jo never coped with the window placement. Imagine now the pleasure that filled her as she washed her dishes looking out the window of her new townhouse. The garden in the community area of the complex might not be as impressive as the one at the farmhouse, but here she could watch the bugs flutter around the koi pond and the neighborhood kids running up and down the street. She felt connected to the community even if they'd hardly met any of their neighbors yet.

She'd been speaking aloud to Richie, who responded when he heard a silence, but he didn't take care in hearing her words. "They're setting up tables outside the complex," she noted. "Didn't the paper say something about a festival? I believe it mentioned something about crafts? I love a good craft fair. I wonder if it's a regular thing. Maybe I can get back into stitching in my down time and put a few things in the fair? Oh, it would be a nice way to meet people and see what other creatives this town has. Maybe I'll find a club to join?"

"Sounds great," Richie responded.

There was a sudden rumble and the few figurines Jo had packed into her suitcase rattled on the window sill. She leaned over the sink, looking through the small window to the clear sky above. Her hands were still wet and left water droplets on the sill as she scanned the sky, looking for the source of the sound.

"Did you hear that, Richie?" she asked.

"Sonic boom," he answered matter-of-factly. "Probably the military doing some testing."

"Out here? The nearest base is hours away."

"Do you see a jet in the sky?"

"Well, no."

"Exactly." He smirked.

"Smart ass." She sighed. She wiped her hands on a kitchen towel and wiped down the wet countertop. "Are you going to be ready soon? I'd like to see if I can find some cute things to decorate our new kitchen."

Richard was in the arm chair in the living room. One moment he'd been sitting up chatting and the next, he rested his head fully back with his eyes closed. He didn't respond to Jo.

"Richie?" She moved to his chair and gave it a whack. "Richard!" she yelled.

He furrowed his brow and leaned forward.

"Are you feeling okay?" she asked, worried.

He rubbed a hand over his face and then his neck and when his eyes went to her, they were glistening and bright. "Yeah, my dear, of course I am." He smiled. "I'm going upstairs to get ready."

He stood a bit wobbly, holding his ribs, and moved slowly up the stairs. Jo watched for a moment but was suddenly distracted when she noticed his unwashed and empty coffee cup.

"This man," she huffed.

There wasn't a stitch of smoke visible in the air, but the smell of it burned their noses. The site was flattened as though it had been struck by a tiny atom bomb, leaving not even a trace of the altar left to be seen. If it wasn't for the crater in the ground, Naomi and Ben would have never found the site.

Both were wordless as they stared at the crater, knowing and still not knowing what to expect next. They barely had a plan, just an inkling of a plan. As far as they were concerned, the crater before them was a preview into what Pickleberry was about to become.

They heard rustling behind them and Naomi turned sharply, ready, only to see Glenn Beasley pushing through the brush, completely winded.

"Glenn," she gasped, lowering her hands.

"Did you run here?" Ben asked.

"Down the creek bed. There is an explosion in this town, you think I'd just mosey on over to it?" he asked.

"How did you even see it?" Naomi asked. "The smoke was gone in a second!"

"I saw it a split second before it disappeared. What happened? Was this you guys?"

Ben and Naomi exchanged looks.

"All right, I stood by and let you take the lead on the murders and all. And I know you handed some responsibility off on me, but you were very vague about it. I don't think I can keep standing by. What the fuck is happening in this town?"

They shared looks again.

"I climbed into the grave. This one's on you," Ben said to Naomi.

"We don't have time to completely fill you in, but hypothetically, if something horrible was about to happen to this town, would you do anything in your power to stop it?" she asked Glenn.

"Yeah, of course."

"Cool... There is a demon who wants to do something terrible to this town. We don't know exactly what it is, but we have some good guesses. And he means to use the hearts that were in this altar somehow. We know you moved them, which is why this happened. Who else knows where they are?" she asked him.

Glenn's brain seemed frazzled as he tried to process Naomi's words and put aside all his questions to answer hers. "Uh, I mean some of the staff at LMH know we brought something in, but they don't really know what. But other than me… uh, Jamie knows. She helped me move them," he said.

"Maybe you should call her. She could help?"

"I could try, but she isn't answering my calls. We had a bit of a moment, and I'm pretty sure I fired her."

"Do you know where you could find her?" she asked.

He thought for a moment. "Uh, shit, no. I've been calling her mother's house and she hasn't seen her in a few days. She's been talking about some collector guy that she met, but I don't know anything about him. Maybe he has a shop in town or in Springfield?" he asked.

"Collector?" Ben asked.

Naomi swallowed a lump. "The chances that it isn't Eddow are very, very low," she said.

"It'd be better to check it out to make sure," Ben agreed.

"I'm going to need some more info," Glenn said.

"You have weapons at the station?" she asked.

"We have some."

"And reinforcements?"

"Um, no, even the sheriff wouldn't bother coming in if I called," he admitted.

"Okay, we'll take what we can get and fast. Ben, go with Glenn and fill him in as much as you can. I'll get The Den. Meet me at LMH as soon as you can," Naomi said.

Ben nodded.

"Wait!" she stopped him. "Here." She pulled Stormrider from her pocket and handed it to him.

"What the fuck is that?" Glenn asked.

"I don't have time to teach you how to use it, but I think you'll manage. Don't lose it and be careful," she told him.

Ben looked momentarily unsure at the notion of her entrusting him with the gun. "You'll get this back," he told her.

"I better."

Ben headed down the creek bed and Glenn started to follow before she stopped him. "Wait," she said, pulling the picture he'd given her from her pocket and holding it for him to see it. "I think you should keep this."

"What? Why?"

"I just think it belongs with you," she pushed.

"You don't recognize him."

Naomi held his gaze and wanted to deny it, but with the world crashing around them, she couldn't bring herself to lie. "I don't know why, but I don't know who this is," she said. "I think that is intentional, like someone wanted it that way. But... in any sense, you should keep this. Maybe someday..." She trailed off, trying to think of a situation but finding none.

Glenn took the photo and put it in his chest pocket. He couldn't pretend like he understood all that was happening, but he didn't think this moment was the best to pursue the matter. "I'll hold onto it until you do," he said.

She nodded. "Go on, I'll meet you."

Glenn followed Ben, hesitating to look back at Naomi only for a moment.

In his memory, Glenn couldn't name a time when he'd used both the siren and the lights on his cruiser. He'd used the lights before, as a precaution, and the siren to scare maverick cattle back into their pens, but never both at once. As he sped across town to the station, he used both though even then it felt like overkill. The drive was over in moments, and Ben hardly had a chance to fill him in at all.

"When you say *demon*—" Glenn began as he threw the car into Park and climbed out, leaving his door open. He ran to the station door and Ben tried to keep up.

"I mean demon, Beasley. Like from hell but prefers earth. Massive and terrifying and has a way of coaxing people into doing his bidding, but making them feel as though they're doing good. The altar with the hearts was his, but he didn't collect a single one of them. They were all given to him by some crazed zealot who thought he was doing good," he said. He stood back as Glenn unlocked the station, listening intently.

"And what does this demon want with Pickleberry?"

"From the best we can tell, he wants to take it over. He's trying to raise an army. My guess is so that he can have his own form of hell on earth," Ben said.

"But why here?"

"I know you're a little slower, but not even you can pretend like weird shit doesn't happen in this town."

"All right, all right. Naomi did vaguely tell me about some stuff," Glenn said. He entered and unlocked the storage room. He shoved the evidence board aside and pulled out the only set of riot gear he had. They both looked at it. "You take the vest. I have one already," he said.

"And the rest of it?" Ben asked.

"We divvy it up?" Glenn suggested.

Ben sighed. "What about weapons?"

"A couple of shotguns and pistols, but not much in ammo," he said. He looked to the wall behind Ben, showing him what they had.

"Does this department get paid in peanuts?" Ben asked. He pulled the helmet from Glenn's hand and shoved it on his head as Glenn tried to gather anything and everything that might be useful.

"The worst this department sees is cows on the highway. You don't need a shotgun to herd cows," Glenn said.

Ben sighed again.

"So what about this Den? What is that about?"

"The bar on the hilltop," Ben answered. "It isn't a bar. Well, I mean it has a bar, but it isn't a people bar."

"I fucking knew it!"

"It's run and owned by vampires, and they have their fingers in pretty much everything in this town."

"That old rumor?" Glenn scoffed.

"For a general rule of thumb to make this all quicker, if you heard a rumor about it, then it's probably true," Ben said as he shoved things into Glenn's bag.

Glenn stopped. "So the mayor…?"

"It hasn't been confirmed, but we can't deny it either."

"Wait! So Naomi went to The Den to get help. Ben, tell me honestly, is the safety of this town really at risk?"

Ben sighed. He zipped up Glenn's bag and threw it over his shoulder. "If we had more time, we would have tried to evacuate the town. Beasley, if you have family you want to be safe, I would make that call now," he said, thinking of Ginger and Allie.

Glenn nodded as his hands fumbled for his phone.

43

Trina had spent the better part of an hour making sure the display on the crafts table was just right. She didn't have a creative bone in her body. Mini made all the crafts with love and dedication. She worked to teach Deena the trade so the creativity would grow within the family, but Trina never had the touch. Her specialties lay elsewhere. She could manage books and work with customers. Trina had a knack for soothing any disgruntled patron whether they be a pair of teenagers in her home or an annoyed Pickleberrian. There were very few things on this earth that caused her to lose her patience, but figuring out how to present Mini's doilies just might do it.

At the moment, Mini was busying herself getting dressed. Deena was hiding away, reluctant to help with the craft fair, and everyone else outright avoided involvement (volunteering to take shifts in the café). This left Trina to pretend she knew what she was doing. The end product was presentable, but it looked like a proud kindergartener displaying their artwork.

She sighed. "Where is Benjamin?"

Ben had the touch. He didn't know how to create towel hangs or jewels or whatever else Mini invested her time into making, but he knew how to make things look nice. It always surprised Trina, considering the constant state of his room. In the past several years, he'd been the one to direct her and help her lay out the tables for the shoppers. And they always got comments on how beautiful it looked.

This year, he was nowhere to be found. While Trina had been happy to see that he'd met someone to spend time with, she worried when he didn't show up. Family had always seemed important to him. She pushed away the thought that maybe he was drifting away from them.

"No Ben?" Gabe asked, appearing at the bottom of the stairs and behind Katrina.

"He must be busy," she said, finally giving up and showing Gabe her work. "That's okay, I don't think I need him."

Gabe examined the display and winced. "Maybe we should call him?"

"Oh, hush you," she said. "This will be fine. Wherever Ben is, I'm sure it's really important." She glanced to the street lined with vendors and music playing farther up the block. "How is the café doing?"

"Bustling!" Gabe said, grinning. "I love festivals!"

"Let's get the door open and sell these, then," she said, starting for the door.

"I got it," he told her, meeting her there and pushing the screen open and locking it.

Trina let her husband do the work, watching as the street filled with patrons and familiar faces. Most of the attendees went to the café to get a drink before walking the tables and enjoying the nice day, but as they opened the doors, a few started to come her way.

Trina stepped aside, smiling and welcoming people. "Hello, welcome. Have a look around. If you have any questions, Gabe or I'll be here."

"Hello, beautiful shoppers! We have the finest collection of hand-crafted goodies straight from the upstairs bedroom. My dear auntie has spent day and night working her fingers to the bone to make sure this month's collection is even more impressive than last's." Gabe allowed his booming voice to carry over the growing crowd. He played up the goods, hoping to get some laughs, if anything.

"Here we have table circle things crafted with homespun yarn. The white ones are spun from alpaca and the brown ones are spun from the very hair on Mini's chin—"

"Gabe!"

"I kid, I kid!" He laughed and playfully nudged a man who was suppressing a laugh. "It was probably from her legs."

Trina couldn't help but laugh at her husband's antics. As she was about to follow the last customer in, she heard someone call from down the bottom of the steep driveway. "Hi, hello! Hi, there!" A woman waved.

Trina waved back from the porch. "Hi, there!"

"Oh, hi! I'm Jo. My husband and I just moved in down the road. I was hoping to meet some of our neighbors today," she said. The poor man was close behind her, but he moved like sludge. After a bit, Jo grew tired of waiting for him.

Trina left the porch and met Jo in the middle of the driveway. "I'm Katrina. My husband Gabe is inside and most of my family also lives here. You'll see them scattered about, I'm sure. Welcome to the neighborhood!"

"Oh, thank you, we love it so much. We came from the country, which was nice for a while, but so isolating. Nothing this fun happened out there."

"Our festivals are modest, but I do enjoy seeing the community come together at least once a month. It's a great time to see all Pickleberry has to offer in one place."

"You know, I thought from the moment we came here that there was something about this town that just feels like home," Jo said. She was looking over the structure of Katrina's renovated house as though she'd seen it before but couldn't place it. "Your home… It's so lovely and quite unique from the others on the street."

"Thank you." Trina looked it over. "It was a small family home when we moved in not long ago, but after some renovations we've been able to run a business and share the space with family. I'm blessed to have my family so close."

"Family is so important," Jo agreed. She barely glanced over her shoulder as she spoke. "Isn't that right, Richie? My husband Richie, he's moving a little slow today," she said.

"Is… is that your husband?" Trina gestured to him as he slowly lowered to the ground as though the weight of gravity was becoming too much to handle. She didn't wait for a response from Jo and hurried to meet him.

"Richie? Richard!" Jo cried.

"I'm fine… I'm fine…" he said. The hollows of his eyes were growing deeper and darker by the moment and his skin was clammy. He stared into space as though his eyes couldn't focus, but he spoke consistently as if to convince those around him and himself. "Everything is fine. I feel fine, Jo."

"You're not fine, you're ghost white," Jo said, holding him upright.

Richard's distant gaze settled on Jo, but he looked through her. The words that came from his mouth were less coherent and soon enough, he was just mumbling sounds.

"Gabe! Call an ambulance!" Trina called.

Naomi was relieved to that her meeting with The Den was uneventful, and it took little convincing for Rik and the others to agree to help. But when faced with the dilemma of sunlight, she knew they would have to go without help until it was no longer an issue. She took whatever help she could get and hoped that they could manage to hold their own for just a couple of hours. The sun wouldn't set for several more hours, but soon there would be enough shade from the hospital. Naomi was less than optimistic that they would help at all until she mentioned LMH. Suddenly, all of them, including Nora, seemed keen to protect the hospital, though Naomi was sure it had nothing to do with the massive blood bank on the hospital grounds.

In the meantime, Naomi teleported around Pickleberry, checking shops and houses and any place imaginable for Jamie. She hoped to find her before Eddow did. She wasn't sure of their relationship and imagined it wouldn't end well for Jamie if she had information Eddow wanted. That was, unless she offered it to him freely. That was far more frightening than the thought of him torturing it out of her.

Naomi spent as much energy as she could sacrifice looking for Jamie but came up empty. With feigned optimism, she hoped she'd just missed her. She had no choice now but to meet Ben and Glenn at the hospital and pray that this entire thing was a massive overreaction.

Ben and Glenn had been sitting in the parking lot of the hospital for nearly half an hour. Ben had told him anything and everything he could think of about Naomi, Eddow, and all the ghouls and creeps of Pickleberry. And for his part, Glenn only partially processed it because if he allowed himself to fall deep into the void of the information Ben had given him, he felt like he would need to be committed to LMH's psych department.

Since then, the two had sat wordlessly watching every direction of the hospital for either a giant demon or Naomi.

Glenn clutched his shotgun nervously.

"You all right?" Ben asked.

"The academy doesn't really tell you how to fight demons. And the Navy kind of skipped over that too," he admitted.

"If it makes you feel better, I've only fought demons once and it was kind of a shitshow," Ben said.

"Yeah, not really, man," Glenn said.

Ben frowned.

An ambulance pulled into the parking lot, holding their attention.

"That's not good," Glenn said. He turned on his radio but only heard silence. "I missed that call. Hopefully, Freeman got it."

"Trouble at the festival, you think?" Ben asked.

"Who knows," Glenn responded, and they watched as the EMTs pulled out a man on a stretcher and carted him inside, shortly followed by a woman Ben immediately recognized.

"That's Naomi's mom," he said.

"What?"

"That's probably her dad," he said, his face losing a bit of its color.

They sat in tense silence, watching for several moments as the EMTs emerged with an empty gurney, climbed into the ambulance, and drove off. Moments later, Naomi appeared a few feet from the entrance, but neither Ben nor Glenn moved.

"If she knew they were in there… how do you think she would react?" Glenn asked.

Ben watched her closely. He watched her pant and bend over her knees to catch her breath. "Everything she does is for them," he said. "If she knew…" he started but stopped.

"She's not holding it together very well," Glenn said, watching her from the car.

Ben nodded. "So we agree?"

"Tell her later." Glenn nodded.

With hesitant looks, they agreed and left the cruiser to meet with Naomi.

"Where have you been? What did you get? Did you get a hold of Jamie? I searched this entire town for her, but I couldn't find her anywhere," she said, panting and using the wall for support.

"You're drained," Ben said.

"I'm fine," she told him, forcing herself to stand, but her shoulders stayed hunched forward.

Ben rolled the sleeve of his jacket up and held his wrist in front of her face. "Just enough to get you through," he said. "Don't argue, we're useless without you."

Naomi wanted to fight but knew he was right. She pulled his wrist to her mouth, biting deep and feeding.

"Um, well, no one told me about that, but okay," said Glenn, looking on in disgust. "No contact with Jamie. We brought everything we could. I have no idea if it will be enough or not. Honestly, I have no idea about any of this."

Naomi gave him a comforting nod through her feeding.

"And you? The Den? They'll come?" Ben asked her.

She nodded but glanced at the sun.

"But they'll be delayed, won't they?"

She nodded. Black started to form around her eyes like veins, and she pulled her mouth from his wrist. She pulled a bandage wrap from her pocket and wrapped it around the bite wound, and then used the back of her hand to wipe her mouth. "They need at least the shade from the building. But there might be too much of a risk still," she said. "I can't say if they'll show or not. Rik does like to protect his investments, so I'm cautiously optimistic."

Ben pulled Stormrider from his belt and handed it to her. "You should be the one to use this," he said. "I have no idea how and we can't waste the bullets."

She took it and thought. "Let's be realistic." She handed Stormrider to Glenn. "My hands will be too busy to use it, and you're the one with the training," she said. "There are only six bullets. Don't waste them. If we take out Eddow, the rest should follow."

Glenn was hesitant to take the pistol. The metal was cool and smooth and as it touched his skin, he felt sparks of electricity. He handed his shotgun to Ben, gave him a brief lesson in how to use it, and put Stormrider in his holster.

They let the tension of the day settle around them as the shadow of the hospital grew farther across the parking lot.

"What if he never comes here?" Ben asked.

"Then we have over prepared, and that's fine," Naomi said.

"What if he went somewhere else?"

"Ben, if he wants his army he has to come here. If he left Pickleberry to start a new collection somewhere else, we can't do anything about it. At least not right now. But I get the feeling he's far too sentimental to leave all this behind," Naomi told him. She looked to Glenn. "How are you holding up?"

He nodded. He opened his mouth to speak but choked instead, and just nodded.

She also nodded. "Let's hope he found a hole to sulk in and this is an uneventful night all due to an overreaction," she said.

44

As the time ticked by, they thought for a moment they would get lucky. The sound of the music from the festival carried over the hill and through the town to a dull echo in the parking lot. The sun dropped lower and lower and while there was still no sign of The Den, there was no sign of Eddow either. For the briefest of moments, Naomi actually had an ounce of hope that all of their predictions were wrong and nothing would come of the night.

But when she heard his voice like a hiss over the wind, she felt herself fall hard back to reality.

"Oh, a welcome party," he said. "You shouldn't have gone through all the trouble."

Ben and Glenn were both facing the open and emptiness of the parking lot. Their skin was covered in goosebumps and they tried to hide the trembling of their hands.

Glenn heard his voice. He heard his footsteps on the gravel and concrete, but he saw nothing. He thought he was losing his mind until he stole a look at Ben, whose face was ghostly white and sweaty. He swallowed down his nerves and looked back to the empty space before them.

Eddow wasn't there one moment but appeared as if from nothing the next. He wasn't alone either, appearing with his Titan to his right and a nervous Jamie to his left.

Glenn felt his mouth fall open at the sight of Eddow and his terrifying and mysterious statue, with his best friend's face stretched over his head like animal hide tanning in the sun. He didn't give himself the time needed to process Brian's face but focused on Jamie trembling to the side of the demon.

"Jamie? Jamie!" Glenn called. "Come here." He pointed Stormrider at Eddow, but when Eddow laughed he lowered it, feeling uneasy.

"You think she wants to leave?" he asked.

Glenn couldn't comprehend the idea. Instead, he shook his head and looked at Jamie again. "Jamie, he's forcing you. You don't have to help him. I know you had no choice but to lead him here," he said.

"No, I wanted to tell him," she said.

Glenn nearly dropped Stormrider.

"Eddie is so brilliant. He's bright and kind and loving, and when he told me that we were stealing his collection, I felt so devastated. I had no idea what we were doing! I'm just acting under your orders, as always, and well, I can't stand by anymore. Eddie promised to show me great things." She beamed up at him with dewy eyes.

Naomi suppressed a gag.

Eddow looked at Jamie, caressing her cheek carelessly, and then looked back to the trio, his features darker. "This is one of those rare occasions where one mask works for more than one person," he said.

"Is he calling Brian's face a mask?" Glenn whispered.

Naomi nodded. "It doesn't fit you. I can see the edges cracking," she said.

"I have been robbed and acted emotionally," he said. "I know I'm not human, but I am allowed reactions, my love."

His eyes wandered to Ben, who looked as though he was about to pass out at any moment. He was so visibly shaken that Naomi could hear the shotgun rattling in his hands.

"This one, on the other hand," he said. "This one sees nothing. My, my, after all this time, you managed to find one on your own, Naomi. I would be proud, but you never even bothered to mention him to me."

"You can't have him," she said.

"Vampiric claims mean nothing to me."

"No," she said shortly. "You can't have him, or these hearts."

"They belong to me. You can't stop me from reclaiming what is mine."

He then inhaled deeply, and the three felt the air grow dense. The sun seemed to darken above them. When he released his inhale, everything returned to normal, but on his face his grin grew unnaturally wide, causing the skin of Brian's face to split at the corners of the mouth.

"I can feel them here," he said. "You know, all I have to do is wave a hand and they will come to me." His eyes lingered on Ben. "But if I had someone like him…" He trailed off. He examined Ben from afar, and the wicked grin on his face spread wider.

"Someone like him could open the door for me. I wouldn't have to lift a finger, and my children would be indestructible."

Ben swallowed hard.

"I could have this world in my hand, Naomi. Isn't that what we always wanted?"

"It's what you wanted," she said.

"You wound me." He pouted. "But I've got things to do and my darling here is surely suited to clear the way." He looked to his beast, who offered a grunt.

Naomi formed fists as her tattoos shifted from her forearms to her knuckles on each hand.

"It would be a waste to see you die," he said.

She stood firm.

"Very well." He sighed. "Darling?"

Eddow's Titan squared up his shoulders. He pulled from his back a large mace that looked to be made of thick tree roots knotted and woven together to form the handle and the head. He slammed it into the concrete of the parking lot, letting out a roar that was meant to intimidate Naomi.

She didn't flinch, but Ben and Glenn stepped back a few feet.

"Naomi," Glenn said in a hushed tone.

"Don't waste it on him," she told him. "If you get a clear shot of Eddow, take it, but only if you're sure."

Glenn nodded.

The beast raised his weapon, charging Naomi, and she met him. Ben's blood allowed her to be exceptionally agile in their fight. She was able to avoid the Titan's slow attacks and counter, landing a blow here or there, but she found his skin far too tough for her to do any real damage. Still she hacked and slashed, avoiding a swing and a punch until he started to pick up on her moves and predict them. She took one hard hit that sent her into the side of the building, but she pushed to her feet, charging again.

When she took two more blows, feeling several of her bones crack and repair in less than a minute, she found it hard to get to her feet and before she knew it, the beast had her by the throat, holding her in the air. She was losing breath when Ben fired the shotgun. The shot didn't do enough damage, but it caused the beast to stumble back a bit. Glenn joined with his own shotgun, hurting the beast enough that he dropped Naomi to the ground.

She gasped, forcing herself to her feet while she coughed. She rushed the beast, tackling him to the ground and pulling her shadow blade back to plunge it directly into his face like a punch, when something happened.

"I'm bored." Eddow sighed. He reached his hand, palm up, to the building, and curled his fingers toward himself. "Children," he said.

The ground shook.

Naomi lost her balance and fell from the chest of the beast, looking around. Behind them, the hospital creaked and groaned as suddenly, the front section that held the ER caved into the earth. The hole wasn't large enough to take the whole hospital down, but it was big enough to compromise its structure, sinking part of it into the earth.

Ben and Glenn leaped out of the way before they were crushed with rubble, but all they could do was watch in shock.

"There are people in there," Ben gasped.

"I've… I've… I've got to call for help," Glenn said, barely able to get his words out. He'd just managed to grasp his radio and organize his panicked thoughts to put in the call when a sound from within the hole held his attention.

It started subtly, the tumble of settling brick cascading over the mountain of rubble. Soon the rocks seemed to rise rather than fall and before Glenn could get his eyes on the emerging being, he heard cries. Mournful, harrowing pleads for help.

"Heeeelllllpppppppp usssss," they came, high-pitched whines that carried to Glenn and caused his stomach to tie into a knot.

"There's sooooo much blooooodddd, heeeelllllpppp usssssssss…"

The sound dragged out until any resemblance to human cadence was lost. It increased in volume and pitch until the cry was so piercing that Glenn dropped his radio to cover his ears.

Ben did the same, screaming in pain and feeling blood immediately pool into his hands.

Rubble seemed to shoot in all directions now, striking Ben and Glenn and anyone near enough. Before the two could gather themselves, they watched in horrified anticipation to see what emerged.

They came out fast, these things, these monsters oozing and bleeding all at once. They moved in swift motions, stretching their limbs and getting a feel for their legs, as having appendages was a completely new sensation to them. But they were quick learners, and they leaped in heaping bounds over each other and from the hole that was once LMH. Some landed on the pavement of the parking lot in shambles, knocking each other about in the process. They snarled and hissed at one another, snapping great jaws connected by blue-and-red vessel-like tendons and gnashing teeth that looked as though they were formed from calcified wood.

A few stood at full height, but most cowered toward the ground in terrified confusion or unsure how to manage such large frames under the weight of gravity.

They began to fight among themselves, confused and unguided.

Ben's hearing was shot. He'd endured so much damage between Naomi firing Stormrider so close to his ear and the screams of these… these things. But even with busted eardrums, he could hear the snap, snap, snapping of teeth in flesh as he watched one creature pin another and rip out its throat without hesitation.

They were lost, these children of Eddow. They were but newborns birthed from rock and destruction in bodies that resembled nothing they'd been promised in a previous life. But when he spoke, when their father called upon them, they fell silent.

"Babies," Eddow hissed. The red glow from under his coat grew brighter as he looked at them. "*My* babies. My children, bring me the Seer and kill the others." He waved.

Each head had been turned in his direction, but when he spoke the order, the horde turned in unison to look directly at Ben.

"What the fucking fuck?" Glenn's hands fumbled with his gun. Ben was completely paralyzed by fear, and Glenn tried to keep his cool long enough to protect him.

The horde moved fast. They were ravenous and rabid.

Glenn reloaded quickly, firing two shots. He managed to maim a couple of the creatures but barely did enough to slow the mob.

Ben snapped from his gaze. He stumbled with the shells to the shotgun as they neared and Glenn's efforts did little.

"Uh, Naomi?" Glenn called, but she was back to battling with the Titan.

Ben could nearly smell the mob's putrid breath when a rush of wind drew their attention away. There was a great blur that moved so swiftly the children of Eddow were unable to pinpoint it. They twisted and turned, leaping at their own shadows on the ground or snapping at the air, hoping to capture something.

No matter how they reacted, they could only watch those around them get picked off. Their injuries varied from having their skulls completely smashed in or being pierced completely through their midsection by something that left massive, gaping holes.

Those nearest to Ben dropped to the ground and those following began to cower back toward the safety of the crater that was once LMH.

Once the line retreated, the blur came to a stop in front of Ben and Glenn. It was a woman, tall and lean, clothed completely in black and swinging a chain. She'd stopped so suddenly the gust of air made Ben tumble over.

"Fuck!" Glenn jumped.

"You're so cute when you're jumpy." Nora smiled. She wore a catsuit with a black corset and heavy boots. She stood with one hand on her hip while the other tossed her swinging chain into the air, grasping the spike that was attached at the end of it. "Are you even remotely useful down there?" she asked, leaning close to Ben, but when the demons advanced again, she shrugged off any response he might attempt to muster.

She attacked, moving so fast he never even saw her travel, just appear in one spot and then another, swinging and piercing demons with her chain and spike so gracefully she could have been dancing.

"Allow me, Deputy." Rik offered his hand to Glenn, who took it shakily.

"It's D-detective," he corrected, hardly able to form the words.

"My apologies, of course it is."

Ben took notice of the axe Rik held, the dual-sided head of which likely weighed fifty or more pounds. It was impressive in both magnitude and beauty as it was inscribed with runes and Nordic sigils not even the most seasoned of historians would be able to translate. Each side of the head was curved with sharp toes and heels, but they seemed to serve different purposes. While one side looked exactly like what one would expect to see in a Nordic museum, the other presented a sharper and more pointed toe. Ben could only assume Rik would use it to pierce and hook into a victim, making them unable to pull away.

The handle of the axe was long and thick, much thicker than that of a typical axe. It was a smooth, dark wood that seemed to be unlike any tree Ben had seen before. A length of gray leather was wrapped around the handle several times just above the knob. It bore deep grooves, grip marks only put there from years—maybe centuries—of wear. Ben imagined Rik's finger fit into the grooves as though it had been molded with his grip in mind. It could be wielded with one hand by someone like Rik, but its true power was felt when held with two hands.

In the heat of it all, Ben couldn't help but admire it. The history, the legends surely surrounding such a weapon were likely endless. He was certain that if he or Glenn were to attempt to brandish it, they would barely lift it from the ground. But Rik held it single-handed as though it were a mere hatchet.

Rik lifted Ben to his feet and gave the axe a twirl with one hand before settling both hands at the knob of the handle. "Excuse me." He gave a smile and began to smash away at hissing, screaming, oozing, horrifying monsters as though they were daisies and he a small child gallivanting through a field.

Rik and Nora had brought with them a team of elite Den soldiers, none of whom Ben recalled sitting around The Den when he'd been there, as he would have noticed men garbed in thick body armor and carrying assault rifles. They spoke little but were effective in combat against the emerging demons.

The demons were decimated in a matter of moments, leaving only Naomi and Eddow's beast standing.

Naomi had done well to keep the beast busy, but dodging his hits were draining and his punches were starting to take their toll as she felt her bones take longer to reform.

Rik rushed in, sliding under the beast's stride to strike each knee, taking him down with Nora gracefully leaping over his head and pinning him down with her chain around his neck. Naomi mustered her strength, crossing her arms on either side of his head and slicing with both blades, decapitating him.

His head rolled across the parking lot to Eddow's feet.

Naomi didn't hesitate. She vanished her blades and stretched her hands toward Eddow, spawning a black portal behind him. It pulled him in slowly as he resisted.

"Now, Glenn!" she shouted, feeling blood drip from her nose, feeling as though her head were to explode holding him in place.

Glenn raised Stormrider, putting Eddow's chest in his sights. He fired as Naomi closed the portal around him and the demon disappeared.

Jamie lay on the ground, dazed and confused.

Naomi fell forward, resting her hands on the body of Eddow's dead beast. She was breathing so heavily she thought she might pass out. "Did it work? Did you get him?" she asked.

"I didn't see," he said. "I think so, but I never saw it hit," Glenn said.

A stillness descended over them. They heard only the settling of rubble behind them and the crackling of fires that were starting in the collapse of the emergency department.

"Is it over?" Ben asked. His hands were finally working and he was mindlessly reloading the shotgun just out of precaution.

Glenn had rushed to Jamie, grasping hold of the collar of her shirt and dragging her from the place where Eddow had stood.

"Get your fucking hands off me, Beasley!" she shouted. She kicked and fought him, but when they reached the edge of the parking lot and he tossed her to the ground, she fell still and quiet.

"We're going to need to talk about this, Jamie. Jesus Christ." He sighed.

She made no motion to acknowledge him. She only lay on the ground, petting her hair and mumbling under her breath. Her features were hollow and Glenn struggled to recognize her.

"He'll come for me, he'll come for me," she whispered. "No cock-suckers. No faggots. No sinful sacrilegious sluts. No usurpers. No ignorant masses. Only him. Only *my love*."

"Goddammit, Jamie, what did he do to you?" Glenn muttered.

Rik and Nora sighed, barely breaking a sweat looking around at the carnage. "Was that the blood bank, Fredrik?" Nora asked.

"No, fortunately, the blood bank is on the other side of the building," he said. "Still, it will cost a pretty penny to rebuild. Oh dear…"

Naomi let her legs relax in front of her and fell back, still on the headless body of the beast. She breathed so deeply her lungs hurt, but she felt as though she could cry from happiness. "He's gone," she said. "He's really gone." She began to sob.

"Naomi?" Ben asked.

She looked at his frightened face and saw him staring at where Eddow had last stood.

It started small, like a black dot in their vision that grew and grew as it filled the air. It was an amorphous cloud of black and shadow and when there appeared to be nothing, Eddow stepped into the dim dusk light, standing tall and vanishing the portal behind him. "How irritating," he said.

"No," Naomi gasped.

"You are created by me to be what I cannot be. Do you think you can simply banish me to a realm where I am already king?" He chuckled to himself, wiping dust arrogantly from his trench coat. He settled his large hands on the collar of his coat and shook his head like a disappointed father. "I really thought you were better, smarter than this, Nay," he said. "Look at this mess you've caused. You've taken my gifts from me."

"You can't call stolen hearts gifts," she said.

"They were stolen *for* me. You wouldn't understand. You wouldn't understand that kind of love and devotion. You've never known it."

Naomi watched his face. She watched it shift from Brain to Taylor before settling on a chubby-cheeked child. His face wore this mask for only a moment, but to Naomi it felt like eternity. It sparked a memory in her and she was able to fill in the spaces where Eddow's mask lacked, like her blue eyes.

She'd forgotten how blue her daughter's eyes were. How they shifted from dimensions of blue to yellow to gray, changing with the time of day. And how they glowed. The darkest of shadows couldn't cloud one's mind when looking into those eyes. In her deepest memories, Naomi looked into those eyes and saw life's abundance. Even at the worst times, the shine never dulled.

But what was her name again?

Naomi knew time was fleeting. She knew that in a moment Eddow would change masks and she would look at her face, the face of her baby, but maybe, just maybe, if she could remember her name… Maybe she could hold onto something. She forced herself to not blink.

"You forgot her face, didn't you?"

Her eyes started to water.

"Tsk, tsk." Eddow shook his head. His face shifted back to Brian's cracked and distorted mask. "They promised love eternal, but where are they now?"

Naomi squeezed her burning eyes shut and felt the tears fall down her cheeks. She bowed her head over her knees to hide them.

"It's a sign," he said. "If you forgot her, she must not have been that important."

"No, I couldn't just forget," she whispered.

"But you did. A mother who has forgotten her own child. Naomi, if you need more of a sign that you don't belong among them, I can't think of one. Even your mother and her poisoned mind didn't forget you."

"I didn't forget her!" Naomi cried. "She was taken from me, and… and…" She struggled. She tried to search for a reason. To search her mind for anything that would tell her why she couldn't remember her daughter's name, but it never came and she broke in heaving sobs. "I can't recall…"

"My dear, *dear* girl," Eddow hissed. His voice was different now, softer and warm.

Naomi found a nostalgic comfort in it but took care to keep her eyes averted.

"He's trying to get into your head!" Ben called, breaking the silence.

"I am the only one who ever loved you," Eddow said. "And no one will ever love you like I do."

"Brian loved you!" Glenn shouted.

"He's gone," she said, choking on her tears.

"Well, I fucking love you," Ben said. "You're part of my family now and nothing is changing that."

"You don't love me. You don't know what I am."

"Doesn't matter. You could've let me die a dozen times and you didn't. No monster would care enough to do that. And maybe I don't know you, but you know more about me than I will ever understand, so I can't let you go."

"A man's love is temporary," Eddow interjected. "You know where you belong."

"Naomi, please," Ben said. He tried to pull her attention to him, but she refused to look.

"I'm just so… tired of living, Ben," she said. "Tired of fighting and tired of failing."

"You have—"

Before Ben could get his words out, Eddow raised a hand and lifted her face to meet his. "You don't have to be," he said. Brian's face smiled at her. The frayed edges around his eyes and mouth were becoming more obvious, and it was as though his face began to age the longer Eddow used it. Naomi didn't see him as the man she knew, but she still knew him well enough to find a familiar comfort in it. "Let me carry your burdens."

Naomi felt the touch to her cheek despite the great expanse between Eddow and her. She was confused by the comfort as when she raised her hand to her cheek, she felt nothing but her skin chilled from the night air. The butterflies that had been in her stomach were devoured by flame and sorrow. She could hear Ben's voice but couldn't make out his words. She heard only the hiss of Eddow's cooing voice and the absence of tangible warmth on her cheek.

She dropped her hands as though to push his touch away and felt her blood burn. None of it mattered. She wasn't the girl who ran away; she was the woman who was created to be useful. Here, atop her master's demolished beast, she felt far from useful.

Naomi raised her fist over her head and brought it down into the chest of Eddow's beast. It cracked under her punch. She struck again and again, her knuckles bloodied, until the chest caved in completely. She pulled at the thick layers of bone and bark-like skin until she could reach her hand deep inside of him. When it emerged, it was covered in thick, coagulated blood and held the heart from which the beast had formed. Dozens of tendrils attached it to the inner workings of the cavity. They were thick and difficult to break, stronger than any vessel, muscle, or ligament found in a human body. But Naomi tore them like twine. She severed the connection and held before her the still red heart of Steve Owens. But she found it was cold despite appearing plump and lush.

"A gift," Eddow swooned. "A gift given by a dying man for a truly worthy cause. An admirable sacrifice."

In savage bites Naomi devoured the heart, tearing and ripping at the flesh until there was nothing but a mess of gelatinous blood in her hands that fell in clumps to the chest of Eddow's beast.

Her skin became unbearably hot and she tore at it, beginning near her eyes and working to her forehead. She stripped her face down to the muscle, which allowed the horns that protruded from her head to grow larger than they ever had before. The inner workings under her flesh were exposed for only a moment as a smooth layer of black pitch covered every inch. She stood, her muscles constraining and growing in size in moments. Her mass increased to such a magnitude that it caused the beast to crack and cave under her feet like he'd been made from paper mâché. With aching and jolting movements, she stepped from the remains and toward Eddow.

She held her arms outright, every movement causing her immeasurable agony. She opened her mouth to howl, but nothing came initially. After a delay, a piercing cry erupted from deep inside her throat so loud and overwhelming even the vamps had to shield their ears. It was the cry of a thousand souls trapped within her, begging to be released, and the longer she cried, the louder it grew. It was a war siren bellowing over the hills and valleys.

Eddow smiled so wide the corners of Brian's mouth finally split fully apart, his jaw now operating completely separate from the upper half of his face.

While the humans and supes alike cowered on the ground, covering their ears and shielding their eyes, Eddow applauded. He was a proud father who had spent his entire life putting his child through the most rigorous athletic training to finally see her bring home the gold medal. His devotion, his dedication—all of it had paid off and before him stood his perfect weapon ready to do anything he asked of her.

"This town is mine. It was gifted to me by one whose blood runs deeper in the soil for longer than your feet have stood on it."

"Naomi?" Ben said. It was a sound trapped in his throat but loud enough for her to snap her attention to him.

"Bring him to me. I will take care of the rest," Eddow ordered. He raised his hand to the hospital and the ground started to rumble again.

Emerging now from the crater was a second wave of demons. Their skin was white and thick and the ligaments that held their appendages in place appeared like thick vines rather than the supple vessels of the previous group. Though they moved more slowly, their thick exteriors provided more of a challenge for The Den's members who engaged them.

Ben crawled backward from Naomi, who was stretching and flexing, getting a feel for her new skin. She was nearly the size of Eddow now, but faster, jumping from shadow to shadow toward Ben.

When Ben backed into Glenn, he grasped him by the collar. "Stormrider! Where is Stormrider?!"

Glenn was lost. His mouth moved, but no words came. His eyes were wide and shaking. It wasn't until Ben slapped him across the face that he broke his gaze from Naomi. "What the fuck, what the fuck, what the fuck, what the fuck, what the FUCK?!"

"You have to shoot her!"

"What?"

"Beasley! Get your shit together!"

Glenn fumbled with the pistol, noticing more demons crawling from the debris of the hospital.

Naomi had nearly reached Ben when she was intercepted by Rik and his axe. The two squared off, Naomi easily deflecting his attacks and landing a few blows of her own. Any moment Rik found himself on the ground, Nora swiftly stepped in. Together, the pair took turns holding her attention while Ben and a group of vampires fended off the emerging demons.

Glenn retrieved the pistol. He lined it up with Naomi and fired, but she vanished in a shadow before the bullet could hit her.

Silence fell as Rik and Nora looked in every direction for Naomi to emerge. Ben reloaded his shotgun with shaking hands, scanning both the rubble for more demons and the space around him for Naomi. Every moving shadow caused him to jump.

Eddow raised his hand again, calling another wave of demons just as Naomi leaped from a portal behind Rik. She opened her jagged mouth wide and latched onto his trapezius muscle near his neck.

"Fredrik!" Nora cried. She wrapped her chain around her hand and plunged the spike into Naomi's back, causing her to release Rik.

Rik fell forward, holding his shoulder, but he wasted no time pushing to his feet to pull Naomi off of Nora.

Naomi had grasped Nora by the throat and slammed her hard enough into the concrete to leave a crater. By the time Rik reached her, Naomi was stomping her deeper and deeper into the ground. She wrestled Rik now with no weapons or shadows; they just held and ripped at each other until they wore each other's blood.

The soldiers of The Den, who had been fighting off the emerging demons, were dropping rapidly. They were unable to provide ample coverage for the two humans and soon enough, Ben and Glenn were left exposed and unprotected.

Glenn took aim again and fired, but Naomi moved so fast he only managed to graze her arm. Still, the touch caused her arm to ignite with lightning and she stopped to grasp it, letting out a howl.

Her black flesh still held the singed pattern of lightning from shoulder to forearm.

Rik took his chance and struck her with his axe, landing firmly in the space between her head and shoulder at the side of her neck. It dug deep into her skin, but she didn't react. She simply grasped the axe, holding his gaze with her large, white eyes. She spun quickly and flung Rik against the collapsing side of the hospital. The wall broke apart, giving way and tumbling over the ancient vampire, who remained motionless under the concrete blocks.

Ben backpedaled farther. Nora hadn't moved since Naomi stomped her into the ground, Rik was useless under a pile of blocks, and the rest of The Den's reinforcements were scattered, barely able to hold their own against the emerging demons. Glenn oscillated between trying to comprehend the horrors he was seeing and recalling his training, but his training had never told him how to fight demons and his best friend's monster widow.

Ben pointed the shotgun at Naomi. He wasn't sure it would do anything against her, but he hoped the threat would hold. As she neared, he squeezed his eyes shut and fired, but the bullet merely passed through her as though she were made of smoke.

Naomi knocked the gun from his hands, and he tumbled backward. She stepped on either arm, and Ben felt his bones crush under her weight. She reached low, holding his face in her clawed hand, digging in and causing blood to drip from his cheeks.

Glenn held the gun steady, her head directly in his sights, but he couldn't pull the trigger. "Come on, Glenn, come on," he growled.

"What… what about your mom and dad?" Ben managed to speak though Naomi held tight to his face. "If you let him win, they'll die and all of your sacrifices will have been for nothing."

He wasn't sure there was any part of her left to appeal to, but that didn't stop him from trying. He felt her grip loosen slightly.

"This town is full of good people who don't deserve this, Naomi," he said.

The white saucers that replaced her eyes seemed to shift and wander in consideration.

"My baby girl…" Glenn choked on his words. "My Allison," he said, seeing her head turn to him. "If you kill this town, you kill her, and I can't let you do that. But I don't want to do this, Naomi. I don't want to do this to Brian."

Naomi hesitated. She looked at the shaking pistol in his hand and then to Ben's bleeding face.

"Your girl was taken. Please don't take mine," Glenn pleaded to Naomi, spit trailing down his chin and tears streaming from his eyes..

Naomi let go. She stepped off Ben's arms and stumbled back a few steps.

Ben pulled his broken arms to his chest and curled into a ball. "Beasley, you're gonna have to shoot her," he said.

Glenn swallowed hard. "Am I, Naomi?"

There were screams of Den members being devoured by demons behind her. She tilted her head to listen but brought her attention back to Glenn.

With shaking hands, he lowered the gun and placed it on the concrete beside him.

Naomi didn't turn but raised her hand, opening a portal. From the portal, long tentacles reached out and pulled the demons from the remaining Den members into the darkness on the other side.

She turned her attention to Eddow now, watching Brian's face melt.

"You can't kill me," he said.

Naomi's head tilted.

Behind Brian's face, she could see his red eyes shifting. He raised a hand suddenly to the rubble of the hospital as more demons emerged, but before they could touch the surface, Naomi lifted the pieces of building under them and shot them into a portal. Each time Eddow summoned them, she would mangle and dispose of his children in another portal until there were no more hearts to call upon.

With no one left for him to call upon, Naomi took her chance. She was fast, but Eddow was stronger.

Glenn had moved to Ben's side and was trying to comfort him, but he couldn't take his eyes off the behemoths that destroyed the parking lot and caused the hospital to settle farther in the ground with each punch.

Rik had recovered from his hit and climbed from under the cinder blocks. He used his axe to stand and only took a moment to watch Naomi fight Eddow. He moved to Nora's side and lifted her from the crater.

"LaNora, dear, you know how I feel about sleeping on the job," he said, trying to rouse her, but she could only manage a groan.

He pulled her body next to Ben and stood to his full height, stretching. He looked at Naomi and Eddow, steadied himself, and let out a battle cry. He charged forward, hitting Eddow hard with his shoulder in the center of his mass.

Eddow stumbled, allowing Naomi a chance to land a punch or two, knocking him down. He was on his feet in time to avoid Rik's axe but not Naomi's claws.

She shredded his coat and exposed his spindly body beneath. His chest was hollow, like an old log, and a red glow from within illuminated Rik and Naomi's silhouettes. Naomi slashed and ripped at his face, cutting her husband's face to pieces until the bits fell to the ground. For the first time she looked upon his face, his true face, and even in her berserk state it caused her to stumble back. Of all the horrors she'd seen, nothing compared to Eddow's unmasked face.

He had no eyes, just glowing, empty red holes that focused like a camera lens. His face lacked the structure and features one would expect to see in a face. It was rounded like the face of a decaying tree but hollowed in the space where cheeks should have been. His mouth operated as though hinged at the jaw with a clasp barely connecting his jaw to the upper half of his face. Now exposed, it hung agape as though he never had control of it to begin with but had disguised it as functional under the flesh mask of another person.

There was no flesh on Eddow's face, only rough, bark-like skin that could have been rotten and molded in the same instance, being as dehydrated as petrified wood.

But his skin crawled. It moved in waves, shifting in one direction until there was no space left, only to turn and shift in the other direction. It took Naomi a second look to realize his skin wasn't skin or bark or even rotten wood. It was composed of beetles, black and tiny that scurried when exposed to the air. They searched for shelter under his mask but when none was found, they retreated deep into his gaping mouth, which dripped maggots. This left his face exposed, hollow, the skeletal remains of molded, rotten, and festering wood left to the whim of nature.

The sight was so startling that even in her current state, Naomi had to release her hold on him.

In her moment of hesitation, Eddow struck his hand through her chest and reached deep inside. Naomi felt his hand close around her heart.

"This… is… mine. If I die… we die together…" he grunted.

Rik raised his axe over his head two, three times, each time bringing it down on Eddow's arm until he'd severed it completely.

Naomi fell to her knees holding the bit of arm still left in her chest.

Eddow howled in pain but reached back and struck Rik hard, knocking him unconscious.

Black leaked from Naomi's mouth as she gasped and choked for air, holding tight to Eddow's arm. She pulled it from her chest, fighting through bile.

Eddow's sight landed on Ben. "So gifted you can't even see it," he said. "You're exactly what my collection needs and just special enough I will have to collect you myself."

He started to stumble toward Ben but stopped abruptly. He staggered for a step but rose to the tips of his toes and stopped, looking down at the black horn that was impaled through his back and out his chest.

Naomi held his shoulders as she shoved her horns deeper into him until he could no longer stand. With great strength, she regained her stance, hoisting Eddow like a prized kill atop her horns.

His blood splattered her skin like a renewing rain shower. She felt it run down her cheeks and over her shoulders and caught it in her hands. It mixed with her own blood that spilled from her chest. She twisted her head to look at Ben and Glenn, Eddow howling in pain at the motion.

Naomi let the blood spill over her body and though she was shrouded in Eddow's shadow, she glistened. A portal opened behind her and moved forward around them. As it started to enclose them, Eddow fought in protest.

"You cannot kill me!" he cried. "I am the only love you have ever known!" He twisted and writhed, only causing her horns to pierce deeper.

Glenn fumbled. He found the gun, lined his shot, and fired, hitting Eddow directly in the glowing cavity that was his chest.

It started from within, the growing lightning that spread over his body like a forest fire. As his body began to turn to ash in Naomi's hold, he screamed the scream of every mask he'd ever worn. They heard each scream distinct and isolated. They never heard the last of the screams as the portal closed, leaving Ben and Glenn staring at a void of air with the image of Naomi's brown eyes against her inky skin burned into their minds.

45

"It was a terrorist attack, Maggie."

"Here in Pickleberry? Nell, why would anyone do that?"

"What else would it be? Who would attack a hospital?"

"I don't think it was an attack."

"What would it have been then?"

There was a clatter of dishes from the kitchen, and the three women looked around the café. It was the tail end of the morning rush and while people still came and went, no one paid much mind to the table of town gossips.

Nell leaned forward and in a hushed voice carried on, "I think the city cut corners building that place. The structures were practically particle boards. It could only hold for so long before the whole place collapsed."

"You know, I heard it was an invasion of the undead that came from the morgue. The morgue was under the ER, after all, and when they rose, they broke the structure down, causing the ER to collapse," chimed in Charlene, stirring her coffee without meeting either's gaze.

"Zombies, Charlene?" Nell asked.

"Why aren't there zombies out roaming Pickleberry?" Maggie agreed.

"Well, maybe they blend in with us?" Charlene suggested.

"Maybe we should petition LMH to put funds toward the psych ward when it opens back up?" Nell spoke from the side of her mouth in between sips of her coffee.

"What about the sound it made when it collapsed?" Charlene asked.

"I've heard something similar on the History Channel when they do those specials about the world wars," Maggie said.

"You think it sounded like an air-raid siren?" Charlene asked.

"Pickleberry doesn't have any air-raid sirens."

"How do you know, Nell?"

"Why would we need it?" Nell responded.

"You tell me! Why would they attack a hospital? What else in this town is worth bombing?" Maggie asked.

"Maggie…"

"Either way we look at the tragedy, it is just that—a tragedy," Charlene said.

"That we can agree on."

"Supposedly seven dead." Nell said after a long pause.

"What do you mean *supposedly*?" Charlene leaned closer to Nell.

"Yeah, two nurses, a young doctor… What was his name? The new one?"

"Dr. Allard," said Maggie.

"Dr. Allard, right. Jim the maintenance guy was there too, the fool. He should've taken the day off like everyone else."

"He was doing upgrades and didn't like doing it during normal business. His poor wife and littles." Maggie refolded the napkin on the table, taking care to press the crease three times.

"All right, so two nurses, Dr. Allard, Jim, the front desk girl, and…"

The ladies were silent in thought.

"Who *were* the other two?" Charlene wondered aloud.

"Weren't they the couple that just moved into the townhouses down the street? I never knew their names, but I remember seeing them at the festival," Maggie said.

"Oh, yes. Remember, they had to call the weewoo for the husband?"

"The *weewoo*? How old are you, Nell? People died."

"Yeah, well, I heard they never found his body," Charlene added.

"What?" Nell asked.

"Why would they say seven died if they never found his body? Bless your heart, Charlene." Maggie shook her head at Charlene and her tendency to believe anything she heard.

"Because they did the intake. They knew he was in the hospital when it went down, but when they got the rescue crew in there, they only found his wife."

"How would they miss that? They've cleaned up all the rubble. Where else would it be?" Maggie asked.

"Maybe it was one of the zombies, eh, Char?" Nell smirked.

"Maybe it was," Charlene whispered, eyes wide.

"Give me a break." Nell rolled her eyes and resettled in her chair, reaching her threshold for Charlene's conspiracies.

"Well? What else, then?" Maggie asked. "I doubt he just up and walked away."

"Ladies…" Trina approached the table of women. "We're all confused about what happened, but let's not forget that real people lost their lives in the tragedy. Might I ask you to be a little more respectful of those families?" She offered a warm smile and refilled their coffees.

"Of course, Trina. We didn't mean anything by it, but it's all anyone in town can talk about," Maggie said.

Nell nodded. "You can't expect people to not wonder."

"Well, maybe you should pay your respects at the memorial service and see the faces of the mourning families before speaking so wildly and loudly about it," Trina said.

The women grew quiet.

Trina left their table, catching a glimpse of Ben in the back room of the café. She put the coffee pot back on the warmer and met him at the door. "What are you doing here?" she asked.

But he didn't answer. He was attempting to pick up the last of the dishes that had fallen to the kitchen floor.

"Ben?"

Still he didn't answer.

"Ben!"

At this he jumped, nearly dropping the plate in his hands. "Jes— Oh, Mom! I didn't hear you."

"When they get the hospital up and running, you should see the doctor about your hearing," she told him.

"The EMS told me the right ear is probably shot from trauma alone, but you're right," he said. "Maybe I will. I have a follow-up to get these removed anyway."

He tried to gesture to casts on his arms, one of which extended further up his arm, past his elbow.

"What are you doing here, my love?" she said, looking at his broken arms with pity.

"Dad said Audrey was sick and you were a little swamped. I just wanted to do some dishes and help out before I left," he said.

"Ben, you have two broken arms."

"They're not that broken," he said, then winced as he tried to pile coffee cups onto a tray while having one arm in a sling and the other a cast. The cups tumbled and fell to the floor, shattering one and chipping another. "All right, maybe I'm doing more damage than good," he admitted.

Trina took his face into her hands. "You were very brave for what you did to help at the accident, but you have to know when it's time to help and when it's time to rest."

Ben held her gaze for a moment but couldn't maintain it for long. Lying to his mother wasn't something that came easy and living with the lie was even more difficult. He couldn't bring himself to look in her eyes for long, knowing she would get the truth out of him eventually.

"You shouldn't get those casts wet anyway." Trina pushed him away from the dishes.

"You're right. I wanted to help, but I think I'm adding to your work. I can hunt down Jonah for you." He sighed, leaning against the cool metal of the dishwasher. "I just can't sit around anymore. I've got to do something with all the reading I've been doing. Maybe things aren't as bad as we think they are, but I'll have to do more research before I can come up with anything definitive. I know it sounds crazy, but I think that the things I'm reading about will help all of us understand better, and I might even be able to bring..." He paused abruptly, catching himself. "To bring closure... Closure for the victims' families." His voice cracked, and Trina watched tears brim his eyes.

"Benny," she said in a hushed voice. She moved to embrace him, but he wiped his eyes on his sleeve and sniffled. "It was an accident. A tragic disaster. That's all. What else could bring them closure?" she asked, wiping the tear from his cheek.

"I have to go." He picked up the backpack sitting behind the door and kissed his mother on the cheek. "Bye, Mom," he said and left.

In the days that followed the incident, the community of Pickleberry pulled together as though trauma-bonded by the devastation to their fathers, brothers, sisters, mothers, and neighbors.

For days, mourners gathered at the south end of the hospital to watch the recovery efforts at LMH. First was the clean-up. Rubble was cleared in what seemed like a day, a feat the locals claimed was testament to the town's ability to pull together in tragedy and not at all relating to the crew sent by The Den to clear the mess.

Second came the memorials, the candle-lit vigils and monotonic singing of "Amazing Grace" while the town's pastors each took turns praying over the carnage. This lasted for several days while crews worked to rebuild the hospital. Though it was nowhere near operating condition and remained closed to the public, people gathered religiously. On the final day of gathering, Mayor Charles Luncor addressed the mourners. He praised their devotion and their commitment to each other and released them from their guilt by promising a memorial garden at the south end of the hospital to honor the departed.

Any obligation to publicly mourn fell off after this. In the coming days, the beginning of a garden was established. A wooden bench was placed at the center of a concrete circle surrounded by empty but freshly laid flowerbeds.

A local artist, a bit of an eccentric type, thought the concrete slab too bare. He crafted a statue, carving it from a large oak trunk with an old chainsaw. He called it a placeholder, but the image was all that mattered for now: a woman holding close to her chest a bleeding heart. He called it *The Heart of Pickleberry*. A community that bleeds for its loss and embraces those in need.

Ben found the irony of the statue something Naomi would have probably chuckled at. She would have shaken her head and asked if the next statue would show the woman eating the heart of Pickleberry.

This version of Naomi prevented Ben from being bitter about the on-the-nose art. The laugh she left in his head was comforting, but when he remembered it was just a memory he was likely to forget, his smile faded.

Ben looked at the seven memorial spots that surrounded the feet of the statue. Each small pile boasted a collection of photos, flowers, and notes—except for the last vase of flowers. In front of this pink-and-purple vase were two names, "Richard and Joanne Dodds." No pictures. No notes of love lost. Just their names alone under Pickleberry's bleeding heart.

In the dusk of the evening, headlights shone over the sculpture from behind Ben. With a glance over his shoulder, he noticed Glenn waving from his cruiser in the hospital's empty parking lot.

"It's come a long way," Beasley said of the memorial as Ben settled in the cruiser.

"It's not close to done," he said.

Beasley rolled his eyes. "I think you need to be realistic."

"Why not them?"

"They didn't have any pictures. They lived in the town for such a short time and met so few people."

"If we'd told Naomi, they wouldn't need pictures at all. They could've been holding the candles," he said.

"Ben…" Glenn sighed.

"Don't do that. Don't use that same tone everyone uses. You're just as guilty as I am."

"And you don't think I know that? We both agreed not to say anything. We both did. This is on both of us. No one could have known how things were going to go down," Glenn said.

Ben turned his gaze out the window. "This is pointless."

"Yeah, something we can agree on, I guess, but we're gonna do it."

"She's not there," Ben said.

"We don't know *where* she is," Glenn snapped back. "She could be dead. We just know she's not dead here. She's probably dead in a black hole or some other weird shit."

"But doesn't that bother you, Beasley? Not even where is she, but *what* is she lost in?" Ben rubbed a hand over his face. "It might not bother you, but I have too many questions to simply forget about her."

"You think I'll forget about her?" Glenn asked. "My best friend's widow randomly pops into my life, turns into a giant, horned demon, kills another demon, and then disappears. Oh, no, there is no forgetting this for the rest of my life."

"You don't get it," Ben said.

"Enlighten me."

"She wasn't a demon. She wasn't a monster or even the bad guy. She was a victim, like everyone else who was hurt."

Beasley didn't speak. He stroked his mustache, watching Ben from his side view.

"You got pulled into this, like, ten minutes before it all went to shit. Aren't you a little curious?"

"Ben, I don't think I know enough about any of this to ask questions. I'm just trying to do my best by this town. I got people asking me questions every day about what happened. I got a deputy locked up in the psych ward at LMH who won't stop rambling on about that… that demon thing. Not to mention my own family to worry about. I can't afford to fall into crazy like you." Glenn pinched the bridge of his nose, knowing how it sounded.

"Well, if I'm falling into crazy, let me be the one to tell you the questions you should have, like where the fuck is she? What is she? What was that thing she was fighting and why did eating its heart turn her into a bigger thing? Oh, and the other thing, the giant fucking demon that has pulled every string in her life? What about that? What was he? We know he wanted an army, but why? And what part am I supposed to play in that? Rik once said something about a doorway and a key. He could have been facetious, but what if he wasn't? What if there is a doorway and Naomi is the key? Or I'm the key? Or fuck, I don't know."

"I don't know, man. I just want to let it all go and figure out how to move forward." Beasley was losing interest in Ben's erratic questioning.

"I can't let it go. We're missing too much." Ben shook his head. He spent the rest of the drive lost in thought, but Glenn found the silence far more comfortable.

After a while in the silence, Glenn turned down a gravel road and drove for nearly a mile before reaching an open field where two shadows stood in the dark. He parked the cruiser and exited with Ben.

They met the shadows standing just short of a mound of dirt.

"You've done it already?" Glenn asked.

"We work quickly." Nora smiled.

They stood wordless around the pile of dirt.

"Is this all?" Glenn asked.

"Who else is there? Her employers, her pet, and…" Rik gestured to Glenn, pausing. "I'm not really sure what your connection is."

Glenn looked at the ground. "Family," he said.

Rik and Nora exchanged looks.

"If either of you would like to say anything…" Rik said.

Glenn looked to Ben, who hadn't taken his eyes off the dirt pile and cleared his throat. "Uh, I didn't know you as well as I would've liked, but Brian was the best person I ever knew. If he picked you to share his life with, I can only imagine you were as good or better than he was. You were brave, strong, and selfless. Because of you, I get to go home to my little girl. I wish I had more to say, but…" He sighed. "Does this feel silly to anyone else? It's an empty grave."

"It's more of a formality," Rik told him.

"I don't think this is for her sake or ours."

"Are you done speaking, Detective?"

Beasley shifted his weight and bit his tongue.

They all looked to Ben, who hadn't said a word.

Glenn cleared his throat again, still mildly uncomfortable with the creatures of the night who stood before him. "I'll give you a moment, Ben," he said. "I'll just be in the car."

Glenn sat in the cruiser while Ben wordlessly looked at her grave.

"You know," Rik began, "it takes a human of exemplary courage, among other things, to put yourself through what you did. You possess many of the traits I admire in an employee."

"Not to mention your little gift," Nora said.

"What she means is that we would like to offer you a position with The Den. I foresee you doing great things with us." He grinned.

Ben bent low, put his hand to the mound of dirt, and held it for a moment. When he stood, he rubbed the grains of dirt between his fingers and looked at Rik. "Go fuck yourself," he said. He walked off past the cruiser, ignoring Glenn as he disappeared into the mist that settled in the night.

"Well, Naomi would have been proud of that, I think." Nora grinned.

"Indeed, she would." Rik smiled.

Sneak Peak: Into Black Bile

The door to Rik's office opened, and Nora gestured for the woman behind her to enter. Nora didn't need to be told, but she left the pair alone in the office.

The woman had silver hair cropped above her shoulders in an angled cut. In the shadows near her neck, Rik could make out a black streak of hair, but the rest shone like the moon. She had an oval face with a long nose and a set of radiant sapphire blue eyes. Rik had heard stories about them, but he'd never had the chance to look into them until now.

"A pleasure to finally meet you," he said.

"We'll see. What is it you want? It smells like pennies and destroyed dreams in this bar."

Her mouth was the second thing he'd heard stories about. Rik sat forward in his chair and gestured for her to sit. She did so. "I appreciate you taking the time," he said.

"Something I have both not enough and too much of. Sorry I was delayed. I don't get much say in my workload and this wasn't on my list of priorities."

"And yet you're here, listening to my offer."

The woman smiled. She leaned back and stretched one leg over the other. "It's hard to skip an offer like this," she said. "It's most of your wealth, I'm sure."

"Money has a way of replenishing itself. Besides, it's not like you will live forever."

"Right." She chuckled, settling her hands on her lap. "Thing is, I'm not entirely sure I'm the one for the job."

"Surely, if there was one person who could do it, it would be you."

"If she were dead, that would be different."

"Isn't she?"

"No," she said, her tone certain.

Rik settled back, surprised.

"I know every soul that has passed. I've escorted them personally, because if I'm stuck doing this shitty job, the least I can do is offer souls one last smile along their way. If she died, I never escorted her."

"Maybe you just haven't encountered her yet," he suggested.

"Not possible. I hear their cries in my sleep. Their scared wails and confusion. Even if they don't mean to, they call to me," she said, her features growing dim in thought.

"Even if they aren't in this realm?"

The woman thought. "So, she's lost?"

"Would you still hear her?"

She pondered. "I'm not sure. I've never had to expand to other realms. I'm not even sure of the rules there. You would have to question my boss on that one."

"I think it would be best to leave your boss out of this one."

"What will he do? Fire me? Make me normal again?" she scoffed.

"If she were lost, could you find her?"

"If she were lost *and* I could find her, I can't speak on the condition that she would return. I'm not even sure I would want to face her. I'm talented, but I'm still a realist. It would be easier if she were dead."

"If she were lost and dead—?"

"I could do the job. I could bring her back."

"To the dismay of your boss?"

"Fuck 'em."

Rik swiveled in his chair as he thought this over. "If you found her, lost but alive, and she were to suddenly become dead, you would—"

"I'm not in that business anymore."

Rik raised his hands to push off any accusations she had. "I'm just tossing around ideas."

"Tell you what: I'll search around. If I find her, I find her. You may or may not get her back, but I'll see what I can do."

"I thought I'd lost the deal for a moment there."

"With a payout like this?" she said. "I could live through millennia and do a lot of good with that kind of money."

Rik extended his hand to the woman, who took it firmly. "Pleasure doing business," he said.

"Pleasure is mine."

ABOUT THE AUTHOR

B. C. Dombrosky hopes to one day achieve the title of "Jack of all Trades". Until then, she'll pick up any hobby that crosses her path and write down the endless stories that float around her noggin.

Her short stories have been published in anthologies, and her plays have been performed in Chicago. Now, she presents her debut novel, "Home to Pickleberry".

She lives in Missouri with her kid, cats, and other critters. She spends her time making art with her monster and hunting for Justin Herbert base cards.

ACKNOWLEDGEMENT

A special thank you to Casey Laine, who was the first person to give my writing a chance. Your sharp mind and endless guidance is the only reason I've made it this far.

Thank you to my editor, Donna, who alleviated all my fears and concerns by sifting through my manuscript with a flea comb.

Thank you to my boss, Stephanie, for initiating creative accountability lunches and taking away my one excuse for not working on my book.

Thanks Mom and Dad for suffering through my first draft but lighting just enough fire under me to finish the damn thing. Mom, thanks for reading anything and everything. Dad, thanks for your honest voice and your willingness to swap crazy stories.

Thomas, thank you for teaching me to "fuck 'em". Thank you for helping me find value in myself when others didn't. Thank you for the patience, for the laughs, and for the food. Love you, Nerd.

www.ingramcontent.com/pod-product-compliance
Lightning Source LLC
Chambersburg PA
CBHW030347120726
47901CB00007B/1946